SHATTERED LIVES

A Lives Trilogy Novel

JOSEPH LEWIS

Black Rose Writing | Texas

First printing

This is a work of fiction. Names, characters, businesses, places, events, and incidents are either the products of the author's imagination or used in a fictitious manner. Any resemblance to actual persons, living or dead, or actual events is purely coincidental.

ISBN: 978-1-68433-784-2
PUBLISHED BY BLACK ROSE WRITING
www.blackrosewriting.com

Printed in the United States of America
Suggested Retail Price (SRP) $20.95

Shattered Lives is printed in Garamond

*As a planet-friendly publisher, Black Rose Writing does its best to eliminate unnecessary waste to reduce paper usage and energy costs, while never compromising the reading experience. As a result, the final word count vs. page count may not meet common expectations.

Shattered Lives is dedicated in love to my two daughters, Hannah and Emily Lewis. They are the greatest gift my wife, Kim, ever gave me, and I can't possibly express to you how proud I am to be their dad.
I love you- always have, always will.

SHATTERED LIVES

"Whoever fights monsters should see to it that in the process
he does not become a monster."
–Nietzsche

PART ONE
A NOT QUITE SAFE HAVEN

CHAPTER ONE

Waukesha, Wisconsin

. . . He faced the man with the gun. He couldn't quite make out his features, but he seemed to be medium height, maybe shorter than that, and well-built but not overly so. At least he didn't seem to be a bulky, weightlifter kind of man. His voice was cold and flat, his eyes were a pale blue, which is what George would remember the most about him. That and the gun pointed at the boy next to him, a boy George did not know.

Jeremy was George's bookend on the other side of the boy. Behind the three of them was a door to a room that George didn't know. He didn't know the room he stood in, but somehow, he knew the room and the house they were in. At least, the house and room seemed familiar to him. He just couldn't place it.

But more importantly, Jeremy, the boy and George stood between the man and the door and George wasn't sure what or who was on the other side of the door, only that the three of them formed a human shield between it or them and the man with the gun.

As the man took aim, George knew with certainty that Jeremy would step in front of the boy. George couldn't let that happen, so he moved in front of Jeremy and the boy as the gun went off . . .

George slammed upright in bed, gasping for breath and pulling the sheet up to his chin, yanking it from Billy who slept soundly next to him facing the wall, mouth slightly open on his left side in a semi-fetal position. Billy didn't seem to notice or care that he was no longer covered. The night was warm and the breeze so light a sheet wasn't needed, even though the windows were open and the ceiling fan was on. Jeremy Evans, the father of the twins Randy and Billy, didn't like to run the air-conditioner at night, preferring open windows and night breezes.

The room was on the small side and made even smaller now that Billy had the idea to substitute the single bed he had slept in for the past two years, for the double bed in the spare room so that the three of them could sleep in the same room. He and George shared the double bed. George looked over at Randy three feet away on the other side of the room, who was sound asleep on his back, one knee up, arms almost spread-eagle, head off his pillow, breathing deeply and slowly just as Billy was.

He covered Billy with the sheet again and slowly, quietly, swung his feet over the side of the bed and sat with his elbows on his knees, his head in his hands trying to remember the dream. His dark, handsome, and almost noble face, along with his chest and back, the color of bronzed copper, were covered in a sheen of sweat. His hair, the color of midnight and hung down just passed his shoulders, and with his head down, it covered his face. His dark eyes were squinted shut as he tried to grasp the wisp of the dream that turned to vapor and disappeared as quickly and easily as he tried so determinedly to remember it.

George didn't know the man with the gun who had faced the three of them. He couldn't see him clearly in the dream. He didn't know who the boy was, and he wasn't certain it was the boy the man had come to kill. Perhaps it was whoever was on the other side of the door that was shut behind the three of them.

Confusing, odd, and disturbing.

George was a traditional Navajo and he believed, as some of the elders of his people believed, that dreams were messages from the spirit world. The trouble with dreams is that they almost always needed someone to interpret them. It had always been his grandfather who had helped him understand what the spirit world was trying to tell him, but his grandfather was no longer there to help him.

His grandfather was dead.

He had been murdered- executed- along with his mother, grandmother, two brothers and sister because George had witnessed the murder of a fourteen-year-old boy and had come forward to report it. He was now alone with no one to return home to except for his Navajo people and a cousin. Jeremy and the twins had asked him to live with them, but he wasn't certain if he was going to accept their offer or if he'd return to Arizona and his Navajo Nation. Waukesha, Wisconsin was a long way from Arizona. All the trees and the city life were different from the Arizona desert and rural life he had grown up in.

Quietly, slowly so as not to wake up either of the twins, he got out of bed, smoothed the sheet over Billy and picked up his knife. It sat on the nightstand along with Billy's iPod dock that served as music for the three boys, as well as the alarm that would get up first George at 5:00 AM and then the twins at 6:00 AM. The clock face read 1:17 AM, far too early to get up, but George did so anyway.

The knife was a gift from his grandfather for his twelfth birthday two years previous in a coming of age ceremony on top of a plateau near their ranch. The razor sharp blade was eight inches long and the handle, made of elk bone, was an additional four inches bound to the blade with leather. It fit his hand perfectly and he had practiced each morning since receiving it under the guidance of his grandfather. To the casual observer, the movements looked oriental, such as with Tai Chi or Karate, and it was defensive in nature. George could use the knife in either hand effectively and he had done so earlier that week.

The knife had been returned by Detective Jamie Graff just the morning before, along with a permit to carry it. It had been taken by the police because George had used it to kill a man sent to kill him, Jeremy, and the twins. It was a dream and *vision* of his grandfather that led him to the side of the house where he found the man with the gun intent on murdering them. But the police and the district attorney had judged that George had acted in self-defense since the man had a gun and a rap sheet dating back more than twenty years.

Self-defense or not, a man was dead and George had killed him. He had told the police, the FBI and the Evans family about the dream and the *vision* of his grandfather, but George was certain none of them had understood the Navajo belief about dreams and visions. He was sure it had sounded crazy to them and he couldn't help but feel that it sounded crazy to him too.

And now a new dream- a dream he didn't understand. He was certain he wouldn't share it with anyone unless and until he needed to- *if* he needed to.

George tip-toed down the hall, down the stairs and out the kitchen door and sat down on the steps to the back patio that faced the yard beyond it just as he had the other night when he had spotted the man in the hedge line in the backyard and killed him. He shivered slightly at the memory and hugged himself. George turned and looked at the corner of the house, half-expecting to see someone rounding the corner with gun in hand. Of course, no one was there.

Just before he confronted the man, Jeremy had come out of the house and sat on the step next to him and had asked George to consider living permanently with him and the twins. But that was before George had killed the man and even though Jeremy had made that offer again afterward and even though the twins had told him they wanted him to live with them, George wasn't sure how he had felt about it.

It had been a difficult day.

Jeremy and Randy had traveled to a hospital in Chicago so they could talk to the boys who had been held in captivity as part of a human trafficking ring, so George didn't have much of an opportunity to talk to either of them. He and

Billy spent most of the day planting flowers for Miss Bert and Mr. Jon, the Lanes who lived next door and who seemed to be unofficial grandparents to the twins. At least, that was how they treated the twins and how the twins treated them. George liked them. While Billy acted as if nothing unusual had happened, and while the Lanes said nothing about what had happened, he knew the Lanes knew about it, and it seemed that at least they had treated him differently. Maybe it was just his imagination.

The kitchen door opened and was shut quietly, but instead of Jeremy, it was Billy. He was barefoot and dressed just as George was in boxers and wrapped in a light blanket. He sat down next to George and gave half of the blanket to him, who wrapped himself in it and the two boys huddled together.

"Sorry if I woke you up," George offered after a bit.

Billy yawned, shrugged and said, "I couldn't sleep either."

George knew he was just being polite, but he accepted his statement.

"How come you're up?" Billy asked.

George didn't say anything and he stared out at the backyard not focusing on anything.

"When I was little and had a bad dream, my dad would sit up with me while I told him about it. It made it go away. Now, Jeremy does, but I don't have bad dreams that much anymore."

George looked at him curiously.

Billy shrugged and said, "I was adopted twice. My first dad died of a heart attack."

George nodded.

"So?" Billy said.

George shook his head.

Changing thoughts, he asked, "Have you decided if you're going to live with us?"

George shrugged noncommittally. As many reasons as he had for staying, he had an equal number of reasons for not. Well, not really as many reasons for not. Actually, not that many at all. Truth was he was scared: scared of staying, scared of leaving. Just plain scared.

Billy had come to know George well enough in the last two days to understand that George was quiet and only spoke when he wanted to, so he gave up trying.

Billy and Randy were identical twins and only those who spent time around them knew how to tell the difference. Both had brown hair cut short in the same style. Both had large brown eyes, though Randy's seemed sad even when he smiled. Billy had a bit of a crooked smile and had a habit of cocking his head when he listened. He was older by eight minutes, born four minutes before midnight, while Randy was born four minutes after midnight. The twins were fourteen-years-old, a month or so older than George, and all three boys were headed for eighth grade in the fall, one and a half months away.

George liked them both and felt he could easily become friends with them. Randy was gentle and a listener. Billy was a joker and a talker. Even though Billy was older, it was Randy who made the decisions. Most of all, George liked watching Jeremy interact with them. He saw the love they had for each other and envied them and it reminded him of just how lonely and alone he was.

Billy sighed and not really understanding why, said, "I think I killed my first dad."

George turned to look at Billy who quickly wiped away some tears on the blanket wrapped around them.

"Why do you think that?"

Billy looked down at his bare feet and then out at the yard.

"I was pissed at my mom for not telling me I was adopted. My parents got divorced and I lived with my dad but spent a lot of time with Jeremy and Randy." He wiped more tears off his face with the blanket and said, "My dad missed my mom and he was lonely. He died of a heart attack."

George nodded, letting the silence envelope them like the blanket wrapped around them.

Billy shrugged.

"Are you happy living with Mr. Jeremy and Randy?"

Without any hesitation, Billy said, "Oh yeah. I love them. Jeremy's my dad now, and Randy's my brother. They're my best friends." Then he was quiet for a moment and said, "I just miss my first dad every now and then."

George nodded.

"When my dad died, I was hoping Jeremy would let me live with him and Randy. He adopted me like he did Randy, but I kept my dad's name, you know, out of respect, kind of." Billy shrugged and said, "It seemed like the right thing to do."

George nodded. That seemed right to him too. He thought that if Mr. Jeremy would adopt him, he'd keep his last name, Tokay, out of respect for his family, his grandfather in particular.

That thought startled him.

No one had asked him if he had wanted to be adopted. There was the offer to have him live with them, but he didn't know if he was going to accept it, and didn't know if that meant Jeremy would adopt him.

"You and I are sort of alike," Billy said, shaking him out of his thoughts.

"How?" George asked.

"I didn't have anyone after my dad died and there was no way I was going to live with my mom. Jeremy offered to have me live with him and now he's my dad and Randy's my brother. He's always been my brother, but you know what I mean. You don't have anyone and dad asked you to live with us." He shrugged and said, "We're kind of alike."

Not wanting to get into it, he said, "It's late. We should probably get back to bed."

He got up and Billy followed him back into the kitchen and up the stairs to bed.

CHAPTER TWO

Indianapolis, Indiana

His idiot partner had tipped him off accidently by calling to let him know that two Feebs showed up at the precinct carrying a warrant and telling a story about his involvement in a nationwide human trafficking ring. His partner knew it couldn't possibly be true.

It's not possible, right? Some sort of mistake, right? his partner had asked.

He had fooled his partner, just like he had fooled everyone else. He was, after all, smarter than any of them.

He had just finished his workout at the gym when his partner had called, so he had to get back to his house and get in and out before the Feebs showed up. Had to hurry, because he knew they'd eventually come to the house if he didn't show up at the station. He had no intention of doing that, though he had told his partner that he'd be there to straighten it all out in about an hour. He thought that might buy him some time.

He told his partner to chill. That was his partner's favorite word and it was one of the many things he had hated about his partner. That and his picking his teeth with his long-ass fingernails after each and every meal, listening to hip-hop crap on the radio trying to fit in with the Spades and the Spics on the force, and drinking green tea like a fucking Yuppie.

He hated his stupid-ass, farm-boy partner and if the opportunity ever presented itself, he'd take his .45 and pull the trigger sending a slug smack dab into the middle of his forehead so it would rattle around in his empty skull and blow a baseball-sized chunk out the back. Would serve him right, the stupid asshole.

He had seen the first reports of the human trafficking ring bust while working out at the gym. He had stepped off the treadmill and grabbed a towel, wiped down his face and draped it across his shoulders. He grabbed his water bottle, drank deeply and walked over and stood at the back of a crowd who had stopped their workouts and watched one of the several flat-screened TVs mounted on the wall. Three of the screens were tuned to CNN; two to ABC; two to CBS; and three to ESPN. No one paid any attention to the ones tuned to ESPN.

The group he stood behind listened to and watched a talking head while a videotape played on the half-screen showing cops wandering around the street and walking in and out of a building in Chicago. EMT trucks and cop cars had been coming and going all morning, but the cameras hadn't shown any of the passengers.

He had recognized the building in Chicago, because he had been there many times.

Every now and then it would cut away to Kansas City or Long Beach. The stories were the same: A human trafficking ring had been busted. Prominent local, state and national political officials, religious leaders, sports and entertainment figures arrested. Kids- all boys who had been kidnapped and held captive, some for more than two years- had been freed and taken to local hospitals to be checked over before they were released to their parents.

Walking nonchalantly to the locker room, he had gathered his things and left without showering. He had to get home and get moving. He had things to take care of. It was on his way home when his partner had called.

Driving slowly, taking care not to draw any attention, he parked a block from his house on a side street of a normal-looking tree-lined drive with white picket fences and bright, sunny flowers growing under front windows and around mailboxes. Bicycles, skateboards and scooters sat in driveways. He stayed in his car with the window down breathing deeply of recently mowed lawn. He got out of his car and locked it, but didn't bother to wipe it down because a simple check on his tags would tell everyone who it had belonged to. By the time they got around to looking for it, he'd be long gone anyway.

Slowly, he surveyed the streets and houses for anything or anyone out of the ordinary.

Nothing.

He crossed the street to the alley and walked down it as if it were something he did every day.

At six-two, two-hundred and twenty pounds, he moved like the athlete he was. He worked out at the gym three or four days a week with free weights. He pounded a heavy bag now and then. He jumped rope for twenty minutes every day and ran six to ten miles before dawn in any kind of weather. He was proud of his body and the shape he was in, viewing it as an asset, a weapon.

He knew this day would come eventually and had been planning for it. He had salted money away and had created an account at a different bank from the one he used to pay the bills. He had created two other identities complete with social security cards and drivers' licenses using a Weasel from the streets who specialized in creating identities. One of the many Weasels he had cultivated from his years on the force. He had secured credit cards with large available balances under both names, along with a car titled and registered in a garage of a townhouse in a northwestern suburb of the city, leased under the name of one of the identities he had created.

Knowing the day would come is different from the day actually arriving.

He had rehearsed. He had planned. He had already tied up loose ends. Like the Weasel.

The Weasel no longer existed. Body gone. Any evidence vanished in a fire described as suspicious, more than likely arson and it was done so there was absolutely no possible blow back to him.

At the back of his house, he paused at the garbage cans lined side by side in the alley pretending to tidy up a bit, but watching and listening for anything out of the ordinary.

Nothing.

He moved quickly to the backdoor, pulled the screen door back and used the key he had pulled from his pocket to unlock the deadbolt. He entered quickly and shut and locked the door behind him and pulled his gun from the pocket of his navy-blue Indianapolis Colts hoodie as he did so.

No sound.

Moving quickly, he went to the guest bedroom, knelt down and loosened the thread in the carpet just to the left of the closet and lifted it up revealing a twelve-by-twelve square piece of three-quarter inch plywood. He used the point of his key to work around an edge of it and lifted it up revealing a drop box of sorts.

He pulled out a fully loaded, unregistered Glock .9M and two magazines loaded with .9M hollow point bullets. The serial numbers had been filed off making the gun temporarily untraceable, courtesy of another one of his Weasels, this one a cocaine dealer who supposedly died in a drug deal gone bad. Not coincidently, the bullets found in his skull came from a Glock .9M just like the one he shoved into his waistband. Temporarily untraceable, because the firing pin like any other firing pin had a serial number few, if any gun owners, knew about.

Underneath the gun were ten banded bundles of cash, all fifties.

A half-million. Emergency money.

Underneath the money were a passport and a wallet with a driver's license and social security card of one of his identities, two credit cards in the same name and a set of keys.

He took a careful look out of the corner of the living room window and satisfied that there wasn't anything unusual, he pulled the hood over his head and left the house as easily and as quickly as he had arrived. He carried two duffle bags with the money split evenly between them and some clothes on top to help conceal it.

Four easy blocks away was a metro bus stop that would take him downtown to the station where he'd catch another bus to the North side suburb where his townhouse was located. The trip would take him thirty-seven minutes.

He knew this because he had rehearsed.

He was ready to disappear. At least, for a while, but he would be back. He had unfinished business to attend to.

CHAPTER THREE

Chicago, Illinois

Brett didn't sleep well and it wasn't from the pain in his shoulder from the gunshot even though it hurt like crazy. It wasn't the intercom chimes that preceded announcements for Doctor So and So to call this number or that number, and it wasn't the fact that in his twenty-two months in captivity, he hadn't slept much at night except in snatches.

This morning at some point, he was going to see his parents again and he was nervous, if not scared, to see them.

He had been trying desperately to remember what they had looked like, how they might have changed, and mostly trying to remember the sound of their voices. He had tried to picture his house and his room, but those memories seemed smoky and faded like an old photograph. That, too, had scared him, but left him mostly sad. During the time he was in captivity, he had often wondered if they would remember him or if they had given up on him.

Mostly, he had wondered if he had somehow disappointed them, especially after they found out what he had to do during the time he was in captivity.

Brett had watched Tim meet his parents for the first time in over two years. While that reunion seemed to go well, he had learned from Tim that his parents weren't comfortable with him talking about all that he had been through. They explained to him that it might be best if he let the past stay in the past and that he should just move forward. Neither Brett nor Tim had understood how that would be possible given all that had happened to them.

Brett had watched Stephen struggle with his father, and Stephen had only been missing one night. But his father had spent time doting on Michael who was abducted with Stephen. The difference was that Michael had suffered, and suffered badly.

Stephen had confided in Brett and Tim that he thought his dad was ashamed of him for not putting up a fight, and that maybe his dad liked Michael more because of all the abuse he suffered.

"Not putting up a fight?" Tim had asked quietly as they sat in the sun room at the end of the hall, their favorite place to sit and talk. "Doesn't he realize that you *couldn't* have put up a fight? You would have gotten killed!"

Stephen had shrugged.

"Didn't Randy's dad talk to him?" Brett had asked.

Stephen had shrugged again and said, "Jeremy told them, but I think my dad thinks I'm gay and that I wanted all this shit to happen to me."

"You're not gay, Stephen," Tim had said. "None of us wanted this to happen to us. We had no *choice*. *You* didn't have a choice."

"I don't think he believes that."

And so, the conversation went. Mike was uncomfortable with Stephen's dad's attention and wanted to be left alone. Mike had even told Brett that he was afraid of losing Stephen's friendship and when Brett had mentioned that, Stephen just shook his head and wept some more.

So, that left Brett worrying about meeting his parents and what might be in store for him.

The other guys seemed to do okay with their parents, guys like Ian and Patrick. But he had watched his friends and he had worried. All of the other boys had gone home, except for Tim, Mike, Stephen and Johnny. Brett worried that Johnny might not ever make it home because he had heard doctors and nurses talk about him in hushed tones. Johnny's parents hadn't shown up yet either.

Brett woke up tired. A fairly typical morning after a fairly typical night for him as far as sleeping went. He kept his eyes closed and he lay still listening to the sounds of the hospital. He had learned to listen well and to use his sense of smell to his best advantage. Captivity and the constant threat of being whipped or branded would do that.

He had learned to know the guards by their smell and the sounds of their shoes and the distance between their steps. Their faces were permanently etched in his brain and it would take a million years to forget them and what had happened to him.

In this same way even after just the one day and one night he'd been in the hospital, Brett knew the sounds the different aides and nurses made, as well as the smell of their shampoo and their deodorant.

His shoulder ached. The bullet had come from a .38 and left a jagged and quarter-sized hole, dark like molasses against his normally dark complexion, and he was still heavily bandaged and in a sling. It had entered his left shoulder, exited out his armpit and lodged in his tricep. He had spent a couple of hours in surgery the morning before and that same afternoon had his first physical therapy session which hurt like hell.

He took the medicine that would prevent any infection and one that reduced inflammation, but he had refused any pain medication. Brett refused because he didn't want to be out of it or *loopy* as he and the rest of the boys described the sensation.

Twenty-two months ago, he was taken late in the afternoon after school as he peddled his bike to a pick-up basketball game at the middle school five blocks away. Like all the other boys, they had drugged him and he hated the zombie-like feeling.

He and the other boys were given two pills to take each morning before their breakfast and shower. One was something to keep them in submission and under control. So, while they stood in line waiting for their turn in the shower, Johnny and Tim had devised a plan and had coached the boys to fake taking that pill. They ended up fooling the guards. It was just a matter of finding an opportune time to spit the pill out and dispose of it without getting caught. Risky, but the boys took that risk.

The doctor at the hospital had told Brett he was lucky. Had the bullet been from a larger caliber gun and had struck an inch or so to the right, it would have hit his lung or heart. As it was, if he had listened to Skip, he wouldn't have been shot at all.

Brett turned slightly, opened his eyes and looked at Skip who was curled up on two chairs at the side of his bed, sleeping with what looked like a grimace on his face. Evidently the dream he was having wasn't a very good one.

Brett was an expert on bad dreams. For him, every night ended with a bad dream and was a prelude to a bad day. One bad day after another. One bad day leading to one bad night and over and over on permanent rewind and repeat for twenty-two months.

He watched Skip sleep under only a flimsy white blanket, knowing that even though he had worn his clothes, he must have been cold. The hospital seemed to not have any warmth at all and ever since arriving, Skip and Brett and the other boys had had a chronic case of goose bumps. No cure for that except warmth and the hospital didn't believe in that.

Skip Dahlke was a forensic scientist in Wisconsin up until yesterday. He had been recruited for the siege on a building in Chicago that would eventually free thirteen boys held in captivity and he had been an almost constant companion of Brett ever since. Brett wasn't sure why he had spent so much time in his room or why he chose to sleep there, but he welcomed his presence. He felt reassured somehow, and more importantly, safe. The fact that there were cops guarding either end of the hallway helped too.

All of the major networks and CNN had carried the story of the boys' rescue: thirteen boys in Chicago, four boys from a motel in Kansas City and twelve boys from a building in Long Beach, California in three separate but simultaneous raids by a coalition of FBI, police and sheriff deputies. The raids also brought the arrest of 123 men from across the country, but that number was in a state of flux. Originally, there were 147 warrants issued, but the FBI had figured that by the time it was all said and done, there would be more because the initial reports put the number at 117. Several had committed suicide upon hearing the news reports, while still others couldn't be found or located. U.S. Marshalls and police departments had arrested those they could find, many of whom argued and objected that it was a misunderstanding and a mistake.

Not a mistake, but a human trafficking ring run by Victor Bosch, AKA Gary Sears, or *The Dark Man* as the boys had called him. These men had taken part in the kidnapping, abuse and torture of the boys who had been saved, along with the murder of others who hadn't been as lucky. Some of these same men were actually responsible for identifying and targeting the boys.

Just as Brett's uncle, Detective Anthony Dominico, had done.

Brett couldn't wait to confront him.

Bosch had a horse ranch outside of Conway, Arizona, a suburb of Phoenix, but his *real* business was the human trafficking of boys in Chicago and Long Beach, as well as a mobile component that moved kids around the country. He and two former FBI agents were confronted in Sheraton restaurant in downtown Chicago. Bosch and Agent Douglas Rawson were arrested and taken away in handcuffs, while Agent Thatcher Davis had grabbed a knife and stabbed it deeply into his neck and bled to death before he could be arrested.

Brett and the rest of the boys who had ranged in age from twelve to fourteen had been abducted off the streets in their hometowns and had been forced into a life they had never dreamed existed, nor wanted. The boys had been forced to do whatever a sick, perverted mind could imagine.

He shut his eyes to push those thoughts away, but they were there and weren't going anywhere for a long, long time. Brett was smart enough to know they might not ever go away.

He opened his eyes and found the clock on the wall that read 5:12.

Almost morning.

The light from the window was brightening, though there were clouds in the sky and not much sun. Moving quietly, silently, Brett swung his bare feet over the side of the bed because he had to get going. This was a big day, an important day.

Using his good arm, Brett yanked one of the blankets off his bed and placed it over Skip carefully so as not to wake him. He stood at the doorway looking out into the hallway and across from his room at the nurses' station.

His chestnut eyes missed nothing. Carol, the night nurse sat at her desk, her back to him, pecking away on a computer keyboard. Her shift had officially ended at five, but Brett knew his mother, also a nurse, had often worked longer to catch up on the pile of paperwork that had accrued during her shift. To his right and down the hall towards Tim's and Mike's room, Rodney, one of the day orderlies leaned against a wall and flirted with Dee.

"Brett McGovern, what are you doing up so *early*?" came a harsh, but playful whisper from his left.

Monique, a big woman and Brett's favorite nurse, stood in the hallway with her hands on her considerable hips, feigning anger.

"Shhh . . . Skip's still asleep," Brett whispered. He pulled his door to a crack and smiled at her.

"Hmm, hmm, hmm. That boy could come to my house and sleep in my bed any time, but instead, he sleeps in a chair in your room. I must be slippin' or somethin'."

"Monique, you know I have dibs on him," Carol said getting up from her computer. "Brett, honey, give me my morning hug."

She scooped Brett up in her arms, careful not to press against his shoulder, and kissed the top of his head.

"How's our angel this morning?"

Blushing, Brett shrugged his good shoulder and said, "Ok."

"Brett, you know why Carol puts in extra time? Just so she can steal Skip from me," Monique said. And to Carol, she said wagging a finger, "An' don't you think I don't know that."

Turning back to Brett she said, "Give Big Monique a hug, Angel."

Brett was immediately enveloped by the big lady, but gently and tenderly. She kissed the top of his head as Carol had done, took his handsome, young face in both of her hands and looked him squarely in the eye.

"How did you sleep and don't you dare give me no BS. I want an honest answer."

Brett made a face and shrugged his good shoulder.

"That's what I thought. Honey," Monique said shaking her head at him, "Carol and Dr. Blaine said you aren't taking any pain meds. Why?"

"I don't need to. I'm okay."

She waved her arm from left to right and said, "My BS meter works just fine, Angel."

"I'm okay," Brett repeated quietly.

"Carol told me you barely ate your supper. I can count every one of your ribs, Child," she said poking a finger at his stomach tickling him.

Brett danced out of the way, but didn't comment and just smiled up at her. Truth was he didn't have much of an appetite. Twenty-two months of fast food menu items would do that. He, like the other boys, came to the hospital malnourished and dehydrated. Monique knew hospital food wasn't the best in the world, but it was damn site better than any fast food restaurant.

"You have to promise me you'll eat some breakfast and take your vitamins, okay?"

Brett blushed and nodded.

Monique held onto his cheeks and gave him a most disapproving frown, before she softened and hugged him again.

"I need one more hug before I get going. Where are you off to? I don't think anyone else is up yet."

By anyone else, she meant Tim and Mike. Stephen had moved to a hotel nearby with his parents.

Tim had been in captivity longer than Brett had been and had become Brett's closest friend. Besides Johnny that is. But Johnny was on the second floor in intensive care fighting to make it. He had been sick for about a week before the boys were freed- coughing, sweating, and weak. He hadn't gotten better and Brett knew the doctors and nurses had been particularly worried about him. They didn't say too much, but Brett knew anyway. It was in what they *didn't* say that told him Johnny was in trouble.

Tim was a little taller than Brett, a little on the lanky side with longish blond hair. He looked like the smart twin on *Suite Life On Deck*, a TV show Brett used to watch way back when. Tim was the boys' acknowledged leader and Brett was Tim's closest confidant and his right-hand man. Dark and brown-haired to Tim's light complexion and blond hair. A perfect complement- not only in looks but in personality: Tim the thinker, Brett the doer.

The night before they were rescued, Tim had a date- *The Cop*- who liked to use his nightstick on the boys. Brett had been on the receiving end of the nightstick himself. Tim had surgery and ended up with a half-dozen stitches and Brett took on the role of helping Tim when he needed to use the toilet and even helped him with his Sitz baths.

Tim had requested that Mike room with him.

Mike had suffered the most of all of the boys because he *wasn't* the one *selected*. Mike just happened to have had the misfortune of being with Stephen when the two were abducted off the streets of Waukesha, Wisconsin. Stephen was the boy they had targeted and wanted, while Mike would only be around for a couple of days for the guards to use before he was disposed of. Besides the black eyes- one was swollen completely shut- he had two teeth missing and one other loosened. Like Tim, he had about a half-dozen stitches and Brett took care of him too.

Michael had suffered far beyond anything physical though. He had developed a severe stutter on both hard and soft consonants, as well as on some vowels. Stephen had told the doctor and Tim and Brett that Mike had never stuttered as long as he had known him, and they had been friends since elementary. Brett and Tim had privately worried that Mike might never talk normally again.

"Brett, you've been such a help to Tim and Michael that we felt we needed to get you something to say '*Thank You*'," Monique said motioning to Rodney and Dee to join them and snapping Brett out of his reverie.

Carol moved back behind the nurses' station and took a Dick's Sporting Goods bag and handed it to Brett. Blushing, he took it, peeked inside and smiled, and pulled out a Chicago Bears t-shirt.

"We know you're a Colts fan, Angel," Monique said.

"But we're Bears fans, so when you wear this, you have to think of us," Carol said.

Brett smiled at them and fought back tears. He looked down and blinked rapidly, and swallowed mightily at a lump in his throat that seemed to grow to the size of a boulder.

"Thank you," he said thickly.

Rodney gave him a 'man hug' and a high five. Dee gave him a hug and a kiss on the top of his head, as did Carol.

Monique held his face in his hands and said, "Angel, we're gonna miss you!" She hugged him once, twice, and kissed the top of his head, and then brushed tears off her face.

CHAPTER FOUR

Waukesha, Wisconsin

Jeremy Evans lay in bed enjoying the silence of his house and the light, cool breeze puffing his bedroom curtains, knowing George would be up shortly. Jeremy had become a morning person during his undergrad years at the University of Wisconsin – La Crosse. Morning was his time to say his prayers, read some scripture and think. Perhaps worry, because he was a first class, A-number one worrier.

He was single, had never married and since the sixth grade, had toyed with the idea of becoming a priest. However, the idea of celibacy drove him crazy, not that he was ever promiscuous. It was the concept of priesthood he had thought about seriously: the mysticism, the prayer life, the religiousness all appealed to him. Just not the celibacy.

Jeremy generally had a ready laugh, was quiet in new situations and surroundings, and was considered by others to be friendly. His brown hair had thinned out and had begun to turn gray. His face was scarred from a major bout with acne as a teenager, but everyone seemed to look past it because he was considered kind and understanding. Jeremy, however, saw it each and every time he looked in the mirror.

At thirty-six, he was a high school counselor who was on-call for police and sheriff departments and the FBI. Formerly, he was a social studies teacher and a head boys basketball coach, but never a priest. With the twins already, his family might grow again if George decided to stay with them.

It had been a long, strange road. Some people collected coins or stamps. Others collected beer cans or some dumb thing like that. Jeremy collected kids, not that he had ever tried to do so.

Fourteen-year-old Randy, his first, had run away from an abusive home and was placed into foster care. Because Jeremy was on the foster list in hopes of eventually adopting a child, he ended up with Randy a little over two years previous. Billy, Randy's twin came along a little over a year later.

The twins were born to a school-aged mom and were given up for adoption, and because neither family had wanted a set of twins, the agency agreed to separate them.

Randy had known from little on he was adopted because his adoptive father had shouted it with every punch and shove, along with the admonition, "We should ship your ass back to Milwaukee where you came from."

Billy had no idea he had been adopted until Randy had shown up. Billy's parents hadn't told him. A picture and story about Jeremy and Randy appeared in the paper and Billy was the first to see it starting a war in the Schroeder household that ended when Robert and Monica divorced.

Monica had moved out of the house to live on the east side of Milwaukee and Billy had refused visitation weekends, so eventually Monica gave up trying. The boys met and became close friends. One would begin a sentence and the other would finish it. They didn't need words to communicate and it was scary how much conversation took place nonverbally.

One early September afternoon, Billy had come home from school and found Robert lying in the upstairs hallway clutching two chocolate chip cookies, dead from a massive heart attack.

There was a legal battle.

Robert's will gave most of his money to Billy, with Jeremy the executor of a trust set up by a huge life insurance policy. Monica had a lawyer who demanded not only the money, but also that Billy live with her because she was the original adoptive mother. Jeremy had a pricey lawyer bought and paid for by his best friend, Jeff Limbach, an international bestselling author. No way could Jeremy have afforded the meetings, the briefs, the- *crap*- as he put it, without Jeff's help.

Billy refused to speak to her or to her lawyer, but it was his threat to run away any chance he could that eventually wore Monica down. She gave up and moved out of state and Billy hadn't had any contact with her since, even though Jeremy had encouraged him to. Eventually, Jeremy had given up too.

So, Jeremy had a set of twins, each going by different last names: Randy Evans, who was eventually adopted by Jeremy, and Billy Schroeder. He was also adopted by Jeremy, but out of respect for his original adoptive father, he had kept his original last name. It was confusing to outsiders, but perfectly normal to those who were close to the twins.

And now there was George.

Two days previous, FBI agent Pete Kelliher, a guy Jeremy had never met, called and asked to meet him. Being curious, Jeremy agreed. Kelliher brought George in tow and asked Jeremy to watch over him while he and the members on his team investigated a human trafficking ring across half of the United States.

Pete had no idea when George would go home, and now it seemed that he might not *ever* go home except to tie up loose ends.

The problem was that George didn't have a home to go home to. He had witnessed a murder- an execution, really- of a boy his own age while tending his family's sheep on the Navajo reservation in Northeast Arizona. He stepped forward as a witness and in retaliation, his grandparents, his mother, his sister and two brothers were murdered and his house set burned to the ground. The only reason George wasn't murdered was because, at the request of Kelliher and the FBI, he was in Wisconsin at a scene of yet another child murder, identifying two perpetrators- found dead alongside the boy.

George had never really known his father and the only living relative he had was a twenty-six-year-old single cousin who was a Navajo Nation Policeman living in a trailer by a creek bed that was more dry than wet.

What worried Jeremy, what kept him awake at night and the puzzle he prayed about and tried to solve early each morning before the boys awoke, was how he was going to afford the twins and a third fourteen-year-old boy, on a high school counselor's salary. George hadn't come with anything other than the clothes on his back, the Adidas shoes on his feet and a small, beat up duffle bag that contained his cowboy boots and moccasins, and a small plastic Target sack that included a toothbrush, toothpaste and deodorant, socks, two t-shirts and three pair of boxers purchased by Kelliher when he had dropped the boy off. Thankfully, the three boys were almost the same height, though George was more narrow and lankier.

Jeremy had also wondered and worried how the boy was coping. He couldn't fathom the loss, the loneliness, the emptiness, and the confusion the boy must be feeling. Only knowing George for a day, Jeremy and the twins had asked the boy to live with them. They hoped he would, but George hadn't given them a clue as to what he was thinking.

The toilet down the hall flushed. Water ran in the sink and a moment later, a shadow appeared in the doorway.

At first, nothing was said. Then in a whisper, George said, "Mr. Jeremy?"

"Good morning, George. Come in."

George stood at the foot of the bed, hugging his bare chest.

"You're making me cold, Kiddo. Get yourself warm," Jeremy whispered in a laugh.

George sat down on the edge of the bed, still hugging himself.

"What's on your mind?"

George didn't answer. He merely lowered his head, his shiny, shoulder length, black hair obscuring his face. Jeremy could see the knots of the boy's spine as George hunched over. He could even count his ribs. He waited patiently.

"I don't know what to do," George finally said.

Jeremy got up out of bed and sat next to him on the end of the bed.

"What are your options?"

George looked up and Jeremy saw tears.

"Move back home to Arizona or live here," George said quietly.

"What are the advantages of moving back to Arizona?"

George lowered his head and was silent for a time, and then said, "I'd be back among my people, in my land. I'd be with my cousin."

"Any other advantages?"

His friend, Rebecca and her brother, Charles flashed through his mind, but in the end, George shrugged and then shook his head.

"What are the disadvantages?"

Without much hesitation, George said, "I don't have a family anymore. I have nothing." He began to weep.

"Hey, Kiddo," Jeremy said slipping his arm around the boy's shoulders. It broke his heart to see the boy like this, any kid like this. He kissed the side of his head.

"If you live here, what are the advantages?"

George shrugged, wiped his eyes with his hands, and then wiped his hands on the sheet beneath him.

"Randy and Billy and you. Mr. Jon and Miss Bert next door."

"And?"

George shrugged and said, "What?"

"You'd have a home. You'd have a family. You'd have people who care about you and want you."

George wept and Jeremy gave his shoulder a squeeze and kissed the side of his head again.

"The Navajo believe in balance."

"I know . . . I mean, I don't know a lot about Navajo customs or beliefs, but I've been doing some research," Jeremy said softly.

"I think I'm upsetting the balance between Randy and Billy."

"Huh . . ." Jeremy said. He hadn't noticed any rift between the boys, so he asked, "How's that?"

"Randy and Billy are best friends. They're different, but the same. They had their own bedroom, but now I'm there."

"I thought it was Billy's idea to move the double bed into their room and move the single bed into the spare room," Jeremy said.

"It's *their* room. I feel like I don't belong," he answered and wept some more.

"But again, it was Billy's idea to move the bed into the room and to sleep with you. I think Randy agreed to it, didn't he?"

George nodded.

"Why else do you think you're disturbing their balance?" Jeremy asked.

"They don't get to spend as much time with each other. You don't get to spend as much time with them." He shrugged and said again, "I'm upsetting the balance."

"The boys will always be together, George. Billy walked away from his adoptive mother to be with Randy, and Randy ran away from home to find Billy. I don't think anyone will come between the two boys." He paused to let that sink in and then said, "I play continue to play tennis with Billy and golf with both boys. We will go to Billy's baseball games. Randy and I will find things to do together. But honestly, I think I need to spend more time with you."

George turned to look at Jeremy and wiped some tears off his face and dried his hands on the sheets.

"George, love isn't like a cake you divide up into pieces. Love is magical in that the more you give it away, the more you end up having. Randy finds time to be with me. Billy spends time with me. They will find time to be with each other and with you. You and I will spend time together. And much of the time, just like any family, the four of us will spend time all together."

George shrugged but didn't say anything.

"I have an idea, Kiddo, but I need you to hear me out before you say anything, okay?"

The boy nodded.

"Don't make *any* decision yet. Later this morning, my friend Jeff Limbach and his son Danny will pick you guys up and you'll drive to Chicago to meet me. Just like we planned, we'll travel to Arizona so you can see your cousin and make peace with your family.

"It will take ten days, maybe longer and along the way, we'll spend time together and see parts of the country you and the twins have never seen. Jeff has to drive Danny back to Omaha because that was the arrangement he had with Danny's mother.

"But I'd like you to come back with us for the rest of the summer. Make your decision then, *after* you get to know us. It's a big decision and you shouldn't rush it. Take your time. Get to know us."

He stopped and George didn't say anything. Jeremy stroked George's hair and kissed the side of his head again.

"George, I promise whatever decision you make, the boys and I will support it. If you decide to live in Arizona with your people, I hope you'll stay with us during the summer and for some of our holidays. If you decide to live with us, we'll make sure you get to visit your people and your cousin. That's a promise."

George turned towards Jeremy, pulled a leg up under him, facing him, and pushed his hair behind his ear.

"If I live here, I might lose who I am. My grandfather warned me about living with the *biligaana*, white people, because Navajos who do, lose their way. I'm Navajo."

Jeremy took hold of George's hand and smiled.

"Absolutely. You're Navajo, but being a Navajo is more than just a name. It's a way of life. It's *being*."

Jeremy tapped George's bare chest.

"Being a Navajo is in your heart." Jeremy tapped George's head. "Being a Navajo is in what you believe. It's in your blood, your skin. It's a way of life." He paused and asked, "How many mornings have you missed practicing with your knife in the backyard or saying your morning prayers facing the rising sun?"

George frowned and said, "None."

Jeremy smiled and said, "Exactly. Even though you're two thousand miles away and living with people you just met, you still kept up the Navajo traditions your grandfather taught you."

George nodded.

"I think you've learned more from your grandfather than you give yourself credit for, George. No matter where you live, you'll always be Navajo. That's something to be proud of, something to share and teach others, like Randy, and Billy, and me. We can learn from you, and I think you can learn from us. That's what being a family's all about."

George nodded again.

Jeremy thumbed some tears out of George's eyes and held his face gently.

"Don't make your decision yet. You're not ready. When it is, you'll know." He tapped George on his chest. "When it's time, you'll know."

George didn't say anything. He didn't nod and didn't attempt to move. He had a distant look in his dark eyes and Jeremy thought he could hear gears spinning.

"What are you thinking?"

He had thought about sharing the dream with Jeremy, but instead, George shook his head once and said nothing.

"You have a lot to think about. Promise me you and I can talk like this every now and then in the next few days?"

George nodded.

"Kiddo, I have to get moving so I can get to Chicago before this one boy's parents arrive." Jeremy got up off the bed and stretched.

George climbed off the bed and moved towards the door, but turned to face Jeremy.

"Come here, Kid," Jeremy said holding out his arms.

George stepped quietly towards Jeremy and they embraced. They stood there and held onto each other. Jeremy let go, but held George's face in his hands.

"You'll be okay, George. It won't be the same. It will be different, but you'll be okay. I promise."

George nodded and hugged Jeremy again, and then turned and left the room.

CHAPTER FIVE

Waukesha, Wisconsin

Like most of America, he had watched the news reports coming out of Chicago, Kansas City and Long Beach. A cold sweat broke out over his skin. His stomach lurched and he had to run to the bathroom to throw up. When he was finished, he rinsed his mouth out with water from the sink and came back and sat on the edge of his couch and stared at his TV. He had tried three times to access the website, but couldn't get to it. It had disappeared, so he decided to stop trying because he was afraid his efforts might be traced back to him.

He nearly passed out when the reporter spoke of the arrest warrants. He hastily threw some clothes and toiletries in a duffle bag. He gathered his checkbook, laptop, cell phone and wallet. He grabbed his keys, locked up his house and drove to the Holiday Inn Express on Bluemound Road. After checking in and dumping his duffle on the bed, he turned on the TV to catch the latest. There wasn't anything new, so he made a quick run to an ATM, withdrew cash, drove to a 7 Eleven and picked up a six pack of cold Mt. Dew and a family-sized bag of Peanut M&M's, and drove back to the motel and hunkered down in front of the TV, zoning out on caffeine and sugar and his name wouldn't be mentioned.

He had a lot to lose.

He didn't have a wife or any children, but he did have a mother who lived in an assisted living complex in Whitefish Bay and an older brother and his wife and their two children living in Wausau. What would they think if he was arrested- not to mention his partners and co-workers?

He got up from the edge of the bed holding his can of Dew, stepped to the side of the window, moved the curtain with his forefinger, and peered out into the parking lot expecting to see squad cars with cops pouring out of opened doors, all running to the lobby.

Nothing except for a few parked cars. No one running in the parking lot or even walking for that matter.

Bluemound Road, which stretched out like a long gray arm just beyond the Holiday Inn Express parking lot was a two-, sometimes three-lane road running east and west from Milwaukee to Waukesha and beyond. Traffic was heavy any time of day or night, and it was no less heavy now.

He watched absent-mindedly, thinking about his next steps and wondering what he should do and where he should go. He didn't know how much time he had before they found him. If they found him.

If they were even looking for him.

With each minute, each hour that went by, he gathered hope like a snowball rolling downhill that he had somehow escaped.

He jumped when his cell chirped, but he didn't move to answer it. The small hairs on the back of his neck stood ramrod straight. His stomach tightened and he had the sudden urge to run to the bathroom and throw up again, but he didn't. Instead, he stood at the foot of the bed, biting his knuckle hard enough to draw blood, and he continued to bite it for a full two minutes after it had stopped chirping. Finally, he picked it up to see who had called.

Bonnie, the receptionist.

He dialed up his voicemail, punched in his password and listened.

Hey there. Just wondered if you'd be in today. We're celebrating because they found the two boys in the Amber Alert . . . Stephen and Michael, and they're coming home today. Isn't that wonderful? Give me a holler to let me know if you'll be in. Later!

He listened again to try to catch any sign of a trap or if they had suspected anything, but didn't find anything remotely suspicious. Bonnie was just being Bonnie: happy, bubbly, efficient. Just to be sure, he listened one more time. He tossed the phone on the bed, drained his Mt. Dew, threw the empty into the garbage can by the little desk, and then ran both hands over his face. He sat down on the edge of the bed to watch the news reports, flipping between Fox and CNN.

CHAPTER SIX

Chicago, Illinois

Skip Dahlke was a twenty-seven-year-old who looked more like a seventeen-year-old. He had dishwater blond hair and was perpetually pale no matter how much sun he got. If anything, he would burn bright red, then peel, and turn back to white. Never tan. He was a skinny young man, perhaps twenty-five pounds underweight who chose to wear wire rim glasses instead of contacts. He stood only five-ten, and maybe weighed a hundred-fifty pounds soaking wet.

He was also incredibly bright, having earned an undergraduate degree in Chemistry with a minor in Biology from Carroll College in Waukesha, Wisconsin and a Master of Science in Forensic Science from Michigan State. Up until a day or so ago, he had worked in one of the state crime labs out of Wausau in Northern Wisconsin. He was the lead forensic technician called to a crime scene near Pembine involving a dead boy and two dead male adults later identified as the individuals who had executed a boy in Arizona. But after he had participated in the raid to free the boys in Chicago, and while waiting for Brett to get out of surgery, he had received a phone call from a co-worker that the Wausau lab was being shut down because of budget cuts. He was invited to apply for a position in either the Madison or Milwaukee lab, but neither had openings and neither one was hiring at the moment.

Agent Pete Kelliher, who was co-leader of a team called the Crimes Against Children Unit that operated within the FBI, contacted Deputy Director Tom Dandridge. Dandridge was an old friend and the boss above Pete's immediate supervisor. Because of that phone call, the day Skip lost his job, he gained a new one, a better one, working in a forensic lab for the FBI and had become an unofficial member of Pete's unit, or Kiddie Corps as many of the agents called it. Of course, he'd have to go through the academy in Quantico where he would eventually be stationed, but he'd have a steady job doing what he loved doing and working with a team he had gotten to know and who he enjoyed being with.

He had a lot to thank Kelliher for, including the nickname that seemed to stick. Most people in the hospital didn't even know his given name was James or at least, didn't seem to care because everyone addressed him as Skip.

Dahlke spent his days with Brett and the other boys and then spent each of his nights in Brett's room, because he didn't want Brett to be by himself. He also had to admit, to himself anyway, that he was responsible for Brett getting shot.

Yes, Brett was bullheaded to the nth degree. But Skip should have demanded that Brett stay in a room or at least, after delivering his line to the guards holding Kelliher prisoner, *"Butch sent me to get you . . ."* should have either gone back into the room or around the corner out of harm's way. But Brett had insisted that he could take out one of the men who had kept him and the boys captive. Instead of just taking out one guard, he tried for two and was shot in the left shoulder for his effort, leaving Skip to finish off the other guard.

So Dahlke suffered from a boatload of guilt.

After getting up and seeing Brett's bed empty, he gathered up some clothes and a towel and showered, shaved what little whiskers he had, brushed his teeth and then stepped out into the hallway. He saw that cops were still posted at either end of the hallway and he walked over to the nurses' station.

"Um, good morning," he said smiling at the nurse at the computer.

"Well good morning yourself," Dee said. Then she looked over her shoulder and said, "Hey, Carol, look who's awake."

Skip smiled and blushed scarlet.

"Oh, Hey. Good morning," Carol said coming over to the counter.

"Um, hi," he answered, smiling shyly and blushing some more. "Have you seen Brett?"

"He got up about a half-hour or forty-five minutes ago," Carol said looking down the hallway. "The other guys aren't up yet, so I think he went down to see Johnny."

"How's Johnny doing?" Skip asked.

Dee and Carol exchanged a look that said it all. Dee shook her head and said, "Not too well."

Carol added, "I'm worried about him."

Skip nodded, wondering how the boys, Brett and Tim in particular, would react if Johnny didn't make it. He glanced down the hallway in the direction of the boys' room.

"I'll look in on Mike and Tim, then head down to see Brett and Johnny," Skip said already moving down the hall at a slow walk.

His cell went off and he answered it as he stood in the hallway leaning against a wall near Tim's and Mike's darkened room. An aide pushed an empty gurney one way and another aide went the other way carrying an armful of blankets and boxes of supplies.

"Dahlke."

"Skip, this is Kelliher. Where are you?"

Dahlke noticed an edge in Pete's voice and answered, "At the hospital on the third floor."

"Are cops still on the floor?"

Skip looked to his left and saw a young-looking cop who had rocked back in a chair as he read a folded sports page. Then he turned to his right and saw an older cop with a graying crew cut and with arms folded on his chest, head lowered, perhaps dozing.

"Yeah, they're here."

"Agent Vince Cochrane out of the Chicago office will be up there in five, maybe ten minutes. Watch for him. I'm about twenty out because of the damn traffic. Find Cochrane when he shows up. I gave him your number. Don't leave the boys."

"What the hell, Pete? What's happening?"

"Where's Brett?"

"On second with Johnny, why?"

"It's probably nothing. Get to him, but don't alarm him, got it?"

"Pete, what's going on?" James began moving to his right towards the nearest stairwell.

"His uncle is in the wind, gone. They fucked up in Indianapolis and we don't know where the fuck he is."

Dahlke reached down and touched the .45 holstered on his hip.

"I'll find Brett."

CHAPTER SEVEN

Between Indianapolis and Chicago

Victoria McGovern sat in the front passenger seat of the blue Dodge Durango staring out at nothing in particular. Houses turned to farmsteads and beyond that, turned to nothing but country. Various billboards advertised this and that. Cars and trucks either passed by or were passed by. She saw all of it, but none of it, lost in her thoughts, worrying about what her son would be like, how he had changed, if he still remembered them.

She had given up hope of ever seeing Brett again long ago, perhaps at the one-year anniversary of his disappearance or perhaps even earlier than that. In her mind, that made her a terrible mother. She suspected that her husband Thomas had given up hope too, but she didn't know because they had never talked about it past that first year. In fact, they didn't talk much at all anymore. Period. Like the laughter, the sex, the time spent together- everything had stopped, including the talking. Talking always seemed to be the first to go, but all of it had pretty much stopped about the same time as when she, perhaps they, had given up hope.

Around the one-year anniversary mark, Victoria had begun taking on extra shifts at St. Vincent Heart Center. Being an RN, it was easy because the other nurses were always looking to take a three-day weekend or a night off. Thomas hadn't seemed to notice and if he had, he didn't seem to care. He was an English professor at Butler University in Indianapolis who had written a thesis as a doctoral student comparing Poe to Hawthorne and parlayed that into a fairly successful book with even more successful reviews. He had also written a textbook on Early American Authors, which was also very successful. Thomas had taken on extra classes or just stayed on campus to grade papers. The time he and Victoria had actually spent together was, well, missing just like their oldest son, Brett.

Both of them had an unstated rule, however, that one or the other would be home for Bobby, their youngest. Bobby, eighteen months younger than Brett, spent a lot of his time at friends' houses or with his cousins. He was more bookish like his father and not as athletic like Brett. Until fairly recently.

They looked alike. It was often said that Bobby was a smaller Xeroxed version of Brett. Friends and family teased them that they looked like miniature Tom Bradys, obviously shorter and younger and without the cleft chin. This didn't sit well with either of them, particularly Brett, because they were rabid Colts fans and Brett's favorite football player was Brady's archrival, Peyton Manning.

Victoria wasn't exactly athletic, but she had always figured Brett's athleticism came from her side of the family, the Dominico side. Her younger brother, Tony, excelled in everything he did. Like his Uncle Tony, Brett was a natural. Whatever Brett did, he did well, especially football, basketball and track. The one trait that she and her husband shared and seemed to have passed onto both boys was stubborn determination.

Detective Anthony Dominico, or Uncle Tony, was on the Indianapolis Police force and specialized in narcotics. Before Brett was abducted, Tony had spent time with Brett- Colts games, Pacers games, or at the river shooting. Recently, Tony had begun spending time with Bobby.

Uncle Tony had never missed one of Brett's games and when Brett went missing, the detective had spent hours- on and off the clock- running down every lead he could to find him. He spent weekends away, telling Vicky and Tom that he had gone underground among perverts and pedophiles looking for Brett. He had come up empty each time, but swore that he'd never quit until Brett came home.

And now, Brett was coming home.

Bobby had spent the evening before at a friend's house while Thomas had worked late at the university and Victoria had worked late at the hospital. No one was at the house when the call came telling them that Brett was found, alive, and was at a hospital in Chicago recovering from a gunshot wound. Neither had checked the answering machine that evening and it wasn't until the following morning after Victoria had gone off to work at the hospital that Thomas had seen the blinking light and played the message.

At first, he thought it was a hoax.

The voice identified herself as Agent Summer Storm with the Crimes Against the Children Task Force of the FBI. *Who would possibly have a name like 'Summer Storm'?* he thought.

Then he replayed the message, listened again, took down the number and dialed it.

Less than an hour later, after making sure Bobby could stay at his grandmother's house, he threw some of his wife's clothes in a small red suitcase, topped off the gas tank and picked up Victoria from the hospital. He hadn't said anything when he showed up, but he was agitated and ghost-like, so she had assumed the worse.

It was only when they got into the car in the hospital parking ramp that he turned to her and repeated the message from the FBI agent. She stared at him in disbelief, searching his face for any clue that it was a sick practical joke. He seemed shaken and anxious, but earnest and sincere, so she changed out of her whites as they drove to Chicago.

Two hours later north of Indianapolis on Interstate 65, about forty-five minutes from downtown Chicago, Thomas reached over and took hold of Victoria's hand. It had been so long since they had held hands, so long since there was a touch of any kind that she had stared at their hands, their fingers intertwined.

When she looked over at him, she noticed that he was weeping.

She didn't know what to say, much less how to say it. It had been so long since they had comforted one another, had even tried to comfort one another that she was out of practice, so she just held his hand.

"Vicky, I don't know if Brett will recognize us," he said quietly, wiping his eyes with his other hand, holding the steering wheel temporarily with his knee. "I've been thinking about what he went through, what he was forced to do . . ." he didn't finish. He just shook his head.

Victoria began to tear up and turned to look out the window so Thomas wouldn't see it.

"I think both of us thought we'd never see him again. I expected a phone call telling us he was found dead. I never, not in a million years, thought we'd get a phone call telling us he was alive."

He paused and made another swipe at his eyes.

"Hell, we even made his room into a guest room and packed his things away." He stopped and shook his head. "Jesus! This is so unbelievable!"

Victoria searched frantically for something, anything to say but came up empty. Gratefully, her cell chirped. She freed her hand from Thomas' so she could get to her phone.

Puzzled because she didn't recognize the number, she said, "Yes?"

"Vicky, don't mention my name or let on that it's me," the man said. Victoria knew who it was and had recognized the voice immediately.

"Okay," she said quietly.

"By now you've heard the news. You're going to hear all sorts of lies and fabricated stories."

"Yes, but-"

"-let me finish. I've been undercover and I still am. You're going to hear things about me that aren't true. You have to believe me. They aren't true. In time, I'll explain everything. Do you understand?"

Victoria frowned, turned her head to the passenger window and said, "No, I don't, not at all."

"But I promise you will in time, all of it. But it's important that you believe me and not the lies you're going to hear. Can you trust me, Vicky?"

She nodded and whispered tentatively, "Yes, I guess so."

"It's important, Vicky. Don't tell anyone it was me. Tell Tom it was a call from the hospital. You can make something up. When I can, I'll call to give you updates."

"Yes, okay," Victoria said nodding.

"Who's that?" Thomas asked. "Is that the FBI? How did they get your number?"

Victoria waved at him to be quiet.

"Stay in touch, please . . . okay?" Victoria said.

"Yes . . . gotta go." And with that, the call ended and Victoria held a dead line, more puzzled and confused than when the trip began.

Thomas asked, "Who was that?"

Victoria shook her head absentmindedly, very confused. "The hospital. Nothing important," she said more to herself than to him.

CHAPTER EIGHT

Chicago, Illinois

Brett stepped quietly into Johnny's room and stopped in his tracks. There were more tubes and machines hooked up to his friend than there was the night before. An oxygen tube helped Johnny breath. There was a tube collecting urine and emptying it into a plastic bottle attached to his bed. There was a similar machine that Brett was on after his surgery that collected Johnny's blood pressure and heart rate with tabs and wires stuck to his chest and ribs with a Vaseline-like substance. His mouth was closed as were his eyes and his skin was pasty and sweaty.

Brett crept up to the bed and gently took hold of his friend's hand, careful not to disturb the finger monitor. His hand was cold and damp. With his other hand, he smoothed Johnny's hair off his forehead and whispered, "Johnny, you have to fight. You gotta fight, Johnny, please."

He leaned over the bed and touched his forehead to Johnny's and whispered, "We're safe now, Johnny. It's time to go home, so please fight Johnny, please."

Perhaps it was his imagination but he thought he felt Johnny's grip tighten.

"That's it, Johnny, fight back."

The grip relaxed and Brett brushed his lips on Johnny's forehead and said, "You're one of my best friends and if it weren't for you, I wouldn't have made it. Never." He paused and added, "I owe you, Johnny. All of us do, so please stay with us, okay?"

Again, he felt Johnny's grip tighten and Brett added, "I'm going to go get cleaned up, but I'll be back with Tim, I promise. Be tough, Johnny, fight. Please?"

Johnny's grip relaxed and Brett eased his hand away. He smoothed Johnny's bangs again, though he didn't really need to do that. He did it more for one last touch before he left the room.

He knew Johnny was in bad shape and getting worse and was torn between getting ready for his parents and staying with Johnny. Someone should be with him from now on to help him fight. He took hold of his hand with both of his, gave it a squeeze, let go and then took a couple of steps backward, turned and left the room, but stopped in the hallway and leaned against the wall just outside his room and wept.

• • •

"There is no way my brother would do any of that, especially to Brett!" Victoria said, leaning forward, teeth bared, finger rapping the polished faux mahogany conference table. They sat in a modestly furnished conference room where doctors met with patients and their loved ones to give them unwanted news or in some cases, messages of hope and relief. This was not an occasion of hope or relief. "No way!" she repeated for good measure.

Just as he had done with each of the boys' parents, Jeremy sat on one side of the table with Dr. Blaine Flasch on his left and Agents Pete Kelliher and Vince Cochrane on his right. Flasch was the surgeon and attending physician for their son, Brett.

Initially, the meeting was as grim as the previous meetings Jeremy had had with Tim's, Mike's and Stephen's parents. Disbelief, yet relief. Anger and frustration. Horror, shock and revulsion. He spoke about how the kids seemed to be more mature and older. Even though they looked young, perhaps because of what they went through, each boy acted older. Lost was the playfulness and the laughter. Instead, there was a somber attitude, a serious attitude that belied the fact that they were only thirteen- or fourteen-years-old.

He talked about Brett's caretaker role with the boys, cleaning up after Tim and Mike and he asked, "How many fourteen-year-old boys would do that? How many do you know who would ask for that kind of help from another boy his own age?"

Victoria and Tom stared at him in silence.

"But when you think about it, their childhood was ripped away from them. Stolen, if you will. Each boy acts older than his age. Each boy seems serious. There isn't the laughter or teasing you would find in boys their age. But as I said, that's understandable given what happened to them for so long."

Dr. Flasch explained the shoulder wound and the resulting surgery and the proposed rehab Brett had begun and would need to follow up with. Arrangements were made for the transmittal of records and x-rays. There were questions as to Brett's overall health, which was surprisingly good, except for the fact that he'd have to be tested every six months for the next two years or so for HIV. He explained that, like the other boys, Brett had suffered from malnutrition and dehydration. He added that Brett had refused any pain medication other than Ibuprofen since coming out of surgery.

Unlike Jeremy's previous meetings, there was open hostility towards Kelliher and Cochrane as well as a refusal to believe, at least on the part of Victoria, anything they had to say about her brother, Brett's uncle, Anthony Dominico. She would not hear anything about him having anything to do with Brett's kidnapping, his captivity or that Dominico had any knowledge of Brett's whereabouts during the twenty-two months Brett had been in captivity.

Speaking quietly, actually softly, Thomas asked, "What you're suggesting is that Tony had Brett kidnapped, forced him into this . . . ring, had him held captive and knew where he was all along?"

Victoria shut her eyes and shook her head, refusing to believe.

Pete patted a manila folder and said, "We have pictures of Dominico entering and leaving the building where Brett and the boys were held captive. We have pictures-"

"-no!" Victoria said, leaning forward, fingertip pointing at the agent.

"-pictures of Dominico engaging in sex acts with your son and with the other boys-"

"-no!" she repeated, more forcefully this time.

"-as well as movies on DVDs of his encounters with Brett and several other boys-"

"-no! No! No!" she yelled, coming out of her chair. "Those are faked. They're lies. You're mistaken. You're framing him."

Thomas reached for Victoria's hand, but she batted it away, and said, "Tony said you'd be telling us lies . . ." she stopped, knowing she had slipped and said too much.

Cochrane's eyes darted towards Kelliher and then back to Victoria. Jeremy looked over at Kelliher, then back at Victoria.

"When?" Thomas asked. He had turned to his wife, shocked, and asked, "When did he tell you this?"

Victoria sat back down, placed both hands in her lap and glanced up at Kelliher and then down at her hands, refusing to say anything further.

Pete ran a hand over his face, sighed and said, "Do you believe your son to be honest?"

Thomas looked at his wife, then back at the men facing him and said softly but with force, "Absolutely. To a fault."

Pete shrugged, looked at Jeremy and said, "It was Brett who first told us about his uncle."

Victoria went white. Thomas covered his face with his hands and then ran them through his hair.

He looked from one agent to the other, then at Jeremy as if pleading for help. "What you're . . . suggesting . . ." he didn't finish, but merely shock his head.

"I know this is a shock," Jeremy began to say.

"It's a mistake . . . a misunderstanding," Victoria said quietly.

"On who's part?" Pete asked a bit more angrily than perhaps he should have. She shook her head dismissively.

"What do we do now?" Thomas asked after the silence in the room thickened like congealed gravy.

"We'll take you to your son. He's anxious . . . nervous to see you," Jeremy said.

"Nervous?" Thomas asked.

Jeremy nodded and said, "It's been a long time and a lot has happened to him. He's a tough and resilient boy, one of the leaders in the group. A boy the others looked up to and sought out. They still do actually, but he's still a fourteen-year-old boy. He's scared you might not remember him, and he's worried about what you might think of him. Maybe that you'll be disappointed in him."

"Disappointed in him?"

"Please take us to our son," Victoria said standing up. "Now."

"One more thing," Pete said.

"No! No more! I want to see my son!"

"If Dominico contacts you, we need to know because we believe your son and the other boys are in danger with him on the loose." Then he added for good measure, "He's a wanted felon, and harboring a felon or aiding and abetting a felon is also a felony." This last he said specifically to Victoria.

Victoria shook her head dismissively, but said nothing.

"If he contacts you, we need to know," Pete repeated, looking first at Victoria and then at Thomas.

Thomas looked from one man to the next, and then nodded slightly at Pete. It was slight, but noticeable by everyone, including his wife.

CHAPTER NINE

Northern Suburb of Indianapolis

He had hoped he wouldn't be the only one, but didn't know for sure. Each of them knew it was a possibility that the ring would be broken. Strike that, a probability, if not an eventuality.

Each of them had a clean, unused Gmail address with a clean user name that only they had known about. He had come up with the idea and the plan and had shared it with nine others who had shared the same urges, appetites and tastes, and who had been paid well for the protection they had provided.

So much for protection. It was over- at least in its present form.

The question was, how many of them got away and were in hiding? He needed to know.

He sat in front of his laptop and piggy-backed on an unsecured wireless network from one of the neighbors who lived close by.

Idiots! he thought. *When would they learn?*

He logged onto Gmail, clicked on Mail, then New, and typed in the nine e-mail addresses he had memorized. In the subject line, he typed, *Survived!* In the body of the message, he typed,

New location and new identity. Enough money to last a long time. Would like to get back at them. Maybe begin again. How about you?

He sat back and considered his message, and then went back to the subject line, deleted *Survived!* and instead typed, *Free!* He then considered the message and thought it was too direct and perhaps, too reveling, so he deleted the first two sentences. It was still direct, but fairly innocuous. Besides, if anyone snooped looking for him, they'd find someone else's IP address.

Now he'd sit back, wait, and see who would respond.

If anyone did.

CHAPTER TEN

Chicago, Illinois

"Dammit!" Brett slapped the water once, then twice sending water up over side of the tub and onto the linoleum floor. He raised his bare, wet knees to his chest, hugging them with his good arm and hung his head. He was beyond frustrated. Tears sprung to his eyes, which made him even angrier.

Tim, who had been in the other room, but near the closed door, stepped into the bathroom, shut the door behind him, knelt down in a puddle on the floor next to the tub. He rested his chin on his arms, trying without much luck to keep from smiling. Biting down on his tongue didn't help either.

"Need some help?"

"I want to take a bath by myself!" Brett shouted. "For two years . . ." he shouted, sobbed, then quieted a bit and said through clenched teeth, "for two years, that fat fuck Butch washed us, and did other shit to us, and I'm sick of it!" He sobbed again and said, "After two years, now when I get the chance, I can't wash myself because my left arm is fucking useless!"

Tim smiled at his friend, took a plastic cup, dipped it into the water and poured it on Brett's head, and then ran his hands through Brett's thick brown hair getting it thoroughly wet. He set the cup on the side of the tub, picked up the shampoo and squirted it into his hands, lathered them up and began washing Brett's hair.

Brett hadn't changed position, but had stopped crying.

"This is embarrassing," he muttered into his knees.

"Really? Embarrassing?" Tim asked with a laugh. "Mike and I take a shit and you have to wipe our butt. *That's* embarrassing. *This* is nothing."

Brett glanced at his friend and said, "I don't mind."

"Yeah, but you gotta admit that's more embarrassing than helping you with a bath."

Tim rinsed Brett's hair and when all the soap was out, took a bar of soap and started on Brett's back.

He washed Brett's chest and his legs then told Brett to kneel and handed him the soap. "I think you can wash down there, right?"

Brett didn't say anything, but took the soap from Tim's hand and washed himself. He tried to wash his backside, but had a difficult time turning, wincing at the pain.

When Brett finished and after he sat back down, Tim said, "You're clean, you smell reasonably nice, and I've done all I can. You're still ugly, but hey, can't have everything."

Brett smiled for the first time since he began his bath.

• • •

His long brown hair still damp, but scrubbed and shined, Brett perched nervously on the end of his bed wearing khaki cargo shorts and a blue and yellow striped polo shirt that Skip had purchased for him. He had his right hand out so Tim could clip his fingernails. Tim held Brett's hand gently and snipped away, starting with Brett's pinky.

"You concentrate better with your tongue hanging out?" Brett asked quietly.

Tim smiled at him.

Mike was in the same bathtub behind them with the door shut soaking and humming some tune neither Tim nor Brett recognized.

"Think he'll stop stuttering?"

Tim shrugged. "Hope so."

Brett stared intently at his friend as Tim finished with his right hand and reached for his left.

"I did the best I could on it," Brett said. "I can't do my toes 'cause my sling gets in the way." Then he added as an afterthought, "Sort of embarrassing you having to help me like this."

Tim stopped, looked up at his friend and laughed, "We've been through this already," and he laughed some more.

Brett smiled, shrugged his good shoulder and said, "I guess."

Tim started on Brett's toes.

"You're my best friend, Tim," Brett said shyly.

"I know. And you're mine," Tim said without looking up from what he's doing.

"Promise we'll stay that way?"

Tim stopped clipping Brett's toenails, looked up at his friend and said, "I promise. Nothing will change that."

Brett nodded.

When Tim finished, he got up off the floor and flopped down on the bed and Brett lay back with him, resting his head on Tim's shoulder.

"Jeremy told me to tell you that your parents are here."

Brett sighed. "I know. Monique told me."

"Nervous?"

Brett nodded.

"It's gonna be okay, Brett."

"What if they don't remember me? What if they don't like me anymore?"

"They knew you for, what, twelve, fourteen years? I've only known you for two years and I know I'll never forget you," Tim said with a yawn, moving to his side and propping his head up on an elbow to face him. "It's gonna be okay, Brett."

"Will you and Mike be nearby, like in the hallway or close by?"

"Promise. Mike will be there for sure, and Stephen should be here any time. I'm going to run down and visit Johnny, but I'll be back."

"Skip said Johnny's mom is here. She flew in late last night."

"Just his mom?" Tim asked.

Brett nodded. Neither boy commented, but they had the same thought. Johnny's parents must have split up, just like Ben's and Ian's did. Their parents had shown up together, but before the two boys had left- Ben with his parents to St. Paul and Ian with his parents to Des Moines- their parents explained that they had divorced. It had saddened the boys, and even though their parents had explained that neither Ben nor Ian had anything to do with it, neither boy had believed them. Two of the other boys, Cory and Patrick, had sent a text to Stephen that their parents were shaky.

"Know what I can't get used to?" Tim asked softly.

"What?"

"That I can leave my room and go pretty much wherever I want." Tim paused and said, "That first morning here? Mike and I didn't know if we could leave our room."

"I can't get used to wearing clothes," Brett said with a laugh.

"I know," Tim laughed. "That first night, Mike and I slept naked."

Brett laughed. "I was going to, but Skip said I might want to wear the hospital thingy in case the nurse came in to check me."

"Those things don't cover much anyway. Our butts were always hanging out."

The boys were still laughing as Mike came out of the bathroom wrapped in a towel as Stephen came in from the hallway.

"Your parents are coming up from downstairs," Stephen said as he plopped in a chair by the side of the bed. "They were just coming out of the conference room with Jeremy, Pete, Dr. Flasch and the other agent guy."

Brett sat up and took a deep breath.

"It's gonna be alright, Brett," Tim said for the third time.

"I b-b-better get d-dressed," Mike said disappearing back into the bathroom after grabbing his clothes off the back of the chair Stephen was sitting in.

"Need help?" Stephen asked.

"N-no, I g-got it," Mike answered as he shut the bathroom door behind him.

"Is he getting any better?" Stephen asked in a whisper to Tim and Brett.

Tim made a face and shook his head. Brett didn't answer. He just stared at the door to the hallway as if the two other boys weren't in his room.

"Stephen, can you and Mike hang out in the hallway, while I go visit Johnny?"

Stephen nodded, and looked back at Brett who seemed to be in another world, a shade whiter, licking his lips nervously.

He got up, knocked on the bathroom door and asked, "Mike, almost done?"

In answer, Mike stepped out of the bathroom dressed except for bare feet. He carried his Nike sandals.

He walked over to the bed, put a hand on Brett's good shoulder and said, "W-w-we'll b-be i-in the h-h-hallw-way, ok-kay?"

Brett nodded, but continued to stare at the doorway, expecting his parents any moment.

Tim's parents didn't want Tim to talk about anything that had happened to him. Stephen's dad thought Stephen was gay. Ben's parents were divorced, as were Ian's. And Patrick's and Cory's parents were probably headed that way.

Given all that, Brett had no idea what might be in store for him.

CHAPTER ELEVEN

Waukesha, Wisconsin

Even though the morning was both hot and humid, George liked being outside, because it was where he was most at home. Jeremy had a list of chores that needed to get done before the boys left for Chicago with Jeff and Danny Limbach, so George, Randy and Billy split them up. George chose the outside work- lawn cutting and trimming and pulling a few weeds. Since the Lane lawn was about the same length as the Evans lawn, he decided to cut and trim their lawn too. Randy and Billy took care of the inside- dusting, vacuuming and bathrooms with a little laundry. Jeremy, Randy and Billy had packed up the night before and Jeremy had taken their suitcases with him so the Limbachs wouldn't have a huge load to carry. And when it was all said and done, George didn't have much to pack by way of belongings.

Running the lawnmower around the two yards was pretty mindless and it gave him time to think. Despite the fact that he had actually never mowed a lawn- living in the desert of northeastern Arizona didn't call for much lawn mowing- he caught on quickly after Billy showed him. He liked the smell of freshly cut grass. He liked the physical activity of the work. Mostly, he felt he was somehow paying Jeremy and the Lanes back for the kindness they had shown him, at least in a way that dusting and vacuuming wouldn't do. It was solid and tangible.

It took him a little over an hour and a half to do both lawns and another half an hour to trim each yard. Weeding didn't take him long at all, but by the time he was finished, he was dripping in sweat and had a layer of dirt and flecks of grass on his legs, chest and back that made him itchy. Still, he felt good, satisfied with what he had done.

George pulled the garden hose from the tan, plastic, portable carrier to give him some slack and turned on the water. It wasn't terribly cold, but cool enough to refresh him and clean off the dirt, the grass and the sweat. He tilted up his face and held it over his head, shaking out his long hair.

Reasonably clean, he sat in the sun on the back step and admired his work. Jon and Bert Lane came out of their back door and walked across the adjoining yards with a brightly wrapped package and a pitcher of lemonade and some glasses.

"You look thirsty," Bert said.

"A little," he admitted. He tried drinking from the garden hose, but the water smelled and tasted like rubber and was lukewarm. At least it didn't have the sulfur smell that the well water had on his small ranch back home.

Jon pulled out two of the lawn chairs from around the small patio set and asked George to sit in one of them. Then Jon went up the back steps, opened up the door and yelled for the twins to join them.

Both Jon and Bert were older. How old, George couldn't tell. They were old enough to have retired and to have a son who had graduated from college working in downtown Chicago, but young enough that George couldn't tell how old they were. He knew they weren't nearly as old as his grandfather or grandmother. At least he didn't think so. Yet, they were older than his mother and Jeremy.

Randy and Billy bounced out the backdoor and joined them on the patio. Billy sat in the chair next to George and Randy sat on the Chaise Lounge. Bert poured each boy a glass of lemonade with ice which Jon delivered to each of them like a waiter.

"George, Jon and I want to give you something to remember us by," Bert said handing George the wrapped package. It felt light and it wasn't very big.

"Thank you, but you didn't have to," George said to both.

Jon said. "It's not much, but it's something we wanted to do."

"Go on, open it up," Billy said giving George a playful elbow.

George took off the ribbon and bow, and then slid his forefinger under one of the flaps that had been taped down and lifted it up without ripping it. Then he did the same to the other side.

"You need some serious lessons on opening presents," Billy laughed. "Just tear it."

George smiled but ignored him and slid his finger under another taped flap, which was the last of the flaps. He opened up the paper the entire way, slicking the tape to the inside of the paper leaving it completely intact.

"My mother told us to save the paper and bows for another day," George said quietly.

"Sounds like a smart lady," Jon said with a laugh. "I think I heard that a time or two myself." Bert gave him one of her looks, but laughed along with the rest of them.

George then proceeded with the box and opened the white tissue paper to reveal a small photo album. Randy got up from the recliner and leaned over the back of George's chair to view it, resting his chin on George's shoulder. Billy leaned over to get a better look.

The first photo was of the three boys, smiling, mugging for the camera with their arms around each other's' shoulders. George remembered the morning they posed for Jon and the photo brought a smile to his face and a laugh from Billy and Randy.

Billy added, "I'm the best looking."

"Not on your best day," Randy replied with a laugh.

The second photo was of Jeremy and George sitting on the back step talking. George remembered the day, but didn't know they had been photographed. And page after page the photos went: Randy and Billy; Jon, Bert and George on the Lane Front step; Billy and George planting flowers; a similar photo of George helping Bert plant flowers; a group photo of George, Jeremy, Randy and Billy; and the last photo of Jon and Bert with George in their backyard.

"We know you're faced with a difficult decision and we know we might not see you for a while," Jon said, "but we wanted you to know you're very special to us."

George had tears in his eyes and he blinked rapidly to control them.

"We know what took place the other night, George," Bert said. "It showed tremendous courage, love and selflessness."

George could not raise his eyes to look at them, but instead, he flipped to the photo of Jeremy, the twins and him, and stared at it, touching it gently with his fingers. Billy turned a bit to the side and away. Randy gave George's shoulder a squeeze.

At last, George stood up and embraced first Bert, getting a kiss on his cheek, and then Jon, who kissed the side of George's head.

"Don't forget us," Jon said, "and make sure you visit us from time to time, okay?"

George nodded.

CHAPTER TWELVE

Suburb of Indianapolis, Indiana

The man was naked except for the towel wrapped around his waist and he stood in front of the sink staring at his reflection in the bathroom mirror. He had showered, but hadn't shaved, thinking that facial hair would help him blend in and disappear. As tall and built as he was, blending in would be difficult and disappearing nearly impossible.

He had had a good life, and now, it was gone.

The anger had been building. At first, it was a spark, an ember. There was never any fear, just the urgency to get away. But the fact that he had to run started the anger. The ember became a flame and the flame grew into a raging fire. He wanted to lash out, strike back and hurt someone.

Not just anyone, but those who had done this to him.

There were several on his list. Each target important, essential. Each had to be dealt with and disposed of.

Each had to be taught a lesson and the lesson was simple, but painful. The lesson would have to be painful. That would be a very important part of the lesson: pain. That would give him satisfaction. It always did. After all, they had done this to him- taken away his life.

It would take planning and preparation- two things the man was particularly good at, which was why his lifestyle had been undetected for so long. His secret would still have been undetected if that Indian kid hadn't come forward. The man or one of the others would definitely have to take care of him.

Then there were the two FBI agents- the woman and the old guy. He had never met them, but the paper and the TV hadn't seemed to tire of showing their pictures, their faces and telling anyone who had tuned in what a fantastic investigation they had done.

The man would be patient. He would plan.

The man would take care of business.

And there would be pain.

CHAPTER THIRTEEN

Waukesha, Wisconsin

Randy sat next to Danny Limbach on one side facing George and Billy on the other. On the end sat Jeff Limbach. He was about the same age as Jeremy and had dark-hair flecked with gray and had piercing blue eyes and a warm, engaging smile. He seemed friendly and gentle and it was clear that the boys had liked him.

Before the Limbachs had arrived, Randy had explained that Jeff was a famous author. Each of his last six books debuted in the top five on the New York Times Best Seller List and each had climbed to the top spot. Four of his books had been made into movies and Jeff had written the screen adaptation for two of them, and in one, had a bit part. George didn't read much, didn't watch much if any TV, and had never been to a movie, so he had never heard of him, which the twins could hardly believe.

Billy told George that when Jeff was eighteen, he was riding his motorcycle home from a football game late one Friday night. A drunk driver or someone who the police had assumed was a drunk driver, pulled up alongside of Jeff and squeezed him into the guard rail dragging him and the cycle for thirty yards before throwing him off the bike and into a field, where a farmer had found him early the following morning. It was the helmet he had worn, the moist, muddy earth he had landed in, and the grace of God that had saved his life.

As it was, Jeff had spent several weeks in the hospital, suffering agonizing surgery after surgery. An equally painful rehabilitation followed up each surgery. He had to relearn to walk and his football playing days were over, which was a tough way to end his senior year in high school. As a lasting remembrance of the accident and of the many surgeries he had suffered through since that accident, Jeff had an ugly scar and a permanent limp. He used a fancy cane made of dark wood with a pearl handle to help him get around. The only good that came from all of those long stretches in the hospital confined to a bed was that Jeff developed a love for books and writing.

Danny Limbach didn't look anything like his father, except for the piercing blue eyes and smile. He had a fresh, scrubbed look and a perpetual smile. His hair was cut short and worn in a preppy, gelled and spiky look. George couldn't tell if his hair was light brown, dark blond or light red.

He wore a blue polo shirt and khaki shorts and dockers with low cut socks. On his right wrist was a gold bracelet inscribed with the words *Love, Always!* It had been given to him by his father on his tenth birthday, the year his mother had divorced his dad and moved to Omaha, Nebraska, and the only time he ever took it off was when he showered. He considered it his most cherished possession.

Danny was almost three years younger than George and the twins and was a close friend to them. He was also something of a musical genius. He had spent parts of the past two summers at Julliard in New York studying classical piano and guitar, though Danny had a penchant for rock and country with a bit of the blues.

Danny, who could play just about any instrument easily and well, had posted a video on YouTube of himself singing and playing guitar, piano and organ on the REO Speedwagon song, *Roll With The Changes*. It had caught the eye and the ear of Paul Schafer, band leader for the David Letterman Show when it was still on. He was invited to perform the song with Schafer's studio band. Since then, he had appeared on the Letterman Show three other times. Even after the show ended its run on TV, Schafer and Danny still had a friendship and had texted and emailed each other.

Currently, he and Randy were writing songs. Randy would compose the lyrics and Danny would set them to music. Both Randy and Danny could play guitar, though Danny was way better than Randy, and they harmonized with each other easily with Randy usually singing the lead. Their plan was to get one or more of their songs into the hands of a country artist. That was their dream, but both knew they were a long way off from that.

Randy had told George that Danny had close to an eidetic memory, though it wasn't ever actually tested, and when someone would comment on it, Danny would only laugh and say that his memory *'was pretty good'*. Quite the understatement because Danny could remember anything he had heard, read or saw. Billy added that Danny had skipped two grades, from fifth to seventh and in the fall, would be in the same grade as the twins. The principal of Danny's middle school in Omaha had wanted him to skip three grades, but Jeff and his ex-wife, Karen, said that the social aspects of skipping that many grades would be difficult for Danny to handle and that the school would just have to supplement his coursework.

The five boys looked at Jeff curiously, George more so than the others. He had a glass of orange juice in front of him, while Billy had a glass of milk. Randy and Danny had ice water, and Jeff had a half-emptied coffee cup that he was rotating in small, clockwise circles.

"George," he began, "Randy and Billy are my god-sons. Well, Randy is, but I treat Billy as if he was too." He paused, smiled at the boys and then continued in a softer voice. "Jeremy told me about the other night. I don't want to think about what would have happened if something had happened to you or if you had failed." He paused, stared intently, but kindly at George, who nodded, then lowered his eyes to the glass of orange juice he held firmly in his two hands.

Jeff looked over at the twins and said, "I know I never told you this, but your dad is my best friend. When Danny's mom and I divorced, it was a tough time."

He paused, looked at Danny who squirmed in his chair although his expression hadn't changed. He briefly made eye contact with his dad, but then he lowered his eyes to his hands.

"I went through a tough time and your dad helped me out of it," Jeff said.

He looked over at Billy and said, "When your father passed away, he left you a sizeable sum of money."

Billy blushed and nodded.

"Jeremy is the executor of your father's estate and he and I set up a trust fund for you."

Billy didn't like to talk about his father or his money, and he didn't like being the topic of conversation.

"What you don't know, and what Randy doesn't know . . . not even Jeremy knows, is that I set up a trust fund for Randy in the same amount at that same time. I didn't want either of you to lack for anything and I didn't want Jeremy worrying about college or helping you get on the right foot after college. It was my way of trying to thank your dad for all he did for me."

Randy and Billy exchanged a look of surprise and then looked back at Jeff.

"That money is distributed in several accounts and earning interest, so by the time you need it, you'll be taken care of."

Randy cleared his throat and said, "Thank you." Billy nodded.

Turning to George, Jeff said, "This morning, I set up a trust fund for you in the same amount that Randy and Billy have now with the same time lines for dispersal."

George was normally slow to show any reaction because it wasn't the Navajo way to show one's emotion, but clearly, he was shocked. He had never met this man or his son before. They didn't owe him anything and to be honest, he didn't feel very deserving of anything. He glanced at the twins who looked over at him smiling and then he turned back to Jeff.

"Why?" he asked.

Jeff smiled at him and said, "I love these two boys and Jeremy is my best friend. You saved their lives and I wanted to repay you for that."

"But I don't know you," George said but not disrespectfully. He was merely trying to understand.

"No, but that's okay."

"I haven't decided whether or not to live here," George said.

Jeff smiled and said, "Living here is not contingent on whether or not the money is yours. Jeremy told me you want to be a forensic scientist or a policeman and that's a fine goal. This money will help you pursue that goal."

Randy cleared his throat again and said, "My dad doesn't know you did this?"

"Not yet. I'll tell him at some point today or tonight and I'm asking that you allow me to tell him, okay?"

Randy nodded and Billy said, "Okay."

George said nothing, but stared at his glass of orange juice with a frown, holding it with both hands.

"One last thing," Jeff said.

The boys looked at him expectantly.

"George, as I understand it, you lost your family and everything you own." He said this gently, kindly.

George didn't raise his eyes right away, but when he did, he looked at Jeff squarely not betraying the conflicting feelings he had.

"You, Randy, Billy and Danny are going shopping. You need clothes. You need a cell phone so you can talk to the boys and to Jeremy, and hopefully, to Danny and me. I think you need a laptop for school and because you live in a desert, you'll need a satellite hook-up. You also need some luggage."

George's eyes widened. He clearly was not able to hide his feelings any longer.

"Boys, I think between the four of you, you'll come up with things I haven't thought of, right?"

Billy laughed and said, "I'm a pretty good shopper."

George shook his head.

"What?" Jeff asked.

"I don't understand."

"I believe in giving back, in providing opportunities for people. I know I can't give you your family back. I can't imagine what it's like losing your home and all your belongings."

George lowered his eyes and set his jaw, determined that he wouldn't lose control.

"I think you and I can agree that you need clothes."

George nodded.

"I think we can agree that you might want to keep in touch with the twins and Jeremy . . . I mean," he struggled for the right words to use, "whether or not you live here or in Arizona."

George nodded.

"So, we need to go shopping. Jeremy asked you to not decide yet, but in the event that you do, if you do decide to stay in Arizona with your cousin, you'll have your clothes and whatever you need to . . . you know what I'm trying to say," Jeff said flustered.

Frowning, George said, "But I don't know you."

"But you've come to know the twins and Jeremy, right?"

"Yes, Sir."

"I love them very much. I know that if anything happens to me and to Danny's mother, Jeremy would take Danny in and love and care for him in the same way he loves and cares for the twins. In the same way, if something would happen to Jeremy, I'd take the twins and I'd love them as much and in the same way as I do Danny."

George said nothing.

"It's true, you don't know me, but I know you recognize love. Jeremy said you're a bright young man, so I think you understand why I want to help you."

George blinked and then nodded.

"Randy, do you have a piece of paper and something to write with?" Jeff asked.

Billy got up, went into the family room to the desk and grabbed a piece of paper from the computer printer and a pen out of the Wisconsin Badger mug filled with pencils and pens, and brought both back into the kitchen.

"Why don't you guys make a list of everything George might need," Jeff said. "Start with what you guys have and George can either say yes or no."

The whole time Danny watched and listened to his dad, he couldn't help but feel proud. His dad smiled at him as he got up to refill his coffee cup.

Danny leaned across the table towards Billy who had already began ticking off items he felt were important. George listened, not sure when or how he was supposed to approve or disapprove of anything on the list.

While the three boys were deep in conversation mentioning this or that and adding to the growing list, George caught Jeff staring at him with a smile while leaning against the counter sipping his coffee.

George smiled back and mouthed, "Thank you."

Jeff smiled and nodded back.

CHAPTER FOURTEEN

Chicago, Illinois

He hid in plain sight because no one knew about him, so no one looked for him. But in order to remain hidden, he'd have to tie up three loose ends. Two would be tricky, but not impossible, while the other one would be fairly easy.

The planning had begun the morning of the raids when he had found out that two of the loose ends, Bosch and Rawson, had been arrested. The spineless Thatcher Davis had stabbed his own throat leaving him out of the equation, but it still left two powerful men who could potentially ruin everything for him. Two powerful and dangerous men and one not as much powerful as he was dangerous.

Dangerous because he was a cop on the second floor of the hospital.

No one as of yet had claimed responsibility for the nightstick that had been shoved up the cop's ass or responsibility for the cop's fried dick due to the tazer clamps that had been attached to it. He had his suspicions, but there was no confirmation because no one volunteered information.

However, it was fortunate that somebody had done this because the cop was close by and incapacitated and not going anywhere for a while.

The man knew the cop was a step or two from the morgue.

He'd have to be careful. He was almost home free. No suspicions so far.

He had to keep it that way in order for him to be able to live his life as he pleased.

CHAPTER FIFTEEN

Chicago, Illinois

No one had ever accused him of being patient. Tim had given him a hug before he left to visit Johnny, and Stephen and Mike had told him they'd be just outside the door. Before they had left the room, Mike turned around, came back, put his hand on Brett's good shoulder and said, "It's g-g-gonna b-be al-r-right, B-Brett." Brett couldn't even respond, not even with a nod, certainly not a smile. He licked his lips and stared at the door.

It was no more than a minute or two later when Monique ushered Thomas and Victoria into Brett's room and at first, the three of them stood just inside the doorway. Brett sat on the edge of his bed, but sat up straighter. Monique began to tear up, then turned and left the room.

"Brett?" Thomas asked.

"Mom? Dad?"

His parents rushed forward and Brett got off of the bed and hugged them fiercely, refusing to let go with his good arm and even though his father put too much pressure on his bad shoulder, Brett didn't care. And there were tears.

Victoria took Brett's face in both hands and looked at him closely, scrutinizing him as only a mother would. Then she kissed his forehead and his cheek and embraced him again.

Brett buried his face into his mother's chest.

Thomas stood behind them with one arm wrapped around his stomach while the other hand was pressed against his forehead as he wept silently. Not a particularly religious man, he thanked God his son was alive.

"Dad, it's okay," Brett said quietly.

"Brett, I'm so sorry . . . so sorry," was all Thomas could answer over and over as he stepped forward and embraced his son, burying his face in his son's hair, holding him gently.

After his parents regained composure, they stepped back and took stock of their son. Both noticed how much smaller he was, skinnier than before he was taken, and suspected that their younger son, Bobby might be as big and the same height as Brett. Even though Brett was only twelve when he was taken, he had

had a football player's set of shoulders and his chest, leg and arm muscles were defined. He had had a chiseled look with a six pack.

The definition was now missing. His arms were skinny and instead of a six pack, his parents felt his ribs through his polo shirt. His face was thin and gaunt, hollow and sunken. His eyes, holding a haunted look.

Brett looked past his parents towards the door and asked, "Where's Bobby?" after wiping his eyes with his good hand.

"He's with Grandma Dominico," Thomas answered. "You'll see him after we get home."

Brett recalled that neither Tim's nor Stephen's sisters had come with their parents, and Mike's brother nor sister hadn't come with his parents.

"I . . . we . . . didn't think we'd ever see you again," Thomas said with a sob, shaking his head. "I can't tell you how happy I am right now."

And that started everyone's tears again.

"Me too, Dad. I didn't know if I'd ever get out of there," Brett said quietly. "There were so many guys taken away. We never saw them again."

"I can't imagine what you went through." Thomas paused and then added, "Are you okay? I mean, I know you were shot, but are you okay?"

Brett nodded and said, "I'm okay, Dad."

"How did you get shot?" Victoria asked as she dabbed at her eyes with a Kleenex from the box on the table by the bed. "They never told us."

Brett told them things about the siege that CNN didn't and couldn't report, because they weren't in the building as he and the other boys were. He told them about the two men who had come through the door holding Pete Kelliher hostage and about the plan that wasn't executed as it should have been. "I screwed up," Brett said apologetically.

"You shouldn't even have had a gun," Victoria answered. She turned to Thomas and said, "I think we should talk to a lawyer about negligence."

"It was my fault, Mom," Brett said. "I took the gun and wouldn't give it back. Skip and I had a plan and I didn't listen to him. It was my fault."

"You're a boy, Brett," his mother answered patiently. "They were the adults and they almost got you killed."

"*I* screwed up and I *didn't* get killed," Brett said a bit more forcefully than he should have. Stephen and Mike appeared in the doorway. "We're not suing *any*body, except maybe my fuckin' Uncle Tony!"

"Don't talk about your uncle like that!" Victoria said. "He spent his weekends looking for you!"

"Looking for me? *Really?*" He laughed bitterly. "Well, he found me almost every weekend."

"Don't!"

Stephen and Mike stepped fully into the room and stood next to Brett, Stephen on his left and Mike on his right.

"Don't *what?* Didn't they tell you what he *did* to me?"

"There has to be a mistake," Victoria answered quietly. "A misunderstanding."

"*Really? A* misunder*standing?*"

"Victoria, stop please," Thomas said quietly, placing a hand on her arm.

"No mistakin' his dick up my ass or in my mouth. Not much to misunderstand about that!"

"Stop it!"

"Why? You don't believe me, do you?"

"Brett, we do believe you," Thomas answered.

"She doesn't," Brett said, almost spitting it out, pointing at her.

"I think you're mistaken, that's all," Victoria answered.

"*Mistaken?* He's the reason I was taken. He knew where I was all along," Brett said, stepping up to his mother.

"Don't talk to me like that!"

"I'll talk to you any way I want! You didn't think I was alive anyway! Good ol' Uncle Tony told me that! He said you turned my bedroom into a guest room and packed all my stuff away!" He saw the shock register on his mother's face. "Yeah, that's right," he said bitterly. "You didn't even know I was alive and the whole time, that fucking pervert-"

He didn't get to finish. Before Stephen or Mike could react, Victoria reached out and slapped Brett hard across the face, snapping his head back.

Three things happened. Thomas stood in front of Victoria and roughly grabbed her by the upper arms.

Stephen caught Brett who was rocked backwards by the blow and then stood in front of him so as to shield him, while Mike stood in front of both Stephen and Brett and pointed a finger at her and in a clear voice without any stutter at all, yelled, "Don't you ever fucking touch him again!"

Thomas turned around without letting go of Victoria and stared at the three boys.

Mike stood statue stiff, eyes blazing, face contorted in a snarl.

"Brett, she didn't mean that," Thomas said, pleading.

Ignoring his father, Brett placed a hand on Mike's shoulder and said, "No big deal, Mike. You and I've been hit harder than that, right?" He laughed when he said it, but there was no laughter in his voice or eyes. "I'm done here," he said, pulling Mike towards the door.

"Brett, please," Victoria said. "I didn't mean to." She added with a sob, "I'm sorry."

Stephen backed out of the room after Brett and Mike left and said, "Don't you ever hit him again. Not ever!" Then he turned around and left.

CHAPTER SIXTEEN

Waukesha, Wisconsin

The hotel room seemed cramped. He was bored. A half-day cooped up waiting for a knock on the door by the police with pointed guns and an arrest warrant in hand will do that. CNN covered the story over and over with no additional information. His cell hadn't gone off since the receptionist had called, and it appeared no one was looking for him.

Yet he was anxious and worried, and his sugar high was long gone.

He paced the room during commercials and from time to time, switched from the national networks to local Milwaukee channels. The local stations no longer covered the story, instead broadcasting regularly scheduled programs.

He went back to the window, stood to the side, and moved the curtain with his index finger and peered out. The parking lot was empty.

He pulled out his cell and speed-dialed Bonnie, who answered after two rings.

"Hey, Bonnie, I'm not feeling well, so I won't be in. Thanks for your phone call though."

"Oh, I'm sorry you're not feeling well." Then breathlessly she asked, "Isn't it great news about Stephen and Michael and those other boys? It's a miracle none of them were killed."

He took a deep breath and said, "Yes, it is certainly fortunate for them."

"We've been glued to CNN. It seems unbelievable that something like that could happen."

"Yes, unbelievable." Then adding a bit of puzzlement to his voice asked, "Has there been any news on the people arrested or the ones the FBI are looking for?"

"No. The only thing CNN is saying is that warrants have been issued and a number of arrests have been made. Fred has a friend in the police department who said that almost all of the arrests have been made in our area."

"Most of the arrests? There still might be more?"

"Well, all he said was that most of the arrests have been made. I don't know if there will be any more."

"Well listen, I think I'm going back to bed. I'll try to be in tomorrow, okay?"

"Don't rush it if you're feeling crummy. You'll get the rest of us sick."

"Okay, Bonnie. Thanks."

He hung up and stood in the middle of the room thinking. If as she said *most* of the arrests were made, maybe they weren't looking for him. The only way to be sure would be to drive by his house to see if anyone was there. Maybe they'd stake out his house and wait, so he'd have to be careful.

He'd have to think about that.

CHAPTER SEVENTEEN

Indianapolis, Indiana

Luke Pressman sat in his navy blue '09 Charger that was parked in the driveway of his modest two-bedroom one story ranch. The motor purred quietly like a tiger ready to pounce on its prey. He gripped the wheel with both hands.

Pressman replayed the ass-kicking he had received, first from his unit chief, then his precinct captain, and finally by the chief, who led him into a room to be hammered by IAB, who first interrogated him, and then chewed his ass just before he was placed on administrative leave by his precinct captain and the chief, who had tag-teamed him in yet another ass chewing.

He had made the grand, grave and God-awful mistake of contacting his partner, Detective Anthony Dominico to ask him about the two US Marshalls who were waiting for him with an arrest warrant. Then, he had to defend himself against the accusation by IAB that he was one of the perverts who had molested, abducted, and perhaps murdered boys across the country.

He allowed his personal cell phone to be examined and downloaded in search of any pornography or any contents that might indicate he was involved. Only when it came back clean did he get it back. He also allowed his laptop and his personal e-mail account to be searched by the cyber-crime guys in the unit, and then he consented to sit for a lie detector that he had passed, which was the only reason he wasn't booked as an accessory and behind bars.

He turned off the engine, took his hands off the wheel and lowered them to his lap momentarily, then he grabbed a handful of his sandy-blond and curly hair with both hands and sighed audibly, wondering how he could have been duped for so long by his partner- a partner he obviously hadn't known in the three years he had worked side by side with him. *How was that possible?*

He slammed the steering wheel with both hands, once, twice, and then three times, before he pulled the keys from the ignition. He was angry with himself, but also humiliated. *How could I have been so stupid?* He opened the door and unfolded his slender, six-foot body out of the car, slamming the door shut behind him.

Pressman leaned against the front fender. *How was it possible that Dominico duped him and everyone else for so long?*

He was angry, baffled and stunned. No answers came to him and for a detective that wasn't acceptable. He ran his hands through his hair and then folded his arms, still leaning against the front fender.

He had been on the force for six years, the last three partnered with Dominico working narcotics. In those three years, there was nothing that Pressman had noticed that would give any indication, any hint of the hidden life Dominico had lived. Yes, Dominico was controlling and bossy, but Luke had passed that off as the fact that Dominico had been on the force longer and had more experience than he had. He knew that on teams, one partner was generally in charge, so that had never bothered him. He had noticed intolerance in Dominico for anyone other than Caucasian or male, but Pressman passed that off as a personality quirk. The two of them had gotten along as most partners do, but they weren't close, nor were they confidants. Even ordinary friendliness like catching a movie or grabbing a beer and a game of pool had always been rebuffed by Dominico.

Pressman had grown up on a farm in western Indiana, two miles out of Attica which was a black dot on the Indiana map that highway 41 ran through, giving it at least one four-way stoplight. It was a small, conservative and a Republican community made up of other farmers, some of whom had given up the farm to live in the small city, but who had never given up their farmer mentality. There was an earthy stubbornness about them. A little awkward. A little backward. Simple. Perhaps unsophisticated, but not dumb. And Pressman was certainly one of them.

He walked up to his front door, inserted the key and entered his small foyer, shutting the door behind him.

Luke sensed that he wasn't alone. It was more than a feeling and more than the tell-tale smell of cologne, faint, but there. And recognizable.

He reached into his right front pocket where his cell was.

While on stake out, he would practice dialing first with his right hand, then his left. He could text with very few mistakes. Besides crossword puzzles and sports magazines, cheap, stale sandwiches and watered-down crappy coffee, what else was there to do? So, he had sat, waited and watched, and during that time, had practiced texting and dialing his cell.

With his left hand he placed his badge on the little table, but kept his gun under his arm in his holster. With his right hand slightly in his front pocket, he dialed 9-1-1, and then took his hand out of the pocket, while keeping the phone in it. A faint voice spoke, "9-1-1, what is your emergency?" Luke ignored it but kept the phone on, knowing that 9-1-1 always recorded their conversations and traced the location of the caller.

He moved to the living room and slouched down into his recliner and said loudly, "So, you didn't go into work today. How come?"

Luke heard movement from the back of the house where the bedrooms were. Dominico appeared holding a heavy revolver with a metal suppresser pointed in Pressman's general direction.

"Well, well, well. Detective Anthony Dominico! Welcome to Detective Luke Pressman's home. I think this is the first time in three years you've been here other than to pick me up."

"Shut the fuck up, Hayseed!"

"That's rude, considering you've broken into my home and you're pointing a gun at me, with a suppresser no less. Are the news reports true? Are you really a pervert responsible for kidnapping, raping and murdering young boys?"

Dominico smiled coldly and lowered the gun just a hair while he sat down on the couch opposite him.

"So, it is true. You're responsible for raping and executing eleven-, twelve-, thirteen- and fourteen-year-old boys. How sick are you, Dominico?"

"You know absolutely nothing and you call yourself a detective."

Pressman nodded and said, "Yeah, you had us fooled." He paused, looked at the gun that was again pointed directly at him and said, "But where are you going to go? They're hunting you down, Man!"

"Got it covered, Asshole. They won't find me because as far as anyone knows, Anthony Dominico is dead. He's gone. He's disappeared and off the grid."

"Oh, I see. So, who are you now?" Pressman had to keep up a running commentary to cover the 9-1-1 operator from trying to speak. "A fake, made up identity?"

"Something like that," Dominico answered with a laugh.

"I suppose the name is going to match the strawberry blond hair you have now. Hell, you even dyed your eyebrows. You have to admit though, you look sort of gay, but then again, you must be if you're raping young boys, right?"

Dominico snarled and put a bullet into Pressman's left knee. Luke leaned forward and grabbed it. The pain was intense and blood ran freely down his leg and onto his beige carpet.

"Jesus! What the fuck, Dominico? Why?"

In the distance, there were sirens.

"Why?" Dominico repeated. "Why? Because I think the world would be better off without a hick like you. I have a list of assholes just like you that need to be erased. You're the first one on that list."

Pressman had to keep him talking until the cops arrived, but the pain was overwhelming.

"Are you that fucked up that-"

The gun spit again, this time in his right knee cap.

"Jesus!" Pressman yelled. "Fuck!"

"Oo . . . taking the Lord's name in vain," Dominico said mocking him.

Knowing Dominico was running out of non-lethal body parts to shoot, Pressman asked through clenched teeth, "A list? Who else is on that list?"

Dominico laughed coldly and seemed to be picturing the faces that went along with the names.

"We made a list of those we need to dispose of. Some are personal just to each of us. Some are common to each of us. Whoever ruined our lives."

Pressman stared at him and as the sirens got closer, there were several things that went through his mind.

The first was that he was never going to get married or have children. He had wanted one boy and one girl and a wife to come home to each night. He knew that facing Dominico with a gun, that wasn't going to happen. The second thing that went through his mind was the question of who was going to find him. He didn't know, but he also didn't want anyone to mess up his house. He knew that thought was silly because he'd be dead. But it was a worry nonetheless.

The last thing that went through his head was a speeding hollow-point bullet that rocketed out of the barrel of the gun held in Dominico's hand.

After that, there were no more thoughts whatsoever. Just . . . nothing.

CHAPTER EIGHTEEN

Chicago, Illinois

Dilaudid is a powerful pain reliever that depresses the central nervous system, so the normal dosage is usually only one or two milligrams. Most pharmacies or hospital dispensaries have it in one, two or four milligram vials and if one uses a three-centimeter syringe, one can collect twelve milligrams of Dilaudid and inject it into an IV port with little problem. Of course, twelve milligrams would be lethal, especially if the patient had two milligrams of Dilaudid already in his system.

That was exactly what he had in mind.

It wasn't hard to swipe a green orderly top and bottom and change into it in the deserted locker room. For good measure, he grabbed a stethoscope hanging in an open locker and slung it around his neck.

The man said hello to Juan Ortiz, the young officer seated outside Robert Manville's hospital room on the second floor and chatted with him, asking him how the pervert was doing, telling him that he needed to check his vitals.

"He's sleeping, but you can try." Ortiz said doubtfully. "Do you mind if I go get some coffee and use the restroom? It's been a while since I had a break."

"Absolutely," the man said congenially. "I'll wait here until you come back, but take your time. I'm in no rush."

The officer thanked him and left. The man watched Ortiz leave the floor and then turned and stood just inside the doorway.

Robert Manville, formally of the Chicago PD, lay sleeping in his hospital bed in dimmed lighting. An IV bag hung on a metal arm over the left side of his bed and the tubing led to a port that had been inserted into his left forearm. His chest rose and fell in steady rhythm, and he had a slight grimace on his face. Every so often, his leg would twitch, as would his cheek.

He had been arrested and had been taken into custody when the boys were freed from captivity from the building in Chicago. He was found in one of the locked rooms with Tim and then was dragged off the boy and thrown on the floor and cuffed by Waukesha Police Detective Jamie Graff with FBI Agent Pete Kelliher backing him up.

At some point early that morning during the siege, someone, perhaps more than one person, had taken his nightstick and shoved it up his ass all the way to the handle, and then had taken his tazer and shot him, frying his penis into something that resembled a burnt hotdog. Hence, the hospitalization and the sedation using Dilaudid as a pain medication.

The man took the three-centimeter syringe out of his pocket which had already been preloaded with twelve milligrams of the drug.

He moved to the side of the bed and inserted the syringe into the port and depressed the plunger. Within seconds, almost instantaneously, Manville's breathing slowed and then stopped. His face slacked and his body went limp.

Quickly, but not desperately, the man wiped the syringe clean and dropped it into the bio-hazard container that hung on the wall. He watched Manville for any tell-tale signs of life and when satisfied that there weren't any, stepped to the doorway and looked in both directions. Satisfied that he didn't see anyone paying any attention to him, he walked down the hallway. He had never intended to wait for Ortiz.

Who he didn't see was Tim, who had walked out of Johnny's room just after the man left the cop's room. Tim saw him from the side and then stopped to watch him walk the length of the corridor, thinking that he had seen him before.

Puzzled, he turned and walked to the other end of the floor and paused before he went through the doors back up to the third floor to find Brett, Stephen and Mike.

What Tim didn't see was the man in disguise stop, turn and look down the hallway just before he went through the doors. He spotted Tim before the boy had disappeared into the far stairwell. As he watched Tim leave, the man wondered if he had been spotted and recognized.

If so, this would be a problem that would need to be taken care of.

CHAPTER NINETEEN

Chicago, Illinois

Johnny died.

He died peacefully and soundlessly and with what seemed like a sigh. He stopped breathing and his heart stopped beating and Johnny stopped being.

Johnny's mom wept. She had her head down with her lips pressed against his left hand. Brett held Johnny's right hand, while Tim had one hand gently on the back of Brett's neck and his other hand on Johnny's chest. While Johnny's mother cried silently, neither Brett nor Tim shed a tear. That would come later.

Mike and Stephen stood at the foot of the bed. Mike had his head down with his hands clasped tightly in front of him like he was deep in prayer, while Stephen stared at Johnny, shifting his gaze to Johnny's mother, to Brett and then to Tim, watching them quietly, wondering what each was thinking and not understanding what his own feelings were. He stood next to Mike, his shoulder and arm touching Mike's. He had the urge to slip his arm around Mike's shoulders, probably more for his own support than Mike's, somehow feeling the need to touch and be touched.

Jeremy stood in the doorway quietly observing the boys.

Next to Jeremy stood Skip Dahlke, head down, jaw clenched, hands balled into fists.

Behind Jeremy and Skip stood the boys' parents: Tim's, Mike's, and then Stephen's. Behind them all, stood Thomas and behind him- not next to him- stood Victoria. The parents wept, except for Stephen's father, Ted Bailey, and Thomas and Victoria. Ted looked rather bored, while Brett's parents looked and acted bewildered.

After about fifteen minutes, which felt like fifteen days, Dr. Flasch came in and asked everyone to leave with the exception of Johnny's mother. She lifted her head, nodded at Tim and Brett and tried to smile, but the smile dissolved into a grimace and more tears. The boys went to the other side of the bed and embraced her, first Tim, then Brett. After they were done, Mike and Stephen did the same.

Brett turned back to Johnny, brushed his bangs off his forehead, and then bent down and kissed his cheek, murmuring something no one heard. That was okay because whatever was said was meant for Johnny. After Brett, Tim did the same.

That completed, the adults filed out into the hallway, while Brett and Tim lingered in the doorway. Without taking his eyes off of Johnny, Brett whispered, "Maybe Johnny had the right idea."

Tim shook his head, slipped his arm around Brett's shoulder, and said, "He never had a chance. He was too sick."

"It doesn't seem fair," Brett said tiredly.

Tim didn't say anything, but gave Brett's shoulder a squeeze, turned and walked out of the room leaving Brett alone with Johnny, his mother and Dr. Flasch.

And it was then that Brett wept silently and alone. Not just for Johnny and his mom, but for himself and Tim, for Stephen and Mike, and for Patrick and the rest of the boys.

CHAPTER TWENTY

Chicago, Illinois

Kelliher's cell beeped.

He pulled it out of his sport coat pocket and glanced at it. The sender was Deputy Director Tom Dandridge and it simply read, *Urgent! Get your team to a secure location for a conference call!*

Kelliher phoned Cochrane to meet him in the conference room and then told Skip and Jeremy to follow him, leading the way back to the first floor and the other end of the hospital. Kelliher didn't volunteer any information on the way down and neither Jeremy nor Skip asked for any.

They entered the room and sat down facing each other with Kelliher and Jeremy on one side and Skip and Cochrane on the other. Using the phone in the center of the table, Pete dialed up Dandridge and put him on speaker. The four of them tensed, listening to the phone on the other end ring.

"Hold on a minute. I'm having MB Wilkey join us from Indianapolis," Dandridge said, sounding a bit distracted. In the background, they heard him yell at his assistant, "Rita, do you have her yet?" They didn't hear an answer, but heard a 'click' and then Dandridge said, "MB, are you there?"

"Yes, Sir," came the reply in a light, but confident female voice.

"Gentlemen, joining us is Agent Mary Beth Wilkey." To Mary Beth, he said, "MB, on the other end of the line are Agents Pete Kelliher, Vince Cochrane, Skip Dahlke and an advisor we use in sex abuse cases, Jeremy Evans."

"Gentlemen."

"MB, bring them up to speed."

Pete had never heard of her. Like the other three men in the room, he pulled out a pen ready to take notes on the yellow legal pad in front of him.

"Using his cell at 11:43 AM, Detective Luke Pressman phoned in a 9-1-1 from his house in Indianapolis. With him was Detective Anthony Dominico."

Skip raised his eyes up from his pad, glanced at Kelliher, who had set his jaw and who had paused in mid-word on the pad in front of him. Jeremy set his pen down on the pad and folded his hands in front of him, waiting.

"I'm going to play the 9-1-1 tape. It runs for three minutes and thirty-seven seconds . . . at least the pertinent conversation between Pressman and Dominico."

Wilkey played the tape through once so Kelliher and the others could listen to it. Kelliher asked her to play it again and this time, he and the others took notes.

After the tape played through a third time, Dandridge said, "Thoughts?"

"Who do you have running the crime scene?" Kelliher asked staring at Dahlke.

"No one yet. I have it sealed up," Wilkey responded.

"I'd like to send you Skip Dahlke."

Dandridge said, "Thought you'd say that." Then to Skip he said, "How soon can you get there?"

"About two and a half hours," Dahlke responded.

"We'll fly you in so that will cut the time considerably," Dandridge said. "Do you have any gear with you?"

"No, Sir. Most of it's still in Wisconsin," Dahlke answered. "The only things I have access to are the basics I brought with me to Chicago."

"If you fax me a list, I can get you what you need from our CSI team in Indy." Wilkey said.

"That'll work. Give me the number and I'll get you the list."

"Any other thoughts?" Dandridge asked.

Jeremy cleared his throat, leaned forward a little and said cautiously, "Dominico mentioned a list."

"Yes, what do you make of that?" Dandridge asked.

"Actually, two lists," Jeremy clarified. He had never met Dandridge. He was also not fully an FBI agent, so he didn't know how much input he should provide.

"Who is that?" Dandridge asked.

"That was Jeremy Evans," Kelliher said. "Jeremy, what are you thinking?"

"Well, Dominico said the list was made up of those individuals who were *personal* to them, and the second group was made up of those individuals who were *common* to each of them." Jeremy paused looking down at his notes. "We need to look at Dominico closely to determine who might be on each list."

"Dominico also said, *'we'* and *'them'*," Cochrane said. "Who is *we* and *them* and how many are we talking about?"

They sat in silence each thinking that over, and then Pete and Jeremy began writing down names on their yellow pads.

"MB, what do you have on Dominico?" Dandridge asked.

"I've looked at his service evaluations and at best, they're marginal. On one, he's described as a loner, a sexist and a bigot. Not actually in those words, but that's what his supervisor said to me when I met him. On another, there's a comment about one of his confidential informants who turned up dead in an alleged drug deal. I was curious as to why it showed up on his evaluation."

"Sounds like someone questioned the death," Cochrane said.

"That's what I thought," MB said. "I can tell you that he wasn't particularly liked by his superiors."

"Why do you say that?" Pete asked.

"It wasn't so much in what they *said*. It was more in what they *didn't* say."

"Besides the evaluations, what kind of guy is he?" Jeremy asked.

"That's Jeremy, right?" MB asked.

"Yes, Ma'am," Jeremy answered.

"He's described as a fitness freak and narcissistic, almost compulsive. He's considered arrogant. His lieutenant said Dominico thought he was better than everyone else. His captain said that Pressman had lasted the longest of any of his partners."

"What happened to the rest?" Cochrane asked.

"They put in requests for reassignments."

Pete looked over at Jeremy, and Pete said, "His former partners should be interviewed."

"I agree," Cochrane said.

"Back to the lists Jeremy mentioned," Dandridge said. "What do you guys think?"

"The *we* part in the 9-1-1 bothers me," Cochrane said. "Who are we talking about and how many are we talking about?"

It occurred to Pete that he had already mentioned that, but he didn't comment on it.

Oblivious to Cochrane's comment, Jeremy said, "I jotted down some names that came to mind."

"Okay, let's begin with the list that they . . . whoever *they* are . . . have in common," Dandridge said.

"Well, you have to figure anyone connected to law enforcement that had a hand in freeing the boys," Jeremy said.

"That would be Summer, me, Skip, Chet Walker, and maybe Logan Musgrave," Pete said.

"But then you'd have to add Jamie Graff, Officer Gary Fitzpatrick, Captain Jack O'Brien, and maybe the others on the teams in Kansas City and Long Beach," Jeremy added.

"And if he or they know about you, you'd have to add yourself and your son, Randy," Cochrane added.

Jeremy nodded and said quietly, "I thought of that." Then he said what the others had been thinking, "Probably George, too."

Pete nodded and said, "They went after him once so what's to stop them from going after him again?"

Cochrane's cell went off. He looked at the number and name, excused himself and stepped out of the room to answer it, shutting the door behind him.

"Okay, those are the law enforcement guys. Who else?"

"I wrote down the McGovern family, especially Brett," MB said. "Anyone on the Indy police force Dominico had a run-in with, which sounds like just about everyone."

"Okay, now what?" Dandridge asked.

"We'll need to put the McGovern family under surveillance, maybe protection," MB said.

"That's going to be hard," Jeremy said. "Mrs. McGovern, Victoria, isn't exactly cooperative."

"Then I suggest we warn them and put someone on them undercover," Dandridge said. "We can't use anyone in Indianapolis either from the PD or from the FBI in case Dominico knows them."

"What about using one or two who helped in the raids?" Jeremy asked.

Kelliher nodded, "I agree. They're already vetted. We could use one or two from the Long Beach raid."

"Unless the . . . *they*, he referred to, know about them," MB said.

Everyone was silent, and then Dandridge said, "Pete, can you call O'Brien and Graff and discuss this with them?"

"I will. Are you going to bring Summer and Chet into the loop?"

"They are. They came up with the same ideas you did." Then to Dahlke he said, "Skip, Chet Walker is going to meet you in Indianapolis."

"Yes, Sir."

"At some point, we need to discuss protection for Stephen Bailey," Jeremy said. "We know each boy was selected by someone in the ring. From what Jamie Graff said, we don't know who targeted Stephen. That means he, or they, are still out there. And that means both Stephen and Mike, and maybe their families are in danger."

Dandridge said, "Pete, I'm guessing Graff and O'Brien are already on that, but when you call, find out what they're going to do for the boys and their families."

"Will do."

"Jeremy, what about you and Randy and George?" Skip asked.

Jeremy pursed his lips thinking, and shifted uncomfortably in his chair. He tapped his pad with his pen and said, "We're leaving this afternoon to take George to Arizona. It's sort of a vacation for us, but it's also for George to tie up loose ends and give him time to make a decision as to whether or not he's going to live with his cousin or come back and live with us."

"Jeremy, that's a very generous offer you made," Dandridge said. "Pete mentioned that you had reached out to him."

"He doesn't have anyone else and it, well, seems like the right thing to do."

"I want you to know that whatever he decides, you and your boys and George will be taken care of by us. That's a promise," Dandridge said with firmness.

"Thank you, Sir."

"Jeremy, how many people know your plans?" Pete asked.

"Hell, I don't even know our plans. Jeff and I are winging it. The only thing we know is that in ten days or so, we'll be in Arizona, and George will decide whether or not he'll be coming back with us or staying with his cousin."

"So, between now and let's say, ten days from now, no one will know where you are," Pete said.

Jeremy nodded and said, "That's right."

"Keep it that way, but check in with me each day and each night."

"Sure."

"Jeremy, do you have any weapons . . . you know, for self-defense?" Dandridge asked.

Jeremy shook his head and said, "I'm not comfortable with guns around the boys."

"George has a knife," Skip said.

Jeremy nodded.

"What kind of knife?" Dandridge asked.

"A big one," Skip said.

"And he knows how to use it," Pete added. "We made sure that he has a conceal and carry permit."

"Good," Dandridge said. "What about a hunting rifle? George might like to hunt when he gets to Arizona."

Kelliher said. "The first time I met him, he had a rifle, an old .22 Winchester. He said he used it for rabbits and coyotes."

Jeremy looked at him and Skip doubtfully.

"Jeremy, with your permission, I'm going to get him a hunting rifle and I'll have it sent to Arizona," Dandridge said. "When you get there, it'll be waiting for him. I'll walk the paperwork through myself."

"I don't know if I like this," Jeremy said cautiously. "It seems we're giving him permission to use it for . . ." He didn't finish, but shook his head.

"*Hunting,*" Dandridge said. "Just for hunting."

The door opened and Cochrane rushed in, slamming the door behind him. He cleared his throat and said, "Bosch and Rawson are dead."

CHAPTER TWENTY-ONE

Brookfield, Wisconsin

George's version of shopping was to go to the trading post located in Teec Nos Pas, the small town of about 800 people, mostly Navajo, that was near where he and his family lived. It was where he, his brother William, and his grandfather sold the wool from their sheep, and was the only place on the entire Navajo reservation that took in wool. Until the FBI flew him to Wisconsin, he had never been off the Navajo Indian Reservation, so going to the Brookfield Square Mall was an experience like none he had had in his life. It was one fantastical shop after another.

When Billy, Randy and Danny pulled him into Dick's Sporting Goods, he marveled at the racks of clothes, baseball bats, baseballs and mitts. He spied soccer balls, softballs, basketballs and footballs. He gaped at tents, kayaks and canoes. They dragged him to the back of the store where there were more shoes on the wall and on tables than he ever saw in his entire fourteen years of life.

After spending a good amount of time and money, at least by George's standards anyway- perhaps by anyone's standards- they next went to JC Penny and Kohl's. He tried on jeans and slacks, polo shirts and sweatshirts, and picked out boxers, socks and a jacket.

They came out of the store laden down with bags of merchandize and Jeff greeted them, and pointed them towards a western wear store he had spied while taking a walk to a Verizon store.

George felt most at home in this store. He selected a new belt with a bronze eagle buckle, some button down short and long-sleeved shirts, and a new pair of leather cowboy boots. Billy wanted him to get a new Stetson, but George was comfortable with the white cowboy hat he had. It was a bit beat up and stained, but it was his, given to him by his mother several years previous. He viewed a new Stetson as unnecessary.

After shopping at the mall for just over two hours and after grabbing lunch in the food court, they stopped at a Best Buy to purchase a laptop and case, and a cell phone. The Verizon guy explained to Jeff that because George lived in a desert, a sat phone would be the only device that would work effectively or consistently. They didn't have any available, but suggested that Best Buy might and that Verizon could be the plan provider. That worked for Jeff. He decided on just an iPhone like the cell phones Danny and the twins had until he, Jeremy and George knew for sure where he would live.

George had no idea how to use the phone or the computer, but the boys explained that they'd have time during the trip to teach him.

Randy said, "A lot of it you learn to do as you play with it."

Jeff drove the boys back home to pack up George's clothes and other belongings and pick up some smaller items that Randy and Billy were going to take along. After a once-through to make sure windows were shut and locked, faucets turned off and the air-conditioning up to a warm seventy-four degrees, the house was locked up and the boys walked next door to say goodbye to Jon and Bert.

George did his best to keep his emotions in check, but as hard as he tried, a few tears still leaked from his eyes.

"We hope to see you in a couple of weeks, but if not, promise you'll come visit us, okay?" Bert said with both of her hands gently caressing George's cheeks.

George nodded.

"We'll see you, Son," Jon said quietly with an embrace that he held George in for a moment or two. "Know you're always welcome."

George nodded solemnly.

They loaded up Jeff Limbach's black Chevy Suburban and waved goodbye. Billy rode shotgun with George and Randy sitting in the backseat at each door, and Danny between them.

George hadn't been in a big city before, and rode with his face pressed against the window staring out at the gray landscape of tall buildings and asphalt, of cars, trucks and busses passing by or getting passed as they traveled east on I-894. Every now and then, he was pulled back into the vehicle when one of the boys or Jeff asked a question, but he always went back to the window marveling at the stark difference between his homeland and the city.

And this was just Milwaukee.

The weather changed as they drove south on I-94 from blue and sunny to gray and misty. The desert didn't have much rain, so even this amazed George.

When they got into Chicago, he not only stared out the window, but looked up through the sunroof gazing at the tall steel structures that seemed to block out the clouds and the sky.

Noticing the innocent amazement and the awe on George's face, Jeff decided to make a side trip before heading to the hospital where he and the boys were to meet up with Jeff.

Better known as the Sears Tower, the Willis Tower- its real name- was at one time the tallest building in North America. It boasted of a 104-car elevator system in three zones that took a person from the ground floor to the pinnacle at the speed of a bungee jump in reverse.

At floor 103, there was a four-foot glass walkout. The boys watched as groups of fearless family members stepped onto it to get their pictures taken. When it was their turn, Billy tentatively ventured onto the platform first, followed by George, Danny and Randy, while Jeff snapped their pictures. Then it was Randy's turn to take a picture of Jeff and Danny.

None of them realized that the Sears Tower or the trip to Brookfield Square Mall would not be what they would remember about this day.

CHAPTER TWENTY-TWO

Chicago, Illinois

At first, they stared at Cochrane as if he were speaking Chinese. After a moment or two, Skip broke the silence.

"What did you say?"

Cochrane sat down, ran a hand through his hair and said, "Bosch and Rawson are dead. They were murdered in jail."

Silence. Eye blinks. Throats cleared. Kelliher began to write something on his legal pad but stopped and set his pen down and folded his hands in front of him like a principal about to lecture a recalcitrant youth. Cochrane was the one responsible for placing Bosch and Rawson in Cook County Jail rather than Danville Prison like Kelliher had suggested. The move would have been unusual, but unusual was modis operandi for Kelliher and Storm.

"Let me get Summer and Chet back in here," Dandridge said curtly. He punched the sound off the phone on the other end and Kelliher could only presume he was getting his secretary to get in touch with the two agents. Perhaps cursing. A lot.

Summer Storm was the field team leader of Kiddie Corps and more importantly, was partner to Kelliher, though technically his boss. She and Kelliher had planned the raids that freed the kids, and Summer, along with Chet Walker, the team techie and youngest member of the team, and Waukesha Police Captain Jack O'Brien, they had confronted Bosch, Rawson and Davis in a hotel restaurant.

Summer got her name because she was born in the backseat of a station wagon in a raging thunderstorm somewhere between Crete and Lincoln, Nebraska. Her parents first thought of Hailey, but settled on Summer because they liked the way it sounded: Summer Storm. Given a choice when she was recruited by the FBI out of law school at Louisville, she chose Kiddie Corps because as she told her parents, she wanted to do some good and make a difference. Of course, just being in the FBI had made her parents proud.

Chet had red hair and freckles and was, until Skip Dahlke joined up, the youngest member of the team. Rumor had it that he could hack into anything and that anyone was fair game. More importantly, he could do it without detection. A quieter rumor was that Chet was recruited because he was a hacker. However, that was never confirmed.

"Short version," Kelliher said quietly, "what happened?"

Before Cochrane could begin, Dandridge came back on and checked to make sure MB Wilkey was still with them.

"I'm here," she said quietly. Kelliher thought he had detected anger, but not knowing her, he didn't know for sure.

"Hi, Everyone," Summer said quietly. Pete recognized her anger right away, but no one else did.

"Cochrane, what happened?" Dandridge asked abruptly.

"Bosch was found in his cell with his throat slit and Rawson was found stabbed multiple times in a shower room. Both sometime this morning," Cochrane said. "I'm having them pull the tapes and I'll head over there when we're done here."

Silence. Looks exchanged.

"This can't be coincidence," Wilkey said from Indianapolis. "Pressman, Bosch and Rawson killed on the same day?"

Almost in unison, Kelliher and Storm said, "No such thing as coincidence." It was the mantra of their partnership.

"If these aren't coincidences, and I don't for a minute believe they are," Wilkey said, "then someone is working on their list."

"What list?" Cochrane asked.

Ignoring him, Skip said, "Then we need to figure out who else is on that list," Skip said added, "in a hurry."

"My list hasn't changed," Kelliher said.

"Neither has mine," Jeremy said.

Before Summer asked Pete and Jeremy to read their lists, Dandridge said angrily, "Cochrane, get over to that jail and secure the tapes and get them to Chet. He'll be wheels up in thirty minutes so send them in a video link. You can do *that* can't you?"

Cochrane looked up from his notes. He caught Skip's glance, but just as quickly, Skip lowered his eyes back down. No one else looked in Cochrane's direction.

"Cochrane, did you hear me?"

"Yes, Sir. I'll leave now unless you need me to stay until the call is over."

"Now!" Dandridge said forcefully.

When Cochrane left the room and shut the door behind him, Dandridge swore, and then swore again.

"Summer, what's your role on this?" Kelliher asked.

"I'm overseeing your team and the Rapid Response Team. I'm leaving the decisions to you, but keep me in the loop."

Kelliher nodded.

"Pete, keep me in the loop too," Dandridge said tiredly, calming down a little. "Skip, I need you to work your magic in Indianapolis. You, Chet and Wilkey have to find Dominico and until we do, there are too many people at risk, and that includes kids and families."

"MB, keep me posted on what's going on there," Kelliher said. "And take good care of Skip and Chet."

"Will do."

"Pete, what's your plan?" Summer asked.

He shook his head and looked at Jeremy.

"Hell if I know," he said tiredly. "I'm going to wrap up here and then follow Skip to Indianapolis. Jeremy and I are going to have to warn the kids and the families. I'll get a hold of Graff and O'Brien in Waukesha and set up surveillance in Indianapolis. Probably Waukesha too."

There was a sharp wrap on the door and Dr. Blaine Flasch entered. He was pale and sweaty and looked disheveled and unkempt, very unlike the doctor they knew him to be.

"Sorry for the interruption," Flasch started. "But I felt I needed to tell you right away."

"Tell us what?" Kelliher said.

"Robert Manville, the police officer on the second floor . . ." he paused. "He died."

"What?" Kelliher asked sharply. "I thought he was going to be okay."

"He was, and that's what I don't understand . . . yet," the doctor said. "But that's not all."

"What?" Kelliher said, getting up from his chair. Jeremy rose too, wondering if something had happened to one of the boys.

"The officer that was posted outside his door is missing. No one has seen him since a little before noon."

The room went quiet. No one said a word and it seemed that no one had even breathed. Jeremy's mind was racing, his mind working like a cop's. "Either he's the killer . . ."

"Or a victim," Pete finished for him. "Tom, if you don't mind, I'd like Skip to do a once around in Manville's room. I don't expect him to find anything, but I'd like him to look just in case. Is that okay with you?"

"Yes," Dandridge said deep in thought. "Skip, make it quick and then get to Indianapolis."

"Yessir."

"Do you and Jeremy need any help in Chicago?" Summer asked.

"Not sure what we need right now," Kelliher answered. "Summer, I'll keep you posted."

At that, the call ended and Pete, Skip and Jeremy began moving.

CHAPTER TWENTY-THREE

Chicago, Illinois

He stood in the hallway and sent off a text feeling pretty good about getting rid of Bosch, Rawson and Manville. He hoped the cop in Indianapolis would be pleased. He didn't know why the cop in Indianapolis was in charge of what was left of the group. He supposed it was because it was the cop's idea to take care of loose ends and then start everything up again. Still, he thought that logically, he should be the one to call the shots.

As he was slipping his cell back into his pocket, he saw the blond boy walk into the gift shop. The boy was incredible looking, athletic and as a bonus, he was alone, which was rare, because where one boy was, another was sure to be found. Hell, they ran in a pack. He took a quick look in either direction and then slipped his .38 out of his shoulder holster and slid it into his suit coat pocket and waited until the boy came out carrying a bottle of water and a small bag fruit snacks.

He walked up to him and said, "You're Tim, right?"

Startled, the boy jumped, then recognized the man and said, "Yeah," with a tentative smile.

The man was confident. He could be charming. After all, he was good looking and had a great smile, one that sparkled and one that disarmed anyone he came into contact with. That included the young patrolman who had sat outside the dead cop's room. More importantly, he had been able to fool everyone by hiding in plain sight.

Tim was confident, but cautious, made even more so after being in captivity for more than two years. "I thought you were a doctor."

"Why'd you think that?"

"I thought I saw you coming out of the cop's room, but I guess I was wrong."

The man took one last look in either direction, knowing he'd have to take care of the boy. A pity, but he saw this as only one more loose end.

Tim turned away when the man took hold of his right arm and said quietly, "You and I are going to walk through the lobby and out the door, and then we're going to take a ride."

"Why?" Tim said cautiously.

"You were taught not to question. You just broke a rule."

"But-"

"-Not another word," the man said. "Just walk or I'll shoot you and anyone else who gets in the way."

Tim sighed, more tired and sad than frightened. He just wanted to go back home, to start his life over again. Now, well, he just didn't care any longer. Maybe it was seeing Johnny dead. Maybe it was the sadness he saw and felt coming from his friends, especially Brett.

Resigned, he let the man take him by the arm and lead him away down the hallway to lobby, ready to face the inevitable.

It was then he noticed the strangely dressed old man with the long gray hair tied back in a braid smiling at him. He didn't know the old man and had never seen him before and he didn't know why, but somehow, Tim felt reassured and not scared at all.

CHAPTER TWENTY-FOUR

Chicago, Illinois

Jeff and the boys pulled into the parking garage across from the hospital and parked on the third level. George couldn't put his finger on anything in particular, but he had an uneasy feeling. He almost grabbed his knife and scabbard, but decided at the last minute not to.

They walked down the cement and metal stairs with Randy and Danny in the lead, followed by George and Billy, with Jeff limping behind. They came to the ground level of the garage and noticed Jeremy's red Ford Expedition parked in a reserved slip with an FBI tag on the rearview mirror, next to two other vehicles similarly marked. George slowed down and ran his hand along the back of a tan Taurus.

Shadow, be careful, but you need to hurry. The blond boy is in danger.

It was crystal clear and he had no doubt about whose voice it was, having heard it every day his life.

Stunned, he hesitated and fell in step with Jeff.

"You okay?" Jeff asked quietly.

He nodded and walked quickly to catch up to Billy. They stopped four abreast at the corner and allowed two cars, a FedEx truck and bus to pass, and then jogged across to the glass front door under an ornate brick walkway with George leading the way. There were four glass doors with the one on the far right being handicapped accessible. George led the boys and Jeff through the doorway and stood in the lobby, holding his arms out like a crossing guard.

"What's up?" Billy asked.

George didn't answer, but scanned the lobby.

A visitor's booth was directly in front of them with an elderly woman behind it. Behind the booth was a bank of elevators and what looked like a gift shop. To the left and right were hallways, but from their angle, George couldn't see down them. To their immediate left and right were chairs, but only a woman and two small children sat in them. The woman spoke into her cell phone. The little girl read a book, while the little boy colored. The rest of the chairs were empty.

Then George spotted them- a man with his right hand in his suit coat pocket, holding onto the right arm of a blond boy about the same age as he was.

And his grandfather.

His grandfather nodded at George, who remained still, staring at the trio as they walked towards them.

"I think that's Tim," Randy said, starting forward with his hand up in a wave.

George held Randy's arm and said, "Randy, go get Agent Pete. Billy, go get your father. Danny, go find the police or security."

"Huh?" Billy asked.

Not taking his eyes off the man and the boy, George said, "Do you trust me?"

"Yes, but-" Randy said.

"George?" Jeff said.

"Randy, Agent Pete is on the second floor. Billy, your father is on the third floor in the room full of sun. Do as I say. Now." George said urgently. He didn't know how he knew, just that he did.

"The stairs are there," Randy said and the twins took off on a run. As they neared the stairs, Randy said, "George means the sun room at the end of the hall on three."

Danny watched them leave and then jogged towards the visitor's booth.

"George, what's happening?" Jeff asked stepping up next to him.

Shadow, don't let the man leave with the boy.

Ignoring Jeff, George walked directly at the man. As he did, the boy glanced at George's grandfather. The man jerked the blond boy forward, but then stopped twenty yards from the front door. He looked both left and right, but didn't move. The blond boy looked up at him, then at George's grandfather and nodded slightly.

Grandfather, are you talking to Tim?

Shadow, you need to be very careful. You cannot trust this man, this biligaana.

Jeff stepped forward next to George, but George held his left arm out holding him back.

Quietly through clenched teeth, the man said, "You're the Indian boy."

George stared defiantly at the man and said, "There are cameras and they see you very clearly."

The man glanced up at the ceiling and saw that George was right.

"Get out of my way you little fucker or you're dead."

George didn't move, but as Jeff tried to step in between the man and George, George held his arm out preventing Jeff from doing so.

"You are not leaving the hospital with him. Any minute, Agent Pete will be here. The police or security will be here even quicker. Leave now while you can?"

The man looked to his left, then to his right, and licked his lips.

"What's going on here?" It was a short, slightly overweight security man who had emerged from the hallway on the left. Danny followed slightly behind, but stopped well away from them. The security man kept coming, his hand on his .45 still in his holster.

"Nothing, officer," the man said pleasantly. "I'm FBI and we seem to have a little misunderstanding that's all."

"Just walk away," George said quietly.

"I need to see some identification," the security man said.

The man finally let go of Tim, and Tim moved off behind and to the side and it looked to George that his grandfather took hold of Tim's arm and led him away.

Shadow, let him leave before he shoots someone.

George stepped aside giving the man a path to the front door and the man started forward.

"Hold it!" the security man said. "I want to see some identification."

The gun in the man's suit pocket barked loudly, echoing off the steel and glass of the lobby. As the security man fell to his knees, the man pulled his gun from what was left of his suit pocket, pointed it at the security man and shot him again in the chest.

The mother with the two children screamed, as did the elderly woman in the visitor's booth. Several people emerged from the hallway to see what had happened and then just as quickly disappeared back to where they had come from.

George pushed Jeff to the floor, kneeling over him and shielding him as best he could. Danny knelt down next to the visitor's booth and shouted, "Dad!"

The man pointed the gun at George, thought better of it, and raced out the door.

Shadow, watch where he goes, but be careful.

George placed on a hand gently on Jeff and said, "Watch over Danny and Tim." He took a look at Tim lying on the floor and then at his grandfather who smiled and nodded at him.

He scrambled to the security man and feeling for a pulse, found one, but it was faint.

"Call 9-1-1," he yelled to the elderly woman in the visitor's booth. "And get a doctor here right away!"

George grabbed the security man's .45 out of his holster, flicked off the safety and chambered in a load. Then grabbing it in both hands and pointing it at the ceiling, he ran to the front door, squatted down to the side and peered out.

"George come back!" Jeff yelled after him.

A shot rang out shattering glass, but the bullet sailed harmlessly into a wall across the lobby.

"George, come back here!" Jeff yelled again.

Ignoring him, George stepped through the door keeping low and ran behind one of the stone pillars of the walkway.

There were no other shots.

He ran from one pillar to another, until he was at the last one across from the parking garage entrance. He heard a car start up, its tires squealing.

Shadow, be careful.

George watched as the tan Taurus with the FBI tag barrel through the garage and break through the wooden gated entrance.

Never having fired a handgun and more out of instinct than firsthand knowledge, George aimed at the front passenger tire and sent a bullet into it. The Taurus was traveling too fast to negotiate the turn and when the tire blew, the man lost control of the car and it slammed into a parked car ten yards from where George knelt. The horn went off and the airbag deployed. Two oncoming cars stopped and the would-be good Samaritans started to climb out to see if they could help the driver.

Knowing for certain that neither driver should get near the Taurus, George shouted, "Get back! FBI!" The men got back into their cars and one of them locked the door.

He stepped around the stone pillar holding the .45 with both hands, pointing it at the man in the crumpled Taurus just as two Chicago PD patrol cars screeched to a halt.

"Drop your weapon!" one officer shouted. "Do it *now!*"

George lifted one hand high in the air and moving ever so slowly, laid the .45 on the pavement and then held his other hand high above his head.

"Get on the ground, Scumbag! Hands behind your head! Lace your fingers!"

George did as he was told as he watched one officer approach him cautiously. The gun the cop held looked to George as big as a canon and for the first time, he was scared, though he refused to show it.

One officer approached the Taurus and yelled, "This guy's FBI. He's alive!"

"You piece of shit," the officer said, kicking George hard in the stomach.

All the air burst out of George's lungs and he nearly passed out from the pain and lack of breath. One arm was yanked up high, nearly out of its socket and a handcuff was slapped on. His other arm was similarly yanked and cuffed, and then he was kicked again, this time in the ribs.

"Get away from that boy now!"

The officer whirled around and pointed a gun at the voice.

"FBI! You kick that young man one more time and I'll kick the shit out of you!"

Fading in and out, George recognized the voice.

A gunshot rang out and the officer near the Taurus fell to the ground. Another shot rang out from inside the Taurus and blood and brain matter sprayed over what was left of the windows and interior.

The man was dead.

George whispered to Pete, "Tell Skip not to let them contaminate the crime scene."

And then he passed out.

Later when Skip debriefed the scene, he couldn't actually remember what Pete had said for sure, or what, if anything, the cop had said. He remembered Pete throwing a roundhouse at the cop's nose and was certain he had heard bone and cartilage snap. He was certain the cop hit the ground and didn't get up right away, and that the cop's face had dissolved in a mass of blood and snot.

Skip had stayed with George until a nurse, orderly and doctor showed up with a gurney, then he worked the crime scene, though there wasn't much to figure out.

The cop near the Taurus took one in his vest and he'd be sore as hell, but he'd live. Other than that, nothing else to deal with except to fill out reports and sit through a phone call to Dandridge and Storm on one end, with he and Pete and Jeremy on the other.

CHAPTER TWENTY-FIVE

His grandfather looked like he always did: plaid button-down long-sleeved shirt, leather vest, and faded blue jeans with well-worn leather cowboy boots. His long gray hair was braided back and held in place with a leather tie. His face looked like old, brown wrinkled leather, aged by the desert winds and the Arizona sun. His brown, wrinkled hands were clasped behind his back and every now and then, he turned his face to look at the sun, which was bright and shiny. George couldn't look at it because it was too bright. Almost painful. George was a shade taller than his grandfather. The joke between them was that either George was growing or his grandfather was shrinking. That brought a smile to George's face.

'You saved the blond boy, Shadow.'

'I saw you talking to him.'

His grandfather nodded and said, 'He was scared, ready to give up.'

'Give up?'

He nodded again, looked up at the sun and said, 'The blond boy has been through a lot and he thought his time was up. It isn't.'

'You know when someone is going to die?'

His grandfather looked at George, smiled, shook his head and said, 'A feeling.'

George didn't say anything but continued to walk next to his grandfather. He didn't know where they were or where they were going. The only thing that mattered was that he was with his grandfather.

'Grandfather?'

'I can't tell you what to do, Shadow. It is your choice,' he said reading George's thoughts.

George remained silent.

'Your brothers have the heart of a lion.'

Puzzled, George glanced at his grandfather, then back at the ground. It was a dirt road that seemed vaguely familiar to him.

'One quiet, one not. Both love fiercely. Both loyal. Deep as the Canyon. They share the same heart, the same mind.' His grandfather paused and then said, 'They have come to care about you.'

'My brothers?'

Ignoring the question, his grandfather said, 'Your father could be Dine', our people. Your brothers would be fierce warriors, especially the one.'

'You called him my father.'

His grandfather smiled at him but continued walking.

'I should live with them?' George asked.

'It is your choice. It has always been your choice.'

'But you called him my father. You called them my brothers.'

His grandfather stopped walking, looked up at the sun, smiled, and said, 'It is a choice.'

A storm of emotions rose in George. Longing. Love. Fear. Confusion. He didn't know which was the greater feeling, but he felt them all.

'Trust your heart, Shadow. Always trust your heart.' His grandfather smiled at him and nodded.

'Will I see you again?'

His grandfather placed a hand on George's shoulder and smiled warmly at him. 'When there is a need.'

'Grandfather, please don't leave,' George said sadly.

'Trust your heart, Shadow. There you will find me. There you will find answers.'

His grandfather walked away, hands clasped behind his back, face turned up at the sun. As he grew smaller in the distance, George heard him say, 'Yes, I think your father and brothers are Dine'.'

Then he turned and smiled, and faded away.

CHAPTER TWENTY-SIX

Chicago, Illinois

"Cochrane was FBI! He was right *here* with our *kids*, and you didn't know he was part of the group that took our boys!" Ted Bailey yelled.

Pete expected harsh and accusatory words. What made it worse was that he didn't have answers.

Stephen was embarrassed by his father. Mike was embarrassed for Stephen. Tim and Brett listened without emotion or judgment. Jeremy sat quietly, not much help when the discussion centered on the investigation.

It had been a busy morning and afternoon. Manville had been killed by Cochrane, who had injected him with Dilaudid. Patrolman Juan Ortiz was found in a dumpster by maintenance personnel. His neck had been broken. Both Douglas Rawson and Victor Bosch were killed in Cook County Jail. Exactly who did the deeds wasn't yet known, but Cochrane was responsible. Tim was almost kidnapped and who knows what would have happened if Cochrane had left the hospital with him. A security guard was shot and killed in the hospital lobby, and George was almost shot and killed along with him.

What bothered and upset Kelliher the most was that under his watch, three FBI agents were involved in the human trafficking of boys and all three were dead. Dead, along with any leads they had. Hell, they didn't even have a direction in which to investigate.

He had called his old partner, Storm, and explained everything that had happened, and after that phone call, made a second one to Dandridge. He made the same offer to both: turn in his resignation effectively immediately.

Both rejected it.

"How can we trust you?" Ted Bailey asked, standing up.

Fair question, Pete thought. Under the circumstances and in their place, he wouldn't be very trusting either and would probably ask the same question.

"I trust him," Brett said, turning around and staring at the man. He was angry, so he stood up to face him defiantly, daring him, challenging him. "I saw him take on those perverts in that building. He almost got himself shot. He saved us." He stopped and glared at him.

"I do too," Tim said, turning around also.

Stephen and Mike turned to stare at him in silent support.

"Guys, let's quiet down," Pete said, clearing his throat.

Tim, Stephen and Mike turned around. Brett glared at Stephen's father, then turned around and sat back down.

And not for the first time did Jeremy consider that these thirteen- and fourteen-year-old boys were in some respects, older and more mature than the high school kids he worked with. He knew they'd be changed, different after all that had happened to them. He knew that they would be numb and indifferent to much of what kids their age were excited by or interested in. He knew they were certainly more serious than they ought to be, but given the circumstances, that was understandable. He only hoped that they'd regain some of the lost childhood that was stolen from them.

"Here is what I can tell you," Pete said trying to get the conference room back in order. "Our computer guy, Chet Walker, has done some preliminary diagnostics on Cochrane's phone. We know he sent an email to several individuals and we're working on who those individuals are."

"About as quickly as you discovered who Cochrane really was, I suppose," Ted Bailey snarled as he sat back down.

"How safe are our boys?" Laura Pruitt asked.

"Cochrane almost kidnapped your boy!" Bailey said.

"Dad, shut *up*!" Stephen said.

There was silence. All heads turned first towards Stephen and then to his father, who got up out of his chair again.

"What did you say?" Bailey asked through clenched teeth quietly.

"He said, 'Shut up and sit your ass down!'" Sarah Bailey, his wife, said. "In fact, leave." She glared at him and then said, "Stephen and I will ride back with Mark and Jennifer."

Then all the adults turned back towards Pete.

Stephen had never seen his mom and dad fight with one another, so not only was he shocked, he was also scared at what might happen to him for telling his father to shut up.

Brett leaned over towards him and whispered, "That was pretty cool." He paused and then added, "Suicidal, but pretty cool."

Stephen barely heard him.

"Mrs. Pruitt, we think Cochrane tried to take Tim because Tim witnessed him leaving Manville's room. The hospital security tapes support that. We don't think Tim or your family is in any immediate danger. However, as a precaution, we're arranging for protection through West Bend PD."

Laura and Thad Pruitt nodded solemnly.

"Brett, you and your family are in grave danger," Pete said quietly. He looked at both Thomas and Victoria, no longer expecting a protest from Victoria, because all of the fight went out of her when she had heard the 9-1-1 recording of Dominico killing his partner. She had recognized her brother's voice and was appalled at his cold calculation. "We'll be protecting you and your family, but Brett, you'll have to be careful."

Brett showed no emotion and Pete and Jeremy worried silently what Brett was thinking or what he might do if given the opportunity.

"Thomas, we'll need to change the locks and the garage code," Victoria said, leaning over towards her husband. "Tony has a key and knows the code."

"With your permission, we'll send someone over to you home before you get there to check out the premises and to wait there until you return," Pete suggested.

Victoria and Thomas turned towards one another, nodded, and then Thomas said, "Thank you."

Brett watched the interaction. He had not heard the 9-1-1 recording and didn't know what his uncle had done, so he was not expecting this reaction from his mother. She smiled at him and he smiled back. He made a face at Tim suggesting his amazement. Tim did not respond.

Pete continued, "Stephen is in danger, because we don't know who was responsible for targeting him. Remember, each boy found in captivity was targeted by someone. According to the boys," Pete nodded at Brett and Tim, "Stephen would have been visited by him soon after he was taken, but because the boys were rescued, he wasn't. Until we find out who that is, Stephen is in danger and by extension, so is his family. We also think that because Stephen and Mike were taken together, Mike and his family might be in danger. Detective Jamie Graff and Captain Jack O'Brien are arranging protection for both families. Graff will be in touch with you when you get back to Waukesha."

Mark and Jennifer Erickson gripped each other's hands and then Jennifer reached over and took Sarah's hand.

"We believe George Tokay to be in danger because he was specifically mentioned in the email sent by Cochrane. Looking at the security tapes and in talking to Jeff Limbach, Cochrane aimed right at George's head, but didn't pull the trigger." Pete stopped and shook his head. "And if George is in danger, Jeremy and the twins are also in danger."

Jeremy lowered his eyes to his hands, but otherwise kept his emotions masked. Of course, he was scared- not so much for himself as he was for his boys. And he included George as one of his boys.

"We also can't find the men responsible for two other boys, one from Chicago and one from Long Beach, so we think they might be in danger too."

"Who? What boy?" Tim asked.

Pete checked his notes and said, "Cole, rescued from Long Beach, and Patrick, rescued from Chicago."

Brett panicked, stood up, and went white. "You have to protect Patrick. You have to. Nothing can happen to him." He looked from Pete to Skip to Jeremy and pleaded, "Please. You have to take care of him."

As confidently as he could, Pete said, "Brett, we're on it. We're working-"

"-Does he know? Does he know to be careful?"

"Brett, we've spoken to his family and with Wentzville PD and with the FBI in St. Louis. They're on it."

Panicking and pale, Brett paced the room with his head down and one hand in his hair. He stopped and said, "Can I talk to him? Please?"

Brett's parents looked at each other, not understanding the connection between Brett and Patrick. Pete and Jeremy exchanged a look, with Pete shrugging an okay.

"Yes, you can," Jeremy said softly. "I know how much Patrick means to you, but can you wait until we're done here?"

Brett stared at Jeremy and said, "I need to talk to him *now*."

CHAPTER TWENTY-SEVEN

Chicago, Illinois

George's dark eyes fluttered open and it took effort to remember where he was and how he had gotten there. He had no recollection of how he went from the cold, damp pavement to a bed. The room was small. A curtain covered one wall, presumably the door because the room was without one as far as he could see. A TV was mounted up in the corner tuned to Sports Center on mute. He had recognized it because it was the station of choice in the Evans house.

He was sitting up in bed and leaning against several pillows, dressed in a hospital gown with the sheets down at his waist and an IV in his left arm. He tried to sit up straighter, but stopped immediately because his ribs hurt. He moved his gown to take a look at the blue, black and red bruising on his right side. He couldn't breathe deeply with any comfort and it was equally uncomfortable for him to move.

"You're awake," Billy said softly.

George blinked at him and saw Jeff and Danny Limbach behind him.

"Jeremy wanted me to text him when you woke up," Danny said. He pulled out his cell and his thumbs sped rapidly over the keyboard.

"How're you feeling?" Jeff asked.

George nodded and said, "Okay." His ribs hurt, he was thirsty and he had a lot of questions and not many answers.

"You have badly bruised ribs, but otherwise, you're fine," Jeff said. "The IV was a precaution because you had passed out."

George nodded again.

"Your cell has been vibrating like crazy," Billy said. "You must have a dozen or so messages."

"From who?"

"Not sure," Billy answered. "Danny put in a bunch of numbers that Tim and Brett had given him."

George shut his eyes and lay back against the pillow. He must have dozed because when he again opened his eyes, Tim was sitting at his bedside.

"Hi."

George blinked at him and smiled.

"I'm Tim."

George nodded.

"You saved my life."

George shrugged, wincing at the pain.

"Can I ask you some questions?"

George nodded again.

"That was your grandfather?"

"Yes."

"But he's dead," Tim said.

"Yes."

Tim nodded as he considered the answer, not sure how he felt about it, but certain that George had told him the truth. He didn't know how it was possible that a dead person could appear and talk to him like he had done. When he did speak, he said, "Your grandfather said I shouldn't worry . . . that I was going to be okay."

"He told me that he thought you had given up," George said.

Tim lowered his face and kept it down.

George waited patiently, letting Tim gather his thoughts.

Finally, Tim looked up and he wiped his eyes with his hands. "I didn't think I was going to get out of it this time. I thought . . . the others . . . Johnny . . . now me." He shrugged again.

George reached out and took Tim's hand and said, "You cannot think like that. The others look up to you."

Tim shook his head and said, "Not me. Brett."

"You and Brett together." He remembered his grandfather's words in reference to Randy and Billy, and he said, "You share the same heart. You cannot give up because who will the others turn to?"

Tim and George stared at one another in silence.

"Do you think I'll see you or your grandfather again?"

George shrugged and said, "I think if there is a need, my grandfather will be there. And me, probably," he said with a smile.

Tim smiled and said, "I hope so." Shyly he added softly, "I was hoping we'd be friends."

George smiled at him and nodded.

"We're meeting in the sunroom at the end of the hall. Our parents wanted to meet you and say goodbye. We're getting ready to leave," Tim said sadly.

"Why does that make you sad?"

Tim couldn't put it into words, but he and Brett had worried about it for the last several days, both together and privately, and especially since the meeting they had just had with Pete and Jeremy, who had outlined the danger they were in. George watched him mull the question over.

Tim was about the same height as he was, an inch or so shorter than the twins, with longish blond hair and blue eyes. He was handsome with a friendly smile, and was on the skinny side like George was, though both boys had broad shoulders.

Tim sighed. "We've been gone a long time. We don't know what it's going to be like when we get home." He paused, looked George straight in the eye and said, "There are assholes out there who want us dead. I'm scared." He was quiet for a bit and some more tears leaked from his eyes which he wiped away. "Sometimes I wonder if it's all worth it."

George didn't say anything.

"You lost your grandfather and your whole family. Pete thinks they're still after you. Brett's my best friend and his uncle is out to kill him. You saved my life this time, but who'll be there next time?"

The news that someone, maybe more than one person was after him had startled him. That meant that if they were after him, Jeremy and the twins might be in danger, and by extension, so would Danny and Jeff.

Did his grandfather know? If so, why didn't he warn him? His frown was visible and his mind worked overtime.

"What?" Tim asked studying him.

George shook his head still frowning.

CHAPTER TWENTY-EIGHT

Northern Suburb of Indianapolis, Indiana

Dominico read the text and was pleased. Now all they had to do was to concentrate on getting even and then begin again.

Of course, *he* knew why getting even was so important.

They had done this to *him*!

Him!

He felt the anger boil up in him again and let it surge through his brain, his veins, his muscles and his being.

He tapped in a message to the five others: *Get them all. Dispose of the boys and their families. We will begin again. Need three to take care of the Indian kid, the Evans kid and his father and anyone else with them or anyone who gets in the way. Who's up for it?*

He didn't have to wait very long before three stepped forward.

They knew where to go, but not necessarily who they were looking for.

Dominico sent an email with two photos: a head and shoulders shot of George and then a picture of Jeremy and the twins.

The text response was quickly returned: *Got it!*

Dominico smiled. He had a couple of others he wanted to deal with on a very personal level. One at his mother's house and the other would be back in town later today or early this evening. He might even do the kids in front of his dimwitted sister and her idiot husband. Let them all know who was in charge. He had something to prove to them all.

He was the one in charge now.

CHAPTER TWENTY-NINE

Chicago, Illinois

Billy had helped George get out of bed by picking up his legs and placing his feet on the floor and then he helped him get dressed. He led him to the conference room on the first floor where Pete and Jeremy heard him go through his story twice. Pete took notes, while Jeremy listened.

"How did you know, George?" Kelliher asked, puzzled with it all.

George shook his head, shrugged and said, "I heard my grandfather and when we walked into the hospital, I saw them."

"Them . . ." Pete said.

George nodded. "That man . . . Cochrane, Tim and my grandfather."

Neither Pete nor Jeremy doubted him. They didn't understand it, but they didn't doubt him.

George cleared his throat and Jeremy looked at him and said, "What?"

"There is one more thing you should know," George said staring first at Jeremy, then at Pete. "Last night, I had a dream."

Besides George's ability to see and talk to his deceased grandfather, both Jeremy and Pete put stock in George's dreams. His dreams hadn't failed him, or them, in the past.

"What was it about?" Jeremy asked.

George frowned, looked down at the varnished table and then back at Jeremy.

"It was short and unclear, but there was a man with a gun. I never saw him before. He had the gun pointed at a boy. The boy was shorter than me with dark hair . . . brown, I think. The three of us, you were on his left and I was on his right, stood in front of a door. I didn't know the room or the house we were in, but the man with gun was going to shoot the boy to get someone." He looked at both men expecting a question. When he didn't get one, he added, "I am certain he was after someone in particular."

Both men stared at him. Jeremy's brow was furrowed. Kelliher's lips were pursed. George waited patiently.

Finally, Jeremy said, "Either this is just a bad dream . . ."

". . . or one of George's warnings," Kelliher finished for him not taking his eyes off George. Then he said, "Do you think you can recognize the boy or the man if you saw them again?"

George thought about that. First of all, the dream seemed like a lifetime ago and secondly, he didn't see either of them very clearly. Mostly just the height, weight and body build more than anything else. Not much more than that. But to be helpful, George said, "I can try."

Pete speed-dialed Chet Walker, put him on speaker and without any introduction said, "Where are you?"

Walker answered, "About to land in Indianapolis. Why?"

"Send me the pictures of the men in the wind." Presuming he could but not waiting for confirmation he added, "Send them in an email as soon as you can."

"Coming your way in less than five," Chet said. "Is Skip on the way yet?"

Kelliher checked his watch and said, "Should be there by now."

"Okay, when we hook up, we'll be in contact."

Pete said quietly, but firmly, "Chet, you and Skip need to watch your backs. This one's dangerous."

"Aren't they all?" Chet said with a laugh.

Kelliher, not at all amused said, "No, not like this. Take this seriously and both you and Skip watch your ass! I'm *serious*!"

Chet was all business when he said, "Got it. You should have your email any second."

Kelliher booted up his laptop, opened his email and opened the jpg file that was attached, and then spun it around so the three of them could look at the pictures together.

"I have it. Can you also send me pictures of each of the boys who were rescued?"

"Coming your way in five."

"Thanks, Chet."

"Holler if you need anything else."

Pete clicked his cell off and began the slide show.

"George, these are pictures of some men we can't locate. I want you to look at them carefully and see if one of them was the man in your dream."

George took his time as Pete suggested, pausing it here and there and asking about heights and weights. He stunned both men when he asked about their familiarity with guns.

"Why? What do you mean by that?" Pete asked.

George became flustered. He hesitated and then said, "The man did not seem like he had used a gun before, but he was confident. His voice was cold."

"What did he say?" Jeremy asked.

George shook his head and said, "I do not think he *said* anything. It was a feeling."

Both men frowned at him and in the end, there were two that were close and Pete noted them.

"The first man you picked is Detective Anthony Dominico. He's responsible for Brett's abduction and we believe he murdered his partner earlier today."

"He's Brett's uncle," Jeremy added. "Have you met Brett yet?"

"Maybe, but I wasn't very awake." He shook his head. "Tim said he and Brett are best friends."

Jeremy nodded, "They're very close. Brett is also very close to another, younger boy, Patrick."

"The second man you picked out is Detective Mark Fox," Pete said. "He's responsible for the abduction of Patrick Wright, Brett's friend. The man was one of Patrick's soccer coaches. The problem is that Fox is much shorter than Dominico."

He paused, flicked the computer back and forth between the two men, so George could have more looks at the two of them. In the end, George shrugged unwilling to pick one over the other, because either man could be the guy in the dream or neither man could be the guy in the dream. He couldn't tell.

"The other problem is that both men are familiar with guns, handguns in particular."

"Does either of the men have blue eyes?"

Jeremy and Pete glanced at each other, and Pete said, "Why?"

"The man in my dream had bright blue eyes. Strange eyes."

"Both of these men have brown eyes, I think, but I'll check to be certain," Pete said, jotting a note in his little notebook.

George shrugged, disappointed he wasn't much help.

Next, Kelliher opened the other email and showed him the pictures of thirty boys. One by one George looked at them. There were four who could have been the boy in the dream, but he wasn't sure.

"Patrick and Brett are the closest, but I do not think it was either one. The other two, Cole and Eric, are close but if I had to pick one . . ." He shook his head. "Probably Patrick. Maybe Brett. I do not know for certain."

Kelliher frowned, shrugged at Jeremy and said, "Both are going to be watched closely anyway, so I'm not sure how this helps." Then to George he said, "If you have any other dreams, tell Jeremy right away, but call me as soon as you can."

George nodded and then said, "May I ask some questions?"

Pete nodded and Jeremy said, "Sure."

"Why did the policeman kick me?"

Of all the questions he could have asked, even the ones they thought he was going to ask, he asked one that they never expected and one that neither Pete nor Jeremy had an answer for. They looked at each other and Jeremy shook his head and Pete shrugged disgustedly.

"George, I don't have a good answer for you. Actually, none. It's just that some people are assholes, 'scuse my language," Pete said.

Jeremy said, "I think he saw a kid with long hair and a gun and sometimes that freaks cops out. Then, the cop finds out an FBI agent is involved . . ." Jeremy shrugged. "I'm not excusing it because it isn't right."

"Tim said there are men after me."

Jeremy nodded and said, "That's what we believe. However, we think you're safe for now because you'll be traveling across the country. Only Jeff and I know the route we'll be taking. Pete won't even know until I call him with an update."

"A bigger concern is what happens when you get to Arizona," Pete added. "We're going to coordinate with your cousin, Leonard when you get closer. We're not sure who we can involve other than your cousin at this point, because frankly, we don't know who we can trust in or out of the agency. That includes the Navajo Police, other than your cousin."

"But Pete and I've been talking and we think we have a plan," Jeremy added.

George frowned. He was putting Jeremy and the twins and Jeff and Danny in danger. He didn't like the potential of being responsible for their deaths.

CHAPTER THIRTY

Chicago, Illinois

They met in the sun room, a large room at the end of the hall that had more windows than any of the other rooms on the floor and that overlooked a lawn with benches and walkways. It served as a gathering place for recovering patients and their families, sometimes just to visit, sometimes to eat a meal, sometimes just for the patients themselves to sit and relax and get out of their rooms for a moment or two.

The boys had been meeting there since they had been admitted and usually sat in the comfortable chairs and a couch near the windows. Tim and Brett had gravitated towards windows because they had been without them for two years and at times, the two stood and stared out at the Chicago landscape, the sun or the clouds without a spoken word between them. As long as the two boys were together and near the windows, nothing mattered.

George walked in trailing Pete and Jeremy and he didn't get more than two steps inside the door when Billy appeared on one side and Danny on the other. He saw Randy talking with a small group of adults towards the center of the room, while Jeremy and Pete approached a few others.

As George was noticed by the parents, they stepped forward in groups of two or so and when they did, Billy and Danny who were uncomfortable to begin with because they didn't know anyone, drifted to a corner and sat at a table with Jeff.

Humble by nature, George nonetheless accepted each thank you, each hug and each kiss given to him by the parents. The most emotional were Thad and Laura Pruitt.

Thad took hold of George's hand in both of his and didn't let go. He said, "George, I can't thank you enough for saving our son. We're . . ." looking at his wife and then back at George, "forever in your debt."

"We hope you stay in touch with Tim," Laura added.

It was similar sentiments from each of the parents with the exception of Ted Bailey. There was an unfriendly, cold attitude about him and George didn't care for him.

After the parents, it was the boys' turn.

Stephen stood before him after saying thank you to Randy and said, "Billy said you might live with him and Randy and Jeremy."

George blushed and smiled tentatively, but was noncommittal.

Stephen nodded at Mike and said, "We hope so. That way we'll get to see you every now and then." They shook hands, rather formally and awkwardly, but in a friendly manner.

Mike stepped forward and George smiled and reached out to shake his hand, but was wrapped in a gentle embrace instead. Mike made sure Stephen couldn't hear when he whispered, "I'm w-worried about Stephen and T-Tim." Then he clung a bit tighter, a little bit longer and then let go.

George had heard that Mike had developed a stutter, and was pleased that it seemed to be going away. Yet, he didn't respond other than to grasp Mike's shoulders and nod.

Stephen said, "I hope we see you again."

George nodded, wondering what it was that Mike might be worried about. He made a mental note to find out.

Brett stepped forward tentatively with almost a shyness about him, however George wasn't fooled. There was strength and toughness and sensitivity that he was drawn to. They didn't say anything right away, but just smiled at each other. It was George who spoke first.

"You remind me of my brother, William."

"Yeah? How's that?" Brett said with a laugh, wondering how that was possible.

George laughed softly, shook his head and said, "I don't know. You just do," and he laughed again.

"Whatever," Brett said with a laugh and then said, "You saved Tim's life. He's my best friend."

"I know."

"I'd like us to be friends, you know, if you wanna."

George reached out and hugged Brett who hugged back as best he could with his good arm.

"I'd like that," George said.

"Thank you," Brett said choking up and then he added, "Thanks for saving Tim."

George nodded, swallowing to get the lump out of his throat.

"Will I see you again?" Brett asked.

Not knowing why, George nodded and said, "Yes, I think so."

Brett nodded and said, "I hope so." He turned to leave, brushed tears from his eyes, but turned back and smiled, giving George a little wave, who smiled, nodded and waved back.

George shoved his hands in his pockets, looked around, smiled at a couple of the parents and searched for Tim. He found him standing at one of the windows with his back to the room. As he neared him, George saw that Tim had his eyes shut so he stood silently next to him.

Down below in the grassy area, there were patients in robes walking slowly in the courtyard. One or two sat on benches in the grassy area. Others not in robes walked slowly back and forth with those who wore robes and George supposed they were family members of patients who needed fresh air.

"Your grandfather said I was thinking about giving up," Tim said finally opening his eyes but not turning to face George.

George didn't say anything.

"He was right," Tim said quietly. "I still think about it. I think about Johnny, Stephen's dad, all the other guys we watched get taken away in handcuffs." He paused and said, "There were so many. All the shit that they did to us." He shook his head.

George was about to tell him that he couldn't, when Tim said, "I won't."

George nodded.

"I'd miss Brett and I know it sounds gay, but I love him."

George understood immediately what Tim had meant.

"I know I'd miss Stephen and Mike, especially Mike . . . maybe one or two of the other guys, but I'd really miss Brett." He waited a couple of beats and then said, "And you."

George glanced at him, smiled and said, "I feel the same."

"Why did your grandfather . . . ?"

George knew what he was asking. He shook his head and said, "I do not know."

Tears welled up in George's eyes. He didn't know where they had come from or why. His grandfather was- *is* and always will be special to him, and for him to come to Tim meant something important and George knew there had to be a reason.

George knew that Tim and Brett, even Stephen and Mike had become important to him. Jeremy, Billy and Randy had become his family in many ways.

There was the death of his family and wrestling with whether to live with Jeremy and the twins or live back home. He had never felt this much at one time. It was too much.

"I'm glad he did," Tim said quietly, brushing some tears from his eyes.

"Me too," George answered, also wiping away some tears. "Me too," he repeated quietly.

"I won't give up, George."

"I know. You are stronger than you think."

Tim looked over at George, squinted at him, and then said, "Can we be friends?"

"I would like that very much."

The two boys embraced and held onto each other. "I don't know how to thank you."

"You do not have to."

"I love you, George. Thank you."

"Friends," George said, gripping Tim a bit harder.

"Friends," Tim answered.

They broke away, wiped tears from their faces and laughed at themselves and with arms slung around each other's shoulders joined the large group and said their final goodbyes.

Tim motioned for Brett to join him and then called to Stephen and Mike. George and Randy followed, though they stood a step out of their circle, not sure if they should be included. Jeff, Danny and Billy stayed well back, but watched intently, while Jeremy and Pete went off to the side and spoke quietly.

At first, Stephen and Mike stood facing Tim and Brett and the six of them didn't say anything, knowing that in minutes they'd be leaving for home, not sure when, or if, they'd be together again.

Finally, Tim smiled and said, "Stephen, you and Mike have to be careful. Like Randy and Jeremy said, you need to make a list."

"We've started, but we can't think of anyone who would do that to me," Stephen answered.

Brett shook his head and said, "That means you have to keep your eyes open. You have to watch each other's backs."

"Brett's right," Tim added quietly. "Stephen, you've got to be careful." He looked at Mike and said, "As much as you can, stick together."

"Jeremy said Detective Graff is arranging protection," Mike said.

Stephen clarified, "He's going to have a couple of undercover cops watching me . . . us, until they figure out who the pervert is."

"That's good, but they can't be with you twenty-four seven," Tim said, "So you'll need to be there for each other, okay?"

Mike looked at the floor, frowning.

"What?" Tim asked.

Mike jammed his hands into his front pockets.

Tim reached out and placed his hand on Mike's shoulder and said again, "What?"

"I'm . . . p-pissed. This sh-shouldn't have h-happened to us. N-None of it. N-Now we have to w-watch wherever we g-go, who we t-talk to, m-make a s-stupid list. I'm p-pissed."

"Watching out, being careful and making a list makes sense. And, I think we're all pissed off," Brett said. Tim and Stephen nodded in agreement.

Tim turned to Randy and asked, "How did you get over it, you know, being pissed off at what was done to you?"

"And the flippin' perverts?" Brett added.

"Flippin'?" Tim said with a laugh.

"Thought I'd work on my vocabulary," Brett said with a laugh.

Randy smiled sadly and said, "Billy, Dad and I went to see the Bat Man movie, *Dark Knight*. There's a scene where this cop, Blake, talks to Bruce Wayne. Blake said that when his parents were killed and he was put in a foster home, he learned too late to smile and laugh and act like a normal kid, so the foster parents gave up on him and he ended up in an orphanage."

He paused and said, "He said the smile became his mask, like Bat Man's mask."

The four boys already understood where he was going.

"I was so angry, so afraid. I didn't treat my dad very well the first days, even weeks. I didn't trust him," Randy glanced over his shoulder at Jeremy who was listening to Pete.

"Eventually, I started to smile and laugh like other kids. I know I'm not afraid, but it's been over two years and I'm still pissed off. I guess, you could say I wear a mask too."

George had never heard Randy talk like that. He had noticed that Billy had a crooked smile. Randy's smile was sad, and even though he smiled, it never touched his eyes.

"It won't do you any good to be pissed off. No one will understand anyway," Randy added. "So, wear a mask like me and all the other kids this has happened to. Eventually, well," he stopped and shrugged. "Like I said, no one understands anyway."

"Except us," Tim said.

Stephen looked from Tim, to Randy, to Brett and to George and said, "Can we talk every now and then? I mean, like if we have questions or something? Or maybe just talk?"

"Boys, we have to get going," Ted Bailey said impatiently.

Sarah said, "Ted, leave. Stephen and I'll get a ride with Jennifer and Mark."

He didn't leave, but it did shut him up.

Ignoring Stephen's dad, Tim said, "Of course. Brett and I don't have cell phones yet, but we gave you our home phone numbers and we have yours. When we do get cells, we'll make sure you get the number."

"You can call me or Tim anytime, day or night," Brett added. "Chances are we won't be able to sleep much anyway."

"You have George's and my numbers, right?" Randy asked.

Stephen and Mike nodded. Stephen added, "And Danny's and Billy's too."

Quietly, Brett said, "Stephen, every now and then check Mike's butt just to make sure he's healing." Then to Mike he said, "Sometimes you wipe too hard and that one stitch bleeds."

Mike blushed and said, "I s-sort of f-forget."

"I will," Stephen said nodding.

"And Mike, you have to work on your stuttering. You're sounding better, but keep working on it, okay?" Brett said.

Mike blushed and nodded.

"I'm going to miss you two," Tim said. He embraced first Stephen and then Mike. "I'm really going to miss you guys."

Stephen and Mike and their families left, leaving Tim, Brett, Randy and George in the center of the room. For the longest time, Tim and Brett stared at each other, not saying anything. First Randy, then George looked away because it was too painful to watch.

Tim broke eye contact first and said to Randy, "You'll stay in touch?"

They embraced in a long hug and Randy said, "Absolutely."

When they broke apart, there were tears in their eyes.

Tim nodded at George, didn't say anything, then embraced him and whispered, "I promise."

"I know."

Tim faced Brett and again the two of them stared at each other without exchanging a word, but that didn't prevent them from *communicating*. George had noticed that Randy and Billy had done the same thing over the short time he had been with them.

Finally, Tim and Brett hugged each other fiercely with Tim rubbing Brett's back. Before he let go, he kissed Brett's cheek and then gently held Brett's face in both of his hands.

"I'm going to miss you the most, Brett."

"Me, too." Then he added, "I love you, Tim."

"I know. I love you, too."

They embraced again and this time, both boys kissed each other's cheek.

They wiped tears away and Tim said quietly, "Can you do me a favor?"

"Anything."

"Can you wait fifteen or twenty minutes before you leave? I don't think I can say goodbye again."

"Me, neither," Brett said thickly.

George said, "In my language, there is no word for goodbye."

The three boys looked at him waiting for an explanation.

"The closet word is 'yá'át'ééh', a greeting." He shrugged.

The three boys smiled at him and George smiled back, blushing deep crimson, even noticeable under his copper-colored skin.

"So, we don't say 'goodbye'," Tim said, smiling first at Brett, then at Randy and George.

"Sounds good to me," Brett answered.

Tim joined his parents and the three of them left the room, leaving Brett, Randy and George watching them leave.

"I can call you guys, right?" Brett said, not taking his eyes away from the doorway that Tim had just walked through.

"Absolutely," Randy said. "Anytime."

"I hope you do," George added.

Brett turned and smiled at him and said, "I will. I was just being polite."

George and Randy laughed.

"Can I say something?" George asked.

Brett nodded.

"I know you are angry, but when you face him, and I think you will, you cannot be so angry that you lose focus. You have an advantage because he sees you as just a kid. It is the same advantage I had when I faced that man sent to kill us and with the agent who had Tim. Do not lose that advantage. You have to keep your focus. You have to remain calm."

Brett nodded, hugged George and Randy one more time. Then he joined his parents and left the sun room and the hospital, leaving Jeremy, the twins, George, Jeff and Danny, and Pete.

CHAPTER THIRTY-ONE

Chicago, Illinois

"May I talk to you, all of you?" George asked.

Jeremy said, "Sure. What's on your mind?"

"Can we sit down?" George asked.

Billy helped George onto a harder, wooden chair, because it would be easier for him with his bruised ribs. Jeremy and Jeff wore a look of concern evidenced by their wrinkled brows. Danny, Randy and Billy looked at George expectantly.

"I was thinking," George said quietly gathering his courage, "that maybe I should go to Arizona by myself. I could take a plane or bus," George said, first looking at Jeremy, then at Jeff. "It might be safer for everyone."

"No!" Billy said, leaning forward towards his father. "No way!"

Randy placed a hand on Billy's arm to quiet him and to allow George to continue.

"If there are men after me, I could be putting you in danger. I do not want that," George pleaded.

"No!" Billy repeated. "You're not getting on a plane or a train or a bus."

"But-"

"-But nothing," Billy shouted, shaking off Randy's hand. "We're family. Families stick together." He looked from Jeremy to Randy and then back to Jeremy and said, "Dad, tell him!"

"George," Jeremy started. "We can't let you deal with this by yourself."

Frustrated, George said, "Do you not understand? These men sent someone to kill me once before. They will not stop."

Pete leaned forward, his forearms on his knees and said, "George, Jeremy and I have come up with a plan. We believe everyone is safe for now because no one will know where you are."

"For *now*, until we get to Arizona where these men will be waiting for us."

"George, do you trust me?" Jeremy said softly.

"Yes, but-"

"-Billy's right," Randy interrupted. "Families stick together."

George looked from Randy to Jeremy and then to Billy.

"What he said," Billy said, nodding towards Randy.

George tried to stand up and when Billy went to help him, George shrugged himself out of his grasp, wincing at the pain on his right side. He gave up and sat back down.

"Please listen," George said, frantic with worry, frustrated that no one was listening to him. "I have already lost one family. I do not want to lose another."

Billy sat back down and exchanged a look with Randy.

"I do not want to lose you too. Any of you," George said looking from one to the other.

Jeff, who had been listening quietly with interest put his arm around Danny, gave his shoulder a squeeze and both smiled at George.

Jeremy leaned forward and said, "George, I need you to trust me." He paused and said, "Can you do that for me?"

George looked to be near tears, frustrated that he wasn't being heard and embarrassed that he had lost his composure once again. No one should be able to tell what a Navajo was thinking. He felt that his grandfather would be disappointed with him because he had lost his composure far too much in one day.

He took a deep breath and slowed his breathing down, placed his mask back in place, and looked at Jeremy.

"We're going to go on vacation. We all need one, especially after all we've been through," he paused and looked at the twins and then back at George. "In, I don't know, nine or ten days, we'll be in Arizona. Our plans are pretty fluid, but when we get there, we have a plan," nodding in the direction of Pete and Jeff.

Jeremy looked over at Pete and then back at George. "Pete and our friend Detective Graff are working on protection also. George, we have a plan that will keep us all safe until we're done in Arizona and back home in Waukesha. We," indicating Randy and Billy, "hope you'll come back home with us, but if you don't, Pete will arrange protection for you for as long as you need it."

George tried to put on a brave face, but his chin trembled and his mask was in danger of slipping off.

"I . . ." he stopped, unable or unwilling to continue. He cast his eyes down and shook his head solemnly.

In the end, they left the hospital together. Pete said goodbye to each of them, hugging each of the boys and then turned around and walked back into the hospital. Billy told the group that he and George were going to ride with Jeremy, leaving Randy and Danny to ride with Jeff.

There was as much said and felt as there was unsaid and felt by each of them.

Jeremy figured it would all come out at some point during the trip. He just hoped that the plan he, Pete and Jeff had come up with would work.

If not, there would be more dead bodies, his own and the twins included.

PART TWO
RE-ENTRY INTO THE WORLD

CHAPTER THIRTY-TWO

Before leaving the hospital, Pete gave each set of parents a script to be used when the families got home in case media was staked out on their front lawns. There was little doubt that there would be because each of the other boys who had left the hospital in Chicago or in Kansas City or Long Beach experienced a media circus. Most of the kids and parents had held press conferences at their local police or sheriff departments with the guidance of FBI or departmental PR people to help run interference.

There were offers of movie deals, book deals, TV interviews, and TV specials. There were agents, PR firms and managerial firms trying to recruit them, each promising the best representation. None of the boys were interested and their parents, taking the lead from their sons, weren't interested either. As Brett had put it before they had left the hospital, *I want to forget what happened to me. Why would I want a book or a movie to remind me?* All the boys had agreed with him.

Stephen counted six TV trucks with news crews and even recognized one or two from the Milwaukee stations he and his family watched. There were other interested folk milling about as well as photographers trying to take their pictures as they pulled up. As instructed, the Ericksons and the Baileys pulled into the back of the Waukesha Police Station and were hustled inside by a phalanx of officers where they were met by Captain Jack O'Brien and Detective Jamie Graff.

O'Brien was a bald, fit and square-jawed fireplug of a man, stocky and chiseled. His arms bulged out of his short-sleeved navy dress uniform. His dark eyes bore deep into your soul and that was the first and lasting impression left on Mike. Normally slow to speak, a man of few words, he was the first to shake the boys' hands in a grip that could have easily broken fingers and knuckles with one squeeze.

"Boys, we met in the hospital. Let me say once again how happy we are to have you home safe and sound."

Mike and Stephen nodded tentatively.

"Mr. and Mrs. Bailey," he said as he shook their hands in the same manner as he did the boys. "Mr. and Mrs. Erickson."

After acknowledging the parents, he turned back to the boys. "Here's how we're going to do this."

. . .

The boys stood side by side to the right of the podium with their parents behind them. To the left stood the Waukesha County Sheriff Myron Wagner. He was dark-haired, rotund and in his late middle-ages with jowls and a neck almost covered by two chins. Next to him stood Detective Jamie Graff. Graff looked as though he'd rather be anywhere other than on the front steps under the glare of lights and media scrutiny. He scanned the crowd that had gathered below and in front of them and in particular, the people on the fringe. He knew there were two others in the crowd doing the same thing as he was.

At the podium, Captain O'Brien thanked the police and sheriff detectives and the FBI for the operation. "Without this joint cooperative effort, these two boys and the other boys held in captivity wouldn't have been freed." He asked for a moment of silence to honor Police Detective Paul Gates who lost his life leaving a wife and small child behind, and then after, acknowledged Police Detective Gary Fitzpatrick and Sheriff Deputy Ronnie Desotel who had been wounded freeing the boys. He introduced Detective Jamie Graff who led the siege in Chicago. O'Brien's smile was meant to be warm and friendly, but it came across as menacing and threatening and actually, scary.

Cameras snapped while the crowd broke into applause.

After O'Brien finished, Jennifer Erickson spoke on behalf of her husband, the boys, and the Baileys. She stepped forward and the boys flanked her on either side. Reporters yelled questions or otherwise told the boys to look this way or that way. Not wanting to be there, the boys understood it was important for them to be.

"Before any questions, I'd like to say a few words," she stated quietly. "On behalf of my husband, Mark, and our son, Michael, and on behalf of Ted and Sarah Bailey and their son, Stephen, I want to thank the Waukesha Police Department, the Waukesha County Sheriff Department, and the FBI for rescuing not only our two boys, but the other boys held captive in Chicago, Kansas City, and Long Beach. Without their quick action, I don't know what would have happened to Michael and Stephen and the rest of the boys. Our hearts go out to the families of Detective Paul Gates, Detective Gary Fitzpatrick, and Deputy Ronnie Desotel. No words can convey what we truly feel, but we want them to know that our thoughts and prayers are with them. We also want to thank the brave young man who recognized Michael and Stephen in the Amber Alert. Without his quick thinking and his bravery, we would still be looking for our sons and the other boys instead of standing here in front of you.

"In closing, my family and the Bailey family asks that the media respect our privacy, especially the privacy of both Michael and Stephen. They went through a lot, more than any child should ever go through. We will not answer any questions about injuries or anything that took place while the boys were in captivity. Instead, we need to focus on their rescue and what we need to do as a society to make sure things like this don't ever happen to our children. As a society, we need to keep our children safe." She paused, scanned the crowd and said, "Thank you."

When she stepped away from the podium, Stephen and Michael stepped forward.

"Were you scared?" one reporter asked. She was the evening anchor at one of the Milwaukee TV stations.

Mike looked at Stephen, then stepped forward and said, "Yes."

"At any point, did you feel your life was in danger?" asked a good-looking man in a suit. Stephen recognized him from yet a different Milwaukee station.

Stephen stepped forward and said, "Yes, but Mike and I don't want to talk about that. What's important is that we're back home."

The questions and answers went on for ten or fifteen minutes, including a summary from Jamie Graff. He normally spoke even less than O'Brien did, though today both were front and center and uncomfortable in the spotlight.

Graff began his career as a traffic cop and then was assigned as an SRO at North High School and became friends with Jeremy Evans and Jeff Limbach, who together formed the three Js as the three of them were called. Where one was, the other two weren't far behind. A thick head of dark hair and dark eyes and matching complexion, he came across as Latino. Quick to smile and usually sarcastic when he had something to say, he was known for his quick mind and skill in the field. A perfect leader, who didn't really want to be, but accepted the leadership role because he knew he should. Besides, he'd rather trust himself in charge than someone else.

The anchor woman said, "Stephen, there are reports that the man responsible for having you abducted is still out there. Is there anything you want to say to him?"

O'Brien stepped forward to answer, but Stephen held his arm out to prevent him from doing so.

"The only thing I want to say is that I'll do whatever I need to do to make sure he's caught. And when he is, I'll do everything I can to make sure he's in jail for the rest of his life."

Again, silence. Stephen didn't realize it, but his hands were balled into fists and he was glaring at the woman, who shrunk from his anger.

CHAPTER THIRTY-THREE

Waukesha, Wisconsin

The man sat on the hotel bed staring at the TV, glued to the image of the two boys next to the police captain and in front of their parents. This was his first glimpse of the boy since he had received the jpg sent by email when Stephen was in the back of the van the night he was taken. Stephen was nervous and the man liked that.

Most of the time, the shot was only of the boys' heads and shoulders, sometimes together, sometimes separately. Less time was spent on the parents, except when Jennifer Erickson spoke.

The man focused on the boys. The questions began and the boys took turns, first the dark-haired boy, Michael, and then Stephen.

The man liked the sound of boys' voices. It was a musical sound, exciting for him to hear. He liked looking at Stephen's face, his full lips and his blue eyes with long lashes. He found himself getting aroused.

He stopped as the female reporter asked Stephen a question, something about what Stephen might want to say to the man who had him kidnapped. He had missed the exact question, because he was already into his fantasy about using Stephen.

"The only thing I want to say is that I'll do whatever I need to do to make sure he's caught. And when he is, I'll do everything I can to make sure he's in jail for the rest of his life."

The man was stunned. He felt himself getting sick to his stomach again.

He stood up, but then sat back down, his hand covering his mouth. Absentmindedly, he ran his other hand through his hair. He got up off the bed slowly, one hand still in his hair, the other still covering his mouth.

Stephen wasn't supposed to react this way. In his mind, Stephen *wanted* him, *needed* him, and *enjoyed* him. Stephen wasn't supposed to be *angry*.

The man had to think this through.

So far, no one knew about him, though it was clear that they were looking for him. If the police knew it was him, they'd be all over it and he'd be in custody. But a call to his neighbor verified that no one had been to his house. A call from the receptionist confirmed that no one had shown up at the office.

So far, he was in the clear.

That was the first and biggest hurdle. He knew he could work his charm on Stephen and then, if he played it right, Stephen and he would have a *real* relationship.

A relationship.

That was what the man had wanted all along. He had other boys, but Stephen was the boy he had really wanted.

Stephen.

He'd have to plan.

CHAPTER THIRTY-FOUR

Chicago, Illinois

Pete read and reread the text messages Cochrane had sent. He read over the call log, jotting down the numbers. He had already called Chet to give him the phone's pertinent numbers and IP address and he knew Chet was on it.

Pete checked the contact list in the phone, but none had matched the numbers to the text messages or the recent phone calls. He knew this group was gunning for George, Jeremy and Randy. He was less concerned about himself, but was also worried about Chet, Skip and Summer. He also wondered if his team had been compromised. Cochrane had stored the numbers of so many people involved in the hunt, including several of the kids. Jeremy's number was listed too. Luckily, Graff's and O'Brien's numbers were not.

There was something else that nibbled at the back of his mind that he couldn't put his finger on. He knew it was something important though.

He left the conference room in search of Dr. Flasch and found him at the nurses' station on the second floor. He asked if he had given the number of his office phone to Cochrane.

Flasch looked somewhere in the distance as his quick mind searched for any recollection of Cochrane using his office for a phone call, if he had given his number to Cochrane, or if anyone else might have given the number to him.

"Not that I know of, but if you need a secure line, follow me." Flasch took off at a quick walk down the hallway without waiting for Pete to answer.

Pete caught up to him and said, "Wherever you're taking me, we have to be sure Cochrane wouldn't have known about it."

Flasch didn't say anything but continued down a flight of stairs to the main floor and walked past the Information Desk which was now manned with two security personnel and one younger woman, who had relieved the elderly lady just after Cochrane shot the security guard during the kidnap attempt. Behind him, Pete had noticed the thick plywood sheets covering the shattered glass in the entryway, but otherwise, didn't see any other evidence of a shootout. The blood from the security guard had been mopped up, glass from the windows had been swept up and anyone who had showed up in the last hour wouldn't have known that anything out of the ordinary had taken place. The news media was told little and they reported even less.

Flasch knocked on a door, tried the doorknob and found it locked. He looked past Pete to the lobby, caught a security guard's eye and motioned for him to come to him. Puzzled, the security guard obeyed.

"Yes?" said the young, fit guard.

Pete figured him to be in his late thirties, maybe early forties and had an air of ex-military about him. The *36th Air Cavalry* tat on his right forearm confirmed Pete's suspicion. He had short cropped black hair, dark eyes and shiny white teeth, but Pete wondered if the man ever smiled.

Flasch leaned forward to read the guard's badge and said, "Mr. Stevens, this is FBI Agent Pete Kelliher. He needs to use a secure line to make a call. I know Dr. McDonough has been on vacation for the past week, so can you let him in Mac's office to make his call?"

"May I see some identification?" the security man said to Pete.

Pete dug out his creds and held them out for the guard to read. Instead, the guard took the wallet-sized leather jacket from him and read it, glancing at Pete twice to confirm Pete was the guy in the photo. Satisfied, he handed it back to Pete and knocked twice on the door, listened to nothing but silence coming from the other side, and then used his master key to open the door. He pushed the door open, stepped in to make sure the office was empty, then stepped aside to let Pete enter.

"Dial 9 to get an outside line. I'll wait down the hall for you," Flasch said, pushing the lock button and shutting the door behind him.

Instead of calling Dandridge directly, he went through the FBI switchboard and had the receptionist connect him to Rita, Dandridge's secretary.

"Rita, don't say my name, but do you recognize my voice?"

There was a pause and he knew that Rita had begun recording the conversation.

"Yes."

"Good. You have caller ID on your phone, correct?"

"Yes."

"Write down the number and find Whitey. Tell him to call me at this number but he needs to do it from a secure line. He can't use any number that might have been in contact with me in the last four days. Do you understand?"

"Yes."

"I'll be waiting at this number for his phone call. And Rita?"

"Yes?"

"It's urgent."

"Understood."

"This is Whitey," was all that was said when Pete picked up the receiver. Whitey had been Pete's name for Dandridge when they went through training together at Quantico. No one other than Pete had ever dared to call him that. The two men had developed a lasting friendship that didn't stop at the supervisor – subordinate boundary because they had recognized they were different sides of the same coin.

"I think we're good, as long as your end is secure."

"It is. What's up?"

"I have reason to believe Cochrane compromised phone numbers."

"I see," Dandridge said slowly. He paused and asked, "Why do you suspect that?"

"I'm looking at his contact list and there are a lot of numbers in it. Same for the call log. I only have a hunch and no proof. I think he might have passed on numbers to the bad guys. If so, I wonder if they're monitoring phone calls and text messages. I don't know their technological capabilities, but I do know they're resourceful."

Dandridge knew Pete well enough to trust his hunches. "How do you want to play this?"

"Could go a couple of ways."

"Which are?"

"We could warn everyone, but if we do, we have no connection to the bad guys."

"But if we don't warn everyone, it potentially puts them in danger." He paused and then asked, "What do you think we should do?" Dandridge asked the question cautiously as if he didn't want to hear the answer, but also as if he knew what Pete's answer was going to be.

"We use the lines as we normally do, but we use them to our advantage."

"Feeding the bad guys misinformation."

"The problem is it's dangerous."

Pete went on to explain his plan, knowing Dandridge might confer with Summer, but he doubted it. It would be Dandridge's decision and his alone. Like the captain of the Titanic, Dandridge was the kind of man to either sail the ship into port or if he hit the iceberg, go down with the ship. Either way, the decision was his.

Dandridge let his breath out slowly.

"One condition, Pete."

"Of course."

"If at any point it puts kids or other innocents in jeopardy, we call it off and come clean to everyone involved."

Pete nodded and said, "Absolutely. I won't have their deaths on my conscience."

"Nor on mine," Dandridge said. There was a final pause and he said, "Go with it. I'll take care of things on my end and get word to MB."

Pete punched the phone dead, rubbed his eyes, and swiveled around and looked out the window, worrying that if things went sideways, he had just sentenced four innocent lives to death.

CHAPTER THIRTY-FIVE

Chicago, Illinois

He called Chet from a payphone at the airport and told him to get to a secure line. Chet called back using a phone in a library lobby, Pete filled him in on his suspicions, told him to warn Skip but no one else. He also told Chet to contact Morgan Billias.

Billias was a mild-mannered, easy-going middle-aged guy with a wife, two teenage daughters and a preteen son. He had an easy laugh, a ready wise crack, and could find humor in anything. He didn't work for the CIA or the NSA or any of the other alphabet groupings that belonged to the government. Chet had never asked Morgan what he did or where he lived or whether or not he was married and had two or six children. And Morgan had never told him.

He and Chet had met at a computer expo in San Francisco, got to talking about computers, had a couple of beers together and hit it off. They kept in contact off and on with Chet reaching out to him whenever a "puzzle" needed to be solved. Nothing grandiose, just puzzles. He had played a huge part in freeing the boys from captivity, and an even bigger part in saving George's, Jeremy's and the twins' lives.

This time, however, it was Pete's idea to bring Billias into the circle to monitor Cochrane's cell phones and to monitor the phones of those who had tried to contact him.

Billias readily agreed.

CHAPTER THIRTY-SIX

Indianapolis, Indiana

Only the two Indianapolis cops who had responded to the 9-1-1 call and MB had entered the home, so that had made Skip's job easier. He had worked the crime scene in Luke Pressman's home silently, quickly and thoroughly like the professional he was. Pressman's body still sat in the recliner in his living room. Blood had pooled under both legs from the shots to his kneecaps and there was blood spatter on the curtains behind the chair, along with a chunk of brain matter and bits of skull. The fact that Pressman's eyes and mouth were open made the whole tableau gruesome.

Skip had found partials in the back bedroom and possible DNA in and around the toilet. Of course, he'd have to compare these with Pressman's DNA to determine if they were his or Dominico's or anyone else's. He had found indeterminate fiber on the couch facing Pressman and it was sent to the FBI lab to analyze it further to determine what it was and what the origins were.

He felt like he hadn't done enough and what he did do, didn't amount to anything usable beyond what they already knew: Dominico had murdered Pressman and this murder was the first of several with more to come if the 9-1-1 tape was accurate.

He had found even less at Dominico's home. There was nothing, other than the empty hole in the floor of the spare bedroom. One could only speculate as to what was in it. Other than that hole, there was nothing that would help close the case any quicker.

"Is he always so serious?" Wilkey asked Chet without taking his eyes off Skip.

"Pretty much."

"He doesn't talk much."

"Nope."

She watched him work a bit longer and said, "He seems really young. Must be smart."

"His IQ is 166, which is fifteen points higher than mine and twenty-one points higher than yours," Chet answered not looking up from his laptop.

Wilkey glanced back at Chet and said, "How do you know his IQ and how the hell do you know mine?"

Chet sighed, punched a few more keys and then said, "I was burned twice. Once with Rawson and once with Cochrane." He stared and said, "I'm not going to make that mistake again."

MB glared at him, folded her arms across her chest and said, "Don't pry into any of my business again."

Chet went back to his laptop and didn't commit one way or the other. When it came to his safety or the safety of the team, he'd pry into anyone he saw fit.

CHAPTER THIRTY-SEVEN

Fishers, Indiana

Mary Beth Wilkey, or MB for short, stood five-four and a fit 130 pounds. Compact and solid, she had attended Indiana University on a volleyball scholarship and earned a starting spot for four years as the Libero. She graduated Cum Laude in Health and Physical Education in four years with the intention of becoming a high school teacher and coach, but when the FBI called, Wilkey said yes.

She liked the academy, especially the physical aspects of it. After she graduated, she returned to her home state of Indiana and landed in the urban crime section, which normally dealt with inter-state gang-related issues. She also dealt with any crime that had federal written all over it or one that crossed state lines, which was why she was chosen for the Pressman murder.

She wore her dark hair short because she liked the fact that she could step out of a shower and towel it off. Besides, long hair and crime scenes didn't mix very well. She typically wore black or navy slacks with a matching jacket over a white blouse with little or no jewelry other than simple gold or silver posts in her earlobes. She also didn't see the need for makeup and her looks and coloring were of the type that didn't need it.

She had driven Chet and Skip to the McGovern house after the crime scene work at Dominico's and Pressman's homes and met up with Pete who had arrived forty minutes earlier. He sat at the curb in his four door navy Chevy Malibu rental. They eased themselves out of their cars all the while looking up and down the street and into front windows that didn't have curtains pulled shut. MB tapped in the garage code and with Pete, Chet, and Skip providing backup, did a quick sweep of the four bedroom ranch finding nothing but a few breakfast dishes in the sink, the morning paper on the kitchen table and an unmade bed in the master bedroom.

MB stood at the front window with her hands on her hips and looked around at the quiet neighborhood. From the outside, the houses appeared to be the same. Each had a two and a half car garage in the front of the house alternating on either the left or right as you went up the street, and the only apparent variation was the color, but even then, the choice was one of three.

A house kitty-corner and across the street from the McGovern house had a For Sale sign in its front yard and MB wondered absently what price they might be asking. She had saved enough for a down payment, had done a little on-line browsing and had given a fair amount of thought to purchasing a home in the burbs away from Indianapolis where she was based. She looked at the house number and made a mental note to check it out when she had the time.

Chet and Skip lounged around the McGovern living room watching Pete pace with a frown on his face.

Something pulled at the back of his mind, but Pete couldn't quite get hold of it. It didn't help that Summer wasn't partnered up with him. When she was, they'd piece the puzzle out together. No such luck now.

Chet didn't stray far from his laptop. Pete liked Skip and was developing trust in him, and he knew nothing of MB at all.

"What?" Chet asked, puzzled by Pete's manner, which was usually much more direct.

MB turned around from the window, folded her arms across her chest and eyed the older man.

Pete ran a hand through his hair and said, "Tell me what we know about Dominico." He paused and added, "What type of man is he?"

"You mean besides the fact that he's a fuckin' pervert?" Chet said.

Ignoring the retort, he turned to each and said, "Describe his personality."

MB shrugged and said, "The reports said he could be mean, nasty, and in general, unfriendly."

"Pedophiles are into control," Skip said quietly.

Pete pointed a finger at him and said, "Exactly!" He looked at each and said, "If Dominico wanted to *control* a situation or people, this family, what might he do?"

"Orders, maybe even passive-aggressive behavior," MB said.

Pete shook his head and said, "Nothing passive-aggressive about this asshole. He's all about aggression, about dominating and controlling a situation."

"What are you getting at?" MB asked.

Pete turned to Chet and asked, "If I wanted to control the McGovern family, what would be the ultimate control?"

"Withholding information. He did that by not letting the kid's parents know he was alive."

Skip added, "He did this by pretending to be undercover when in fact he knew all along Brett was in Chicago. He knew because he helped put him there and on weekends, went and raped him."

Pete nodded and asked, "But how could he control and dominate the family besides withholding information?"

The four of them looked at each other and then the realization spread over Chet's face. He said, "Oh fuck! No way!"

Pete shrugged reading Chet's mind. "It's possible. Maybe likely."

"Just like-"

"-Stop," Pete said holding up his hand and cutting him off, not wanting to give away too much information in case his hunch was correct.

Chet set his laptop aside, stood up from the couch and looked around the living room. He shook his head and went into the kitchen. Pete followed him with Skip and MB trailing.

"Besides the bathroom, the kitchen and the family room would be the most lived-in rooms in the house. Next would be the bedrooms."

Chet did a slow 360 in the middle of the kitchen, eyes up at the recessed lighting in the ceiling. He dragged a chair over from the kitchen table, climbed up and began unscrewing the small floods sweeping his fingers cautiously and carefully around the socket. On his third light, he left his fingers where they were and stared at Pete, who shook his head. Chet nodded. Realization dawned on Skip and MB. He checked the rest of the lights but found nothing.

Next, he moved to the air-conditioning vent in the ceiling. He pulled out a small pocket knife and unscrewed the cover and opened up the vent. At the top left and almost out of sight, mounted to the drywall, Chet found another. He turned to Pete, motioned to his eyes and nodded, then to his ears and shook his head. Pete made a note on a piece of paper.

The group then went into the family room and Chet examined the stereo system hooked up to the 42-inch big screen. Inside one of the speakers, small and unobtrusive to most eyes, Chet found a small camera. It was motion sensitive and state-of-the-art. He left it where it was, pretending to examine the speaker size. He commented on the fact that he had a similar system at his house, but that the McGovern speakers were of a better quality. He next began examining the recessed lighting and on his second try, just above the couch facing the TV, Chet found a small microphone.

Room by room they went. There was one camera in the master bedroom. There were two microphones and a camera in the study, all three in recessed lighting. There was one camera and one microphone in Brett's former room, now the spare bedroom. There was another set in the other spare bedroom.

They hit the jackpot in Bobby's room, Brett's younger brother. They found one camera in one light over the bed, one in the air-conditioning vent, and two microphones, both in recessed lighting over the bed.

Their search done, Pete said, "Guys, I think we should wait for the family in the driveway. I don't feel comfortable in their house without them being here."

"I agree," Chet said.

They left by the front door, climbed into Pete's car and rolled the windows up though the day was warm and humid. They sat in silence and then Pete asked Chet, "What kind of system is it?"

"Near as I can tell all motion sensitive. If he's recording, he's doing it via remote access."

"How would that be possible?" Skip asked.

Chet started out in geek mode, but switched to common, every-day English when he recognized the puzzlement on Skip's and MB's faces.

"It is as simple as tapping into a phone line or internet. The computer wouldn't necessarily have to be on, but it's a lot easier if it was." Then he added, "Did you notice that the computer was on, just asleep?"

Skip nodded.

"As long as it's on, he has access. Then, he can monitor from just about anywhere, especially if he knows their IP address, which I'm willing to bet he does."

"Why all the electronics in the younger brother's room?" MB asked.

"Yup," Chet said. He stared long and hard at Pete.

"Oh Jesus, no," MB said quietly.

Pete shrugged and said, "He's about the same age Brett was when Dominico first molested him."

"Easy access. Availability. An uncle looking out for his nephew." Skip added looking out the window. "If Dominico is molesting Bobby, I'm wondering who else he might be molesting in the extended family and just how much about it Brett's brother knew."

"Good questions, Skip," Pete said, impressed at the way Skip's mind worked.

"But why?" MB asked shaking her head.

"All about control," Pete said turning and looking at the McGovern house. "As simple and ugly as control."

CHAPTER THIRTY-EIGHT

Indianapolis, Indiana

The car hadn't even pulled into the driveway yet when Bobby burst out the front door waving, dancing from foot to foot, and peering into the McGovern vehicle. It came to a stop and he moved to the rear door where he knew Brett to be and was rewarded when Brett opened the door and climbed out.

Bobby stepped forward, took gentle hold of his brother's shoulders and said, "Brett?"

Brett smiled at him, his eyes tearing up.

"It's over, right?" Bobby said. "It's over . . . done, right?" shaking him a little, hurting Brett's shoulder without realizing he had done so.

Brett nodded and said, "I'm home. It's over."

Bobby broke down, wrapped Brett in a hug and both boys wept.

"It's okay, Bobby. It's okay."

They stood almost the same height, Brett just a smidge taller, but not much more than that. Bobby had filled out to almost the same size as his older brother and at first glance, they looked identical. They even had the same longish haircut.

Eerie was what Brett thought at the time.

"Bobby, be gentle of your brother's shoulder, okay?" Victoria said.

Brett smiled at her through his tears and said, "He's okay, Mom. I missed him too."

Bobby pulled away from Brett, but still gently gripped his shoulders, looking him up and down.

"You're okay?"

Brett laughed and said, "Well, other than my shoulder, I guess so."

Bobby noticed Brett's shoulder for the first time. "Who did that?"

"Don't worry, he's dead."

"Uncle Tony?" Bobby's eyes were huge, wondering if it could possibly be true.

"No, he's still around somewhere," Brett said with disgust.

"Don't talk like that about your uncle," Margaret Dominico muttered.

She had come out of the house just after Bobby, but had stood off to the side, just in back of Victoria and Thomas. She was small and round with white hair tied back in a bun.

She kept her small three bedroom house neat and tidy, though her humble furnishings were old and outdated. Since her husband had passed away, she didn't bother to update anything or buy anything new. She was content and for the most part, happy. Her best work was in the kitchen, believing that any ill, any wrong, or any sadness could be cured with a good hot meal of pasta piled high and buried in rich tomato sauce with garlic bread on the side.

Every now and then she'd consider the fact that though her health was good, she was on the downhill side of eighty and knew her time was coming to an end. It didn't bother her and it didn't make her sad. She had accepted it as fact. More than anything, she was tired. She had a wonderful family and wonderful grandchildren and she had looked forward to times when family could all be together.

All of her family should have been together now that Brett had come home.

Should have been, but it wouldn't be.

She and her daughters had been visited by the police, the FBI and the US Marshalls looking for her baby boy, Tony. *How dare they ask those kinds of questions, demanding to know his whereabouts and accusing him of those disgusting things? Didn't they know he had hunted for his nephew? Didn't they know he had promised to find Brett and bring him home?*

"Mom, stop," Victoria said gently, but firmly.

"Brett glanced at her, then at his mom and then back at his grandmother and said, "Hi, Grandma."

She had been crying but had wiped her face on the apron she had worn over her simple black dress. She didn't know what to do with her hands and settled on folding them behind the apron.

She smiled and said, "Hi Brett. Glad to have you home."

"I'm happy to be home."

She limped slowly to meet him and he met her halfway where they embraced. She kissed his forehead and both cheeks and said, "I need to fatten you up."

Brett smiled and said, "I wouldn't mind that."

Margaret stepped back, smiled and nodded and said, "We've planned a welcome home party for you on Sunday. All your aunts and uncles and cousins will be there."

Brett's smile disappeared as he looked at his parents.

Thomas shook his head and said, "He won't be there."

Margaret stepped away from Brett and brushed past Thomas and Victoria and went back into the house without another word and without looking back, letting the door slam shut behind her.

Bobby slipped his arm around Brett's shoulders and said, "Can we go home now?"

"Yes," his mother said with a smile, though she wiped tears from her eyes. "I'd like that."

CHAPTER THIRTY-NINE

Waukesha, Wisconsin

Stephen roamed from room to room as if he hadn't been there in ages. He couldn't sit still. He'd flap his arms as if he were trying to take off, then he'd stop and move to a different room, flap them again, and so on until he had managed to do several circuits of the Bailey home.

"Stephen, what?" his mother asked. Sarah had been worrying about him ever since Ted's strange behavior at the hospital.

He shook his head, flapped his arms, and left the kitchen for another room, only to come back a short time later.

"Tell me," Sarah said.

He burst into tears, shook his head and said, "I don't know!"

Alexandra, *Alex* for short, came into the kitchen from the family room to see what was happening. She was three years younger than Stephen and resembled her brother and mother in looks, but had her mother's easy-going personality. Like Stephen and her parents, she too was an athlete, though more into dance and softball than soccer.

Sarah moved to her boy and held him while he sobbed into her shoulder. She had dark blond hair and blue eyes and stood the same height as her son. She had been a three-sport letter winner in high school and had been married for sixteen years to Ted, her high school sweetheart, who had also been a three-sport letter winner during his time in high school. His physique had sagged to a paunch and his once powerful pecs sagged and gave him a set of man-boobs. Sarah, however, had barely changed because while in college, she had become a jogger and swimmer and she had stuck with it ever since. While Ted went for a beer and a brat, she would drink unsweetened iced tea and eat grilled chicken over a salad.

Stephen and Alex could claim their athleticism from either parent. In terms of looks, with their blond hair and blue eyes, they looked more like their mother. In terms of personality however, he tended to be quieter and more intense like his father. Just like Ted, he would brood and when enough was enough, he'd explode like a volcano. But unlike his father, once he exploded, he'd soon forget what it was he was angry about and all was forgotten.

"Please, Stephen, what's wrong?"

Stephen's response was to sob.

"Oh, for Pete's sake, what the hell is wrong?" Ted barked.

Startled, Stephen jumped, broke away from his mother and stood at a distance looking from one to the other.

"Stephen, why don't you call Mike and ask if you can spend the night there. I'll pick you up tomorrow morning," Sarah said gently.

"What the hell, Sarah! That's how he ended up in Chicago in the first place! He's not going anywhere near there for a helluva long time if I have anything to say about it."

"You don't, so Stephen, go on back to your room, pack up what you need and I'll drive you over. We can call when we're on the way."

"I said, 'No'!"

Ignoring Ted, Sarah gave Stephen a gentle push, a weary smile and said, "Go on."

"Didn't you hear me?" Ted barked.

"Yes, I did," Sarah said facing her husband with her hands on her hips. "I'm sure half of Waukesha heard you too."

Before he could respond, she left the kitchen and moved down the hallway following her son.

Over her shoulder she said, "Alex, would you like to come with us or stay here?" Then Sarah added, "I won't be gone for more than forty-five minutes or so. Up to you."

Alex decided she'd go along for the ride, not wanting to risk being near her father in the mood he was in.

CHAPTER FORTY

On I-72 Between Springfield, IL and Hannibal, MO

Jeremy followed Jeff, shaking his head at the lead foot Jeff tended to have. The destination had been planned by the two of them that afternoon, so even if Jeff pulled ahead, he knew where to go. They had planned on Six Flags near St. Louis, but because of George's bruised ribs, decided to take it easy the first day. That way, George would have a chance to heal.

Billy sat in the backseat behind Jeremy and George sat next to him. Every so often, he'd grimace when the Expedition went over a bump. For the most part, it was a smooth ride, so he closed his eyes and tilted his head back.

"Dad, where are we headed?"

"You'll just have to wait and see."

"No hints?"

"Nope," Jeremy grinned at him using the rearview mirror.

Turning to George, Jeremy asked, "George, you doing okay?"

"Yes, sir."

Jeremy noticed that ever since that last conversation in the hospital, George had been treating him more formally and ignoring Billy altogether, even though it was Billy who had helped George get into the car.

"Are you really okay?" Billy asked.

"Yes."

"Are you angry?"

Of the twins, Billy was the peacemaker, the one who sought to smooth troubled waters and make sure feelings weren't hurt. Jeremy knew that Billy couldn't stand it if someone was angry at him. Long ago, he had labeled Billy as a classic pleaser.

George opened his eyes, caught Jeremy looking at him through the mirror and turned towards Billy and said, "I'm not angry. My ribs hurt, I'm frustrated and I'm worried."

"Why?"

George sighed, shook his head and said, "Don't you understand that there are men who are going to try to kill me? If you and Mr. Jeremy and Randy are near me, even Mr. Jeff and Danny, they will try to kill all of you too. Don't you understand that?"

Billy shrank back from him, turned away, and looked out his window at the passing scenery.

To the back of Billy's head George said quietly, "I'm not angry. My ribs hurt and I'm frustrated and worried."

Jeremy had been sitting this one out but felt the need to step in.

"George, Pete told me there is evidence that they're going to try to kill us too. It doesn't matter if you're with us or not. It doesn't matter if we stayed in Waukesha or drove straight through to Arizona. At some point, they'll be coming for us. I'm not trying to alarm you anymore than you are now, but that's what the evidence points to." He let that sink in and then said, "Pete, Jeff and I felt we'd all be safer together rather than trying to fight separate battles with people we don't know."

George frowned upon hearing this new information. He had considered the fact that he wasn't the only one these men were trying to kill, so it didn't totally surprise him. But Jeremy saying it out loud confirmed it and made it real.

"George, I love you. Honestly. I think I can speak for Billy and Randy when I say they love you too." He paused and then added, "Because we do, we can't let you fight them by yourself. I'm asking you to trust me . . . us. We have a plan."

George looked out the window, thought for a minute, looked at Billy, then at Jeremy and said, "I meant what I said at the hospital. I already lost one family. I do not want to lose another." He paused again, struggled in thought, seemed to fight for the right words, but settled on, "I . . ." and never finished. He had wanted to tell Jeremy and Billy that he loved them. He didn't know what had prevented him from doing so and for that, he was angry with himself. Somehow, he knew that his grandfather would be disappointed with George for not speaking his heart.

Jeremy smiled at him and said, "Try to relax as best you can. We need this time away. I know it'll be difficult, if not a bit surreal knowing what's waiting for us at the end of this trip, but let's take some time to get to know one another and have some fun. Let's not waste a day or a minute any longer. Please try to believe that we think we have it covered, okay?"

George stared at him, nodded solemnly and shut his eyes.

"So, you're not angry at me?" Billy asked.

George opened up his eyes and stared at him. He had wanted to ask Billy if he had been listening to anything that he had said, but instead, shook his head and said, "No, I'm not angry at you."

"Honest?"

Exasperated, George reached out, backhanded him in the chest just hard enough to make a point, and said, "I am not angry at you, yet. Keep it up and I will be."

Billy turned to the window and smiled.

As did Jeremy.

CHAPTER FORTY-ONE

Fishers, Indiana

The hardest part was believing that her brother had anything to do with this. Yet the proof was on the kitchen table: ten wireless cameras; eleven wireless microphones; one wireless relay that had been attached to their home computer. Throw in the 9-1-1 tape she and Thomas had listened to, there was little doubt.

How could she have grown up in the same house with him and not know him? What had happened that turned him into a monster? She wanted to phone her younger sister and closest confidante, Joan, and ask if she had suspected anything, but at this point, she didn't know if Joan knew the full extent of their younger brother's perversion. She held her head in her hands.

"Bobby," Pete began gently, "I have to ask you a couple of questions that might be uncomfortable." Skip, Chet and MB left the kitchen and stepped outside on the back patio, shutting the door behind them.

Victoria lifted her head and stared at Pete and then at Bobby, who lowered his head so his chin rested on his chest.

Brett frowned at Pete, stared at this brother, and then as the realization hit him, his eyes grew wide and his mouth opened in amazement.

"Bobby, you too?" Brett asked softly.

Bobby wiped tears from his eyes, but never raised his head and never said a word.

Victoria stared intently at her youngest son and then covered her mouth with her hand. Thomas placed both hands on his head, rocked back in his chair slightly, and then got up and leaned against the counter.

Brett placed his hand on Bobby's shoulder and said softly, "Bobby, look at me."

Bobby shook his head and wiped tears from his eyes.

"Please look at me," Brett said.

Even though he hadn't planned it like this, Pete let Brett take the lead.

Bobby lifted his eyes and glanced at Brett, and then lowered them back to his hands in his lap.

"Bobby, please look at me."

Bobby raised his eyes and looked at no one else. He dared not look at his mother or father. He didn't know Pete other than that he was an FBI agent, so he didn't look at him either.

Bobby was a thinker. His personality was fairly the opposite of Brett's up until Brett was abducted. Instead of being involved in sports, he had read, tinkered with the computer and like his father, wrote. Unlike his father, he wrote poems instead of the technical kinds of writing professors do. He had played the piano since he was seven and had begun playing guitar.

After Brett's abduction, he began playing basketball. He began running and weightlifting. He still read and wrote poetry and messed around on the computer. He still played the piano and guitar. But if it was possible, Bobby spoke even less than he had before his brother's abduction. He became silent and brooding. He seldom smiled and spent much of his time alone, except for a few friends, a couple of cousins and, his uncle.

"Bobby, whatever happened wasn't your fault. You've got to believe that." Brett paused to see if Bobby was listening. "I don't know what you did or didn't do, but after two years doing what I did, nothing, and I mean *nothing* you did could be any worse."

Bobby lowered his eyes, not able to sustain eye contact with his big brother.

"Did you hear me?"

Bobby nodded and wiped more tears.

"Pete has to ask you questions, but I'm right here. It's okay."

Bobby shrugged his shoulders and nodded.

Brett gripped his younger brother's shoulder, gave it a squeeze, then reached out and took Bobby's hand and held it. Then he turned to Pete and nodded.

"Bobby, we found the most cameras and microphones in your bedroom. Your father mentioned that in the last six months, you've spent more time with your uncle."

Bobby sat motionless. He didn't acknowledge Pete's statement. He didn't confirm that he had even heard Pete. But Brett noticed that Bobby's grip on his hand had become tighter.

Brett nodded at Pete.

"Bobby, I have to ask if your uncle did anything to you that made you uncomfortable."

Victoria reached behind her and lifted the tissues from the counter and placed them on the table between Bobby and herself. She grabbed one and twisted it in her hands. Thomas leaned against the kitchen sink with his head down and hands in his pockets. Brett lifted his left arm out of his sling and as best he could, held Bobby's hand with both of his.

Bobby breathed deeply and sighed. Keeping his head down and not looking at anyone he said, "Yes."

The silence in the kitchen was a thick, living thing, ugly and grotesque. It seemed everyone had held their breath waiting for Bobby to continue.

"Brett, I'm sorry. I'm really sorry. You have to believe that."

"Bobby, it's okay. I believe you. You didn't do anything wrong."

Bobby looked up at his older brother, shook his head and said, "No, you don't understand. I'm really sorry."

Puzzled, Victoria said, "Bobby, Brett's right, it wasn't your fault."

"NO!" Bobby shouted. "You don't under*stand! None of you understand!*"

"What don't we understand, Bobby?" Thomas asked. "Help us."

Bobby sobbed. He took his hands away from Brett and covered his face and sobbed. He shook his head, took a deep breath, sighed and said, "Brett, I'm really sorry."

"Why?" Brett asked.

Bobby struggled to find the words, shook his head and said, "Because I knew you were alive. I knew where you were five months ago."

It was like a bomb had gone off in the McGovern kitchen. Pete, Victoria and Brett sat back and away almost as one. Thomas flinched as if someone had thrown a roundhouse at his face.

"What?" Victoria asked. "What did you say?"

Bobby sobbed and said, "Brett, I'm sorry. He made me promise. He said he'd have you killed. He said he would have it filmed and then he'd give the video to mom and dad and me to watch."

Brett shook his head, eyes wide, mouth open, utterly and totally speechless.

"Start from the beginning," Pete said softly after clearing his throat. He took out his little notebook and jotted some notes.

Slowly, painfully, Bobby explained that at first, the visits with his uncle were innocent and fun. A Pacers game, a movie, a stop to grab a burger. There were hugs and kisses to the top of his head, to his cheek. At first, it was nothing, but then Dominico became more aggressive. Embraces became longer. One time, Dominico kissed him on the lips.

One night on a sleepover after a movie and shortly after the kissing incident, Dominico pulled out a DVD. Before he turned it on, Dominico said, "Bobby, we're going to watch this together from beginning to end. You won't get up off the couch and you're going to keep your mouth shut."

The DVD was of Brett and Dominico.

Bobby sat and watched it in horror, not believing, not understanding, and yet knowing that what he was seeing was real. It wasn't made up. It wasn't Hollywood.

Bobby wanted to throw up. He wanted to run from the house. He wanted to phone his parents, the cops. Someone. Anyone. He wanted the DVD to end, to stop.

"He said you were still alive and if I ever wanted to see you again, I couldn't say anything to anyone because all it would take was one phone call and you'd be dead."

Brett wept, unable to look at his brother.

"He said he and I were going to do things like in the movie. He said I had to. He said I had to because if I didn't, you'd be killed."

Brett wept some more and nodded.

Bobby looked from his mother to his father and said, "He told me to grow my hair long so I'd look more like Brett."

Brett didn't- *couldn't*- look at his brother.

"Bobby, why were there so many cameras and microphones in your room?" Pete asked.

"Why do you think?" Bobby sobbed incredulously. "He couldn't be with me every night. He'd text me and tell me to do stuff."

"You knew he had us bugged?" Thomas asked.

Bobby shook his head sadly. "Not at first. The first time he texted me, and I texted back after a little while and said I was done. I pretended to do what he asked. He texted me right away and *told* me I was lying. He asked if I wanted to see Brett again and that if I did, I better do what he wanted me to do."

"Oh God!" Victoria said softly. "Oh my God!"

"He watched me in bed," Bobby said sobbing.

"Sweet Jesus," Thomas said.

"Brett, I'm sorry. I know I should have told somebody but I was afraid they'd kill you. Honest!" Bobby sobbed, "I wanted to tell, but I was afraid."

Brett shook his head and said, "Shhhh, it's okay, it's okay."

"I *know* it's not, but I was *afraid*," Bobby yelled.

"Bobby, it's okay. He was right. They would have killed me. It wasn't your fault."

"But maybe you could have been home sooner. You wouldn't have gotten shot," Bobby said.

And maybe Johnny would still be alive and Ryan wouldn't have been taken away. Maybe Stephen and Mike wouldn't have been taken, Brett thought. But instead of saying any of that, he said, "Listen, Bobby. Look at me."

"No," Bobby said shaking his head, refusing to lift his chin off his chest.

Brett got up out of his chair, went to his little brother and hugged him fiercely.

"I need you to listen to me," Brett said. "Please look at me."

Bobby lifted his head and Brett held Bobby's face with his hands, his face inches from Bobby's.

"I should have told mom and dad two years ago when that shitbag stuck his hands down my pants. If I would have, I never would have been kidnapped. You wouldn't have been . . . whatever. I should have said something back then. If I would have, none of this would have happened."

"But-"

"-But *nothing*," Brett said. "But nothing," he repeated softly. "*I'm* to blame. Not you. Not mom. Not dad. *Me. Only me.*"

Bobby tried to shake his head but Brett held it firmly and said, "Yes, *I'm* to blame."

"No, Brett," Victoria said softly. "Neither one of you are to blame. The only one to blame is my brother. He's the only one to blame."

CHAPTER FORTY-TWO

West Bend, Wisconsin

Tim was lost.

That was the only way to describe what he felt like; what was going on inside. He felt like he didn't belong. After the news conference at the West Bend Police Station, he had asked his father to drive past Badger Middle School and St. John's Lutheran Elementary School. West Bend had gotten bigger and at the same time, smaller. While it was familiar to him, it was also different and not in a friendly way. Perhaps he was different.

His sister Christi glanced at him furtively and stayed away from him. His mother doted on him trying to feed him a cookie, a sandwich, a glass of milk or juice. All were politely refused because he wasn't hungry or thirsty. He had no appetite.

His father had proudly shown him that his bedroom hadn't changed during the time he was gone. A museum exhibit of the life Tim had before he was taken. It was neat and tidy, but creepy and frozen in time. It was as if he had never left, never been gone for over two years. It was as if he had just rolled out of bed, spent the day doing this or that, and was now back.

His baseball and basketball trophies lined the shelves above his desk. A picture of him and his two best friends, brothers Caleb and Kaiden Mattenauer with their arms over each other's shoulders laughing at something Cal had said was framed and sat beside the trophies. Tim remembered the day and the joke like it was yesterday, and just like it had done each time he looked at the photo, it made him smile. At the same time, it made him sad.

A picture of Brett Favre leading the Packers to a win in Super Bowl XXXI against the Patriots hung over his bed. His baseball glove, ball and cleats were in his closet just as they were after each baseball game he had played. His uniform was washed and hung in his closet awaiting his next game. He didn't think he was on the team any longer, certain that the coach had long ago selected another player to take his place. It probably didn't fit him any longer anyway. A basketball was on the floor of his closet alongside his basketball shoes, three pair, all fairly new, but probably too small for him to wear.

It all felt strange to him, foreign. Like someone else's room, but familiar enough to be his. His, but not his.

He didn't know how to act. He didn't know what to say. His day was no longer programmed or structured. He wasn't confined to a locked room without a TV or radio.

He could roam the house freely just as he did the hospital, noticing new paint in the living room and hallway. If he had wanted, he could have gone out to the garage, jump on his bike and peddle over to Cal's and Kaid's house to see what they were doing.

If he wanted to.

He didn't.

He didn't want to go anywhere or see anyone. At least not yet. He wasn't . . . ready.

His parents, family and friends were going to throw him a welcome home party tomorrow and he wasn't certain he wanted to attend even though he was the guest of honor.

For now, Tim was content to sit on the back patio on a recliner staring at the late afternoon sun and the clouds and breathing the clean, fresh air. That was enough for him for now.

CHAPTER FORTY-THREE

Hannibal, Missouri

The six of them had finished eating at a Texas Roadhouse and then jumped into the hotel pool for the better part of two hours. Billy had helped George get undressed and into his swimming suit, and both of them ended up laughing to the point where George's ribs hurt like hell. He liked the hot tub the best, but swam with the other guys as best he could with his sore ribs. The swimming and hot tub helped him stretch out and relax his muscles. Maybe the laughter helped too.

The best part of the night, even the day- besides laughing in the bathroom with Billy, was when they wandered into the hotel bar to grab a soda. Danny spotted an older, upright Baldwin piano and sat down on the wooden bench with a twinkle in his eye. He didn't ask the bartender for permission. Before he began an instrumental version of Billy Joel's *Piano Man*, he told Randy to run up to the room and grab their guitars.

Two empty stools sat on a small nicked up stage opposite the bar. Two microphones on adjustable stands sat on the stage along with the piano. The cords led to an amplifier that served as a sound system. After he finished the song, Danny flicked on the amp, turned on one of the microphones and tested the sound level.

The bartender poured dark amber liquid into an eight-ounce cut-glass with ice cubes for a middle-aged man in a rumpled suit. Two other men sat at a corner table munching on peanuts or pretzels, one with a soda over ice and the other with a Corona. The only other table that was occupied was filled with Jeremy, Jeff, Billy and George, each with a soda: a Fanta for Billy; a Coke for George; and Diet Cokes for Jeremy and Jeff.

Randy walked up to the stage carrying both guitars feeling nervous but excited at the same time. He didn't know if he was ready to *perform* on a stage in front of a room full of people, even if more than half were family and friends.

George didn't know much about music. He didn't listen to it all that much, but he liked Randy's voice. It was smooth and easy to listen to. Danny's voice was even better. He soared on the high notes and had a sad, lonely quality. Randy had told him about Danny's musical ability, but George had no idea how good he was until he had heard Danny sing and play.

George loved the songs, but mostly loved Danny's voice. More impressive was how he performed. It reminded him of his grandfather when he prayed each morning. His grandfather had the ability to shut out everything except for the words he chanted. George used to sneak peeks at his grandfather, amazed at his concentration and effort.

Danny was the same way. There could have been a hundred people in the room or no one else. It wouldn't have mattered because Danny was so into the words, the sound, and the song. Danny wasn't on the stage. He was bigger than the stage.

Another five or six people drifted into the bar to listen. A girl with a cell phone recorded. The bartender became busy. The hotel manager stood just inside the door with his arms folded across his chest, listened to a song and left.

When Danny and Randy finished their first four songs, there was applause. One man said, "Hey, you're the kid who was on Letterman, right? The kid who plays sixty different instruments at once."

Danny laughed and said, "Well not quite sixty, but yes, that was me."

"I thought so."

"I'm Danny Limbach and this is my friend, Randy Evans. We'll play a couple more songs, if that's okay with you."

By the time their impromptu concert had ended, there were more than twenty people in the room, and another bartender appeared along with a waitress. Several other cell phones had come out to record the boys' performance.

"Okay, last song," Danny said. There were protests and Danny held up his hands and said, "We really have to go, but we'll leave you with this one."

Danny played and sang, *Set Fire To The Rain* and to George it was the best song yet. Danny sang with intensity, with power, with *heat*. Each note was sung clearly and with what seemed like pain and anguish. It left George silent and shaking his head.

The crowd was silent, into the song, and hanging on each word, each note. When he ended, the crowd stood and cheered. As the boys packed away their equipment, the crowd dispersed and the only ones left in the bar were Jeremy, Jeff, Billy and George, along with the two bartenders and the waitress.

"Hey guys," the original bartender called. "Come back tomorrow. Best entertainment we had all year!"

CHAPTER FORTY-FOUR

Hannibal, Missouri

Back in their room, Billy had asked which side of the bed George wanted, giving him no choice as to who he was going to sleep with, which was all right with him. He had gotten used to Billy's rhythm. He took the side closest to the alarm clock with Billy taking the side nearest the wall.

The TV was tuned to some movie on HBO, but the volume was barely audible and the four boys lounged on George's and Billy's bed. George was propped up with pillows and sat cross-legged on top of the covers. Billy laid half-on, half-off the bed, leaning towards George. After they had gotten back to their room and after brushing teeth, Billy had again helped George out of his clothes and into his shorts as they got ready for bed. George hadn't asked Billy to help him. He had just knocked once on the bathroom door and entered. When George thanked him, Billy shrugged and said, "You'd do the same for me."

"Can I ask a question?" George asked looking at Danny.

"Sure."

"Where do you get the ideas for your songs? The two songs you wrote," George said looking from Randy to Danny, "were beautiful."

"It just sorta happens." He turned red and said, "When Randy writes lyrics, I read the first couple of lines and I sort of know what I want to do with the music." He finished with a shrug.

"Where do you come up with the words?" George asked Randy.

"Things I think about. Things I feel."

Randy had been quiet since the concert. He had yawned a lot and seemed tired, but to Billy, it was more than that. As the guys talked, Billy glanced his way every now and then, but said nothing.

"What?" Randy asked.

Billy shook his head.

"What?" Randy repeated.

"I don't like what this crap does to you."

By *this crap*, Randy knew Billy meant talking to kids and parents about abuse. Listening to their stories. Getting *involved.* He sighed and said, "Billy, I'm okay."

"You're not," Billy answered. "You were like in a different world up on that stage, but as soon as you stepped off . . ." he finished with a shrug.

Randy sighed and said, "Billy, I'm fine."

Billy shook his head. The two boys stared at each other like gunfighters. "Really."

"I'm worried about you. How many times did you check your cell during dinner? How many times did you check it in the last half-hour?"

Randy knew he was busted. There was a rule in the Evans' house that during meals, cell phones were forbidden. He had been on it constantly and still was, mostly to Mike and Stephen, and Patrick. Brett had checked in a couple of times using his brother's phone. The only one he hadn't heard from was Tim.

Billy sat up with his legs crisscrossed under him like George and frowned at Randy.

"Billy, who else can these guys talk to?"

"Dad."

Randy's cell buzzed but he ignored it and said, "We've been over this. These guys went through a lot. They need someone to talk to. I've been through it so I understand. I know what they're feeling."

Billy leaned forward and said softly, "It's tearing you up."

"Billy, I promise. I'm okay." Randy knew Billy wasn't convinced so he said, "I promise."

Billy sighed and gave up. There was no point in arguing because he knew nothing would change anyway.

Danny lay down between Billy and George, but faced them, leaning on a pillow from the other bed. Looking at George he said, "Can I ask you a question?"

George nodded.

"The night you fought that man, were you scared?"

George had thought about it but hadn't come to any resolution. He almost talked to Jeremy about it, but decided he didn't need to. "I was nervous but not scared."

"But that guy had a gun," Danny pressed. "He was going to kill you and everyone else."

George looked at Dan but spoke to the three boys when he said, "My grandfather was with me. I trust him."

"Well, I'm glad you killed him. You, and Randy and Billy and Jeremy wouldn't be here if you hadn't."

George frowned as he said, "He gave me no choice, but I am not happy I killed him. Navajos do not believe in killing."

Randy and Billy nodded.

The twins had noticed that George spoke formally when the topic turned serious.

Danny thought it over, looked at George and said, "Were you scared today? I mean, that guy had his gun pointed right at you."

Billy and Randy turned to face George, eyes wide, mouths open.

It was Billy who spoke for them, "I didn't know he had his gun pointed at *you*."

"He pushed dad out of the way and knelt over him and the guy pointed his gun at George," Danny explained.

Blushing, George said, "I did not think he was going to shoot me."

"But you knelt over my dad protecting him like he was going to shoot *some*body," Danny said.

George explained. "I was not as big a threat as your dad was."

Danny wasn't convinced.

"But that was a huge chance you took," Randy said.

"Huge," Billy repeated.

George looked down at his lap. Sitting cross-legged was uncomfortable for him, but he didn't want his ribs to dictate what he did or didn't do. Besides, the hot tub and the swim, not to mention the pain killer he had taken, had helped.

"Danny, he had just shot the guard. I did not want him to shoot your dad because I know what it is like losing family. I did not want you to go through that. If someone was going to get shot, I would rather it be me and not your dad."

"Shit, George! Randy and I don't want to lose you either!"

George shrugged and said quietly, "Once Mr. Jeff was out of the way, I did not think he was going to shoot anyone else. He had to get away."

"But then you went after him," Danny pressed. "Even after my dad told you not to."

"My grandfather did not want me to let him get away," George answered. This was the truth and the only explanation he could give the boys. "I had to obey my grandfather."

Danny shrugged, not understanding the whole thing about his grandfather, even though Jeremy had tried to explain it to him and to his dad. But the twins didn't question it.

"What?" George asked Danny.

"My dad was really worried about you, afraid you'd get hurt especially after you ran outside with the gun."

George said, "That is when I was afraid. Not because of the agent, but because of the police. Both of them had their guns drawn on me."

"Damn, George! You can't do that stuff!" Billy said emphatically, smacking George's thigh with the back of his hand.

"My grandfather told me to go after him and not let him get away," George answered quietly but with finality.

"But the cops almost shot you!" Billy countered.

"I was careful. I had my hands up and I put the gun on the ground slowly and did what they told me to do." Yet, that was when he was as close to getting shot as ever.

"Don't do it again!" Billy said smacking him on the thigh again, this time harder than the first time.

Ignoring Billy, George turned back to Danny and said, "Is your father angry at me for disobeying him?"

Danny considered the question. Concerned, yes. Worried, yes. Angry, not sure, but he doubted it. He said as much to George.

"Randy, can you help me up?" George asked as he struggled getting his legs out from under him.

"Where are you going?" Billy asked.

"To speak with Danny's father."

As Randy helped George to his feet, he noticed George wince with the effort and asked, "Do you want us to come along?"

"No, I will go alone."

George walked slowly over to the door separating the two rooms, wrapped twice and waited.

"Come in," Jeremy said from the other side.

George stepped into Jeremy's and Jeff's room and shut the door behind him.

The two men were seated at the desk hunched over Jeff's laptop. Jeff pointed at something on the screen and Jeremy nodded thoughtfully and continued to stare at the computer.

"Hi George," Jeff said with a smile.

Jeremy looked up, smiled and said, "Hey George. What's up?"

"May I talk to Mr. Jeff?" George answered.

Jeremy and Jeff exchanged a look and then Jeremy asked, "Would you like me to leave?"

"No," George said shaking his head. He wanted Jeremy present if for no other reason than for moral support.

"What's up?" Jeff asked curiously, folding his arms across his chest.

George wasn't sure how to begin and suddenly became aware that he stood in front of them bare-chested, bare-footed and wearing only his shorts with nothing under them. He wore his turquoise and leather necklace. Even though the men didn't seem to notice or care what he was dressed like, he blushed deep crimson.

"Do you want to sit down?" Jeremy asked.

"No, Sir."

Both men waited. They had changed into shorts and t-shirts and were ready for bed. Jeremy wore flip-flops, while Jeff was barefoot. Several thin jagged white and red lines ran from somewhere under Jeff's shorts to his mid-calf and George knew those were the scars from the motorcycle accident and the surgeries that followed it.

"Mr. Jeff, when I disobeyed you this afternoon, I did not want you to think I was being disrespectful." George decided to begin with that and see where it took him.

"I'm not sure what you mean."

George sat down stiffly on the edge of Jeremy's bed, wincing at the effort. He knew it was Jeremy's because of the bible just off the pillow and the John Sanford paperback he had seen him reading at their house. He knew the other bed must have been Jeff's.

He said, "I tried to keep you safe from the agent with the gun and then I ran after him even though you told me not to."

Jeff nodded thoughtfully, but didn't respond.

"I was worried that the agent was going to shoot you like he did the security guard."

Jeff nodded again. Jeremy glanced at Jeff and then looked back at George.

"That is why I pushed you down."

"But you almost got *yourself* shot, George. That was risky," Jeff said quietly.

"I did not think the agent was going to shoot me. You were the bigger threat because you were the adult. To him, I was just a kid. I needed to keep you away from him."

"But that was dangerous."

"Mr. Jeff, Danny was watching. I know what it is like to lose family." George stopped and stared at Jeremy, then nodded at Jeff. "I did not want Danny to lose you and to watch it happen. If anyone was going to get shot, I wanted it to be me, not you."

Both Jeff and Jeremy sat back, speechless. Neither could find the words to respond.

"I did not think the agent was going to shoot me. My grandfather would have warned me. I am certain of that. The only thing the agent wanted to do was get away."

"But then you went after him with a loaded gun," Jeff said.

George nodded and said, "Because my grandfather told me not to let him get away."

George said it as a matter of fact.

Jeremy and Jeff exchanged a look, but said nothing. George was certain that Jeremy had understood him, but didn't know what Jeff was thinking. However, it was important for Jeff to believe him.

"I do not want you to think I was being disrespectful. I was listening to my grandfather."

"Son . . . George," Jeff said, getting up off the chair to sit down next to George on the edge of the bed. "I never thought you were disrespectful. I was only concerned that you put yourself in danger."

"Yes, Sir."

"What you did was very brave, but it was also very dangerous."

"Yes, Sir."

Jeff considered him and then said, "I think that if you had to do it all over again, you'd probably do the same thing."

George nodded.

Jeff pursed his lips, looked at Jeremy for guidance, but didn't receive any, so he said, "You were willing to sacrifice yourself for me." It was a statement, not a question.

"Yes, Sir. I did not want Danny to lose his father."

They regarded each other for several seconds. Finally, Jeff bent over and kissed George's forehead.

"Kiddo, I'm going to ask that you never do that again, but I know you're going to do what you think is best, especially if your grandfather gives you guidance."

George smiled shyly and nodded.

"I figured as much," Jeff said with a dry laugh. Then he kissed George's forehead once again and the two embraced.

CHAPTER FORTY-FIVE

Fishers, Indiana

MB was on her third lap moving from room to room familiarizing herself with the McGovern house. It was a typical family home, fairly plain and hid the fact that the McGoverns had money, pushing them to the lower limits of upper class. She didn't know for sure, but decided that because Thomas was a university professor, that made him liberal and probably a democrat. She didn't know about Victoria and didn't care. MB wasn't into politics.

MB spent time in the basement checking windows to make certain they were locked. She guessed that if there was a break in, it would take place on the main floor from either the garage door off the laundry room or the slider that led from the family room and emptied into the backyard and patio. She made a mental note to secure the slider with a nail or bolt in the track that would prevent the door from opening more than six inches. That way, it would be too narrow for someone to enter. Satisfied that nothing could be done to secure the house further, she went back into the kitchen and found Victoria sitting alone at the table.

Pete had driven Chet and Skip to a nearby motel that was going to be their base for the time being. Skip had volunteered to stay with the McGoverns and genuinely seemed disappointed that Pete chose MB to stay with the family.

The Quality Inn was a short five, maybe ten minutes away even in traffic so they could get there in a hurry if need be. Skip and Chet were going to get started on the techie things Chet liked to do, while Pete had other plans that he hadn't shared with her. MB was pretty sure he hadn't shared his plans with Skip or Chet either.

A different kind of guy, MB thought.

MB was going to stay at least one night, perhaps more. A lot of it depended upon whether or not Thomas and Victoria wanted her to. So far, they had allowed her, even if they hadn't actually welcomed her.

She had hoped Pete would let Skip stay because this protection duty- babysitting duty- seemed like penance during lent. The family and the house had a stifling feel about it. Hell, all she needed was sack cloth and ashes. She liked the two boys, though she hadn't interacted much with either of them, but the parents, well, they were a different story altogether.

"Ma'am, is there anything I can get you? Anything I can do for you?"

Victoria smiled weakly, shook her head and said, "No, not really."

MB waited, sensing that she might want to talk woman to woman, even though MB was at least ten years younger. Probably more.

"Are you married . . . have kids?"

"No, Ma'am."

"Please call me Victoria or Vicky."

"Yes, Ma'am . . . Victoria," MB said.

There was silence between them, but it wasn't uncomfortable or cold.

"When Brett went missing, I blamed Thomas. I blamed myself. I blamed Bobby for not being with him. I even blamed Brett for allowing himself to be taken," she said shaking her head. She held her head in her hands and then folded her hands on the table.

It seemed to MB that Victoria didn't know what to do with them. Or with herself for that matter.

"I couldn't comprehend it. I tried to find a *why* and a *how*, but . . ." she let the statement drift off to nothing.

MB sat down across from her.

"Never, and I mean *never*, did I suspect my brother. I never suspected him of being involved. It had *never* occurred to me. My own *brother*! Brett's *uncle*! My *God*!" She shook her head and looked off somewhere towards the empty family room.

MB looked into the family room to see if there was anything in particular Victoria was looking at.

"Even after I heard the 9-1-1 tape, killing his *partner* . . . even though I saw those ugly," she twisted up her face in disgust, "*ugly*, disgusting pictures of him doing things to those boys, to *Brett* . . ." she let her voice trail off, never finishing the thought, letting silence finish it for her.

"I can't imagine what Brett went through. I. Just. Can't." she said shaking her head at each word.

MB sat helpless. She felt sorry for Victoria. A woman's instinct is to protect her children. And perhaps it was this instinct, failing her in the case of Brett, and then in the case of Bobby, that made her all the more vulnerable, insecure and, well, pathetic.

MB wouldn't judge her. She had to admit that she wasn't all that enamored with her. Or with Thomas for that matter. But there was no way she was going to judge her. Them. She didn't have the right.

"Do you have a gun or something for protection?"

Victoria smiled and said, "Ironically, my brother gave me, us, a gun. He said it was 'just in case', whatever that meant."

"May I see it?" MB asked curiously.

"It's in our bedroom in the night stand on my side of the bed," Victoria said.

She waited and when Victoria showed no sign of moving, MB got up to retrieve it.

She passed Thomas in the study at the computer. The computer wasn't turned on, the screen was dark, and he sat at the desk staring at, what? MB couldn't tell and wasn't curious enough to ask. She didn't think he had noticed her standing in the doorway.

She passed Bobby's bedroom, peeked in and saw both boys sitting on the bed talking quietly. Neither looked in her direction, though she was certain both knew she was there.

Entering the master bedroom, she went to one nightstand and with a quick look in the top drawer discovered it was Thomas's. It was man stuff: a watch, a bit of jewelry, a finger blood pressure gauge, some books and pictures of the boys. All tucked away in fairly orderly fashion.

She moved to the other side of the bed and opened the top drawer. She lifted out a prescription bottle of Ambien with Victoria's name on it that had only six tablets left in it. There were pictures of Brett and Bobby. The pictures of Brett were dog-eared as if they had been held long and often. In the bottom drawer she found an S&W .38. It wasn't a powerful handgun, but it could be lethal nonetheless. She checked and it wasn't loaded, but a box of bullets sat in the drawer next to it.

She carried it back to the kitchen and sat down at the table. Victoria hadn't moved. It didn't even look as though Victoria knew she had left the kitchen.

MB began taking the gun apart piece by piece. Victoria watched her curiously, wondering how a woman knew how to do something like that.

"Hmmm . . ." MB said.

"What?"

"The firing pin was removed."

"What does that mean?"

MB looked at her with a frown and said, "Without the firing pin, you could pull the trigger all day long and nothing would happen."

"Who . . ." Victoria never finished the question because she knew the answer.

CHAPTER FORTY-SIX

Waukesha, Wisconsin

He lost count of the number of times he checked each of his email accounts. He had even gotten into his car and ventured into his neighborhood cruising past his house. There were no strange cars on the street or in neighbors' driveways. He decided that if anyone had come looking for him, they had left long ago. His neighborhood was as quiet and as peaceful as it ever was.

Perhaps he had over-reacted in not going to work and in getting a room at the hotel. But it was smart to take precautions. And, there was nothing wrong with calling in sick. He seldom took time off.

He lingered in Brookfield Square looking for cute boys. Unfortunately, he didn't see any that suited him, not even in the arcade. He drove back into Waukesha to Frame Park to watch Little League baseball. He hated the game but loved the boys. He even went to the concession stand and stood as close to two boys as he could. He smelled their sweat and their scent. He even brushed up against the better looking of the two, touching his arm. It was soft with light, downy hair. He apologized, smiled charmingly. The boy smiled back, then left with his friend. Driving back to the Holiday Inn, he thought briefly of calling one of the boys he had been with, but decided that might be pushing his luck.

No, he'd have to lay low for a while.

He pulled up the email and the picture of Stephen and the other boy, Michael. He enlarged the picture as much as he could without it getting fuzzy and out of focus.

He'd have to have Stephen.

Sooner or later.

CHAPTER FORTY-SEVEN

Hannibal, Missouri

Jeremy and Jeff popped into the room to say goodnight after the boys settled in for the night.

George looked forward to each of these nightly visits. In a different life, after saying goodnight to his mother and grandparents, George would kiss his youngest brother Robert and the youngest of his siblings, Mary, on the cheek along with a hug each. With William who was just over a year younger, he exchanged hugs. He shared a bed with both Robert and William. Robert would snuggle against George and William would keep to himself on the other side of the bed.

George felt sad that he hadn't done more or told them how much he had loved them and that he would always love them. He regretted it each time Jeremy came in to say goodnight and give them hugs and kisses because it reminded him of his inability to say I love you and that now, he never could. He knew he would regret that the rest of his life.

It didn't take long for Randy and Danny to fall asleep. Randy fell asleep in his usual position on his back with one knee up and arms out. Danny slept with his back to Randy but pressed up against him.

George remembered that the doctor had advised him to sleep on his sore ribs because that way, the mattress would act much like a splint and they'd be better protected. He laid on his right side, his back to Randy and Danny, but facing Billy, who tossed and turned. Billy was as quiet as he could be, but it was clear he was wide awake.

George reached out and touched Billy's bare shoulder and whispered, "What's wrong?"

Billy shrugged but otherwise didn't respond.

Still gripping Billy's shoulder, George shook him gently.

Billy turned and stared intently at George, their faces inches apart. George waited patiently.

Billy lifted his head to see if Randy and Danny were awake. He moved even closer; their noses almost touching.

He said in an urgent whisper, "Promise me that you'll protect Randy and Dad and that you'll take care of yourself."

George frowned at him and considered the remark. He didn't know if he could actually make such a promise. George considered promises a sacred thing, never to be taken lightly.

Billy continued, "I know your grandfather will tell you to do things, but you have to promise me that you'll protect them and yourself. You can't let anything happen to them or to you. Okay?"

George stared at his friend, smiled and said, "I'll do my best to protect father, Randy and you. I promise."

Billy shook his head and moved closer so that their noses touched lightly. George could smell the scent of Billy's minty toothpaste and the clean, soapy smell of his face.

"I don't care about me. I care about Dad and Randy and you. Promise me you'll take care of them and yourself."

George rubbed his nose with Billy's, just as he used to with his little brother Robert and said, "I promise I'll do all I can to protect us. All of us. I promise."

Billy nodded once and then rolled away from him.

George let him settle and then on impulse, tapped Billy on the shoulder.

Billy rolled onto his back and turned his face towards George.

"I love you and Randy and father."

Billy smiled, nodded and then turned away again.

Satisfied, George shut his eyes, smiled to himself and laid his hand on Billy's shoulder.

Billy backed up against him, so George draped his arm across Billy's chest.

It wasn't too long before Billy whispered, "Love you too."

With that, Billy fell asleep. Peacefully.

George stayed awake a little longer hoping that he could fulfill his promise and protect Jeremy and the twins. He knew that he would do his best. He just hoped his best would be enough.

CHAPTER FORTY-EIGHT

Fishers, Indiana

Brett couldn't sleep. He didn't want to be in his old room, now the spare room, so he climbed into bed with Bobby. At some point, he must have dozed off, but that didn't last long. It never did. An hour here, an hour there was the best he could do. It had been like that for most of his captivity because he never knew when he'd be wakened.

Before climbing into bed, he had wandered around Bobby's room looking at the collection of stuff accumulated by his brother during his absence. He had never really spent time in Bobby's room. For that matter, he never really spent a great deal of time with Bobby. He decided that was going to change.

His fucking uncle. How could he do that to him? To Bobby? To both of them? And who else? He had a cousin one year younger and wondered if Good Ol' Uncle Tony got to him too.

Brett was surprised to see his autographed poster of Peyton Manning in Bobby's room hanging on the wall. When Bobby saw him staring at it, Bobby had said, "I know it's your favorite thing." Brett had shrugged but didn't comment. Then quietly Bobby had added, "When you were gone, I wanted to have it in my room because then I could have a piece of you. It was the only way I could think of . . ."

Bobby never finished the thought and Brett remained silent. In the end, Brett told Bobby to keep it. Bobby protested, but Brett had insisted, saying, "We can share it, but I want you to have it in your room." Bobby hung his head on the verge of tears, so Brett put his hand on Bobby's shoulder and said, "Bobby. It's okay. Honest."

As quietly as he could, Brett slipped out of bed. He picked up a blanket that either he or Bobby had kicked off and carried it into the family room. MB was nowhere to be seen, so Brett wondered if she had fallen asleep in his room. Or the *spare room* as he referred to it.

Quietly, he opened the patio door and curled up on the lounger and wrapped himself in the blanket and stared up at the moon and stars.

He missed Tim and Patrick, Stephen and Mike. He missed Johnny and thinking about him brought tears to his eyes. He missed Ian who could always crack him up with some wiseass comment. He missed George and Randy and wished he could have spent more time with them.

He was lonely.

No matter how many times he had called or texted one of them using Bobby's phone, it wasn't enough. He still felt far away from them.

He heard the slider open and shut softly. He knew it was his mother by the smell of her perfume and without turning around and looking at her said, "Sorry if I woke you up."

Wrapped in a robe and slippers, she sat down on a cushioned chair next to him, wrapped her arms around herself to keep out the chill and said, "You didn't. I haven't slept well for a long time."

There was silence between them as they looked up towards the heavens. The night was calm, still and warm, but cooling off. Not much of a breeze. Brett could smell the flowers his mom had planted just off the patio. Every now and then a dog would bark in the distance and the bark would echo down empty streets.

"Brett, I'm sorry I slapped you. Honestly, I didn't mean to," his mother said quietly.

"Mom, it's okay. It's no big deal."

"It is to me. I hadn't seen you in months and the first chance I get . . ."

Brett knew from the catch in her voice she was weeping.

"Mom, let's forget about it. It's over. It's okay."

Again, there was silence, but not very comfortable for Brett. Probably not for Victoria either. He didn't know what else to say and maybe she didn't either. Besides, he didn't really want to talk. He wanted to sit quietly letting the night embrace him as tightly as the blanket was wrapped around him.

The slider opened and closed, and MB sat down on the back step. Brett turned around just to make sure, and he was surprised she was still dressed as she was earlier that evening. She didn't have that I-just-got-out-of-bed-look someone gets when they have been sleeping. She didn't even look like she had been dozing.

"Guys, I don't think it's a good idea for you to be outside this late." She let that percolate and then added, "It's dangerous." Then to soften it she added, "At least for the time being."

Brett didn't say anything. For twenty-two months he'd been shuttered in a room without windows. For twenty-two months he had never ventured off the floor he was held captive on. He wasn't going to argue and he wasn't going to go back inside.

Screw it.

If he was going to come after him, let him. He wasn't about to exchange one captivity for another.

So, the three of them sat there not moving, not talking, and at some point, Brett fell asleep.

CHAPTER FORTY-NINE

Fishers, Indiana

He had driven around the neighborhood, but not down that particular street. It didn't look like anything was out of the ordinary. He knew someone had to be watching the house. A Car? Someone's house that was commandeered for the time being? He wasn't sure. If it were him, he'd have them in a box: one or two out front and one or two behind. But that was him. They probably hadn't thought of that because they were not as smart as he was.

What he was sure about was that at least one agent would be in the house. What he didn't know was what would happen if one or more family members left. He knew Thomas would eventually go back to the university. He had classes to teach and office hours to keep. As for Vicky, maybe she'd take a leave of absence or eat up some vacation time.

It didn't matter. It was only a matter of time before he'd get even, before he'd tie up loose ends.

There was no way he could just walk away and start over. No. Not an option.

They had done this to him and because of that, he was going to take care of them. He didn't know exactly when yet, but he was sure it would happen soon.

That made him smile.

CHAPTER FIFTY

Mike and Stephen had been best friends since the second grade. The sleepover routine was always the same: movies, homemade nachos heavy on the cheese or some popcorn drenched with butter. There'd be sodas to drink, and a video game or two to play. It never varied. It was a rhythm as much as breathing and hearts beating. Buddies, together forever.

They attempted to watch a movie, *Remember The Titans* with popcorn and a Fanta for Mike and a Sprite for Stephen. But the popcorn went mostly uneaten and the drinks barely touched. Neither cared about watching the movie, and neither cared for playing a video game. So earlier than normal, they got ready for bed and lay down on the carpeted basement floor under blankets with heads resting on pillows they had grabbed from the couch.

Stephen lay on his back with his eyes wide open, staring at the ceiling. He wasn't the least bit tired or ready to sleep. Sensing this, Mike was wide awake too. He lay on his stomach, silently watching his friend.

He concentrated very hard on his words, his pronunciation, determined to not stutter. "What?" Mike asked finally.

Stephen's only reaction was a slight shake of his head.

Mike reached over and playfully flicked Stephen's nose. Mike smiled but there was no reaction from Stephen, so Mike waited. Typically, he was much more patient than Stephen and he knew that he could, and would, wait him out.

Finally, Stephen rolled onto his side, faced Mike and said, "Mike, I'm really sorry all this shit happened to you."

Mike frowned, rolled to his side and faced his friend, waiting for an explanation.

"They said I was the one they wanted. You were taken because you were with me." His eyes were wet with tears and his lips trembled. "All this shit happened because of me."

Mike frowned and shook his head.

"This happened to both of us. It was *them*. Not you."

"Don't you see?" Stephen reached out and grabbed Mike's arm. "If you and I hadn't been together, it would have just been me. Not you."

"So?"

Exasperated, Stephen rolled onto his back, faced the ceiling and muttered, "Never mind. You don't get it."

Mike propped his head up with his hand and reached out and laid a hand on Stephen's bare chest.

"Stephen, listen to me." He shook him gently and said, "Listen to me."

Stephen wiped tears from his eyes but didn't dare look at his friend.

"In soccer, don't I always have your back?"

Stephen rolled onto his side and started to say something, but Mike was pissed and didn't give him a chance.

"Don't you always have my back?"

Stephen started to talk but Mike placed his hand gently over Stephen's mouth.

"Stephen, we're best friends. Always have been. Always will be." He repeated, "We're *best* friends."

Stephen shook his head to get Mike's hand off his mouth, but Mike said, "Just shush a minute."

He took his hand off Stephen's mouth, but placed it on Stephen's shoulder.

"Let's say I wasn't with you. Let's say that for some reason, they took you and not me. How do you think I'd feel?"

Stephen wiped his eyes and stared at this friend.

"How do you think I'd feel?" Mike continued. "We're best friends. I'd rather be with you than anybody. If you went missing and we couldn't find you, I'd go frigging nuts. They'd have to lock me up in a padded room and throw away the key."

Exasperated, almost frantic, Mike said, "Stephen, you're my *best* friend. I love my mom and my dad. I think I even love my brother and sister sometimes, but Stephen, I love *you*. You're. My. Best. Friend." He said this last with a finger bouncing lightly on Stephen's chest to accentuate each word.

"But look at what they did to you, Mike. Look at you!"

"Yeah, so?"

"*So? So?*" Incredulous, Stephen said, "They were going to *kill* you! They were going to rape the shit out of you and then *kill* you!"

"But they didn't kill me. We're safe now."

"But they were going to."

"But they didn't."

"But-"

Softly, patiently, Mike smiled and said, "But. They. *Didn't*."

"But-"

Mike gently placed his hand back over Stephen's mouth and said, "Shhh."

Mike shifted his hand to Stephen's cheek and said, "We're safe. It's over."

Stephen shook his head and said, "No it's not! It's *not* over. Some asshole is out there who wants me. The cops don't even know who he is. Fuck! *I* don't even know who he is."

Mike smiled, put his hand on Stephen's shoulder and said, "And tomorrow, we're going to make a list of everyone it could be."

"We tried that," Stephen said quietly, the fight almost out of him.

"And tomorrow, we'll do it again. The cops will help us. My mom and dad and your . . . mom, will help too." Mike paused, smiled and said softly, "It's okay, Stephen. It's okay. We're safe."

Stephen stared at his friend. Mike smiled at him with his missing teeth and his black and blue swollen eye, his split lip and his bruised face.

"I really am sorry, Mike. I never wanted this to happen to you. Honest."

Mike rolled closer and wrapped his friend in his arms, his cheek resting gently on the side of Stephen's head. "It's okay. I have your back and you have mine. We're friends."

Stephen nodded and shut his eyes.

Mike did too. Smiling. And very proud he managed to not stutter at all.

• • •

Jennifer and Mark were going to say goodnight to the boys, but stopped when they heard them talking. They sat down on the steps and listened. Both wept and Mark held her tightly and kissed the side of her head.

Without speaking, they got up and went back upstairs.

PART THREE
DANCING WITH THE DEMONS

CHAPTER FIFTY-ONE

West Bend, Wisconsin

Tim sat at the kitchen table eating his fourth strip of bacon, swishing it around his plate to soak up the syrup that had run off the four pancakes he had eaten. Breakfast had always been his favorite meal. He loved the smell and taste of bacon. He loved French Toast and Pancakes with butter and syrup dripping off the edges. He was proud of the fact that he could almost eat his weight in anything his mother cooked for breakfast. At least, he could before he was held captive.

Since then, it had taken him several days to get his appetite back. He still slept lightly and in patches, waking up several times a night. Noises at night that before went unheard, now sounded like crescendos from timpani. Like the other boys, he'd wake up, wander around the house, only to sit in the silence of the backyard gazing up at the stars, the moon and the clouds and if lucky, doze until the sun had replaced them.

Tim picked up and rolled the Truvada between his thumb and forefinger. His mother must have gotten it from the prescription bottle in the cupboard and set it down next to his plate. The doctor at the hospital explained to him and to the other boys that it was for those at high risk to help avoid infection with the AIDS virus, and because of what the boys had been through over the past year or more, they were all at risk. Even Stephen and Mike. Though they had only been held for less than twenty-four hours, they had been forced to do most everything the others had been forced to do. The doctor explained that the precautions were necessary regardless of the length of time they were in captivity.

The boys didn't talk much about the possibility of getting HIV and AIDS. Actually, they tried not to think about it. Ian had summed up their feelings when he said, "Fuck it! We either get it or we don't. Not much we can do about it."

The doctor had also explained that Truvada was expensive. He remembered how his parents stood with arms around each other's shoulders when the doctor told them about it. It was Stephen's father who had asked what the cost was. The doctor explained that it was $1100 a month, but that an anonymous donor had paid for each of the boys to have a two-year supply. He watched his parents blink and his father nod and his mother bring her hand up to her mouth as tears sprung to her eyes. The boys didn't understand the significance until later when Mike had overheard a group of parents discussing what their health insurance would and wouldn't pay for. This anonymous donor, whoever he or she was, must have known that none of the parents could have afforded it, even with the best of insurance.

He popped the Truvada into his mouth and finished off his cranberry juice. He tipped back on his chair and stretched both arms high above his head.

"Tim, did you get enough to eat?"

Laura Pruett was thirty-four when she had had Tim. Now, her blond hair had a mousy look and her body had a more rounded shape than before Tim had been taken. During his captivity, she hadn't taken care of herself as she used to. Her shoulders slumped and instead of walking, she shuffled. Tim felt guilty about that, but didn't know what he could do to fix it. She had always been soft-spoken and reserved, but was more so since Tim's abduction. She was a head shorter than her boy, and though she'd deny it, Tim had always been her favorite.

Oh, she loved Thad and her daughter, Christi, Tim's younger sister. She loved them fiercely. But it was Tim she felt the closest to. The two of them had always talked. Whenever there was a question, a decision, Tim always sought her out. He'd confide in her. Mostly, they just talked about this and that.

Christi, who was three years younger than Tim, gravitated towards Thad. Christi would bake and cook with her, but it was Thad she preferred. Laura would tease her saying, "You have your dad wrapped around your finger." Christi would laugh and blush and Thad would protest, but not too strenuously because they all knew it was true.

They were a happy family. There was energy. There was life.

When Tim was taken, the energy and life went with him. Laura had hoped that now that Tim was back, the energy and life would come back.

The thumping of the basketball in the driveway brought Tim out of his reverie.

Déjà vu. It was as if the two plus years in captivity had melted into never happened.

Laura peered out the window by the sink as she was finishing up the breakfast dishes, watched as she rinsed the plate she had used, and then smiled to herself without turning around.

Tim carried his plate and glass to the sink and set them on the counter. He looked out the window to confirm what he already knew, kissed his mom on the cheek, gave her a little hug, and then disappeared.

He climbed the stairs two at a time and went into his bedroom to the closet and selected a pair of basketball shoes, hoping they wouldn't be too small. His toes were cramped but, what the hell, he'd make them work because he had some basketball to play. He stopped in the hallway bathroom outside his bedroom, brushed his teeth and smeared on some deodorant. He decided he'd skip the shower, because if he played two or three games of one on one or two on two, he'd be sweaty and gross and he'd have to shower again before the party. The deodorant was a compromise.

He took the stairs back down, quick-walked to the kitchen, gave his mother a kiss on the cheek, and walked to the backdoor that led to the driveway. He took a deep breath, and then stepped through the door and stood on the back porch after closing the screen door softly.

The tall boy with longish curly black hair wore a light blue Nike tank top, dark blue gym shorts with two thin white stripes running down each thigh, and expensive looking basketball shoes. He dribbled the basketball in a figure eight around and through his legs, concentrating so intently that he didn't notice Tim watching him. When he did, he stood up straight with the basketball on his right hip and stared at his friend.

"You've gotten better," Tim said with a smile.

The boy didn't say anything, but slow-dribbled the basketball using just his right hand.

Finally, he said, "You're back."

Tim nodded, smiled and said, "I am."

"Your hair is kinda long."

Tim laughed and said, "And yours isn't?"

"You look just like Cody on *Suite Life On Deck*."

That was the second or third time Tim had heard the comparison, so as he walked down the end of the driveway, he decided he'd have to check out the show to see if they were right.

He stood in front of the deeply tanned boy. The boy had grown to at least a half a head taller than Tim and his shoulders and chest had gotten broader. Self-consciously, Tim glanced at his own skinny arms and legs, a shell of what they were before he was taken. He felt embarrassed at how he looked, but determined he'd do something about it.

Usually if Cal was around, so was his brother Kaiden, younger by a year. "Where's Kaid?"

Cal stopped dribbling, held the ball on his right hip, and stared down at his shoes before answering.

"He's mowing the lawn. He'll be here in a little while," Cal said not looking at Tim.

"What's wrong?" Tim asked squinting at his friend.

Tim lived at the end of a cul de sac and Cal and Kaid lived just around the corner on Silverbrook Drive. Cal turned around and looked off in the direction of his house. Off in the distance, they could hear the mower, or at least *a* mower. It could have been Kaid.

"Listen . . ." Cal started. He stopped dribbling, shook his head and said, "Before he gets here, I have to tell you something."

Tim waited. Cal and Kaid were unusually close for brothers. They shared the same friends and were seldom away from each other. The fact that Cal stood in front of Tim without Kaid was unusual because one would generally wait for the other before going anywhere.

"When you were . . ." Cal searched for the right word and settled on, ". . . *gone*, Kaid had a really tough time."

"How so?"

"When you were gone, Kaid . . ." Cal stopped and shook his head and glanced towards his house again.

"What?" Tim said impatiently.

Cal wandered to the curb and sat down, his long legs stretched out in front of him.

Tim followed and sat down next to him.

"When you were gone, for the first couple of days, Kaid would come to your house, ring the doorbell and ask your parents if you were home. Then after a couple days, he wouldn't ring the doorbell, but would sit on your front porch and wait for you. That lasted about a week, maybe a couple days more. When Mom didn't see him around the house, she would send me to go find him and I always found him here, sitting on your front steps," he said jerking a thumb over his shoulder. "I'd get him and bring him home. I think he'd sit there all day and all night if he could."

Cal didn't, maybe couldn't, look at Tim. Instead, he stared towards Silverbrook Drive as if he were waiting for Kaid to appear.

He paused and shrugged before continuing. "There's other stuff. He sleeps with a light on, and if mom or dad turn it off after he falls asleep, he *loses* it. You know his temper, right?"

Tim nodded.

"He has nightmares and screams at night. That really freaks me out," Cal said with emphasis.

Cal paused once more, looked off in the distance and sighed.

"He got in a fight with Gavin."

"With Gavin?" Tim asked. "Why?"

Cal glanced at Tim, shrugged and said, "Just after you were gone, Gavin said something stupid."

"What did he say?" Tim frowned not understanding what Gavin might have said that would be stupid enough to cause a fight between him and Kaid.

Cal turned slightly, faced Tim and stared at him.

"What?" Tim asked again.

"I forget exactly. We were at baseball practice and the guys were talking about . . . you know, what might have happened to you and stuff."

Tim figured that would happen. He also knew it would probably happen again.

"Somebody said something, and somebody else said something, and I could tell Kaid was getting worked up." Cal looked at him intently and said, "You know you mean a lot to Kaid, right?"

Tim nodded.

"Well, Gavin said that maybe if you . . . you know, had to do stuff, maybe you'd end up gay or something. And Kaid punched Gavin and when Gavin went down, Kaid jumped on him and beat the shit out of him."

"Seriously? Kaid beat Gavin up over that?"

Cal opened his mouth to say something, but thought better of it.

"Didn't you try to stop him?"

Cal blinked in disbelief, thinking that Tim would be pissed at Gavin. He said, "It happened really fast. Before I could pull him off, he beat the shit out of him. Hell, when I grabbed him, he swung at *me*. Finally, Coach Schlicht came over, yelled at us, and called Gavin's mom, and Gavin went home, and that was the last we saw him."

Tim leaned back on his elbows stretching his legs out in front of him.

"You said that was the last you saw him," Tim said puzzled.

"Yeah."

"What about games or practice?"

Cal shook his head. "He quit the team."

Tim sat up and ran his hands through his hair, and said, "He quit?"

"Yeah."

"But, geez, Cal. We played basketball almost every day. Didn't you guys play after I was taken?"

Cal shook his head.

"Didn't you make Kaid apologize?"

Stunned, Cal said, "Kaid was sticking up for you. He was pissed at Gavin for saying you were gay."

Patiently, Tim said, "The four of us are friends, Cal. I like Gavin. I like you and I like Kaid. The four of us are friends."

Cal shrugged and looked away.

The two sat for a bit and finally Tim said, "Come on. Let's go get Kaid."

"He's mowing the lawn."

"It can wait."

Tim ran back into the house to change into the shoes his parents bought him when he was in the hospital. The basketball shoes he had on were too small and uncomfortable. He also wanted to let his mother know that he and Cal were going to go to Cal's house to get Kaiden. His mom protested, but he promised he'd be safe and that he'd return in an hour to help set up for the party.

The two boys walked back to the Mattenauer house side by side in silence. Cal wasn't sure what Tim was thinking, and Tim was so deeply intent on figuring out how to fix things between Kaid and Gavin that he didn't catch Cal sneaking glances at him.

"Are you pissed?" Cal asked when they reached Silverbrook and made the right turn towards Decorah Avenue and the Mattenauer house.

Tim wasn't sure. Angry was one feeling. Sad, because two of his friends had fought over him, was another.

"Yeah," Tim answered. They finished the walk in silence.

They reached the yard and stood on the lawn in the path of the oncoming self-propelled red Tecumseh, which Kaid pushed and ran behind to make the mowing go faster. When he saw them, he cut the engine and stared at Tim.

Kaid had the same curly black hair as Cal. He stood almost as tall as Tim and he looked physically bigger than Tim, but wasn't nearly as filled out as his older brother. He had softer features than Cal. Cal had more of a cut-in-granite look, while Kaid's was softer. Maybe Kaid was just better looking, cuter.

Cal watched the two of them stare at each other, lowered his eyes to the lawn, and then finally said, "Well, aren't you two gonna say hello or something?"

Without turning towards Cal, Tim smiled and said with a laugh, "Hello or something."

Kaid slowly walked forward and stood in front of Tim, blinking rapidly.

"Hey, Bud. I missed you," Tim said with a smile.

Kaid broke down and wept and Tim reached out and held him and let him cry into his shoulder, patting his back as he did so, and saying, "It's okay, Kaid. It's okay."

He felt Kaiden nod, but Kaiden's grip never loosened. Finally, Tim took Kaiden by the shoulders and said, "It's okay."

Kaiden wiped his eyes with his hands and then wiped his eyes with the bottom of his shirt. He stopped weeping, smiled at Tim and said, "Kind of a baby, huh?"

"Not really," Tim said with a smile and then he reached out and hugged Kaiden again.

"I missed you, Tim."

"I know. Me, too." Then he let go and asked, "How much more lawn do you have to do?"

"A little. I'm almost done."

"Okay, it can wait. Let's go."

"Where?"

"To Gavin's house," Tim said looking first at Kaiden and then at Cal. "We need to fix things."

Kaiden looked at Cal, but didn't say anything. Cal shrugged at him.

"I don't think he'll want to see me," Kaiden said quietly.

"We have to try," Tim said quietly. "You guys are my friends so we're going to try to get back to normal, okay?"

Reluctantly, Kaiden lowered his head and fell in step behind Tim who had already turned around to walk down the street away from the Mattenauer house, expecting the brothers to follow him.

The short walk was solemn and silent. They reached the Hemauer house and stood on the sidewalk, but the brothers hung back wanting to be anywhere else.

"Come on. We need to do this."

Tim moved forward with Cal a step behind. When Kaiden didn't move, Cal went back, took a gentle hold of his arm and led him forward. Tim stood on the porch and rang the doorbell. Cal and Kaid stood side by side on the sidewalk. Both had their heads down.

The door opened and Ellie Hemauer saw Tim. She covered her mouth with one hand and reached out to hug Tim with the other. Tears sprung to her eyes as she held and kissed him.

"Oh, my Lord!"

"Hi, Mrs. Hemauer."

"Oh my God, Tim Pruett! I've been praying for you. Oh my God!" Then she turned around and said, "Gavin! Gavin! Come see who's here!"

Then to Tim, she said, "Come in! Come in!"

As she was shutting the door, Tim said, "Mrs. Hemauer, can Cal and Kaiden come in? We have to talk to Gavin."

Ellie looked over Tim's shoulder and saw the brothers. She glanced at them without expression, staring mostly at Kaiden, and then turned her attention to Tim.

"I need to try to fix things," Tim said quietly. "Please?"

Reluctantly, Ellie held the door open for Cal and Kaiden, who entered the home quietly, sliding in and away from her, afraid she would smack them.

Ellie led them into the kitchen. Cal and Kaiden lingered in the entry hallway, not quite in the kitchen with Kaiden hiding behind his older brother. Ellie and Tim faced the back hallway waiting for Gavin to appear.

Gavin came out of his room yawning, saw Tim and stopped in his tracks, mouth still open but not from the yawn. He blinked and reached out to touch the wall to catch his balance.

"Hey, Gav," Tim said with a smile.

Gavin stepped into the kitchen and stood in front of Tim. Of the four boys, Gavin had always been the shortest, but now, he stood eye to eye with Tim. He had brown hair, green eyes and a smattering of small freckles on his nose and under his eyes. He was also the quietest. As Cal would often say, "Gav, I don't know if you'd say shit if your mouth was full of it." Gavin would smile and shrug. Tim thought it was funny that whenever Gavin smiled, his eyes disappeared.

He wasn't smiling now.

"Hi," Tim said.

Gavin stared at him and when Tim reached out to place a hand on his shoulder, he flinched. Tim felt sad.

When Gavin spied Cal and then Kaid, he retreated two steps, glanced at his mother, then at Tim, and then back at Cal and Kaid. He took another step backward. The fear on his face was real, and Tim could feel the tension in the kitchen. Ellie stood close to Gavin, but didn't say anything.

"Gavin," Tim said softly, "I want to try to fix things between you and Kaid and Cal. We're friends, or at least we were. I want us to be friends again."

Gavin looked at Cal and Kaiden, then at Tim, then at his mom, and then back at Tim. Tim suspected that Gavin was about to cry.

"Cal and Kaiden, come in here. I have something I want to say to all of you."

The two brothers took a step closer, but more or less stayed behind Tim. They faced Mrs. Hemauer but didn't dare look at her. They glanced at Gavin every so often without sustaining any significant or prolonged eye contact.

Sadly, Tim said, "Listen, please." The brothers looked up and stared at Tim, as did Gavin and Ellie.

"Guys, I don't know what happened and I don't care. All I know is that the four of us are friends."

The three boys stared at him, glanced at each other, and then back at Tim.

"I was gone over two years. I was almost killed twice and I lost a lot of friends." He wiped his eyes with his hands and continued. "My friend Johnny died. He was really sick and maybe if we would have been rescued sooner, he would have lived. But he didn't."

Tim's voice caught and the lump in his chest grew, making it hard for him to speak. He wiped his eyes again.

"The first couple days and nights after I was taken, I was really scared. Johnny helped me. He helped all of us, and I really miss him." He stopped, looked at the floor.

"There was this other guy, Ryan. He was taken away the morning we were rescued. They took him away in handcuffs and they killed him. There were other guys they took away and none of us knew who would be taken next. We just knew that if they came to get us, we wouldn't be seen again. We'd be dead.

"My friend, Brett," Tim wept silently. "He got shot trying to save us and his shoulder's all screwed up. He might never get to play football or basketball again, but he risked all of that to save us."

Ellie reached for a tissue and dabbed her eyes. Cal had started to weep, and he and Gavin wiped their eyes with their hands, while Kaid used the bottom of his t-shirt.

"There's this other guy, George. His whole family was murdered. His *whole family*. He saved my life in the hospital when a man tried to take me. George stood in his way and wouldn't move. He had a gun pointed right at his face, but he never moved. He didn't even flinch. He did that for me and he didn't even know me."

Tim wiped his eyes on his shirt sleeves.

"I can't worry about the four of us because I'm worried about Brett and George. I'm worried about two other guys, Mike and Steve. There are perverts out there trying to kill them. They're my *friends*! I worry about *them*! That's who I have to worry about, so I can't worry about *us*."

The four boys were weeping pretty freely now.

"Gavin, I was really stupid. I was worried about Tim and I lost my temper, and I should never have hit you. I wanted to apologize, but I didn't know how." Kaiden had trouble getting it all out, but felt relieved that he did. "I called, but when you or your mom answered, I hung up. I was afraid, and I'm really sorry. If you want to hit me, you can 'cause I deserve it."

"No one's hitting anyone," Tim said sadly. "Friends don't hit friends."

"I said something stupid, but I didn't mean it the way it came out," Gavin pleaded. He took a deep breath, stared at Tim and said, "I said that if men forced you to . . . you know . . . *do* stuff, then you might be gay. But that's not what I meant to say. I didn't know what I wanted to say, but I know that's not what I meant," Gavin said.

"Kaid, you had no right to beat up Gavin," Tim said staring at Kaiden. "Friends don't beat up friends. You could have said something like, 'That was stupid' and then forget about it. You don't beat up friends."

"I know," Kaiden said to his shoes.

"There's going to be a lot of stuff said about me and you can't beat someone up every time you hear somebody say something stupid. Okay?"

Kaiden nodded, resting his chin on his chest.

Tim held out his arm to Kaiden and said, "Kaid, come here."

Kaiden stepped forward and Tim put his arm around his shoulders. And then to Gavin, Tim said, "Gav, come here."

Gavin hesitated and glanced at Tim, who nodded at him. He stepped next to Tim, who placed his other arm around Gavin's shoulders. He gave both boys a gentle hug.

"Cal, come here."

Cal stepped forward and faced Tim and like him, placed his arms around Kaiden's and Gavin's shoulders.

Tim wept.

"I want us to be friends. We were friends before I was taken. Please, I can't worry about us. I can't. I've got Brett and George and Stephen and Mike to worry about. I worry about the next phone call," Tim's voice caught. He could hardly breathe. He struggled and stammered, "I worry that the next phone call I get will be someone telling me that one of them is dead." He wiped his eyes and in a small, quiet voice said, "I can't worry about us."

It was a relief for him to talk about it, but at the same time, verbalizing his biggest fear brought it all into focus. Perhaps this was what was causing him to feel out of place. Perhaps this was what made him feel like he didn't belong. He needed to be with his friends. With Brett, George, Mike and Stephen. He knew he couldn't, but he knew he needed to be.

"Are you okay?" Cal asked, eyeing him closely.

He nodded and said, "My parents are having a party this afternoon. I want you guys to come. You too, Gavin."

Gavin glanced at his mother. He stared at his shoes, then at Tim, then at Kaiden, but didn't commit one way or the other.

Ellie cleared her throat and said, "We'll be there."

Tim nodded at her, smiled at Gavin, and gave his shoulder a squeeze.

"I missed you." He paused, looked down at his shoes, blinked back tears, and then looked at each boy. "When I was taken, I wondered if I'd ever see you again. All that time, I wondered if you'd even remember me. And then, when I was in the hospital, I was afraid to see you because I didn't know what you thought of me. I was afraid."

"Shit, Tim . . . excuse my language, Mrs. Hemauer . . . shoot, Tim, why would we forget you?" Cal asked.

"Well, you forgot you guys were friends, right?" Tim asked.

The boys looked at one another and then down at their shoes.

Kaiden reached across the small circle, put his hands on Gavin's shoulders and said, "Gavin, I'm sorry. Honest. Please forgive me."

Tim watched Gavin flinch away and he could see the hurt in Gavin's eyes, in his body.

"At school I know guys made fun of you. I know you were by yourself a lot," Cal said. "I . . . shit, I don't know."

"Please forgive me . . . us," Kaiden pleaded.

Gavin looked first at Tim, then at Cal and then at Kaiden.

"I know it might take some time, but we're friends, right?" Tim said.

The boys nodded.

Maybe one less thing to worry about.

CHAPTER FIFTY-TWO

Fishers, Indiana

The room was comfortable but small with typical hotel furnishings: a desk and hard-backed chair, an over-stuffed but uncomfortable chair in a red floral print with a matching ottoman, two queen-sized beds with five or six pillows of various sizes and thicknesses on each, a cheap one-serving coffee machine and two black plastic mugs, four glasses with an ice container that was empty except for a plastic bag that served as a liner, and a four-drawer dresser with a flat screen TV on top of it. It didn't matter if the room was on the first or second floor. Each room was the same except for the color pattern.

Pete's alarm had gone off at 4:30 AM, but he had pushed the snooze button twice so he crawled out of bed a little before 4:50. He had showered, shaved, brushed his teeth and smoothed his close-cropped salt and pepper flat-top. He dressed in a pale blue button-down short-sleeved shirt with a yellow and blue striped tie, and dark slacks that would fit nicely with a light-weight sport coat that hung in the closet. He didn't shop at Jos. A. Banks or S & K. Anything in his drawers or closet could be found in any of the thousands of Sears stores across the country.

He never went anywhere without his .45 stuffed snuggly into his leather shoulder holster under his left arm. Pete opted for the .45 because he didn't like the feel of the Glock .22 or .23 that was issued to new FBI recruits. He was old school and had argued that his .45 worked better for him because of the heft of it, and he knew that when he shot at someone, the slug would tear a whole in and mostly through whatever he aimed at.

Skip and Chet wanted to sleep in, so alone, he drove to a Denny's where he had eaten a breakfast of oatmeal and a chocolate muffin, with a Diet Coke to wash it down. He glanced at the paper and then had driven back to the hotel. He flipped between CNN and the local news searching for anything on his perps. The coverage of the sieges in Chicago, Long Beach and in Kansas City had dried up and had mostly played out, except for what was happening with the *ones who got away.*

Normally, Pete was quiet. He left the media to Summer or others who were better in front of the camera. He didn't want the spotlight and didn't seek the headlines. He was a cop in a suit, an investigator who operated best on his feet out in the field. He didn't like the politics of the job, and just as he did with the media, left that for others.

He didn't leave many messes for others to clean up. While no one mentioned it, the *ones who got away* were loose ends that needed to be tied up because if they weren't, they would become a mess that either he or others would have to clean up.

He was startled out of his thoughts by a rap on the door. With his hand on his gun, he looked out the window and saw Skip Dahlke leaning against the railing outside his room. Skip gave him a nod when he saw Pete at the window, and then Pete opened the door for him to enter.

"Morning," was all Skip said as he stood momentarily just inside the room. He moved to the edge of a bed that didn't have a slept-in look and sat down.

"You eat?"

Skip shook his head. "Not hungry."

"You have to eat something. You're too skinny and it might be a long day."

Skip shrugged and yawned tiredly.

After leaving the McGovern house the afternoon before, he had borrowed Pete's car and using the directions MB had given him, drove out to the mall to pick up a couple of polo shirts, a couple of button-down white shirts, two pair of slacks, and a dark sport coat that would match whatever shirts or slacks he chose to wear. This day, Skip wore a black polo with khaki slacks and loafers. He carried his sport coat and laid it over the arm of the stuffed chair. He wore his side arm on his belt at his right hand. On his left side was his iPhone.

"Is Chet up yet?" Skip asked.

Pete grunted and said, "If he is, just barely."

Chet was a night owl who stayed up late surfing the web, checking leads, and checking in with Morgan to find out if there was any cell traffic. Even having Cochrane's cell hadn't helped. Either the bad guys knew Cochrane was dead and weren't using their cells to communicate, or they were lying low and waiting.

Skip pulled out his cell and hadn't even finished tapping in Chet's number when there was a knock on the door. He leaned towards the window, saw Chet, and then went to the door and opened it for him.

Chet flopped down in the red floral print stuffed chair waiting for orders.

Pete took out his cell, hit speed dial, and turned on the speaker function so the three of them could listen together.

"Right on time," Summer said as she answered on the first ring. "Who's with you?"

"Chet and Skip."

"Chet, any word from Morgan?" Summer didn't waste any time because there wasn't any to waste.

"Nothing," Chet said shaking his head. "There isn't anything coming over Cochrane's cell. No email coming to his laptop, and nothing coming into any other cell that we're monitoring. Nothing."

"Skip, what did you find at Dominico's house."

"Just what I put in the report. Like it was wiped clean other than his own prints."

The three men heard papers ruffling on the other end and then Summer said, "Tell me about the hole in the floor."

Skip sat up straighter, leaned towards the phone and said, "It wasn't a hole. It was more of a cut-out. I doubt if anyone would have found it if it weren't already open. It measured twelve inches in length, twelve inches in width and fifteen inches in depth." He paused to see if Summer or anyone else had any questions. When none came, he said, "I found what seemed to be an oily substance at the bottom. I'm guessing gun lubricant. Other than that, it was clean. Like I said, his house looked like he had wiped everything down."

There wasn't anything new and nothing but dead ends all the way around.

"Pete, any ideas?"

He ran his hand over his hair, looked at both men in the room and then said, "Two options, I think. But first, was anything found at Cochrane's residence or office?"

"Nothing," Summer answered. "He was thorough, not sloppy."

Pete puffed up his cheeks and then blew them out.

"Um . . ." Skip said, waiting for permission to speak further.

"Skip, speak freely. You're part of the team," Summer said.

"I was wondering, in Cochrane's apartment or home or whatever, did they find a hole or cutout like Dominico had?"

They heard Summer shuffling papers and then she said, "No. I don't see anything like that in the report."

Skip frowned and shook his head.

"What?" Pete asked.

"I bet there is one. It just wasn't found."

"Summer, there isn't anything for Skip and Chet to do here. I'd like to send them back to Chicago to tear apart Cochrane's place? If Skip's right, we might be able to find a lead."

"Okay. Guys, get back to Chicago and like Pete said, tear the place apart."

"Will do," Skip said.

"Pete, what will you do?"

"Stay here. The McGovern family is under protection inside and out. It's just a matter of waiting."

"Any other ideas?" Summer asked.

Skip and Chet looked at Pete, expecting him to answer for them.

"I can't help but think we're missing something. Something obvious. I just can't put my finger on what it is."

"Can you narrow it down some?" Summer asked.

Pete shook his head and said, "No. There's something right in front of us, but we're not seeing it."

Chet frowned. Skip tilted his head as he thought. Pete ran his hand over his flattop.

"I don't know what to tell you," Summer said. "Just keep picking at it."

"Yeah, I will."

"Any other ideas?"

Pete lowered his head and then said, "Well one. We could wait and see what happens. The second would be to push them some. We release their pictures, including Dominico's new look according to Pressman's description. That might force them into action."

"Or it could send them running for cover," Chet said.

Pete nodded considering the viewpoint, one he had already thought of.

"Possibly, but I don't think so," Pete said quietly. "These assholes are arrogant. They're used to having it their way. They're used to acting as if they won't get caught. I've read and reread MB's report on Dominico. He *especially*. He won't run. He won't hide. I think it will force him to act."

"Would Brett and his family be safe," Skip asked. "They've been through a lot."

"I've coordinated with Jamie Graff on that, and they should be in place this morning. We already have someone with the family at all times," Pete answered.

"I know I'm new to this, but what if the family gets split up? Brett and his brother go to a friend's house or Thomas or Victoria go to work? What happens then?" Skip asked.

"Good question," Pete said with a smile, followed by a shrug. "That's one reason we need to get this group to act. The longer this takes, the harder it'll be to contain the situation. The sort of protection we're providing is expensive in terms of man hours. We can't account for every contingency, and it won't be long before the McGovern's ask us to leave."

Pete knew he never directly answered Skip's question. He couldn't because he didn't have an answer for him.

Pete continued, "We know that three of them are going to be in Arizona when George, Jeremy and Randy get there. I've set up a net to let them in, but not let them out. Dangerous, yes. Easy, no. But I feel confident we'll be able to protect them as well as get whoever comes after them."

Skip lifted his head and looked first at Pete, then at Chet. "We're sure George and the others will be safe?" Skip asked.

"As sure as we can be, Skip. There are a lot of unknowns and variables we can't control," Summer answered.

"Do Jeremy and George know?"

Pete hesitated, his eyes looking away from him to the phone, darting to Chet, and then back to Skip. "We've given them a plan, but it's fluid."

Both Chet and Skip looked at each other and it was Chet who spoke for them.

"What you're saying is, you're using them as bait."

Pete frowned, opened his mouth to speak, but Summer cut him off.

"Chet, we have a plan. They're aware of the plan and have agreed to it. It's been vetted by Dandridge. They'll be protected and there will be precautions."

"So, they're bait," Chet said firmly.

"It's the only way we know to get these assholes. If we don't get them now or very soon, the time will come when there'll be no more protection or help for them, and then they're sitting ducks. We might as well paint a bull's eye on them."

"Seems like you've already done that," Skip said quietly.

CHAPTER FIFTY-THREE

Waukesha, Wisconsin

Detective Jamie Graff stood about five-eleven or six foot. His dark complexion, dark eyes and dark, wavy hair worn on the short side gave him a Latino look, but he wasn't Latino at all. Of the three Js, he was the quiet one and the most intense, certainly the most serious. It wasn't that he didn't talk or laugh, but mostly, he was an observer, a listener who took in and processed everything around him. Like his eyes, his mind never stopped working. As a detective, he was a chess master who stayed three or four moves ahead of his opponent, and his current opponent was whomever had tried to have Stephen kidnapped.

They sat around the Bailey kitchen table with coffee cups or glasses of milk or juice either empty or nearly so. Stephen and Mike sat next to each other on one side facing their mothers Sarah and Jennifer. Jamie sat at the head of the table. Neither Ted Bailey nor Mark Erickson sat. Instead, they leaned against the counter watching and listening, but kept their distance from one another. Ted glowered in the corner sipping his coffee, wishing it was a cold beer.

The boys and their mothers had been discussing various men in the boys' lives. Barry Miller, their soccer coach, was the first man on the list. The mothers considered him a long shot because he appeared happily married and had two young ones of his own. They discussed two teachers: Gordon Franklin and Richard Reif, both single and who were considered by the boys as being fun, nice guys and good teachers. Franklin taught mathematics, and Reif, science.

"I feel bad putting them on the list," Stephen said quietly.

"You can't feel that way, Honey," Sarah said. "Detective Graff has to consider everyone."

"Your mom's right," Graff said. "Who else is on the list?"

Stephen shrugged and said, "I put Lucky on the list, but I don't think it's him either."

"Lucky?" Jamie asked.

"Stephen takes tennis lessons at the Waukesha Racquet Club and he's one of the instructors," Sarah answered.

"Bob Luchsinger? The dark-haired guy?" Jennifer asked. She and Mike took lessons there too, but she had never worked with him. Mike had on occasion, but only when paired with Stephen.

"Yeah," Mike answered. "He's a good guy."

Jamie took the list from Stephen and scanned the list of seven names, wishing he had his chew.

"Both of you put this list together?"

The boys nodded.

"Stephen, I'm going to ask you some questions, and I want you to consider each one carefully, okay?" He handed the list back to Stephen, and then looked at Mike and said, "Because you're his friend, you're in a good position to notice things Stephen might not, okay?"

The boys nodded.

Jamie had worked abuse cases and sex crimes with Jeremy, and not only took notes on the various kids' responses, but also took notes on the types of questions Jeremy asked.

"Of the men on this list, is there anyone who gave you extra attention, any unexpected gifts?"

Stephen looked at his mom as he thought about it. Jeremy had asked him the same question at the hospital.

"I got a birthday cards from Lucky and Mr. Franklin."

Jamie looked at Mike and asked, "Did you get a birthday card from either of them?"

"From Mr. Franklin. I got one from Mr. Reif, but other guys did too."

Jamie made some notes. His handwriting was small, cramped and unreadable except by him. It was a common complaint in the department.

"Lucky asked me to be his partner for a doubles tournament."

Jamie looked up from his notes. "Do you consider that, I don't know . . . unusual?"

Stephen looked at his mother and shrugged.

Sarah answered for him. "It is a father-son tourney. Ted doesn't play, and Stephen is pretty good."

"The fact that Stephen and Luchsinger aren't father and son, is that acceptable?"

"It happens. Several adults play with kids who aren't their sons," Sarah answered.

"How good a tennis player are you?" Graff asked.

Stephen made a face, shrugged and said, "I'm pretty good, but not that good. Mike's better than I am."

"Maybe," Mike offered.

Graff made more notes.

"Okay, think about this one. Is there anyone on this list who touched or touches you anywhere from your shoulder to your knee?"

Stephen sat back and looked at Mike. Mike cocked his head, squinted in thought and then his expression changed subtly, but enough for Jamie to notice.

"What?"

Mike looked back at Stephen and then at Jamie.

"Franklin hugs kids. Not girls, just guys."

"What do you mean he hugs guys?" Ted asked.

Mike glanced at Stephen and waited for Stephen to respond to his father.

"I don't know," Stephen shrugged. "When we're working on math problems and we ask for help, he'll put his arm around your shoulder like this." He stood up and demonstrated on Mike. He sort of bent over him and slipped his arm around Mike's shoulders, gave his shoulder a little squeeze and said, "Like this."

To Jamie, it looked innocent, like something a caring individual might do for encouragement. The fact that he didn't hug girls was understandable: he was a single guy and hugging girls might get you in trouble, whereas guys not so much unless you hugged the wrong one. And, to Jamie, it couldn't really be described as a hug. Still, Franklin was worth a closer look.

"Anyone else touch you between your shoulder and knee?"

"Well Coach Miller after a game. My goalie coach after a workout."

Jamie scanned the list and asked, "What's your goalie coach's name?"

"We didn't put him on the list," Stephen said apologetically. "I . . . we didn't think of him."

"What's his name?"

"Bill Weston," Sarah said.

"Why didn't you put him on the list?" Jamie asked.

"I don't know," Stephen said with a shrug. "I didn't think of him." He shrugged again.

"Right," Ted said in disgust.

"What?" Stephen asked.

Ted shook his head and looked away.

"What?" Stephen asked angrily.

Ted didn't answer, but glanced at him and then turned away again.

"You think I didn't put him on the list on purpose? Bill didn't do anything to me except give me high fives or punch my arm . . . just goofing around. He didn't do anything to me."

"Mike, why did you think of him?" Jamie asked.

Mike glanced at Stephen and said, "Sometimes after a workout or sometimes after a game, he'd give you a hug or, you know, smack your butt."

Stephen looked from Mike to his mom and then to Jamie said, "But that's nothing. It's no big deal. He doesn't mean anything by it."

"Right," Ted said.

"What?" Stephen demanded.

"Ted, shut the hell up and leave!" Sarah said getting up from the table and facing him.

"You've been an ass since the hospital and I'm sick of it. Pack your bags and get out. Now!"

Ted didn't move. He didn't flinch. He glared at Sarah.

"I said, get *out*! *Now*!" Sarah shouted. "I don't want you around Stephen any longer."

She dissolved into tears and Jennifer stood up to comfort her, wrapping Sarah in her arms. Her tears, however, didn't make her weak.

"Boys, why don't you go to Stephen's room," Mark suggested.

"Don't you tell my son where he should go! This is *my* house!" Ted shouted.

"Folks calm down," Jamie said standing up. He noticed that Ted stood near the kitchen knives, steak knives and butcher knife on the counter in a wooden holder, so as a precaution, he moved closer to the boys.

Mike tugged on Stephen's arm, but Stephen didn't budge.

"You think I wanted all this shit to happen, don't you?" Stephen asked. "You think I wanted to do that shit with those perverts."

Mike tugged on Stephen's arm trying to pull him from the kitchen but Stephen pulled away from him.

"You think I'm gay," Stephen said, tears streaming down his face. "I'm not. I'm not gay. I didn't want any of this shit to happen! *None* of it!" Stephen shouted.

"Ted, why don't you-" Mark started.

"-don't you *dare* tell me what I should or shouldn't do," Ted said through gritted teeth, pointing a meaty finger at him.

Jamie watched Stephen's father knowing he was the dangerous one in the room. Slowly, he placed himself between Ted and the boys, pushing the boys behind him towards the family room and hallway to what he presumed led to bedrooms.

Stephen shook with anger. Mike had his arm around his friend and glared at Stephen's father.

Sarah composed herself and said, "Ted, I asked you to leave. If you don't, I'll ask Detective Graff to arrest you."

"*Arrest me?*"

"I want you out of this house. I'm not asking you. I'm telling you. You can come back later to pick up some clothes. I'll have a suitcase on the front step." Sarah sighed, wiped tears from her eyes and said, "Leave now."

Ted threw his cup in the sink where it shattered. What was left of his coffee splashed on the counter, the floor and on the curtains on the window above the sink. He took one last look, grabbed car keys off the counter and stormed out, slamming the screen door behind him. The car started up and the tires squealed as he backed up out of the driveway.

They stood facing the back door expecting Ted to reappear, but as the sound of the car faded away, each of them began to breathe again.

CHAPTER FIFTY-FOUR

Waukesha, Wisconsin

A half-hour later with Graff pushing and pulling the boys through the list, he felt he had a pretty good idea where he wanted to begin the investigation. They worked through the names and the most likely were the two teachers, Franklin and Reif, the tennis coach, Bob Luchsinger, and the goalie coach, Bill Weston. Or, it could be none of the four, someone else on the list that wasn't as visible as the others or even someone not on the list. Graff had a lot of work ahead of him.

"I almost forgot," Mike said. "Did you give that kid our letter?"

He and Stephen wanted to thank the boy for helping them get freed, but knew it was confidential. They were determined to meet and thank him in person, so they wrote a letter and had asked Jamie to deliver it to him, hoping that the boy would contact them. So far, he hadn't.

Jamie nodded and said, "Gave it to him the day before yesterday."

"And?" Mike asked.

Jamie shrugged and said, "Might take some time. He's a pretty quiet kid."

Mike felt deflated. He was disappointed that he hadn't called either of them.

"Can I ask a question?" Stephen asked.

"Shoot."

Stephen glanced at Mike, then down at his hands, and then directly at the detective.

"How much danger am I in? I mean, is this guy, whoever he is, gonna kill me?"

Graff sighed. He spent two hours with an FBI profiler and came away unconvinced at anything she had suggested because it sounded vague and inconclusive. He wasn't a big fan of profilers, but he had to consider every avenue.

"I don't have a good answer for you." He scratched his head and said, "Until we know who this guy is, we think it's prudent to keep watch on you, Mike, and your families. We know what those other men are . . . *were* capable of. But this guy, we don't know anything about him.

"Here's what I think. I think that if this guy meant any harm to you, he would have acted a long time ago. Think about it. This guy, whoever he is, knows you. He's watched you. Chances are you know him. He blends in, doesn't stick out, and keeps a low profile. I don't mean to scare you, but he wants you for sex, which means he wants you alive."

"I don't want to have sex with him, honest!" Stephen said, his voice rising.

"Honey, we know that," Sarah said, reaching across the table towards her son's hand. Stephen withdrew his hands and put them in his lap, his eyes down at the table.

"All I'm saying is that the likelihood of this guy wanting to hurt you is pretty low," Jamie said reassuringly.

"But you don't know that for sure," Stephen said.

"You're right. We don't know for sure, and that's why we'll have eyes on you and Mike at all times, day and night."

Jamie waited for a question and when he didn't get any, he said, "You two will have to stick together. If for some reason you can't, at least be with one other person. I'd prefer that you don't do anything by yourselves. Make sure your parents know where you're going and with whom. Daylight is always safer than nighttime."

"But if Mike hangs out with me, I might be putting him in danger. Maybe he and I shouldn't hang out for a while."

Mike turned to him and said, "No way! Stephen, we talked about this last night. I'm not letting you fight this by yourself."

"But-"

"-No buts! You're my best friend. We're going to be together."

Stephen looked at his friend. Mike, with a bruised and blackened eye, swollen cheek, missing and loose teeth. His friend, who the night before held him as he fell asleep. His friend who refused to back down and who had assured him that he had his back and always will. His best friend.

He nodded. He didn't agree with Mike. He still felt that Mike would be in danger. But he nodded because Mike was his friend and if there was anyone he had ever wanted to be with, that person was Mike.

Turning to the two mothers and Mark, Jamie said, "If at all possible, try to stay with the boys."

"You said there will be protection for the Mike and Stephen?" Jennifer asked, glancing at Mike.

Jamie nodded and said, "Yes. They will be watched. You won't necessarily know them and chances are, you might not see them. But they'll be around the boys at all times."

Jennifer reached out and clutched Sarah's hand.

Graff smiled at the two boys and repeated his earlier instructions, "Just be careful, think before you do anything, and, this is really important, make sure you stay together as much as possible. Make sure your parents know where you are and where you're going at all times. Okay?"

The boys nodded, grim-faced and serious.

It seemed to Jamie that for twelve-year-olds, Stephen and Mike looked at once both young and old. Prematurely aged. With good reason. Someone was out there who was after them.

CHAPTER FIFTY-FIVE

Fishers, Indiana

"But you have to admit, Purdue is the weakest basketball team in the Big Ten."

Brett had been after Cleve Batiste ever since he had replaced MB that morning and found out he had played basketball for Purdue.

Cleveland Batiste stood six-one and was wiry, muscled and put together tightly. If the man had ten ounces of fat on him, no one knew where it was.

"No, that would be Northwestern," Batiste said quietly sipping some orange juice that Bobby had poured for him.

"What was your best game?" Bobby asked.

"Ohio State my senior year. I had fourteen points, six steals and eight assists."

"State's tough, but still, *Purdue?*" Brett said with disdain.

"Good school," Batiste said into his glass.

"Butler's better," Bobby said.

Cleve faked choking, pounded his chest and coughed. "Seriously, the Bullfrogs?"

"Bulldogs!" Bobby said.

"Yeah, whatever," Batiste said dismissively. "Northwestern and Minnesota, the worst and the *second* worst team in the Big Ten would beat them by fifteen. Maybe twenty."

"Who did you have your worst game against?" Bobby asked.

"Just about everybody," Brett said with a smirk.

Victoria had been semi-reading the paper and drinking her coffee, amused at the conversation in her kitchen. She couldn't help but smile. Thomas was still in the back getting dressed and she wished he was out here listening with her.

"Kid, there's a house across the street with a basketball hoop and I'll take you there and kick your butt!"

"Um, you might not have noticed, but my arm is in a sling?" Brett said lifting it up slightly.

"Oh, I see. Big talker can't back it up 'cause he has an itty bitty booboo," Batiste said faking sadness.

Brett left the kitchen, went to the living room window, looked out, and said over his shoulder to his mother, "Mom, do you know who's living kiddie corner from us?"

"I don't think anyone is, Honey. The house has been for sale."

"I don't see a For Sale sign," Brett said. "Think they'd mind if we went over there to shoot some hoop?"

"Brett, your shoulder isn't ready for that yet," his mother cautioned. "But if you take it easy, maybe you can play horse or something."

Horse sucks, he thought. *Screw it, I'm playing basketball.*

"Well, come on," Brett said, and then added, "I wonder what your FBI friends will say when I kick your-"

"-Brett!"

"-butt."

"There is no way in . . . sorry, Missus M, but there is no way I'm losing to you and your brother."

Bobby ran back to his room, grabbed a basketball and the three of them left the kitchen by the backdoor. Brett threw a playful elbow into Cleve's ribs and he responded by grabbing both boys and placing them in headlocks as they crossed the street.

His eyes, however, were conscious of the street, the parked cars, and anyone looking out windows. His Glock .22 was in a holster in the middle of his back tucked under his t-shirt.

Normally a shirt and tie guy, he knew the boys were athletic and he wanted them to get out for some exercise. Perhaps, he wanted to get out and get some exercise himself, so he wore a black Adidas warm-up suit, an Under Armor t-shirt and a pair of well-worn Air Jordan's. In his duffle-bag were other clothes and shoes he could change into.

He was a four-year letter winner at Purdue majoring in Sociology and Criminal Justice. By Big Ten basketball standards, he was better than average but not outstanding. Originally his hard-nosed college coach, Gene Keady, thought of him as a point guard. But by the middle of his junior year, Keady alternated him between point guard and shooting guard. Keady's style was a little like football: beat up the opponent on defense, take conservative shots, beat up the opponent, pound the boards, and then beat up the opponent some more.

Batiste fit Keady's prototype as a football player who played basketball: quiet, solid, not given to talking trash, determined with a no-quit attitude. It earned him Honorable Mention Big Ten as a junior and senior. That description also fit Batiste as an FBI agent.

"Better check to see if anyone's home," Cleve said.

Bobby rang the bell and a tall, slender brunette answered the door.

"Yes?" She saw the boy with the sling bouncing the ball and the muscular black man next to him. The black man nodded slightly and she nodded back.

"Hi. We live across the street, over there," Bobby said throwing a thumb over his shoulder. "We were wondering if we could use your basketball hoop."

"As a matter of fact, my husband Tom and I were about to play a game of one on one to see who's going to mow the lawn. Why don't we play some two on two or three on two?"

Bobby turned around and gave Brett and Cleve a 'what-the-heck-look'.

"I'm Brooke," she said still in the doorway and then she turned slightly and said back into the house, "Tom, we've got a game to play."

From somewhere in the back they heard a, "Yeah, yeah."

She stepped onto the front stoop wearing a red Wisconsin Badger tank-top, black shorts and a pair of beat-up basketball shoes.

"Oh, man," Brett moaned.

"What?" Brooke asked with a smile.

"You're from Wisconsin?"

"I played at Green Bay and went to the NCAA tournament four years in a row."

"Huh," was all Brett managed.

"Huh, yourself," Brooke said with a laugh. "Keep that up and I'll kick your scrawny butt along with my husband's."

"Hey guys," Tom said coming up the driveway from back by the garage. "Who's kicking whose butt?" He stood maybe five-eleven, thickly built like someone who pumped iron. He had sandy brown hair and blue eyes. "What are the teams?"

Standing next to each other, he stood half a head shorter than his wife. She clapped her hands requesting a pass from Brett who obliged. She took it, pivoted and sunk a twelve-footer that banked off the backboard neatly and cleanly.

"Yeah, what are the teams?" she said with a smile.

"Damn, I'm with her!" Bobby said with a laugh, which earned him a high five and a smile from her.

After introductions, Bobby and Brooke ended up on one team, with Tom, Cleve and Brett on the other. Brett had discarded his sling and struggled with his left arm, grimacing in pain with each pass and each time he tried to dribble left-handed.

Brooke was really good. It didn't matter if she shot from the outside with Cleve in her face or when she drove past him on her way to the hoop, she made everything she put up and ended it with an annoying giggle. That was all the trash talking she did, but it was enough to get their goats.

Tom was a lefty, mostly a shooter, but had a smooth move to the bucket. Not nearly in Brooke's or Cleve's class, but not bad.

It was Bobby that had impressed Brett the most. Brett had no idea his brother could play.

Before he was taken, he couldn't remember Bobby ever playing basketball. He had a really nice jump shot, a nice shot off a dribble-drive, and a nice no-look pass that fooled him several times.

Down by four Cleve asked, "How you doin' Buddy?"

"I suck!" Brett said in disgust. "My left arm is *fu* . . . useless."

"Take a break if you need to," Tom suggested.

"I don't need a break. I need my left arm back."

He could still play defense and he could still pass the ball, but his shot was rusty and his timing was a step or two behind his mind. More than anything, it was the lack of timing that frustrated him. Brett knew what to do and how to do it, but his body couldn't seem to follow orders from his mind.

"You're rusty, that's all," Bobby said.

"I suck!" Brett responded. He sat down on the front lawn at the edge of the driveway court and wiped his sweaty face on the front of his shirt.

"Who's thirsty?" Brooke asked brightly.

"I could use water or iced tea," Tom said. "Anyone else?"

"Water," Bobby said sitting down next to his brother.

"Water for me too," Cleve said wiping his face on the front of his shirt.

Brooke disappeared into the house and came out a minute or two later with five bottles of water and an icepack. She handed a bottle and the icepack to Brett and said, "Here. It's probably swelling. Are you on any meds?"

"I'm using Motrin."

"When was the last time you had some?"

"When I got up this morning. Too early for any more," Brett said taking a swig from the bottle. He placed the icepack on top of his shoulder and held it in place with his free hand. "Thanks."

"Yup," Brooke said as she handed a bottle to Bobby and tossed bottles to Tom and Cleve.

"Are both of you FBI?" Brett asked, eyeing her as he took a drink of water.

She cocked her head and said, "What makes you think that?"

He shrugged and said, "I saw you and Cleve nod at each other when you came to the door. Sort of like you knew each other. Every time a car drove past, the three of you stopped playing and watched it."

"You don't miss much, do you?" Cleve asked.

Noticing everything was the only way he survived. He shrugged his good shoulder.

"Tom and Brooke are on loan to the FBI," Cleve explained.

"We're with the Waukesha County Sheriff Department in Wisconsin. Jamie Graff asked us to help out. I was the team leader in Kansas City," Tom answered. "Brooke is a detective."

"You're not married," Bobby said.

Brooke smiled and said, "No. We're friends, but not married."

"I wanted you boys to meet them just in case. I would prefer that no one else knows, and I would prefer that you don't talk about it in your house," Cleve said.

"You mean, you don't want mom and dad to know," Bobby said.

"I didn't say that," Cleve said shaking his head. "I just don't want you talking about it in your house. Bugs and all."

"I thought they found them all," Bobby said sitting up straighter.

"You never know, Bobby," Brett answered for them.

"You guys are pretty smart. You need to be. You need to use your eyes and your ears. Look for anything, hear everything. Be smart. Got it?"

Both boys nodded.

Tom drained his bottle of water and said, "Has anyone told you that you look like-"

"-Tom Brady," Brett and Bobby said in unison.

"Just about everybody," Brett added in disgust.

Tom laughed and asked, "Well, okay then. Let's play. Same teams?"

CHAPTER FIFTY-SIX

Wentzville, Missouri

He and the rest were pissed as hell. Their pictures were on CNN and on the network and local stations everywhere. Dominico had alerted them, so each had taken the necessary precautions to change the way they looked to avoid detection.

They moved up the timetable. That way, they could disappear for a while before they started it up again.

His blond hair was now black. Nonprescription contacts changed his blue eyes to brown or something even darker, and like the others, he had let his beard grow, though it was no more than lengthy stubble. Eventually, he'd color that too. He stood only five-nine and was slightly built, but in good shape and that would serve him well.

He had money and weapons and a plan.

He pulled to the curb a little less than a half-block away from the house, his Nissan Altima blending in with the neighborhood and the other cars on the street, though there weren't that many. The homes here started at the mid-$500K and went up rapidly from there. They were characterized by long and mostly hidden driveways, sweeping front lawns, exquisite landscaping and most of all, privacy. Most, if not all, had a home security system, but he wasn't worried about that.

He'd been to this neighborhood and this particular house several times, dropping the boy off after a game or practice, and had been here for his team's end of season party. His biggest problem was that he knew the boy and his family, and they knew him, which was a big problem that could prove to be lethal for him. Preferably, them.

He checked his new looks in the rearview mirror for the fifth or sixth time.

He stepped out of the car, locking it with that familiar chirping sound and walked quickly, but not too quickly because he didn't want to draw any attention. His Sig-Sauer was tucked into his belt at the small of his back underneath a zip-down gray hoodie. The hood was down, because he thought that wearing the hood might attract unwanted attention. A suppressor was stashed in the hoodie's front pocket.

Taking a direct approach, he walked up the driveway to the backdoor near the three car garage. As he had hoped, the door was not locked and he walked in without knocking or ringing the bell.

He stood in the entryway to get his bearings and listening. He slipped his weapon from his back waistband and secured the suppressor to it.

He walked quietly into the empty kitchen and heard sounds coming from the back. A television, most likely in the family room. A BMW crossover sat in the driveway so he knew at least one of the parents was home. Probably the mother, since she worked in real estate and kept irregular hours. Lucky for him, unfortunately for her.

Three kids lived in the house with both parents: older sister in high school, the boy in middle school, and a younger sister in elementary. All fresh and pretty and scrubbed and wealthy with the air and sophistication that comes with money. None of them with any cares or worries.

He kept moving to the front hallway where he locked the front door like he had done with the backdoor.

The mother appeared on the stairs and stopped in mid-step. Her mouth formed a perfect O of surprise. The man placed a similar O in her forehead and she tumbled backward and lay sprawled over the top four steps.

"Mom? What are you doing?"

The high school-aged daughter ran to her mother and she soon joined her mother in the land of the dead, also with a hole in her head, though hers was just above her ear.

Two shots, two down.

He moved to the family room and found the youngest girl glued to something noisy and obnoxious on Nickelodeon, and before she had an opportunity to notice him, he shot her.

Three for three, leaving only the boy, just as he had hoped and planned.

He moved from room to room, clearing the downstairs making sure it was empty and then moved up the stairs, dragging the two dead bodies with him. He went to the teenager's bedroom, where he unceremoniously threw them into the closet and shut the door behind him. At the end of the hallway, he heard the shower running and knew where the boy was.

Perfect for him, not so much for the boy.

He went back downstairs, used a blanket that was thrown on the back of the couch to wrap up the girl and carried her upstairs where she joined her mother and sister in the closet.

He went into the boy's bedroom. Shelves were filled with trophies and books. Posters of soccer and baseball players covered the wall along with a poster of Taylor Swift wearing a milk mustache with the caption that read, 'Got Milk?' A laptop sat on a small desk.

He heard the water stop, gave the boy about a minute or two to towel off and then he opened the door, stepped in and said, "Hi Kevin. It's been a while."

CHAPTER FIFTY-SEVEN

Waukesha, Wisconsin

Graff had read the reports so many times that he could almost recite them word for word. The problem was that what he had read and had committed to memory was nothing that would lead to whoever was responsible for Stephen's and Michael's abduction.

It came down to seven names on a list plus the goalie coach. Slim, really slim. Anorexic.

He picked up the phone and dialed.

"Kelliher," said the tired voice on the other end.

"Pete, this is Jamie Graff."

"Hey, Bud. How's it going on your end?"

"I have two scared kids, three nervous parents, and Stephen's father who I'm thinking of arresting."

"On what charge?"

"Being an asshole. You have anything?"

"Hell, I think you have more than I do. I'm sending Skip and Chet back to Chicago. Dominico had some sort of safe or hole in the floor of one of his bedrooms and Skip has a hunch that Cochrane might have one too. If we find it, we might get a lead. Who knows . . ." he trailed off and Jamie could hear the doubt in his voice, as if he had said it to convince himself.

"Hmm." Jamie paused and then said, "The boys came up with eight names. One of them might or might not be the pervert responsible for Stephen's abduction. I was wondering if you could run them forward and backward for me."

"I'll get Chet on it right away."

There was another pause, a bit too lengthy.

"Something else?" Pete asked with hesitancy.

"Well, I wouldn't want you to do anything illegal, not that the Feebs do anything illegal."

"Such as?" Pete asked with a laugh.

"Such as asking the great eye in the sky to check out what Chet might not be able to find."

"Billias isn't really on company payroll."

"That gives him latitude."

Jamie could hear the wheels turning. Pete finally said, "I'll give him a call with your names."

"Thanks. You get any tips on the photos you released?"

"About a thousand. Most of them live right next door to the caller," Pete said tiredly. "I don't know if sending pictures to the press was a good idea after all."

"Gotta do what you gotta do."

"Sounds suspiciously like, it is what it is."

Jamie laughed and said, "Something like that."

"Jamie, something's been bothering me about this case."

Jamie leaned back in his chair and propped his feet up on his desk and said, "What do you mean?"

"I can't put my finger on it. Not just Dominico or the ones who got away. It's about all the kids. I'm . . . we're missing something . . . something we've overlooked or not looked at closely enough."

"Huh." Jamie had thought it was all buttoned up other than finding Dominico, Stephen's abductor, and a couple of other perverts. "Not sure I follow."

Pete rubbed his flattop, frowned and wished like hell Summer was with him.

"I don't know . . . I'll figure it out," Pete mumbled.

After he hung up, Jamie thought about Pete's comment and tried to think of other avenues that were either explored or not explored enough. When nothing came to mind, he reread the paperwork looking for anything that didn't catch his eye the first ten times he had read it.

And struck out on both counts.

CHAPTER FIFTY-EIGHT

Wentzville, Missouri

"Please stop," Kevin cried. "I can't anymore. Please stop."

For almost three hours, Kevin had been with the man.

He lay on the bed with the man next to him. The man either didn't hear him or didn't care.

The man smiled and said, "See, you like this, don't you?"

"No, I don't!" the boy sobbed.

"Sure, you do, Kevin. All boys do," the man said soothingly.

"Please stop!" the boy cried.

"I'll tell you what, Kev. One more time and then we'll take a break. I have a job for you anyway. Okay?"

"Please, no," the boy said, already knowing the man was going to win again.

• • •

The man got up from the bed, stretched and stared down at the boy. Kevin wasn't as cute as Patrick. Not that he was ugly or even homely. Not by any means. By most standards, Kevin was good-looking. It was just that Patrick was special. Exquisite. But Kevin made up for it in other, better ways. Some boys are just better equipped than others. Not fair, but nature isn't fair and neither is life. Just ask Kevin's mother and two sisters.

The man stretched one more time, scratched lazily at his groin and retrieved the boy's cellphone from the dresser. He lay back down on the bed, handed Kevin his phone and reached over to the nightstand and picked up his gun, pointing it at the boy.

"I want you to call Patrick and invite him over. You're going to be very convincing. You're not going to give him any hint of me being here. If you do," he paused, cocked the pistol and aimed it right Kevin's forehead and said, "that will be the last thing you ever say to anyone. Do you understand?"

"Yes."

"Use the speaker so I can hear the conversation. I don't want to hurt you, but I will if you try anything. Understand?"

"Yes."

"Okay, get yourself together and quit crying. I want your best sales job."

The boy nodded.

"Okay, let's do it."

Kevin dialed Patrick's cell, turned on the speaker and waited.

"Hi, Kevin," Patrick said when he saw the caller ID.

"Hi, Patrick. What are you doin' tonight?"

"I'm at the Holiday Inn across from Six Flags with some friends. I'm spending the night and then tomorrow we're spending the day there. It's my first trip since . . ." he stopped, not wanting to say it.

Kevin looked at the man with the gun, unsure of what he should say next. The man waved his gun and nodded at him.

"I was hoping you'd come to my house tonight. You know, like you used to," Kevin finally said.

"Sorry, Kevin. I might be able to when I get back, though," Patrick said hopefully.

The boy read the man's lips and asked, "Who are you with?"

"Some friends I met after I was rescued. A kid named Randy, his brother and his dad. George, and their friend, Dan, and his dad."

The man smiled, gave Kevin the cut sign, so Kevin said, "Well okay. Call me when you get back, okay?"

"I will. Sorry about tonight."

"Me too," Kevin said, though he sounded relieved.

He ended the call and the man took the phone away from the boy and set it on the nightstand, and said, "I want a couple of pictures before I leave, okay?"

He set the gun on the bed out of Kevin's reach, grabbed his own phone and took several of the boy as he lay there.

"Okay, now flip over on your stomach."

"Please no!" Kevin sobbed.

"Don't worry, I just want some pictures."

Kevin rolled over, heard the click of the camera on the phone and saw the flash.

Kevin didn't notice the man picking up his gun, because he had his head buried into his pillow.

"Good," the man said, stroking Kevin's buttocks.

Then he put two bullets into the back of Kevin's head.

The man decided he'd shower since he'd have at least an hour or two before Kevin's dad came home from work. As he stepped into the shower, he was already planning his next move, pleased that he'd have the opportunity to not only get rid of Patrick, but the Indian kid, and Randy and his father.

Originally, he had planned to spend the night at Kevin's house. Not any more, however.

First, he'd have to wait for Kevin's dad to come home from work.

He didn't like loose ends.

CHAPTER FIFTY-NINE

Eureka, Missouri

Patrick Wright was one of the smallest boys rescued in Chicago. He had been there only six months, but was one of the more popular boys.

He had brown hair, cut much shorter than he had to wear it in captivity and was pale, almost ghostly. His large brown eyes shifted and darted from one boy to another. He fidgeted with his hands and fingers and couldn't sit still. Even the 25 milligrams of Hydroxyzine didn't help.

Randy felt sorry for him. He was like a rescue dog: beaten and afraid, not knowing who to trust or if he could ever trust again. Of all of the boys, Patrick was the one Randy was most worried about, which was why when he had found out they were heading to Six Flags Missouri, he asked the others if they minded if Patrick joined them.

Jeremy had suggested that he spend the night with them at the Holiday Inn so they could get an early start to their day and was surprised that Patrick and his mother agreed. After a brief hello and goodbye, she drove off leaving him in the care of people neither she nor Patrick hardly knew. She was much more trusting than he would have been under similar circumstances.

The boys sat or lounged around their room talking. It was small talk mostly. What sports they were best at. What they liked to do. TV shows or favorite movies they watched.

George mostly listened. He didn't play any sports like the others did, at least not on an official team. He seldom if ever had watched TV because the little ranch he grew up on didn't even have electricity, and had never been to a movie.

And he felt a tickle at the back of his head.

He wasn't sure when it began or what it was from. It was more like there wasn't one and then there was. It wasn't an alarm and it wasn't his grandfather.

The best way he could explain it was that it was a tickle, an expression he had heard his grandfather use off and on. He decided to say nothing about it for the time being, but to be watchful. That was something he was good at anyway. He was taught to be observant at an early age by his grandfather, the best of all teachers.

Deciding to go swimming, they took turns heading to the bathroom to change, except for George and Patrick who stripped down and changed unselfconsciously side by side in the room.

Randy knocked on the inter-room door to let his dad and Jeff know where they were going.

"Be careful and stay together."

"I'm in charge since I'm the oldest," Billy said stepping out of the bathroom.

"Then you need a baby-sitter," Jeremy answered with a laugh.

They raced out of the room and down the hall to the elevator. Danny pushed the button and then Billy pushed it again.

"Pushing it twice doesn't make it come any faster," Danny said with a laugh.

Billy pushed it again with a grin on his face and said, "Maybe it does."

There were several adults and three younger kids riding the elevator with them, so it was crowded. George found himself standing next to Patrick who was pressed into him. Not sure why he did so, George placed his arm around Patrick's shoulders, gave him a little squeeze and when Patrick looked up at him, George smiled at him. Patrick smiled back. It was the first genuine smile George had seen from him, so he kept his arm around Patrick for the entire ride down and gave his shoulder another squeeze.

They reached the first floor and the elevator opened up and disgorged its occupants. George and Patrick were the last to leave and fell well back from the rest of the group.

"Brett said I should get to know you," Patrick said shyly.

"Good advice," George said with a smile. Then he added, "I would like that."

Patrick smiled up at him again and George placed his arm around Patrick's shoulders again and that's how they entered the swimming area. The five boys picked up towels from the cabinet to the left of the door and staked a claim to a table in the corner along with five chairs.

"Patrick and Danny are on my team," Billy said cannonballing into the pool. As he came up shaking water from his head he added, "Keep away!" holding a little plastic yellow football over his head.

Randy, Patrick and Danny jumped in with Randy landing as close to Billy as possible without actually landing on him and started fighting for the ball. True, they were brothers who loved one another, but they were also competitive. It didn't matter what the game or contest was. It was all about competition. All fun. All games. But competitive just the same.

The tickle was stronger. The small hairs on the back of his neck stood at attention.

George did a slow 360 looking around the pool area, searching the lounge chairs and the tables and chairs set back from the pool. There were several family groupings or at least what appeared to be family groupings in the pool area. He didn't see anything or anyone alarming, but didn't actually know what he should be looking for. He shifted his gaze up towards the four floors of balconies overlooking the pool. There were adults with drinks leaning over the balcony either gazing downward or talking and laughing with each other. Others walked this way or that way. Nothing and no one out of place or particularly alarming.

"What room are you boys in?"

A manager or a waiter in a green blazer appeared at George's side.

"We need to make sure only residents enjoy our amenities," he explained.

"We're on the third floor," George said glancing quickly in his direction, but then looking back up at the balconies. "Room 317."

"Okay, thank you. Enjoy yourselves but be careful and obey the pool rules."

"Thank you, we will," George answered without looking at him, so intent he was on the balconies.

The man disappeared as quietly and as quickly as he had come.

"George, get your butt in here and help me," Randy yelled.

George jumped in and took up the tussle for the football that was being tossed from Danny to Patrick.

The man stood near the door and watched the boys, especially Patrick, and then left. Satisfied that he had done what he had set out to do.

He knew which room they were in.

CHAPTER SIXTY

Fishers, Indiana

"Look, I have to run out and pick up assignments from the TA," Thomas said tiredly. He'd been cooped up and housebound too long and needed to get out. "I won't be gone more than an hour, maybe an hour and a half tops."

"Mister McGovern, if you really need to do this *tonight*, at least let me make a call first." MB was beside herself. "I can't be two places at once."

They had been at each other most of the evening. Thomas insisting that he'd be safe, gone and back in a short time. MB insisting that it could wait until morning given the fact that Dominico was still out there somewhere.

Victoria stayed out of it. Brett had been dosing off and on. Cleve had suggested that the two boys run with him that morning and he had pushed them. Perhaps, the boys pushed him. His shift ended and MB had taken over and Brett was beat. His shoulder was sore so he was wearing his sling and popping Motrin like Skittles. Bobby had been reading a John Sanford book on his Kindle as he sat next to his brother. He wasn't all that tired or out of shape and that bothered Brett a little.

"Okay, make your phone call," Thomas said through a yawn. "I really have to do this though. And I think you'd agree that the later it gets, the more dangerous it is."

MB stepped away, dialed a number, turned her back to them, spoke briefly, and then turned around.

"You'll be followed to and from. Get in and get out. Don't deviate and don't go anywhere else. Park out in the open and stay in well-lit areas. No side trips."

"Okay," Thomas said nodding.

"No side trips," she stated again as a point of emphasis.

"Yeah, yeah," Thomas said. "I got it."

He walked out through the backdoor by the kitchen and MB and Victoria moved to the living room and stood at the front window, watching him pull out of the driveway. Thomas gave a friendly little wave and drove off.

Victoria went back to the kitchen to unpack the dishwasher and the boys flipped on the TV and channel surfed. MB started at the back of the house moving from bedroom to bedroom including the closets, bathroom to bathroom looking behind shower curtains, and finally back out to the family room to check on the two boys.

She should have looked into the kitchen.

She found both boys staring at her. Brett stood a little in front of Bobby.

"Turn around slowly and keep your hands where I can see them."

It was an unfamiliar voice, but MB knew who it was, cursing herself for not locking the backdoor after Thomas had left.

She turned around to face him and the first thing she noticed was the gun with the suppressor. Victoria had moved to the far end of the kitchen with the table between her and her brother. The blood had drained from Victoria's face and she was clenching and unclenching her hands.

MB moved slowly backwards towards the boys and to a position between him and them, wondering how she could get to her gun at the small of her back hidden under her loose sweatshirt.

"You're the best the Feebs could come up with to protect my sister and her family?" he said with a sneer. "What a joke!"

"Tony, leave," Victoria pleaded. "Go away and don't come back."

"Shut the fuck up, you dumb bitch and sit your ass down!" He glared at his sister, trying to intimidate her. The trouble was that Victoria didn't intimidate very easily, even facing her brother who was not only a pervert but a killer. A killer, perhaps a sociopath, who had a gun. A gun he had no qualms about using. She remained standing, refusing to sit. The pure hate on Dominico's face thickened as the silence and battle of wills went on.

During that exchange and the lengthy stare down between the brother and sister, MB not so much heard Brett move forward behind her, but felt it.

Her gun was no longer in the small of her back, and no one witnessed that Brett had even moved.

FBI training kicked in.

The most lethal person in the house was Dominico, who had the gun in his hand. His attention was focused totally on his sister. For a cop, he didn't seem all that steady or sure of himself in spite of the tone of his voice.

The wildcard in the room was Brett.

She had heard of Brett's bravery in Chicago, of his ability to shoot with accuracy under duress. She also knew that like his mother, he was bullheaded and stubborn. He did things his own way with little regard for rules or for himself. And now he had a loaded gun.

"Please, Tony! Don't hurt the boys," Victoria said quietly, much like the big sister she was to her unruly, unreasonable and recalcitrant younger brother. "Kill me if you need to kill someone, but not the boys!"

She moved in their direction but he barked, "Stay where you are! Don't move."

"What do you want?" MB asked.

"Shut the fuck up! If you were doing your fucking job, I wouldn't have gotten in." He added, "I should double-tap your ass on account of that."

He regarded MB as the only threat in the house. His sister was nothing but ineffectual and weak. The boys, well, they would do what he told them to do. He might have to rough them up, but he'd have his way with them like he always did.

"Brett, move away from her and stay with your brother. I'd hate for an accident to happen, like the bullet going through her and into you. We wouldn't want that, would we?"

"Please, Tony!"

The bullet spat inches from Victoria shattering the salt shaker that sat on the counter behind her.

She jumped, as did MB. Even Bobby jumped.

The only one who didn't was Brett. Having been kidnapped, tortured, shot at, wounded and almost killed, numbed him. There was nothing that had shocked him any longer. Perhaps wouldn't ever again.

"Hey, Fuckhead! You're nothing but a coward," Brett said softly, but clearly and loudly enough for everyone to hear.

Dominico focused his attention on Brett, regarding him malevolently.

"Don't ever talk to me like that again," he said through clenched teeth.

"Or what?" Brett said with a laugh. "You'll shoot me? Kill me?" He laughed and then he said, "You're a fucking joke!"

"You and Bobby and I are going to have some fun tonight. Just like old times," Dominico said darkly.

"There's no fucking way I'm doing anything with you except kicking your ass!"

"Oh, you're a tough guy now," Dominico said. "Even with a shot up shoulder."

"And you're a fucking pervert," Brett spat. "You have to fuck boys because you can't get it up for women."

Dominico moved forward and when MB moved to intercept him, he shot her twice in the stomach. She tried to block his path, but stumbled and fell to her knees and then rolled over onto her back. She groaned and moaned and held her stomach as tightly as she could, but blood oozed between her fingers.

Dominico stood where he was, looking down at her with loathing.

"Oh my *God*! Tony!" Victoria screamed. "*Why?*"

He turned around towards her and yelled, "Because I can!"

The nurse in her kicked in and she moved to help her.

Dominico pointed the gun at his sister and said, "Stay where you are."

"Hey, Fuckhead," Brett said calmly.

Dominico turned towards Brett, but his gun had lowered towards the floor.

Brett had taken MB's Glock.22 out of his sling and before Dominico could react, Brett shot his hand, sending the gun to the floor. Brett followed the first bullet with a second into Dominico's forearm rendering his power hand and arm useless.

"You little-" but that was all that he said before Brett shot him in the right kneecap, sending Dominico to the floor. Now his power leg was all but useless as well.

Dominico's gun was within reach of his left hand, but before he had the opportunity to snatch it up, Brett shot his left hand. Now both hands were useless, and as Dominico started to get up, Brett shot his left kneecap, making it impossible for him to walk.

"You little *Prick*! You *Cocksucker*!"

Brett said, "You got me confused with yourself, Fuckhead."

Then he turned to his mother and said, "Mom, can you help MB?"

Not sure if one of the neighbors had heard the gunfire, he turned to Bobby and said, "Call 9-1-1. Give them our address; tell them we have two gunshot victims and tell them we need two ambulances. Tell them we have an officer down."

Bobby picked up the phone and did what Brett had told him to do. Victoria grabbed hand towels from a drawer and ran to MB.

"MB, listen to me," Victoria said soothingly. "An ambulance is on the way. I want you to focus on me. Look at me, nowhere else."

MB couldn't focus her eyes, blinking rapidly, sweating profusely.

Brett never took his eyes from Dominico. The man licked his lips nervously. He tried to get up and Brett put another slug into his uncle's right thigh. He yelled and swore at the pain, holding his legs as best he could with damaged hands.

"It's not much fun getting shot," Brett taunted. "Is it?"

Bobby finished the phone call and Brett said over his shoulder, "Bobby, go get Tom and Brooke. Tell them what's happened, but be quick."

Bobby ran off, banging through the front door, but was met in the street by Brooke, who had heard the gunshots and was on her way to the rescue. Bobby told her what had happened.

Brett moved further into the kitchen and kicked Dominico's gun into the family room, as far away from Dominico as he could get it, and then stood over him.

There was no fear and no panic. Brett was calm, focused, and breathing easily. There was no expression on his face.

He aimed the gun at his uncle's crotch and fired.

The gunshot startled Victoria who uttered a gasp.

Dominico grabbed at his crotch and screamed, mixing curses towards God, his mother, Brett, his sister, everyone.

"That's for Johnny and Tim and Patrick. That's for Stephen and Mike. Mostly, that's for Bobby and me. You won't be fucking any of us again."

"My God, Brett, that's enough!" Victoria said. "Don't kill him!"

"I'm not going to kill him. I want him to stand trial for being a Fuckhead. He's a pervert and I'm going to make sure he goes on trial and I'm going to testify."

CHAPTER SIXTY-ONE

Eureka, Missouri

The boys sat or sprawled on George's and Billy's bed. They were tired out from messing around in the pool and full of pizza and cookies, soda and water. The boys had settled into quiet conversation, jokes and laughter. Little attention was paid to the television.

Randy had noticed that every now and then, Patrick smiled and laughed. It wasn't often, but when he did, his eyes lit up and the only way Randy could describe it was angelic. It made Randy all the more sad, hoping that one day, Patrick would regain the inner strength and confidence he must have had before he was taken.

When he talked, which wasn't much, he did so quietly, feeling his way out from whatever it was that still held him captive, even though he wasn't in a locked room or on a floor in a building he couldn't escape from. He usually had one hand on Billy's shoulder or forearm, and Billy didn't seem to notice, but if he did, he didn't seem to mind.

Randy observed George glancing at him every now and then and when Patrick saw him, the two smiled and Patrick would reach out and touch George's leg or arm, but the other hand never left Billy.

"Patrick, since you've back, has everything been okay?" Randy asked.

Patrick shrunk back into himself. His hand left Billy's shoulder and joined his other as they fidgeted in his lap. His eyes lowered and he didn't answer at first.

Randy felt awful. He glanced at Billy and George, not knowing what to say, wanting to apologize but unsure how. Seldom was Randy speechless but he found himself so now.

"My parents are getting a divorce," Patrick said quietly.

Danny perked up. Of the boys in the room, both he and Billy had been through that. Danny bounced from his mom in Omaha to his dad in Waukesha and back again.

"They want me to pick who to live with," Patrick said. "I can't. I don't know how."

"Have you thought about the pros and cons of living with your mom or your dad?"

Patrick glanced up at Randy, shrugged and fidgeted even more. He shook his head.

"What're your sisters going to do?" Billy asked. "You're what, the middle kid?"

Patrick nodded. "I think my two sisters are going to live with my mom."

The boys waited, each of them uncomfortable with the silence.

George realized he paralleled Patrick in that he had to decide between living with the twins and Jeremy or returning to his homeland and his Navajo people. In George's case, it was hard because the decision came down to living a different life and lifestyle, one that was different from the one he had been living. The other thing that made it different was that George no longer had a mother or family to choose to live with, only his cousin.

"I don't know how to choose," Patrick said.

Danny said, "Look, Patrick . . . you don't know me very well, and what I'm going to say stays in this room," he looked right at Randy and then at Billy. "Patrick, no matter what decision you make, it's gonna suck."

All eyes turned to him.

"Divorce sucks. I know it happens. I know sometimes parents don't get along. But it's us who suffer."

As close as Danny was to Randy, Danny never hinted that he felt that way.

Danny stared at Randy, then at Billy and George. To Patrick he said, "I love my dad and I love my mom. When I'm with my mom, I think of my dad all the time and want to be with him. When I'm with my dad, I think of my mom and want to be with her. It sucks and I can't stand it."

Randy reached out to touch Danny's arm, but he pulled it away.

Ignoring Randy, he said, "The thing is, Patrick, no matter what you decide, it's gonna suck. So, what you have to decide is, what's gonna suck the least, living with your dad or living with your mom? That's how you make your decision. It's what's gonna suck the least."

Both Patrick and George nodded. They understood. Both had a decision to make and the decision sucked. It sucked much worse for Patrick than for George, but it still sucked at least a little.

CHAPTER SIXTY-TWO

Chicago, Illinois

"We got it!"

Pete sat up straighter, gripping his cell tighter. "What did you find?

Chet was in hyper-mode, running on God knows how many Diet Cokes and Snickers, talking so quickly the words tumbled out of his mouth. Pete had this picture of him, his green eyes wide, his red hair mussed, hands and arms flailing as he paced- if not ran- around the room.

"You remember the false cupboard in the TV stand Rodemaker had at his house?"

Pete had to think back. Jim Rodemaker was a pedophile in Waukesha, Wisconsin. A kid named Garrett reported him as the possible perp responsible for the abductions of Stephen and Mike after he saw their Amber Alert. Garrett played soccer on Rodemaker's soccer team and he and several teammates had been molested by him. When Pete and Jamie Graff showed up with a Knock-Search and a SWAT Team at Rodemaker's house, they found one of Garrett's teammates on a couch with Rodemaker. He had a laptop full of porn and a lot of digital microphones and digital cameras hidden throughout house. The laptop contained the website that led to Victor Bosch and the human trafficking ring that held the boys captive, including Tim and Brett and the others freed in Chicago, Long Beach and Kansas City. Rodemaker, however, wasn't responsible for Stephen's or Mike's abduction.

In a hidden cupboard in Rodemaker's TV cabinet, Chet and Pete had located a digital recording system. Conveniently, Rodemaker had catalogued and titled the various videotapes of his exploitations. All of it was bagged as evidence and this evidence, along with his confession, would be used to help convict Rodemaker of the rape and sexual abuse of preteen and teenaged boys. Pete hoped he would serve a life sentence in prison.

"There was a recess in a wall in Cochrane's condo," Chet laughed. "I still don't know how we found it. We were just tapping on walls and stuff."

"What did you find?" Pete said.

"$350K and three passports, one in Cochrane's name and two others with his photo but with different names. A Sig Sauer Pro with two loaded mags, and a burn phone. I gave the number to Billias and he's monitoring it just like the others. I'm downloading what I can from it and cross-checking the numbers and texts with what we have."

Pete stood up and began pacing back and forth in his room.

"And this is really important, I did a hunt and found that the other names he used, the ones on the passports, had two different checking and savings accounts at two different banks. He also had another condo in Thornridge on the Southside of Chicago. We've got a warrant and we're going there now."

The gears in Pete's head spun, thinking of next steps and the steps after that.

"Who knows about this?"

"You, me, Skip, Summer and Morgan."

"Okay. I'll let Dandridge know. I want a lid on this. There are people out there running around and we aren't sure who's playing on what team, at least for sure."

"No problem. Once we check it out, I'll be back in touch."

"And Chet, you and Skip stay together and be careful. I mean it."

Finally, a lead. Pete didn't know where it would go or to whom it would point to, but it was a lead.

CHAPTER SIXTY-THREE

Fishers, Indiana

"Bobby, stay here on the front lawn and wait for one of us to come get you!"

Brooke didn't wait for Bobby's answer. She took the three steps up to the front door, stood to the side, turned the knob and pushed it open.

"FBI. Brett, I'm coming in."

"We're in the kitchen," he yelled back. "My fucking uncle's not going anywhere."

She stepped in low and fast and cleared the front entrance and living room. She moved down the hallway and entered the kitchen.

"We need an ambulance," Victoria said.

Brooke determined that the crime scene was secure.

"Brett, I need your gun."

He dislodged the magazine and ejected the bullet in the chamber and then handed her the gun by holding on to the barrel and put the magazine and bullet in her other hand.

"It's MB's. I took it when Fuckhead wasn't looking."

She stared down at Dominico. He lay on the floor of the kitchen, bleeding from multiple wounds, and holding his crotch and writhing in pain. A puddle, wet, dark and sticky had pooled around him.

She looked at Brett. Indeterminate expression, at least none she could discern.

They heard sirens.

In a flat, emotionless voice, Brett said, "His gun is over there on the floor. He fired three shots. One towards my mom. It hit the salt shaker over there on the counter. You can see the bullet entry. If he were actually aiming at her, he would have shot her. He fired two shots at MB hitting her in the stomach."

"Abdomen, lower left quadrant," Victoria said. She turned around looking grim. "We need an ambulance," she repeated.

"It's on the way. What do you need me to do right now?"

Victoria glared at her brother and said, "Arrest that son of a bitch on the floor. You can do that."

Pete showed up after the ambulance and two sets of squad cars. Police tape had been set up and the house had been cordoned off. Neighbors had gathered on front lawns and front porches and watched nervously. They were like moths to a flame, except in this case, the flame was the light bar on a cop car.

He held out his creds and nodded at this cop or that cop and entered the house and found paramedics working over MB. Another group had stabilized Dominico and had loaded him up on a gurney and started an IV drip. Pete walked over to make sure he was handcuffed to it, and he was. Just to be sure, he yanked the cuffs causing Dominico to yell and one of the paramedics to say, "What the hell?"

He found Brooke standing in the family room, one hand on her holstered gun, the other relaxed at her side. She was standing in front of Victoria, who sat on the couch with her arm around Bobby and her other hand on Brett's knee. He couldn't tell what they were feeling because of their flat affect.

Pete turned to Brooke and asked, "Has Thomas been contacted?"

Brooke nodded and said, "He's on his way back. Tom Albrecht said they're ten or fifteen minutes out."

When Albrecht got the call from Brooke, he and Thomas were already at the university. Tom had cleared the second floor and Thomas' office, then went back down the hall and had waited by the main stairs, while Thomas went into his office. Upon receiving the call from Brooke, Tom raced down the hall and burst in and found Tom and his TA in an amorous position on his desktop.

Disgusted, Tom said, "While you're here groping a coed, Dominico showed up at your house and pulled a gun on your *wife* and your two boys. The agent assigned to your family's protection was shot and in serious condition. Perhaps that's more important than copping a feel or getting laid. I'm leaving. I suggest you do the same."

• • •

Albrecht arrived well ahead of Thomas and jogged up the driveway and into the house. He found the boys sitting on the couch with their mother. Bobby spoke with one detective who knelt in front of him with a small notepad, while Brett spoke with another who had pulled up a kitchen chair. Both boys gave their accounts of what had taken place.

MB and Dominico had been taken away by different ambulances. A Crime Investigations Unit worked the scene. He counted one taking photographs and one videotaping the scene in the kitchen. Each wore plastic booties and latex gloves, which Albrecht could never understand because there were cops and agents all over the place traipsing around mucking up the scene without gloves or booties. He wanted to yell at them and if he were in Waukesha, would have. He wasn't, so he didn't.

Brooke re-introduced him to Pete and they shook hands. Just as Brooke began filling him in on what had transpired, Thomas entered the house and walked immediately into the family room.

"Dad!" Bobby yelled, interrupting his debrief.

Brett smiled at his dad, who smiled back briefly, and falsely, then looked at the floor.

Thomas looked at Victoria, who sighed and turned away from him, burying her face into Bobby's hair as she pulled him closer to her.

Brett took it all in. He looked at his mother curiously, and then at his father, who stood there awkwardly in front of them with his hands stuffed into his brown plaid sport coat pockets. Brett looked back at his mom and understood.

His dad had been cheating on his mom. And, his mom had known it was happening.

CHAPTER SIXTY-FOUR

Eureka, Missouri

Their cells went off almost simultaneously, either buzzing or chiming or a musical ringtone depending upon whose cell it was.

Pete called Jeremy. Stephen called Randy. Tim called George, and Brett called Patrick. Billy and Danny knew something big had happened and were hoping it wasn't someone dead or dying. The boys mostly listened and seldom spoke.

Typical of him, George was stoic, devoid of expression thus giving away nothing. Being polite, Randy had a habit of speaking softly and turning his back on anyone who happened to be in the room when he spoke on the phone and this night was no different. Patrick paced, head down, one hand holding his phone and the other on top of his head.

The first inkling that it was good news was when Patrick pumped a fist in the air and yelled, "Yes!"

George, who had been sitting on the floor by the inter-room door, nodded and smiled up at him, then smiled at Danny and Billy, and then nodded at something that was said on the other end. Randy hadn't turned around, but hugged himself as he listened. That left Billy puzzled.

"Brett wants to talk to you," Patrick said, holding the phone out to George. Then he turned to Billy and Danny and said, "Brett shot his uncle and his uncle was arrested! Brett's safe!"

"Tim, can I give you to Patrick? Brett wants to talk to me," George said. "Yeah, sure. Talk to you soon. Bye."

He held the phone out to Patrick who took it and began speed talking. Billy and Danny listened closely as Patrick retold the story he had received from Brett.

"Hi, Brett," George said. "Tim told me what happened."

"Yeah."

George waited, but frowned when nothing further came from him.

"You okay?" he asked quietly.

Brett spoke quietly. "Can we talk . . . in private?"

George stood up and stepped outside the hotel room, shut the door behind him, and sat down beside the door. Noise from the pool area below their balcony echoed off the walls and glass ceiling. The smell of chlorine caused his eyes and sinuses to burn.

The closest person to him was several doors down and he was holding a can of Miller Lite and staring at someone in the pool below them.

"You okay?" George repeated.

"I think I'm fucked up," Brett said.

George couldn't tell whether Brett was crying or not. His voice didn't have the confidence he normally had. George pictured him in darkness, by himself and alone somewhere either in his house or in his yard.

"What do you mean?"

Brett sighed. He couldn't put into words what he was feeling. He had never felt the way he did and had no reference for identifying it.

"Can I ask you a question? I mean, just you and me? No one else?"

"Sure."

"When you killed that man that one night, what did you feel?"

George had tried to bury that memory and those feelings as deeply as he could, but when he shot the tires of Cochrane's car at the hospital in Chicago, that same feeling came back to him. Especially when Cochrane shot and killed himself.

"Not good."

"What do you mean?"

George waited until a mother and daughter had walked past him on their way to their room three doors down. The girl, about five or six, looked at him curiously and then smiled. George smiled back. The mother carried three bottles of soda and a bottle of water while trying to open their door.

"Navajos respect life. We don't believe in killing another human being. We only do that if there is no other way. That man didn't leave me a choice. He tried to shoot me and then kept going for his gun."

Brett longed to speak with him face to face. He wanted to read George's expression and study his body language. Being two states away, the only thing he could do was listen closely to the tone of his voice and the words he chose.

"Why do you ask?"

George was certain Brett was crying. He heard muffled sobs and sniffles.

"I think I'm fucked up."

"Why?"

"When I shot my uncle, the first two shots were to get the gun out of his hand. I wanted to make sure he couldn't use his right hand. Then I shot his right knee because I didn't want him coming after me or Bobby or my mom. Then I shot his left hand because his gun was close and I knew he could shoot with either hand."

This made sense to George and he nodded in agreement.

"But then . . ." Brett sobbed. "I shot him in the leg again."

George didn't understand why this upset Brett because he thought Brett was just trying to disable him.

"Then, I don't know," Brett said. "I was pissed. I kept thinking of all the stuff he did to me and all the stuff he did to Bobby."

George waited patiently.

"He was sitting on the floor holding his legs. He was bleeding all over the place. I stood over him, and I shot his balls off."

George blinked and reflexively drew his knees up to his chest.

"I didn't have to, but I was pissed. You told me not to lose focus. You told me to be in control." Brett sobbed and said, "Fuck, George. I didn't have to shoot him there. I didn't have to."

George couldn't put himself in Brett's place. He didn't have any experience like this. Killing the man that was sent to kill him, Jeremy and the twins, was defensive. He didn't do anything *additional*, nothing that was more than *necessary*. The man left him no choice but to kill him.

"What's wrong with me?" Brett sobbed.

"Nothing, Brett."

"But I didn't have to do that. I know what he did to me, Bobby, and the others, but I didn't have to do that."

"I know."

"Am I . . . I don't know . . . bad or something? Evil?" Brett sobbed again.

"No, Brett. You're not evil."

"But when I shot him, I wasn't in control. I think I liked it. But I don't now. If I could take it back, I would."

"That is why you are not evil," George explained. "If you were evil, you would not feel like you do now. You are sad. You are not happy about it."

"Fuck no!" Brett said with a sob. "I feel awful!"

"That is why you are not evil. You have a good heart, Brett."

Brett sniffled back and George pictured him wiping tears on the front of his shirt or on his sleeve.

"I don't think I have a good heart."

"You do, Brett," George said with a sad smile. "If you didn't, you would not feel this way."

"You think so?" Brett asked hopefully.

"I am sure. I would not like you if you did not have a good heart."

There was silence. Even though it went on quite long, neither felt compelled to break it.

Finally, George said, "My grandfather told me that in all of us, there are two wolves. One is good and one is evil. We make a choice each day to feed one wolf or the other. The one we feed the most determines whether or not we are good or evil. I believe you feed the good wolf."

Brett was silent and the only thing George heard was sniffles.

"You don't think I'm fucked up?"

George shook his head and said, "No."

"I wish I could be there with you."

"Me, too."

"Are we still friends?" Brett asked shyly.

"Yes, Brett. We are friends."

"Okay."

Brett sniffled again, took a deep breath and said, "Can you do me a favor?"

"Sure."

"Don't tell anyone what we talked about, okay?" Brett asked, and then added, "Please? Not Jeremy or Randy or anybody. Okay?"

"I won't. I promise."

"Thanks."

"No problem."

"Well, okay," Brett said sadly. "Well, goodbye."

"Navajos don't say goodbye," George teased. "There's no such word."

"So, what do we say?" Brett said with a small laugh.

"We say, "Yá'át'ééh". It's a greeting from one friend to another."

Brett said, "I remember. How about if I say, 'Talk to you again soon'?"

George laughed and said, "I'd like that." And then on impulse, George said, "Brett?"

"Yeah."

"I love you, and you are my friend."

"Me, too."

George turned off his phone and sat with his head pressed against the wall and his eyes shut.

CHAPTER SIXTY-FIVE

Eureka, Missouri

He had a bad feeling.

He had not heard or seen his grandfather, but he had a bad feeling.

George stared up at the ceiling, listening to night sounds and waiting . . . for what? He didn't know.

He turned to his right. Patrick was curled up against Billy. One arm was thrown over Billy's chest, his head on Billy's shoulder sleeping quietly, peacefully. His mouth was partially open and a bit of drool had seeped out. Billy had turned slightly towards Patrick, their heads touching. He turned to his left. Randy lay on his back, arms out to the side, right leg up. Danny faced the window and away from Randy, but up against him.

George looked at the window. The heavy rust-colored curtains weren't pulled all the way shut. Just the thin, white privacy curtain was pulled. It allowed ambient light into the room, but didn't allow anyone from the outside to see in. At the side of each door along the hallway, there was a small light that allowed someone to walk comfortably and securely, which was important on the second, third and fourth floors.

He saw a shadow of a man appear at the window, stop and peer into the room and then slowly pass by.

George sat up and without thinking slipped his feet into his moccasins and he took hold of his knife that was on the nightstand.

"What?" Billy asked groggily, raising his head from the pillow. Patrick hadn't stirred.

George motioned to him to be silent, and Billy slowly sat up in bed and absently wiped the drool off his shoulder while he stared at George, and then at the window.

George waited, frozen in his spot, not ready to relax even though the shadow had moved on.

Minutes passed.

Billy had lay back down, but his eyes were open.

George stood up and stepped silently to the side of the window, looking first in the direction the shadow had moved, and then to the left. There was nothing he could see without moving the curtain and he dared not do that. Even though his vision was limited and he was not about to move the curtain.

Neither Randy nor Danny had moved. Billy had raised his head and watched George. He had a hand on Patrick's back.

As George turned back to the window, the shadow appeared again. Same height. Same shape. A man.

George heard Billy gasp and again, George motioned for him to be quiet.

Mere inches from him on the other side of the glass and privacy curtain stood someone staring into the room. Certain that he couldn't be seen, George stood motionless, his knife pointed in the shadow's direction.

Seconds passed, perhaps minutes.

The shadow moved off to the right again, but slowly.

George silently, but quickly picked up the stuffed, padded chair and placed it down against the door. He stepped away staring at the door, certain that someone was on the other side.

George went to Danny, placed a hand over his mouth and spoke in a whisper. Danny got up quickly, quietly, took his phone, turned it on and crouched down by the inter-room door.

George heard something at the door and then saw the knob move, but it was locked and the safety chain attached.

He stepped over to Randy, placed a hand over his mouth and whispered to him to get on the floor between the two beds, between the nightstand and the head of the bed. Randy did so without question, eyes wide, but trusting George.

Billy watched as Randy and Danny had moved and when George looked at him, he placed a hand over Patrick's mouth and whispered into his ear. He watched Patrick nod franticly, and then Billy took him in both of his arms and rolled quietly over the side of the bed in the narrow space between the bed and the wall.

George moved backward still watching the door and stood next to Danny. Between them and the door was a dresser with the flat-screen TV on top. Feeling he needed to further secure the door, George whispered to Danny, who went to the TV and lifted it off the dresser. When he did, George pushed the dresser against the chair tightly. It had made more noise than he had hoped.

Danny had just replaced the TV back on the dresser and had moved back next to George, when the first of two quick, silenced shots went through the door zinging past them into the wall between the closet and the bathroom.

George pulled Danny to the floor, wrapped him in his arms, and laid down on top of him. He watched Randy ball up and cover his head.

"I don't wanna die, Billy," Patrick whispered, more of a whimper.

"Shhh, George is going to take care of us," Billy whispered back.

Two more shots that seemed a little louder than the first two spat through the door and the dresser, both inches above George's head. He pressed himself down on top of Danny who had his eyes shut tightly.

The door rattled. Someone was trying to get in, so both George and Danny pushed the dresser as tightly as they could against it.

Seconds ticked by. The shooting had stopped.

George whispered into Danny's ear and felt him nod once in return.

Danny crawled out from under George and across the floor. He reached up, turned the knob on the inter-room door and pushed the door open, crawled inside, and shut the door quietly behind him.

The shadow was at the window and there was no mistaking the gun in the shadow's hand.

It spat through the window two, three times. Chunks of glass rained down on the bed where moments ago Randy and Danny had slept. Their bed was riddled with bullets and glass fragments. Two more shots to the head of the bed, not a foot from where Randy lay on the floor.

Patrick whimpered and cried and Billy tried to reassure him.

Nine shots. George knew the man was reloading.

"Boys! Are you all right?" Jeremy called out, not quite a yell, but not quite a whisper.

Neither Randy nor Billy answered and that was good. To do so would betray their position in the room.

George answered for them. "Call 9-1-1 and Agent Pete." And then as an afterthought he said, "Stay down and away from the window and door."

Shots rang out, this time in his direction. More rang out slamming into the back wall and the bed where he, Patrick and Billy had slept, penetrating the mattress and pillows. The light on the nightstand above Randy shattered as a bullet slammed into it and the wall above him.

The window had holes and chunks missing, but was surprisingly intact.

"What the devil is going on out here?"

In answer were two shots, then a third at the man and his family next door. There were screams from the neighbor's wife and children. A yelp and groan from the man.

He had counted the shots. Three left. He needed the man to empty it, so he grabbed somebody's shoe and threw it at the window. Two shots. A third. And a click on an empty chamber.

He had to act now.

CHAPTER SIXTY-SIX

Eureka, Missouri

George hurtled through what was left of the window, and it exploded on impact. He had crisscrossed his arms in front of his head which was lowered protectively. He led with his right leg, knowing he was going to get cut up. He also knew that if he didn't act, one or more of them would get shot or killed.

Between the gunshots, the screams of the neighbors, and the exploding window, whoever wasn't awake certainly was now.

As he flew out of the window, he slipped on broken glass, slid along the balcony floor, and landed at the feet of the man with the gun. He held the gun in his right hand, a magazine in his left.

George had to act or he'd lose the advantage of surprise.

Still sitting in the broken glass and shell casings, he jabbed his knife upwards into the man's groin with both hands and then sliced it outward rather than pulling the knife back out.

The man stumbled backward and leaned against the balcony railing. A look of horror and shock spread over the man's face as his intestines and other vital organs fell out of the rip in the man's pants.

George sprang to his feet and slammed the knife up under the man's ribs and then ripped it downward in an arc across the man's abdomen. He knew he had destroyed the man's lung and severed an artery because blood and other organs and fluids gushed and fell out of the man's shirt.

The man sunk to his knees. He tried to hold himself together, but it was impossible. His mouth opened and closed, but only a steady stream of bright red blood came out.

Finally, the man rolled to the side, still staring at George, but his eyes were lifeless.

Exhausted, George stood above the man, his knife dripping blood. His sucked air in great gulps but couldn't get enough. He fell to his knees and hung his head waiting for help to arrive.

"George! George!"

He heard Jeremy calling him in panic, but he neither had the strength nor the will to answer.

"Dad, is he okay?" Randy asked. He was near panic and near tears.

He wasn't the only one.

"Billy. Stay. With. Patrick. Stay. With. Patrick." George stammered. It took all he had to yell it.

Jeremy sprinted out of his room yelling, "George! George!" and then in a much softer voice as he knelt next to the boy said, "George, are you okay? Son, please!"

George did not have the strength to answer. He was in pain. His left thigh up near his groin, his right hamstring high up just under his buttocks, his arms and hands, all throbbed and stung. He looked at himself and saw chunks and shards of glass sticking out of his hands, arms and legs. His own blood dripped out of him, mingling with the blood of the man he had killed.

Jeremy said softly, "My God, George! Son, are you okay?"

George tried to look at him, but either he couldn't or didn't want to.

"Mister, that boy saved my life!" the neighbor said. "That man shot me! Hit me in the arm, but that boy saved my life!"

George said haltingly just above a whisper, "Father, we need to secure the crime scene." He took a big gulp of air and said, "Father, we need a camera. Take a picture of the man's face and send it to Agent Pete."

"Here, use mine," Danny said as he appeared next to Jeremy.

"I don't know how it works," Jeremy said.

Danny stepped over to the man, gagged repeatedly, but took three pictures of the man's face.

"Randy?" Jeremy said. "I need your help."

"What can I do?" Jeff asked coming out of the room with Randy close behind.

George pointed his knife at the man and said, "Pocket. Wallet . . . identification."

Jeremy moved to the man and felt his backside and found the wallet.

"Thumb . . . and . . . finger. Watch . . . prints," George gasped.

"Jesus, George," Jeff said softly. "Shhh, don't talk."

George thought he had nodded, but didn't know whether he actually did.

Jeremy shouted, "Where's the fucking ambulance? Where are the cops?"

Randy and Danny stood off to the side, worried about George, and refusing to stare at the dead man on the balcony.

There was the sound of running feet and shouts. "Step aside. Police! Step aside!"

Jeremy held the wallet between his thumb and forefinger and said, "George, I have it. Now what?"

George nodded, gulped air and said, "Picture to Agent Pete. Name. Address. License."

That was the last George remembered because he passed out in Jeff's arms.

CHAPTER SIXTY-SEVEN

His grandfather was dressed as he had appeared earlier. However, his face looked older. His brown, wrinkled hands were clasped behind his back. George walked silently beside him.

'You are angry, Shadow.'

George didn't respond. He felt confused and sad and angry, so he didn't know how to respond.

After what seemed like a long time, his grandfather said, 'You did not need me.'

George glanced at him. A man had come to kill Patrick. The man shot at and him and his brothers. A man in the next room was shot. How could his grandfather say that he didn't need him?

'You did not need me,' His grandfather repeated.

They walked along a familiar path in silence. George had a lot to consider. A strange combination of peace and anger. Perhaps not so much anger as frustration, but over it all, peace.

'Grandfather, I think I want to live with my brothers and my father.'

His grandfather nodded and said, 'If this is what you want.'

'Is this what you want me to do?'

The old man smiled and said, 'Shadow, it is not what I want or not want.'

George nodded. 'It is my decision then.'

His grandfather stopped, smiled up at the bright sun and said, 'It was always your decision.'

George nodded.

His grandfather turned to him and smiled and in a very gentle voice said, 'Shadow, you did not need me.'

'The man had a gun and was shooting at us.'

'Yes, but he was arrogant and ignorant. A biligaana.'

'My brothers and father are biligaana.'

The old man smiled and said, 'In their heart, they are Dine'.' He glanced back at the sun and said, 'They have good and gentle hearts.' His grandfather turned to look at him and placed a hand on George's shoulder. 'The man was evil and it is good he can no longer hurt others.'

'But I took his life,' George said sadly.

'He was evil and you saved the lives of your brothers, your father, and your friends.'

George nodded and said, 'I love them very much.'

'And they love you. You will be good for them and they will be good for you.'

'I miss you and Grandmother. I miss Mother and William, and Robert and Mary.'

His grandfather walked away slowly, his hands behind his back, staring at the sun.

'You did not need me,' he said looking upward at the sun.

George watched him walk away. His heart was sad and unsettled.

'I love you,' George called after him.

His grandfather waved without turning around and walked on.

CHAPTER SIXTY-EIGHT

Eureka, Missouri

The emergency room wasn't busy. A young couple sat in a corner filling out forms on a clipboard. A mom and dad comforted their crying seven-year-old son who had an arm wrapped in ice. A plump, older Hispanic woman in a wheelchair and covered in a blanket sat next to a younger woman who asked her questions in Spanish as she filled out forms. A tired, older security guard read the local sports page and a receptionist worked on a computer behind the desk.

Jeremy had ridden in the ambulance with George. Before leaving for the hospital, Jeff and the boys had moved everything into two rooms on the fourth floor as far away as they could get from the scene of the shooting. The rooms for two additional nights were free, compliments of Holiday Inn.

Billy and Patrick had been inseparable ever since the shooting. Patrick had been so frightened that he had peed on both of them, so after the police came, Billy took Patrick into the bathroom, started the shower and both climbed in together. Patrick had apologized, and Billy assured him it was no big deal.

Patrick sat between Billy and Randy, and Danny sat next to Randy. Billy had his arm around Patrick's shoulders and Patrick had his head resting on Billy. Patrick's parents met them at the emergency room and sat with Jeff across from the boys and talked quietly about nothing in particular.

Pacing in the waiting area, Jeremy had a one-sided conversation directed at Pete Kelliher, much of it through clenched teeth. After, he called Jamie Graff and told him what had taken place, but spent more time listening than talking. Both conversations were out of earshot, but Jeff knew he'd be filled in later.

They had been there an hour and a half when a tall, thin, middle-aged doctor wearing bloody green scrubs and a green surgeon's cap pushed open the heavy steel door and stepped into the waiting room. He wore his glasses down on the end of his nose and a stethoscope around his neck. He caught Jeremy's eye and motioned him over.

"He's quite a young man," the surgeon said tiredly.

Jeremy waited nervously.

"We had to use a general anesthetic because he has, hell, I don't know over one hundred stitches. I thought I was sewing a blanket," he added as he rubbed his eyes. "There are two deep wounds that we had to suture inside and out. There is another bad one, but not quite as deep as the other two. A bunch of others," he said shaking his head. "He lost blood and he's weak, but he'll be fine, provided he takes it easy for a couple of days. Ordinarily, he shouldn't get the stitches wet for twenty-four hours, but on those three wounds, not for forty-eight. An antibiotic ointment will need to be applied and I'd like to keep gauze on them for at least forty-eight hours. The gauze will have to be changed as needed, but at least twice a day and the ointment reapplied each time."

Jeremy nodded and asked, "George is going to be okay?"

The surgeon nodded and said, "He'll need to take it easy. No lifting anything over ten pounds. I would like him to stay overnight, but he insists on leaving."

The surgeon took off his glasses, rubbed his eyes and said, "He's in post-op now and he's been asking for you."

Jeremy followed the doctor down the hall, where he was pointed to George's room. He entered and stood in the doorway. George's heavily bandaged right arm lay across his eyes and his right knee was up. His bandaged left arm was above the covers at his side. There were no stitches on his face or on the part of his chest and stomach that Jeremy could see.

He moved to the side of the bed and ran the back of his hand softly against George's cheek.

"How are you doing, Kiddo?"

When George answered, it was soft and sad and Jeremy had to lean in to catch it. "I don't like killing."

"I know."

Tears leaked out from under his arm.

"You saved lives, George. That has to count for something."

George didn't respond.

Jeremy sat on the edge of the bed, took light hold of George's hand and said, "Anything I can do?"

George shrugged and wiped his eyes with his other hand.

"George, I love you. The boys love you. Nothing has changed, but I understand what you're feeling." Jeremy said.

"I killed a man . . . another man. I ruined the trip to the park," George said quietly.

"First of all, you saved lives. Secondly, we can wait another day or two for the park. It's no big deal."

George looked at him doubtfully and Jeremy added, "Really."

He looked away and Jeremy asked, "How much pain are you in?"

George's head whipped back and he answered quickly, "I don't want to stay here. I want to be with you and my brothers."

"You didn't answer my question." Jeremy said with a smile.

"I am sore. I hurt a little, but I am okay."

"It wouldn't hurt to spend a night here. I can stay with you if you like."

George set his jaw and his eyes narrowed. "No, please. I want to be with my brothers."

The use of 'my brothers' was not lost on Jeremy.

A gentle silence grew between them and then George said in a small voice, "Do you still want me to live with you? I mean, I killed two men."

There wasn't the confidence Jeremy was used to. He smiled and said, "But you saved lives both times." He paused and asked, "Do you want to live with us?"

"If you want me to."

"I do," Jeremy answered with a smile. "I know the boys do, too."

George studied Jeremy closely; his dark eyes never blinked. Jeremy had the idea that George searched for the truth, and Jeremy was certain that he had spoken it.

Only after George was satisfied, did he say, "I was thinking . . . Mister Jeremy is very formal." George blushed. "But 'Dad' is not respectful enough."

"The twins call me 'Dad'."

George shook his head slightly.

"What are you thinking of calling me?"

George licked his lips and eyed him nervously. "I was thinking of calling you, 'Father', if that is okay with you."

Jeremy smiled and a lump grew in his chest. "I'd like that."

"I was thinking that if you . . . you know . . . want to adopt me, I would keep my last name like Billy did. I would be George Tokay, out of respect for my family." Then he added, "If that is okay."

Jeremy smiled and asked, "You want me to adopt you?"

George's face turned deep crimson.

"I would like to adopt you, Kiddo," Jeremy said gently. "But adoption is something we should decide together."

George blinked at him, swallowed and said, "Well, I would like to be adopted, that is, if you want to adopt me."

Jeremy smiled and said, "I would be happy to adopt you."

George exhaled deeply as if he were holding his breath.

Jeremy bent down and kissed his forehead and George embraced him and kissed Jeremy's cheek. Jeremy rubbed noses with him and said, "I'm proud to be your dad . . . father."

"I am happy and proud to be your son."

CHAPTER SIXTY-NINE

Fishers, Indiana

With each spoonful of cereal, Brett eyed his mother carefully. Victoria knew she was being watched because Brett wasn't subtle about anything. Never had been. He popped his vitamin and Truvada into his mouth and washed them down with the milk that was still in the bowl, then held his juice glass with both hands and stared at his mom.

She folded the newspaper and set it down on the table, took off her reading glasses and said, "I've suspected, actually known, for a while, but I didn't want to believe it. When I found out for sure, I thought that when you came home, it would stop and we'd be a family again."

"Is it because of me?"

Victoria shook her head, tears welling up in her eyes and said, "No, Honey, no. We just grew apart."

"But if I were here . . . you know . . . if I hadn't been kidnapped . . ."

But Victoria had suspected Thomas of cheating before Brett was ever taken and out of any hope that Brett might forgive his father, opted not to tell him that.

"Brett, sometimes these things happen. Your dad got busy at school. I got busy at work," she looked away, shrugged and just shook her head.

Brett was silent and decided that he was as much to blame as his parents whether she said it or not.

"Does Bobby know?"

"Yeah, I know," Bobby said from the doorway, startling both Victoria and Brett. "I knew for a long time."

"How . . .?"

He was dressed as Brett was: shorts, no shirt and bare feet and bed-head. He sat down at the table across from his big brother. He looked first at Brett, then at his mom and shrugged. "I just knew."

The three of them looked at each other and then Brett said, "Now what?"

Victoria didn't have a clue.

CHAPTER SEVENTY

Waukesha, Wisconsin

Sweat dripped off his body. They started with the ball machine firing to Stephen's backhand and then switched to his forehand. Using a two-handed grip, Stephen hammered balls to the corners. His normal game would have been to charge the net after a long volley, but his tennis coach, Bob Luchsinger, had instructed him to remain on the backline. That was like trying to keep a thoroughbred at a trot instead of a full gallop.

"Take a break and get a drink and we'll work on your net game," Lucky said from across the court.

Stephen slipped off his shirt and walked to the wall, leaned his back against it and slid down to a sitting position, knees up. He took a towel out of his bag and wiped the sweat from his face, his arms, chest and stomach. He took a blue Gatorade out of his tennis bag and drank a good quarter of it, spilling some down his chest. He mopped it up with the towel and sat with his head down, one hand in his sweaty hair and knees drawn up to his chest.

He liked coming to the tennis club. As much as the workout, he liked the smell, which was offensive to others. Rubber and sweat. The club had sixteen full courts, six with synthetic turf and ten with a rubber, non-turf surface, and ten racquetball courts whose back walls were plexi-glass. The locker rooms had showers and a large hot tub.

"Stephen, right?"

Stephen looked up warily and said, "Yes?"

The red-haired, freckled-faced man handed him a business card. "You might want to read it and then put it in your bag, but keep it handy. If he asks what we were talking about, tell him I was complimenting you on your game."

He turned around to look for the tennis instructor, who had his back to them talking to an adult on the other side of the court. "You're pretty good, but I think I could take you," he added with a smile. Then he walked two courts away and using the wall, practiced backhand volleys.

Stephen looked at the card.

Detective Paul Eiselmann, Waukesha County Sheriff Department

The card had a seal, a badge number, email address and a phone number. Stephen looked over at the man, who was more intent on his backhand than he was on him. He turned the card over and saw a phone number identified as a cell phone and the message, *Det. Graff says hello. Call me anytime. P.E.*

Stephen watched Eiselmann volley and decided that he'd beat the cop in four sets.

"Stephen, let's go," Lucky called from behind the canon.

He got up, kept his legs straight and bent down placing the flat of his hands on the floor, and stretched. He did two quick squats and jogged up to the net.

"Let's try a little finesse, okay?"

"Whatever," Stephen answered, annoyed.

The ball machine swung on a slight swivel and Stephen moved effortlessly, much like he did in goal on the soccer field, returning each shot, though several went wide. He swung his racket at the net.

"Take it easy," Lucky said. "The net is all about touch, finesse, and placement."

Stephen placed his left hand on his hip and glared at Lucky.

Bob Luchsinger turned off the machine and walked up to the boy.

"What's up?"

Stephen shuffled his feet, tapped the head of his racket on the synthetic turf, but didn't look up.

Bob Luchsinger stood a compact five foot ten. He had thick black and unruly hair on his head. Black hair spilled out of his shirt and onto his arms and out of his shorts and onto both of his legs. He was in his mid-thirties, but looked younger and had a dark shadow on his face even after he had shaved.

"Look, Stephen, I don't know what happened to you, but I don't blame you for being angry. I'd be angry too. But there is a time to be angry and a time to be focused. You're an athlete and a smart kid. You know that."

Stephen looked up and said, "Mike's a better player than I am. Why did you ask me to be your partner instead of him?"

Luchsinger blinked, not expecting the question. He knew the boys were best friends, so he chose his words carefully.

"I like the way you play. I know you better than Mike, so I asked you. If you don't want to play, that's okay. I can get you a refund."

Stephen stared at the man, wanting to ask him the million dollar question. *Are you the fucking pervert who had me kidnapped?* But he didn't. In the end he said, "Let's go."

Lucky frowned at him, tried to read his mind, but gave up. He turned around and walked back to the ball machine and turned it on.

Stephen slowed himself down, placing his shots carefully, bouncing lightly on the balls of his feet.

Fifteen minutes later, his shorts were soaked with sweat. Sweat poured off his chest, stomach and back. But Stephen loved it. He loved working out. He loved the ache and the pain from pushing himself to the limit. But Stephen didn't know what his limit was and each time he played soccer, tennis or baseball, he went all out. *'Balls to the wall!'* was the slogan he and Mike lived by.

Luchsinger turned off the machine and said, "Collect the balls on your end and I'll get the ones on mine."

Stephen walked back to his tennis bag, took a quick drink, set his racket down and ran the towel over his face, chest, stomach, arms and legs. Then he walked around the court picking up stray balls, tossing them to the other side of the net where Luchsinger caught them and dropped them into the large bucket.

When they were done, they met at the net and Luchsinger said, "Listen. If you don't want to partner with me, it's fine. I have no problem with that."

Stephen shook his head and said, "No, I'll play. I just think Mike's better than me, that's all."

"Don't sell yourself short. If I didn't think you could play, I wouldn't have asked you."

Stephen shrugged dismissively.

"I talked to a couple of the other coaches and given the circumstances, if you're uncomfortable using the main locker room and shower, I can let you use the coaches' locker room for a while . . . you know, until you want to use the main room. Mike can too if he wants."

Stephen looked down and then looked back up at the man. He shrugged and said, "Thanks."

Luchsinger smiled at him and said, "Nice job today. Don't forget, the net is all about finesse and touch. Not everything has to be rocket fire, okay?"

Stephen smiled at him, shook his hand and said, "Thanks."

Luchsinger had a mother-daughter lesson and went to the next court where they were waiting.

Stephen turned around and walked back to his bag. As he packed, Eiselmann went to the water fountain which was near and pretended to drink from it.

"Everything okay?"

Stephen didn't look in his direction, but instead glanced at Luchsinger who was busy with the mother and daughter.

"He said Mike and I can use the coaches' locker room if we want to."

"Being nice, maybe."

Stephen shrugged and said, "Before the workout, I told him I had a soccer game tonight. He said he'd come watch."

"Good. Your mom is on court nine. Which locker room are you going to use?"

"I'm just going to go home. I have goalie training at four, then the soccer game at seven. You gonna be there?"

"Yes, but I'll be in the background. Don't acknowledge me, but I'll be watching."

Eiselmann finally took a drink of water and headed towards the lobby.

Stephen waited for his mom, but kept an eye on Luchsinger.

Wondering.

CHAPTER SEVENTY-ONE

Waukesha, Wisconsin

First, a visit with Andy Garber, the family dentist. Nice guy, but Mike didn't like dentists. He determined that Mike would need either implants for the two missing teeth or two bridges because the missing teeth were inconveniently spaced apart from one another, one up and one down. And if that wasn't enough, not one tooth, but two teeth were loose enough for Jennifer and Mark to consider either braces or a retainer.

"I thought I had only one loose tooth," Mike protested.

"Sorry, Buddy," Garber said. "Two, though one is certainly looser than the other. I just want to protect them so we don't lose either one."

Jennifer looked at Mark and both had the same thought: *We can't possibly afford this!*

As if Garber read their mind, he said, "Look. Dentistry is expensive. I'm going to make a deal with you guys, but I want your word that this is between you and me. Okay?"

Jennifer barely heard him. She was adding up the cost of travel soccer for their three kids, plus the credit card payments that were killing any chances they had to get out from under. Mark wondered if either he or Jen would have to pick up a second job.

"Guys, I'm doing this for free. You've been in my care since the kids were little and I appreciate that. And, I know what this young man went through, so all of this is on me."

Jennifer and Mark exchanged a look. Mike, lying flat on his back in the dental chair could only look up and backwards.

"With that in mind, I'd like to do implants. If we do bridge work, it would damage four perfectly good teeth."

He stuck his gloved finger in Mike's mouth and said, "See?" turning to his parents. "This tooth and this one, I'd have to file down and I don't want to do that." He shifted to the lowers and said, "Same with this tooth and this one. He's too young for a bridge. Cosmetically, the implant would be better for him."

Garber looked up and saw Jennifer wiping her eyes and Mark blowing his nose. He paused and said, "Is that okay?"

"I don't know what to say," Mark said. "Are you sure?"

At first, Garber thought Mark was talking about the implant versus the bridge, when it dawned on him that the question referred to free dental work.

Garber was in is late fifties, thick in the middle with a salt and pepper head of wavy hair. His eye brows were thick. Though he had been a dentist for more than thirty years, he took pride in the fact that he had kept pace with new practices and procedures that were common practice among the newer crop of dentists. Unknown to his patients, he spent four weeks each year doing free dental work in Appalachia, feeling it was important to give back. Given all that Mike had been through, it was important to give back to him too.

"If you'll let me, this is something I'd like to do."

Mark looked at Jennifer, then at Garber and said, "I don't know how we can thank you."

"No need. I only ask that this deal is between you and me, okay?"

Unable to answer, both Mark and Jennifer nodded, and then Mark shook Garber's hand, while Jennifer hugged the man.

"Thank you," she whispered.

The second stop was to see Blaise Frechet, a Pediatrician specializing in pre-teen and teen youth, and one of Mike's and Stephen's travel soccer team sponsors. Though he generally had excellent checkups and didn't have any injuries or major illness, Mike cared for doctors even less than dentists.

Frechet was fine-featured and fairly tall but because he was so slightly built, he didn't seem tall. He had thin, straight blond hair with matching eyebrows and pale blue eyes. He had a habit of whistling as he checked over his patients, but Mike had never recognized the tunes and the whistling wasn't pleasant to listen to.

The only thing Mike had looked forward to was getting his stitches removed and getting cleared to play soccer that evening. The checkup was his passport to play soccer.

"Mike, strip down and put on this gown, but don't tie it. Leave it open in the back."

Proud that he was no longer stuttering, he asked, "You want everything off?"

"Yes, please. It will be easier for me to take out the stitches, and given what you have been through, I want to give you a thorough physical. While you get yourself ready, I'm going to go speak to your parents, okay?"

"Sure."

Mike didn't like the thought of getting naked again in front of anyone, doctor or not.

Frechet smiled at him and left the room.

Mike hopped down from the bed, slipped off his Nike sandals, then his shirt and then his shorts and boxers in one quick move. He was confounded by the gown and was fumbling with it, when there was a quick knock on the door. Frechet opened it and came in, shutting it and then locking the door behind him.

Mike tried to hustle into the gown, but Frechet said, "Let's hold off on that for the time being. I'll check you over first, okay?"

Embarrassed, Mike turned dark red.

"First, put your feet together, hold your arms to the side, and look straight ahead."

Mike did so, as Frechet pushed on his arms, and then felt his neck, chest, ribs and stomach. He stepped behind Mike and did the same from behind.

"Mike, all in all, you look good. I see from the bit of hair under your arms and in your groin that you're in the beginning stages of puberty. Looking at the X-rays that were sent from Chicago, I think you're going to begin a growth spurt."

"Really?" Mike had been hoping he'd grow. His voice had gotten a little deeper. He and Stephen had been the same height until the last year when Stephen had gotten taller.

"I looked at the growth plate in your wrists," Frechet took hold of Mike's right wrist, "and in your knees and ankles. That, and in looking at your penis size," Frechet took gentle hold of it, lifting it up, stretching it gently, "you're about to grow."

Mike was embarrassed, afraid he was getting hard. If Frechet noticed, he didn't let Mike know.

"Sit on the end of the table and I'll listen to your breathing and your heart."

Thankfully, Mike did so, trying to cover himself up with his hands.

"Keep your hands and arms at your side. Take slow, deep breaths."

Frechet warmed the stethoscope up with his hands, but it was still felt cold to Mike.

"Breathe in and hold it. That's it. Exhale slowly through your mouth. Again. Good. You're breathing is fine. Lungs sound good. Okay, lie down, head on the pillow, arms at your side." He pulled out the bed extender so Mike could lie down comfortably.

But Mike wasn't comfortable. He was almost erect and there was nothing he could do about it. Again, if Frechet noticed, he didn't let Mike know. And, there was no way Frechet didn't notice.

"I want you to breathe normally in and out through your nose."

Frechet used his stethoscope and listened to Mike's heart and then moved lower to Mike's stomach and then just above Mike's groin.

"Sounds good." He took the stethoscope from his ears and tapped Mike's stomach on either side of his belly-button

"Don't worry about your erection. It's not the first I've seen."

Frechet examined Mike's testicles, first one side and then the other.

"You have bruising on your left testicle. Is this uncomfortable?" he asked as he felt it.

"N-no."

"Good. That means it is healing. I'm going to check for hernias, so turn your head to the wall and cough."

Mike did so.

"Good. One more time."

Mike coughed again.

"Excellent. Mike, I'm going to give you a shot to relax you so I can take out your stitches. It will make you drowsy and you probably won't remember anything after I inject you. You seem to be in excellent shape and I'll finish your exam while the shot takes effect, okay?"

Mike nodded, though he was embarrassed and uncomfortable lying there like he was.

"I think you have a game tonight, right?"

Mike nodded. He watched the doctor fill a syringe from a little bottle, nip it to get air bubbles out, and then squirt it. Mike also noticed that Frechet wasn't wearing any gloves. That was odd. Doctors and nurses always used gloves.

"This is to help you relax."

He took a cotton ball and alcohol and swabbed Mike's forearm at the elbow, found a vein and inserted the needle.

"You'll feel woozy in a second or two."

Mike's eyes fluttered. He tried to fight it off, but couldn't.

"Just fall asleep and when you wake up, you'll be all set."

• • •

His eyes fluttered open. Mike was on his back in the same position he was before he fell asleep.

"Careful. You're not fully awake yet. I'm applying an antibiotic ointment because of that broken skin. I don't want any chance of infection."

Mike blinked, tried to sit up, but couldn't.

"All done. I'll help you get dressed and then I'll bring in your parents and we'll talk about your exam."

Mike kind of remembered getting dressed with Frechet's help. He wasn't sure if Frechet had kissed him on the lips, using his tongue. Maybe he just imagined it.

By the time he was fully awake, he was dressed and sitting on the table and Frechet was talking to Jennifer and Mark.

"He's in very good health. All things considered, that is. The reports from Chicago confirm what I found out today. Stitches came out just fine. For the next day or so, Mike should use Tucks pads, but after that, wipe as he normally would. I'd like him to use the antibiotic ointment he used on his stitches for the next week. Just to be safe, I'd like to see him in two weeks to check it. Other than that, he's good to go."

Frechet smiled at Mike and at his parents, and then stood up, ending the session.

Mike hadn't spoken until he stood to leave and after his parents shook Frechet's hand, Mike said, "Th-th-ank you."

Mike and Jennifer gaped at their son. They hadn't heard Mike stutter at all in the last few days.

"It could be the stress from the exam or from the relaxing agent," Frechet said with his charming smile.

He tried to place his arm around Mike's shoulders, but Mike sped up ahead of his mother and headed out the door.

"Mike's been through a lot. I wouldn't worry about it," Frechet said gently. "He'll be fine."

As they walked to the car, Mark waited until Mike was well ahead, and asked Jennifer, "What the hell happened to Mike?"

Jennifer wondered the same thing.

"It's like someone threw a switch or something." Mark said. "He goes in normal. Everything's fine. And he comes out stuttering like he did in Chicago. What happened in there?"

CHAPTER SEVENTY-TWO

Eureka, Missouri

They hadn't gotten back to the hotel until almost 4:00 in the morning. After Jeremy and Jeff said goodnight to the boys, Danny and Randy fell asleep as soon as their heads hit the pillow. Billy helped George out of his clothes and stayed awake. George couldn't get comfortable because the boxers he wore put too much pressure on the sutures in his groin and on his backside. No matter what the position, his boxers twisted causing discomfort.

"Just take 'em off," Billy said with a yawn.

"I'll be naked," George said.

"So?"

"I don't think I should."

"It's not like we're going to do anything," Billy said with a laugh.

"Go to sleep," George said.

"Suit yourself." Billy turned over on his side but snuggled up against George like he had done the night before and fell asleep without another word.

George tossed and turned a little longer, and finally gave up. He slipped out of bed, removed his boxers and crawled back into bed next to Billy, trying to keep distance between them. But no matter how far he moved away, Billy settled up against him.

Eventually, George gave up and fell asleep, facing Billy with one bandaged arm slung over his chest.

• • •

They had slept in. As the noise outside their room grew, the boys finally roused from sleep with yawns, groans and stretches.

"George, you awake?" Randy asked.

"Yes," he answered through yawn.

"How are you?"

"Tired, stiff and sore."

Billy lifted the sheet and laughed, "He's stiff all right."

George glared at him, but Billy laughed again.

Billy got out of bed, rummaged around in George's duffle and pulled out a pair of shorts and came over to the side of the bed. Moving slowly and with a grimace, George swung his legs over the side and Billy him helped slip his shorts on.

"God, George!" Randy said as he sat up in bed. "I was too tired to notice last night, but you're all cut up."

George looked down at himself.

There were cuts up and down his legs, some with black thread running through them. His arms were bandaged in gauze and tape, but not a scratch on his face, chest or stomach.

"What does my back look like?" he asked as he turned his back towards Randy.

Randy got out of bed and ran his hand gently over George's shoulders and back.

"You have some cuts. There's a long gash with stitches on your left shoulder. A couple of cuts in the middle of your back, and a couple of stitches on your lower back."

Randy lifted up the back of George's shorts slowly.

"My God, George!"

"How bad?"

Billy moved to the side, next to Randy, and Danny got up out of bed and stuck his head between the twins.

"Geez," Danny muttered.

"How bad?" George asked again.

"Well, there's a bandage just under your butt on the right side, but your butt is all cut up. No stitches, but it's cut up," Billy answered.

"You have cuts all over the backs of your legs and you have stitches," Randy said.

George turned back around facing them.

"How far up?" Randy asked.

George didn't answer, but Billy said, "Pretty far."

Randy and Danny waited, so George lowered his shorts to show them.

"How did you not cut your dick and balls off?" Danny asked.

Billy laughed and said, "Looks like he tried."

"I don't understand how you didn't cut them off," Randy said.

George pulled his shorts back up with Randy's help and said, "I'm not supposed to get the stitches wet for twenty-four hours and the ones under the bandages for forty-eight hours. How am I going to get cleaned up?"

Billy chewed on his lip and glanced at Randy, who puffed out his cheeks, placed his hands on his hips and said, "We'll have to help you."

The twins marched George into the bathroom with Danny trailing behind.

"Rock, paper, scissors," Billy said. "One, two, three."

Billy had paper, and Randy had scissors.

"I'll wash George's hair," Randy said.

In the end, they washed George's hair together with Randy washing and Billy rinsing. Rather than using the blow dryer, Randy toweled George's long, black hair to a semi-dry state.

"Okay," Billy said. "Take off your shorts and get in the bathtub."

Embarrassed, George looked from Billy, to Randy, to Danny, and then back to Billy.

"You wanna get clean, right?" Billy asked.

George nodded.

"Well?"

Because of the bandages, he struggled with his shorts. Billy helped him out of them, and Randy helped George into the bathtub.

"Okay, here's how we're going to do this," Billy said. "I'm going to start with your face and work my way down. I think I'll just soap up my hands. You're too cut up for me to use a washcloth. You okay with that?"

Even with George's dark complexion, he knew he was blushing. All he could do was nod.

Twenty minutes later, George was clean. It was embarrassing for both Billy and George especially when Billy washed George's lower regions. Probably embarrassing for Randy as he gently dried the areas.

After the bath, George said, "I can't change the bandages by myself."

"No problem," Billy said. "Let's start on your arms."

It took fifteen minutes, maybe longer just to put ointment on all of George's stitches without the bandages. Then with Randy's help, Billy took the bandages off of George's arms.

"Holy shit!" Danny said. "Damn, George!"

That was repeated several times in the process of changing George's bandages.

It was early afternoon when Jeremy and Jeff faced the boys. George had assured them he was fine, but tired and sore.

"We've been thinking," Jeremy started slowly. "We have some choices, especially given what took place last night."

He glanced at Jeff.

"We think we should spend another day or two here. It was a late night for everyone and I think the FBI is coming over to question you guys. In a couple of days, George can get his stitches wet and we can go to Six Flags . . . that is, if you guys still want to."

"Can Patrick come?" Billy asked.

"If he wants to."

The four boys looked at one another, shrugged, and Billy answered for them, "Sure."

"Okay. That's settled."

"Jeremy called Jamie Graff and told him what happened last night. He's sending two undercover detectives to keep an eye on us. The FBI doesn't know and the three of us, Graff, Jeremy and I, would like to keep it that way."

George cocked his head, squinting first at Jeff, shifting to Jeremy. "Why?"

"I don't have a good answer for you, George." Jeremy shook his head and said, "Just a feeling."

George pursed his lips considering Jeremy's answer. He trusted Pete and Summer and wasn't sure why Jeremy didn't. Yet, George trusted Jeremy, so he nodded.

"After that, we have some choices," Jeff said.

"We can continue on our trip as we planned, ending in Arizona. Or, George and I can go to Arizona, while Jeff takes the three of you to Omaha to wait for George and me to finish what we need to do."

Randy shook his head, while Billy was adamant, "No," he said quietly, but with force. "We're family. Families stick together."

"You saw what happened last night," Jeff said gently. "That man meant to kill everyone in the room."

Jeremy added, "We know there are three men just like him waiting for us in Arizona. They're going to try to kill us, just like that man tried to do last night."

"We know, Dad," Randy said quietly. "But listen, please, okay?" He waited until Jeremy and Jeff nodded.

"I can't speak for Danny, but Billy and I've talked. We want to be with you and George. We're family."

"Besides," Billy added quietly, "Those three men are after you and Randy. That means they're after me too."

"That's why we thought one option would be for me to take the two of you and Danny to Omaha to wait until your dad and George finish in Arizona. Keep you guys safe."

Billy looked at Randy, at George and then back at Jeremy. "No, families stick together, especially if George is joining our family."

"And if we have two cops watching over us, we'll be safer, right?" Randy asked.

"Well, that's the theory."

"Father, I have been thinking." George had a habit of slipping into a formal speech pattern when he had something serious to say. "I know my land. Those three men do not. That is our advantage. They also see me as a child. That is a further advantage."

"Even after last night?" Jeff asked. "Word is going to get out how you killed that man and had a hand in the death of the agent in Chicago."

George blushed and nodded. "I thought of that. But the bigger advantage is that I know my land. I have hunted it. Rode horses on it. They don't know my land like I do. That is our advantage."

"What are you proposing?" Jeremy asked.

George took a deep breath, looked at Billy, at Randy and at Danny.

"We take our trip as we planned. Just before we get to my country, Mister L takes Billy, Randy, and Danny away to wait for us . . . somewhere close by, but safe. When we're done, you and I will meet up with them."

"I'd like to see where you used to live," Randy said.

"Me, too," Billy added.

George sighed and then nodded. "I think we could do that. I lived far enough away from where these men might wait for us, but we'll have to talk to my cousin, Leonard first."

"Danny, are you okay with this?" Jeff asked.

Danny looked down at his hands and then looked up and nodded. "Dad, they're my best friends. I'd rather be with these guys than anyone else. I'd like to be with them as long as possible."

Jeff smiled and nodded. "George's option was actually the one Jeremy and I thought you guys would choose."

"Father, one last thing," George said.

Jeremy smiled and said, "What's that?"

"Can you get pictures and information on the three men who are looking for us?"

"Why?" Jeremy asked.

"They know who we are. I want to know who is hunting us."

"I know the FBI released their pictures, but I don't know how much they know about them. I'll see what I can get from Pete, okay?"

George nodded at Jeremy.

Jeff smiled at the boys and said, "Okay, we have our plan, but on one condition."

The boys waited.

"Our plans stay in this room. No one else, not any of your friends, not the police, not the FBI, not the undercover cops know about this. George, your cousin doesn't find out until Jeremy says it's okay to do so. We think it's safer that way. Okay?"

Except for George, the boys nodded.

George wondered why Jeremy and Jeff didn't trust Pete or Summer or even Detective Graff.

For that matter, why didn't they trust his cousin, Leonard?

CHAPTER SEVENTY-THREE

West Bend, Wisconsin

Things were moving in the general direction of normalcy. Even Christi was getting used to Tim. Laura thought it odd that her son and daughter would have to get used to one another, but after more than two years of being separated, they didn't know one another anymore. However, that was changing.

Laughter helped. Laura Pruitt loved the sound of voices in the house, especially laughter.

Since the day Cal showed up with the basketball, the four boys had been inseparable. Cal and Kaid did most of the talking, with Tim chiming in every now and then, usually prompting a laugh. The only one who didn't talk much was Gavin. Tim had told her what he had gone through the past two years, suggesting that what Gavin went through was almost as bad as what he went through. Laura didn't doubt that Gavin had suffered, but doubted it was as bad as what Tim and the other boys in Chicago had gone through.

The phone rang and she noticed the caller ID. Stephen Bailey.

"Pruitts," Laura answered.

"Mrs. Pruitt, can I talk to Tim? It's important."

Laura frowned and said, "Just a minute, Stephen. I'll get him."

"Tim, phone," she called. "It's Stephen."

Tim came in smiling at something, took the phone and said, "Hey, Stephen. What's up?"

"Tim, something bad happened to Mike. He's stuttering again."

Tim paced the kitchen, one hand on his hip, one holding the phone as Stephen filled him in on Mike's morning. Laura watched her son. There were too many possibilities as she watched Tim's face cloud up.

Cal, Kaid and Gavin came into the kitchen to see what was happening. Christi came out from the back bedroom and stood in the doorway.

"Where is he now?" Tim asked.

"Inside. His mom asked me to call you."

"Did you call Brett?"

"Yes, but he can't come until tomorrow. His mom has a couple of heart surgeries or something like that."

Tim covered the mouthpiece and said, "Mom, I need to go see Mike. Can you take me to Waukesha?"

Laura looked at the clock. Thad wouldn't be home until five-thirty. Christi had dance at six-thirty. She'd have Christi call Jessica to see if Christi could be dropped off there and then together, go to dance practice. Thad could pop a pizza in for dinner and pick up the girls.

Already nodding, she said, "Yes."

Christi called her friend. Laura called Thad and explained what little she knew.

"Guys, something happened to my friend Mike," Tim said to them after he hung up.

"You okay?" Kaid asked.

Tim nodded, straining to keep composure.

"Do you want us to come along?" Kaid asked.

Tim looked hopeful.

"Kaid, we can't. We have a game tonight," Cal said. "Sorry, Tim."

"I can go, I think," Gavin said. "I'd have to ask."

"Can you?" Tim asked.

Gavin went back into the family room to fetch his cell.

Laura hung up and said, "I told your dad that we'll be home sometime tomorrow or the day after. We'll see."

Tim sniffed his armpit and said, "I have to shower."

Gavin came in and said, "My mom said I can go, but she wants to talk to your mom." He handed the phone to Laura, who said 'hello' and began talking as she turned away from the boys.

"Tim, I . . . we," Kaid said.

"It's okay. Hopefully it's nothing, but damn, he's been through so much."

"Maybe we could skip the game," Cal suggested.

Tim shook his head, "No, it's okay. I'll call you when I find out more."

"Are you going to be okay?" Kaid asked.

"Yeah, Kaid. I'll be fine. Promise."

Tim noticed Kaid wiping his eyes.

"It's okay, Kaid."

Kaiden loved Tim. Tim was his friend, a kind of big brother and a hero all in one.

"Really, Kaid. It's okay," Tim reassured him.

Laura came back into the kitchen and said to Gavin, "Your mom wants you to get home and take a shower. We'll pick you up in twenty minutes. And pack for two days, just in case."

The brothers and Gavin left and Tim ran up the stairs to shower and pack.

Laura went to the bedroom to throw some things in a suitcase, shaking her head.

So much for normalcy.

CHAPTER SEVENTY-FOUR

Fishers, Indiana

Pete splashed cold water on his face and then grabbed a white towel off the bathroom counter and dried off. He had been on caffeine non-stop and his stomach had been yelling back at him. Sour and upset. Worse, the caffeine hadn't worked in the least.

He went back to the desk and dialed four sets of numbers, asking each of the previous contacts to hold. When he finished with the last, he clicked the previous three, setting up a five-person conference call with Skip in Missouri, Jamie in Wisconsin, Chet at the townhouse Dominico had purchased under the name Dobbs, and Summer in D.C.

"I'm hoping someone has good news," Pete began.

Chet said. "Dominico had a laptop and I've been playing with it. I have his email downloaded. He has pictures and videos of Bobby and another boy who looks similar enough to be a cousin. Dominico organized from here. There are, or were, a total of six. Cochrane, Fox and Dominico are the three we know about. He sent an email to three others identified with only nicknames. One is Dodger. The other two are Scholar and Diablo. Those are the three who responded to Dominico's text when he asked for someone to go after George, Randy and Jeremy. I know it doesn't help much."

"Chet, can you locate them by cell GPS or IP address?" Summer asked.

"Morgan and I are working on it."

"Any information on the names I gave Pete?" Jamie asked hopefully.

"Nothing," Chet responded. "The only quirky thing we found is that the tennis coach works as a male escort for a legit service out of Milwaukee and makes pretty good money. The others are clean."

"What about the goalie and soccer coach?" Jamie asked, suspecting he knew the answer.

"Clean," Chet answered.

"Skip, how about you?" Pete asked.

"Fox had an ID in another name."

"Send me what you have and I'll check him out," Chet answered.

"His cell has porn taken yesterday afternoon. A blond boy about the same age as the others. I think it was taken in the boy's bedroom and I don't think the pictures were taken willingly. I checked the contact list, texts and stuff, and I came up with the same names Chet did. He referred to Dominico as Dee, but that's a guess. Cochrane was Griffin."

"That's the name for the Invisible Man," Chet said.

Without commenting on Chet's observation, Pete said, "Chet, sift through all the information on the men we can't account for. There's gotta be something on these three guys we missed."

"Is there any way we can ID the boy on Wright's phone?" Summer asked.

"If I show these to Patrick, he might know him."

"No graphic shots," Pete said. "Patrick was almost killed."

"Skip, send them to me as a jpg. I'll doctor them up and get them back to you," Chet suggested.

"Anybody have anything else?" Summer asked.

"I got nothing. This morning, Mike went to a dentist and a doctor. He checked out fine, but he's stuttering again," Jamie said.

"I thought he was done with that," Pete said with a frown.

"Something happened that set him back. His parents said it's worse than ever."

"You said Mike checked out fine?" Skip asked.

"Yeah, nothing. Same as what the doc in Chicago found with the other guys."

Puzzled at the odd question, Pete asked, "Skip, why did you ask that . . . if Mike checked out fine?"

"I've been thinking. Doesn't it seem odd? I mean, Tim was raped, sodomized, forced to do God knows what, and checks out fine except for the stitches he needed?"

"What are you saying?" Summer asked.

As if he had not heard Summer's question, Skip continued, "Same with Brett. Other than the gunshot, he's fine. The kids in Chicago are fine. The kids in Long Beach are fine. These kids get examined at a hospital, have blood tests, and they're healthy as can be."

Jamie sat up straighter. Pete drummed his pen on his little notebook. Summer frowned, and Chet folded his arms and sat back.

"These kids didn't have herpes, or syphilis, or HIV. Given the number of sexual partners, the shitty diet, the lack of water and their living conditions, the only kid who's sick is Johnny, but that's from pneumonia complicated by dehydration. Doesn't any of that seem strange to you?"

"The kids we found, the ones who were dead, most had at least one disease," Chet said.

Pete stood up. Pieces were falling into place.

"The kids were given Viagra and a prescription med to control them," Summer said.

"They had to get meds from somewhere," Chet said.

"Not somewhere, someone. They had to get meds from someone," Summer said.

"And for the boys to be in such good shape, medically speaking, physically speaking," Pete started.

"They were taken care of," Jamie finished for him.

"Doctors," Pete said. "Chet, get us the names and pictures of all of the doctors that were picked up. I want eight by tens sent to Jamie, Summer, Skip and me. Jamie, get in touch with the PD in West Bend and show those pictures to Tim. Chet, you and I'll show them to Brett. Skip, show them to Patrick along with the picture of that boy on Fox's phone. I want to know what these doctors did with these kids other than what we know about."

"My God! How organized were they?" Summer said.

"Very. They didn't leave anything to chance," Pete said.

"I'm wondering if Mike's check-up was a trigger of some kind," Skip said.

Pete shook his head. "No, he was barely in Chicago one, two nights. I doubt there was time."

"But, if the doctor performs a physical, a full physical, it could have reminded him of what he went through," Jamie said.

Jamie went silent as he considered the new information. If a physical was a trigger, why didn't the other boys have a similar reaction? At least, some reaction. None of them did. In the hospital, Mike had a physical and was checked out at the hospital, but was happy, smiling, and normal except for the stutter. By all accounts, Mike's stuttering had pretty much disappeared. Now his parents said Mike is a basket case. Nervous, jumpy, afraid. What's the tie-in? What were they missing?

CHAPTER SEVENTY-FIVE

Waukesha, Wisconsin

Laura Pruitt pulled her silver Honda Accord into the driveway, and Tim and Gavin got out. Mike ran to Tim and burst into tears and held him in a bear hug. Tim held Mike's head gently and rubbed his back, resting his cheek on the smaller boy's brown hair.

"T-T-Tim."

"Shhh . . . it's okay, Mike," Tim answered.

Mike sobbed. Tim struggled to stay in control. Though he didn't know him, Stephen held onto Gavin's arm. Gavin watched Tim and Mike, and hardly noticed Stephen holding him.

"T-T-Tim," Mike sobbed.

"Shhh . . . it's okay, Mike," Tim repeated.

Eventually Mike settled down enough to say, "S-s-s-sorry I'm s-such a w-w-wuss."

Tim smiled, rubbed his back and said, "Mike, you and Brett and George are the toughest guys I know. You're not a wuss."

Mike shook his head, but Tim said, "You're not, Mike. You're strong."

CHAPTER SEVENTY-SIX

Fishers, Indiana

Brett sat at the kitchen table with Pete, Chet, Bobby and Victoria and shuffled through the pictures. Since the night of the shooting, Thomas had moved to a hotel and that bothered Bobby more than it did Brett. Neither boy could tell how his mom felt.

"Once a month, a doctor would come in and give us checkups. Blood pressure, look at our throat, ears, eyes, our . . . *stuff*. We'd get a shot, maybe two shots, and some pills. They never told us what the shots or pills were for."

"You received pills each morning when you showered," Pete asked.

Brett shook his head and said, "The morning pills were to keep our dicks hard . . ." He glanced at his mom and said, "Sorry, Mom." Then to Pete, he said, "Like Viagra or something. The other pill was to control us. It made us kinda loopy."

"The pills the doctors gave you were different?" Pete asked.

"Johnny and Tim figured they might be to keep us healthy. Vitamins maybe. Same with the shots. Maybe Penicillin or something."

"Honey, do you remember any names that might have been on them? Maybe their shape or color?" Victoria asked.

"Not really, Mom. If a guy was really sick, he wouldn't get a shot. They'd eventually take him away and then a new kid would show up."

Brett frowned as he went through the pictures again.

"What?" Pete said.

"There's a guy missing . . . one of the doctors."

"You sure?"

"Positive. A blond guy with a kind of fox face and weird blue eyes."

Pete squinted at him, "What do you mean 'weird blue eyes'?"

"His eyes were really blue, like ice. We called him Frenchy because he liked to French kiss and play with us . . . you know . . . for a long time before he did anything else."

"You're sure," Chet said.

Brett sorted the pictures into groups and said, "These six I've never seen. These three liked me and Patrick and Ben because we had brown hair. These four liked the younger guys. These two liked the older guys. The blond guy is missing. He liked guys with blond hair, like Tim and Ian and Cory. Sometimes Tim and me together. Frenchy probably would've liked Stephen because he has blond hair."

Pete frowned. It made sense that Brett wouldn't know six of them because they were located on or near the West Coast. His eyes went wide and he stood up slowly.

"What?" Chet asked.

Brett, Bobby and Victoria watched curiously.

He needed to get a hold of Jamie.

CHAPTER SEVENTY-SEVEN

Waukesha, Wisconsin

Parents staked out their territory with lawn chairs starting at the half-line and spread down the sideline across from their respective teams' benches. Some parents stood in groups of two or three. Mike's dad couldn't sit or stand in one spot so he roamed the sideline. Tim and Gavin sat away from the parents and watched Stephen's and Mike's team warm up.

Stephen jogged over to the sideline and said, "The guys on my team think you're Cole Sprouse," and laughed. "Cool, huh?" and then he ran back to his team still laughing.

Tim said, "Who?"

Gavin laughed and said, "*Suite Life On Deck*. The smart twin."

Tim shook his head.

Every now and then the other boys would turn around and stare at him, and when Gavin noticed, he'd laugh.

Tim pulled out his cell, did a Google search, and said, "I don't look like him!"

"Yeah, you do," Gavin said with a laugh.

"Bull!"

A sandy brown-haired boy about the same size as Gavin sat down on the grass a short distance from Tim and Gavin.

Tim watched him for a bit and then asked, "Are you the one who called the Amber Alert?"

The boy glanced at him and then looked away, blushed, and then nodded.

"Stephen hoped you'd come. Sit with us," Tim said.

The boy hesitated, glanced at Tim one more time, and then got up, walked over and sat down next to him.

Tim looked around to make sure no one was listening and said, "What's your name?"

"Garrett." He said it quietly, almost in a whisper.

"You saved our lives," Tim said holding his hand out to him. "I'm Tim. I was in Chicago with them. You got us out of that shit hole."

Garrett blushed an even deeper red, but shook Tim's hand.

"This is Gavin," Tim said leaning back so the two boys could see each other.

"Hey," Gavin leaning forward.

Garrett nodded at him.

"I'm glad you came," Tim said. "Stephen and Mike will be happy to see you."

After finishing warm-ups, Stephen and Mike ran over to them.

"Are you . . .?" Stephen asked.

The boy looked up and nodded.

"This is Garrett," Tim volunteered.

Stephen squatted down in front of him, and said, "We played you, right?"

"Yeah," Garrett said quietly. "Mercy ruled us."

"S-s-sorry ab-b-bout that," Mike said with a smile, holding out his hand.

Garrett shook it, but didn't make much eye contact.

"Garrett, wait for us after the game so we can we talk. Okay?" Stephen asked.

"Okay."

"Great. Come on, Mike."

"Th-th-thanks f-f-for c-comin', G-G-Garrett," Mike said.

Garrett smiled shyly.

As they ran back to their sideline, Tim said, "If you wouldn't have made that phone call, Mike would have been dead by now."

Garrett looked at him doubtfully, and Tim said, "Believe it!"

Mike flew over the field stealing passes, stopping runs, and had four slide tackles controlling three of them while sending the other harmlessly out of bounds. The only time Stephen touched the ball was when his defenders dropped the ball back to him. With less than ten minutes to go, Spring City had a three-nothing lead.

"Hey, Foreskin, give any blowjobs lately?"

Three boys sat on bikes ten yards away. A dark-haired boy with thick lips and big ears made the comment. His two wingmen laughed.

Garrett didn't look at them but hunched his shoulders and stared across the field. Tim glanced sideways at him, while Gavin turned around to see who the talker was, then turned back, glanced at Garrett and Tim, but otherwise watched the game.

"Foreskin, I might be in the mood."

Gavin stood up and faced them. Tim stood up along with him. Garrett stood up last.

"Foreskin, I'm talking to you," the talker said.

"He's not interested in talking to you, Murphy."

Two boys, one slightly built with broad shoulders and with long, curly black, shoulder-length hair juggled a soccer ball on his right foot, bouncing it nimbly from toe to heel and back again. He stood directly in front of Garrett and slightly in front of Tim. He was about the same size and age as Tim.

A smaller dark-haired boy with dark eyes juggled a soccer ball from foot to knee and walked up and stood alongside the long curly-haired boy in front of Gavin.

"I wasn't talking to you Denalli," Murphy answered.

"Then I guess no one's talkin' to anyone, so let us finish watching Erickson and Bailey kick butt," the smaller boy said.

"Mind your own business, Girici. Go back to the UN," Murphy said.

"Funny! Like we haven't heard that one before, have we Cem?"

"Murphy, why don't you and your pet monkeys go ride your bikes home or off a cliff and let us watch the game," the smaller boy said.

"It's more interesting than talking to someone with shit for brains like you," Denalli said.

All this took place as Denalli and Girici juggled their soccer balls without stopping. Right foot and right knee for Girici, switching to left foot and left knee, while Denalli juggled with his right heel and toe, then with his left heel and toe. Nonstop, without break.

"I was talkin' to Foreskin. You two think you're so tough. You're parents are probab-"

He never finished the sentence. Denalli sent his soccer ball in a line shot at Murphy hitting him in the face, knocking him off his bike.

Tim hadn't seen Denalli wind up. It was one fluid motion: heel, toe, Murphy's face. It was the hardest, fastest and most accurate kick Tim had ever seen.

Murphy slowly got to his hands and knees, blood dripping from his nose.

"Denalli, you're a-" the boy on the bike nearest Tim and the others never finished.

Girici sent his ball into the side of the boy's head, knocking him off his bike and on top of Murphy, and then Girici casually walked over and picked up their two soccer balls.

"Go away and leave Garrett alone," Cem said as he turned away.

The three boys got on their bikes and left. Blood still dripped from Murphy's nose.

"So, pretty good game, huh?" Cem asked with a smile as he walked back to the other boys.

Tim and Gavin looked at him, mouths open and said nothing.

"Garrett, Cem and I have your back. Just want you to know that," Denalli said.

Embarrassed, Garrett stared at the ground and nodded.

Denalli turned to Tim and Gavin and looked them over. "You guys friends of his?"

Tim smiled and said, "Just met Garrett today. He's friends with Mike and Stephen."

Denalli nodded, smiled and said, "That's good." And then to Tim he said, "Take care of Garrett. He doesn't deserve this shit."

Tim glanced at Garrett and asked, "What's happening?"

Denalli glanced at Garrett who stared at the ground and said, "You didn't do anything wrong, Garrett, but Cem and I have your back."

He took his ball from Cem and walked off.

Cem smiled at them, gave them a little wave, and turned and followed Mario.

Tim, Gavin and Garrett watched them leave and then Tim said, "Who was that?"

"They go to school with me, but I didn't think they knew me," Garrett said quietly.

Tim put his arm around Garrett's shoulders protectively and said, "Evidently they do."

Just up the sideline amongst, but not with, the parents stood a tall, narrow blond man who watched Stephen and Michael intently. Observing. Hunting. He already had Michael. Now he wanted Stephen.

Frechet had watched the two boys pass him as they juggled their soccer balls, caught their scent and they smelled good. He thought they'd be good in other ways and wondered how he could entice them to his home. Maybe money. Most boys liked money.

He watched the exchange with the boys on bikes and watched as they rode away, thinking that the boy with the bloody nose might have a minor concussion, possibly the other boy too.

The tall blond boy was a stallion and beautiful. He looked familiar, like he should know him. He couldn't place him, but the thought tugged at the back of his mind.

He turned back to the soccer game and watched Stephen and Michael. He really wanted Stephen. He needed to have Stephen.

Tonight.

Somehow. Someway. Tonight.

CHAPTER SEVENTY-EIGHT

Eureka, Missouri

He was distracted, maybe frustrated. George couldn't tell and didn't know why.

He and the others spent most of the hot afternoon at the St. Louis Zoo. George, not used to the humidity, was uncomfortable. All of them got sunburned except for George, who just got darker. Jeff and Jeremy had retreated to their room, while the boys ended up at the motel pool. Danny, Randy and Billy swam while George sat on a lounger and watched them. The yelling, screaming and splashing made napping impossible. He felt restless, like he should be doing something other than sitting.

George had easily picked out the two undercover agents. It wasn't hard because either they didn't care if he knew or they weren't very good. He first noticed them at the zoo trailing at a discreet distance: a male and female trying too hard not to look like they were watching them.

She was tall and had long black hair. She carried a small bag and George knew that was where she kept her gun. He was about the same height, muscular and a lefty. The left foot drag told George where his gun was and confirmed the fact that they were cops. They acted like they were married or dating, but seldom held hands. George didn't care.

Something was going to happen soon. George could feel it. He just didn't know what. Or to whom.

CHAPTER SEVENTY-NINE

Waukesha, Wisconsin

Pete had called and had shared his hunch. Having worked with him in Chicago and having watched him in action, Jamie knew Pete was good at what he did, so he trusted Pete's hunches.

And Jamie was frustrated. The West Bend PD couldn't get a hold of Tim or his family, so he couldn't verify the information Brett had given Pete and Chet. He had called the Pruitt residence twice and left his cell, office and home phone numbers with a message to call as soon as possible.

While he waited, Jamie ran Frechet's driver license and enlarged it. He placed it with the rest of the photos and emailed a copy of it to Pete for him to check with Brett. He conference-called Pete and Chet and gave them the license number, address and phone number, along with the address and phone number of Frechet's medical practice. They were going to get it to Billias and have him do some digging.

He shared the little he knew about Frechet. Frechet was one of three principals in a medical practice specializing in pre-teen and teen youth. His name was listed second and it employed a total of thirteen individuals: three doctors, one physician assistant, seven nurses, one receptionist and one accounts clerk. It was hugely successful and took up the entire first floor of a corner red-brick, two-story building kitty-corner from Waukesha Memorial Hospital.

Not knowing what else to do, Graff picked up manila folder holding the glossy eight by tens, his keys, and backed up too quickly knocking his rolling desk chair into the bookcase. He turned off the light and slammed the door behind him.

Eiselmann and O'Connor had tailed the Bailey and Erickson families to Frame Park for Stephen's and Mike's soccer game, so Jamie decided to visit Frechet.

CHAPTER EIGHTY

Waukesha, Wisconsin

They ended up at the Erickson house. It had taken some convincing, but Garrett relented, and sat on the couch in the basement dueling Gavin on Wii Sports. They laughed, elbowed each other and trash-talked like they had known each other forever.

While Mike showered, Stephen and Tim talked quietly and even though he wasn't supposed to, Stephen told Tim about the undercover cops watching him.

"He was at tennis, my goalie training, and the soccer game. He said there were two of them, but I haven't met the other guy."

"Does Mike know?"

Stephen looked away, licked his lips and said, "I wasn't supposed to tell anyone."

Tim smiled and said, "Then we better not say anything, okay?"

Stephen nodded.

"Who were those two guys at the game, the two with the soccer balls?"

Stephen laughed and said, "Probably the two best soccer players in the state. Seriously. They're our age, but they play up an age group. They're in ODP, the Olympic Development Program."

Garrett turned around and said, "Mario Denalli and Cem Girici. They go to my school. Mario's from Italy and Cem's from Turkey."

"Is his name Jim or Gem?" Gavin asked.

Garrett laughed and said, "You spell it C-E-M, but the C sounds like a J. His last name is spelled G-I-R-I-C-I, but the G sound is hard."

"You said he's from Turkey?" Gavin asked. "I thought he was Italian like the other kid."

"No, Mario is from Italy, but Cem is from Turkey," Garrett answered.

"You know how moms and dads and some friends came to our game?" Stephen said.

Tim nodded.

"Well, when they play, everyone shows up, not just parents and friends. This summer they had coaches from North Carolina, Duke, Creighton, Indiana and UCLA. Honest."

"Seriously?" Gavin asked.

"Truth!" Garrett answered. "Mario scores at least once in every game. *Every* game."

"And damn, is he fast!" Stephen added. "He can do stuff with a soccer ball that most guys only dream about."

Gavin laughed and said, "Yeah, we saw. Two of those guys got a really close look at what they can do," he said with a laugh.

"I've heard him say there are three things he cares about in the whole world. His grandmother, soccer, and his guitar," Garrett said in awe.

"His grandmother?" Gavin asked.

"I don't know the whole story, but he lives with his grandmother. I don't think his parents are around, and he doesn't have any brothers or sisters. I don't think he does anyway."

"Who were those other guys?" Tim asked.

Garrett blinked at Gavin, Tim and Stephen. He put his controller down, stared at his hands and then sighed.

"I go to school with them. Murphy, Henderson, and Douglas."

Tim waited patiently. Garrett shifted uncomfortably. Gavin and Stephen remained silent, but were interested.

"My coach is in jail, so our soccer team dissolved. He, the guy I turned in, did stuff with me and some of the guys on my team. He had porn . . . videos, pictures . . . sick stuff. Word got out about him doing stuff and some of the guys blamed me."

"And if you wouldn't have said something, Mike would be dead, and Stephen and me and the other guys would be locked up doing all the crap you did with that pervert," Tim said firmly.

Garrett looked doubtful.

"Look, Garrett. Calling Randy and Jeremy took guts. And what you did with that pervert? I did that shit for more than two years. Every day, all day, all night. Anything you can think of, I did.

"I saw guys get whipped, branded, and dragged away in handcuffs. We . . . I . . . never saw them again. I even had to do stuff with the guys, my friends. So, if anyone says anything to you, remember you saved almost thirty of us. Mike would have lasted *may*be a day or two longer. And then, they would have hung him up, whipped the shit out of him in front of us, and then they would have taken him away in handcuffs and no one would have seen him again. I know it because I've seen it. I can give you the names of other guys, and you can call 'em and ask 'em yourself if you don't believe me."

Tim shook. He didn't realize it, just like he didn't realize he was crying either. Angrily, he wiped his eyes with the front of his shirt.

Stephen reached out and held Tim's arm gently.

"So . . . why did this Mario guy and the other guy defend you?" Gavin asked quietly watching Tim and Stephen.

Garrett couldn't bear to look at any of them. Finally, he shrugged and said, "I don't know."

Mike bounced down the steps two at a time, hair still damp, and asked, "What did I miss?"

CHAPTER EIGHTY-ONE

Waukesha, Wisconsin

At the soccer game, Frechet had overheard the boys talking about spending the night at Erickson's house. He hadn't exactly worked out the details of how he'd get Stephen. Maybe take them for ice cream and then offer to give him a free physical.

He knew deep down, Stephen wanted to be with him. He knew Michael enjoyed the office visit. Michael was more special than he had imagined. But he knew Stephen was going to be even more special than Michael.

He packed a duffle bag with enough clothes for one night. He stuffed a syringe and the vile of medicine into his jacket pocket along with a loaded .38 and grabbed his medical bag.

Frechet turned off the house lights, locked his front door and got into his white Cadillac Escalade, backed out of his driveway, and drove down the street and around the corner.

CHAPTER EIGHTY-TWO

Waukesha, Wisconsin

"Mark," Jennifer said as she came into the living room. "Sarah, Laura and I are going grocery shopping. We'll be back in an hour or so." She gave him a kiss and added, "You have the boys." She gave him another kiss and said, "If they get hungry, you can order pizzas. There's a coupon on the counter near the toaster along with two twenties."

Mark hugged her and buried his face in her stomach.

"Stop," Jennifer said with a laugh.

"You make me horny when you give me orders," he said hugging her tighter.

"A change in the barometric pressure makes you horny," Jennifer laughed.

"The point is I'm horny."

"Mason is at Miranda's house, and Morgan and a group of his friends are at a Chad's house, and the boys will be downstairs, so we'll have the upstairs to ourselves."

He gave her a kiss and said, "I guess my horniness can wait a little while longer."

She kissed him back and said, "You know, it's nice to have a house full of kids."

"Did you notice Mike's not stuttering? A little soccer and a lot of Tim, and poof!"

She nodded and said, "I noticed."

"I wish we knew what the hell happened."

"Me, too." She kissed him again and said, "Gotta run."

Jennifer went back into the kitchen, yelled "Bye", and she, Sarah and Laura left by back door, got in the Erickson van and backed out of the driveway.

• • •

"We have a van leaving the Erickson house. Heads or tails?" Eiselmann said into his radio.

"I'll take it."

Pat O'Connor was slightly built on the tallish side, had a narrow face, and wore his brown hair to his shoulders. He looked like any guy with rough edges who lived on the dangerous and questionable side of life. He had partnered with Eiselmann since joining the Waukesha County Sheriff Department but the two of them were more than partners. They were best friends. He'd work undercover, while Eiselmann worked control because his red hair and freckles made him stick out too much. O'Connor blended in.

The two of them had been on loan to the FBI and had headed up the team that had freed the boys in Long Beach. Graff had arranged through his captain and the Sheriff department for them to keep an eye on Stephen and Michael and their families.

O'Connor waited until the van reached the corner and then pulled out and followed, keeping a block behind them.

CHAPTER EIGHTY-THREE

Waukesha, Wisconsin

Had Graff arrived just thirty minutes earlier, he would have found Frechet climbing into his Escalade. As it was, he rang the front doorbell three times and gave up on the idea that the good doctor would come to the door.

He walked down the driveway and peered into the garage through the window on the side of the house.

No vehicle.

The backdoor was locked. He walked around the house, peering into windows looking for anything suspicious, anything that would give him probable cause to enter the house.

Nothing.

He pulled out his cell as he walked back to his car.

"Eiselmann."

"Where are you?" Jamie asked.

"A couple houses down from the Erickson house."

"Where's O'Connor?"

"Following Mrs. Erickson, Mrs. Bailey and Mrs. Pruitt. They took off about twenty minutes ago. Mr. Erickson is baby-sitting the boys."

"Wait, did you say Mrs. Pruitt? Is Tim Pruitt there?"

"Yeah. His mom, Tim, and another boy arrived late this afternoon."

Jamie pounded the steering wheel. "That's why they never called me back?"

"What?" Eiselmann asked puzzled.

"I'll be there in less than fifteen minutes. If the boys try to leave, stop them."

Eiselmann was left holding a silent cell phone.

CHAPTER EIGHTY-FOUR

They sat in a circle and talked. Cans of soda forgotten. Video game on pause. The shower Stephen was going to take on hold.

At first it was getting-to-know-you kinds of things: what sports they were good at, classes they liked or hated, teachers at school, movies and books and TV shows. Gradually it got deeper.

Gavin, who was the least talkative of the guys, mostly watched and listened because he was interested in what the other guys had to say. Normally a jokester and quick-witted, Garrett felt at a disadvantage because he didn't know any of them, so he took a cautious approach and like Gavin, listened more than talked. Just as in the hospital, Mike and Stephen were open and honest and held nothing back.

Finally, Gavin spoke up and said, "Tim, that night you were taken, what happened?"

Tim squinted off in the distance and said, "I was going to your house and I was at the corner of my street when I was grabbed from behind. They covered my mouth with a cloth and the next thing I knew, I was naked, in a van, and my arms were chained to the wall."

"That's what happened to Mike and me!" Stephen said. "Two guys grabbed us from behind and threw us in a van. I woke up and Mike and I were naked, and guys . . ."

He stopped and looked at Mike, and then said quietly, "All the way to Chicago. Three guys. Mike and then me, and then Mike again."

He turned to Mike and said, "We got to Chicago and the last I saw you, I didn't know if you were alive or dead. Two guys dragged you to the end of the hall. They shoved me in a room and I thought it was just us. At first, I heard you screaming and crying. Then I didn't hear you anymore and I thought . . . I thought . . ."

Mike reached over and took hold of Stephen's arm.

Stephen said, "I was so scared." He looked at Tim and said, "I thought Mike and I were alone until you and Brett came into my room."

Mike looked from Stephen to Tim and back to Stephen and said, "You never told me."

Stephen looked down at his hands, and Tim jumped in and said, "Butch, the ugly fat guard wanted Stephen to make a movie with Brett and me."

"A movie?" Gavin said.

Garrett grew pale. He knew about movies.

"Stephen did me while Brett did him. That way, I could tell him what was going to happen to him and you."

"You did Tim?" Mike asked Stephen. "Brett did you?"

Stephen blushed and looked away, ashamed.

"He had to, Mike. You know what happens if you didn't obey," Tim said gently.

"No, no, that's not what I meant. I didn't know, that's all," Mike said shaking his head. He reached out and held Stephen's arm gently. "It's okay, Stephen."

Stephen wiped his eyes, "I know it sounds bad, but I didn't mind being with Tim and Brett because I knew you and I weren't alone."

"It's okay. Really," Mike said.

Stephen wept and couldn't make eye contact with any of them.

"All new guys have to make a movie their first night," Tim explained to Garrett and Gavin. Then to the group he said, "I think the worst part for me was thinking I was the only one. They put me in a room and the guards took turns. It wasn't until Johnny and a guy named Travis came in my room when I found out I wasn't alone. I was still scared, but I knew I wasn't alone."

Garrett said, "It was different for me. We heard rumors about my coach. Nobody said anything, just, rumors. My friends Phil and Danny went to his house a couple of times."

He shook his head, looked down at his hands, and said, "I wanted to be captain. He said if I did . . . stuff, I could be. He said he had to get to know me better." When he looked up, there were tears in his eyes. "It was sick. I didn't like it."

It was Gavin who slipped his arm around Garrett's shoulders and said, "It's okay."

Mike said, "Been there and done that. Tim, me, Stephen, we all did that stuff."

"Yeah, but you had to. I didn't," Garrett said with a sob. "But I'm not gay, honest!"

"We know that, Garrett," Mike said.

"My dad thinks I'm gay," Stephen said. "I'm not, but he thinks I am."

Frustrated, Tim didn't know what to say and his expression showed it and it was a while before anyone spoke.

"You know, it's like I don't belong here," Gavin said quietly.

"You belong here, Gavin," Tim said. "These past two years you went through hell."

Gavin looked at him and said, "It's not the same, Tim, and you know it."

"For two years, you went through hell, Gavin. How many times did guys make fun of you? Your friends turned their backs on you when guys made fun of you. You were treated like shit and for no reason."

Gavin shrugged.

"For two years, who did you talk to besides your mom?"

"Just my English teacher."

"Wait, why?" Stephen asked. "I don't understand."

"Because I said something stupid about Tim."

"What?" Mike asked. "What did you say?"

Gavin looked at Tim, who nodded encouragement. He told them about the fight at baseball practice and said, "I just wondered if Tim was alive and if he had to, you know, do stuff, if he would be gay or something."

Stephen and Garrett sat back and nodded.

"But I didn't mean it like it sounded." He blushed, got flustered and said, "I was just kind of thinking and it came out."

"I told you, it's okay," Tim said.

"Sometimes, I don't think I am, but sometimes I wonder about it," Stephen said quietly.

"Me, too." Garrett said. "I mean, I didn't have to go to my coach's house."

"Guys, listen. Just because you did stuff with a guy doesn't mean you're gay. The stuff you did, did you like it? You wanna keep doing that shit?"

Gavin, Tim and Mike watched Stephen and Garrett wrestle with the thought, their faces registering disgust.

"You're not gay. You're not!"

Tim let them sit with that thought and then he turned to Gavin and asked, "You forgave Kaiden, right?"

Gavin's face hardened and he said, "Yeah, but I don't trust him."

Tim sighed.

"I'm sorry, Tim. I know he's your best friend, and I know you like him more than anyone else, but . . ." he shook his head and said, "I don't trust him."

"Gavin, I . . ." Tim didn't finish his thought.

"The only person who knows what I went through was my English teacher. He had me write letters to you. Every night before I went to bed, I'd write you a letter. I was pissed at you for not being there. I was afraid you were dead. I really missed you, and I wanted you back. I was, I don't know, just pissed off. I didn't have anyone to talk to. I didn't have anyone to be with. No one liked me. Guys made fun of me." He stopped and shook his head.

"Did Kaiden and Cal make fun of you?" Tim asked.

The hurt in Gavin's eyes was palpable and he was close to crying when he said, "No. But they'd laugh and never did anything to stop the others from making fun of me."

Tim reached out and took gentle hold of Gavin's hand and said, "I'm sorry, Gav."

Tim let go and Gavin said, "When those three assholes showed up at the game tonight and started picking on Garrett, I got so angry because it was like what happened to me all over again." He turned to Garrett and said, "And I wasn't going to let that happen to you."

Garrett smiled at him.

"You're always the first to stick up for someone. I do like Kaid and Cal. Kaid is like a little brother to me, and I've known Cal forever. But Gav, I love you and we'll *always* be friends. I *want* to be friends with you."

Gavin wiped tears from his eyes. Tim embraced him and whispered something to him that no one else heard, but it caused Gavin to smile and nod. Then he said, "Friends?"

Gavin nodded and said, "Of course."

There was silence as the guys wiped their eyes and smiled at each other self-consciously.

Finally, Gavin laughed and said, "I don't know about you guys, but Tim, you changed a lot."

"Well, having some pervert's dick in my mouth or up my ass twenty-four-seven kinda changes a guy," Tim said with a laugh.

All of the guys laughed and Tim said, "How do you mean?"

"Well, I've never seen you cry before. You hug me . . . us. You've kissed me and Mike. You've never done that kind of stuff before."

Tim thought about it and said, "Guys, listen. I almost got killed twice. *Twice!* I decided after George saved me that from now on, I'm going to say what I mean and show how I feel and if guys don't like that, tough shit."

"Some guys might not understand, though," Stephen said.

"And if they don't, who gives a shit?" Tim said defiantly. "I don't."

Mike nodded, "I don't either."

Heads nodded and Gavin reached out and took hold of Tim's arm, and Tim and said, "I love you. All of you."

The guys smiled and nodded and wiped more tears from their eyes.

CHAPTER EIGHTY-FIVE

Eureka, Missouri

The boys sat in the fading sunshine on metal chairs around a small table at a Baskin and Robbins a block away from the hotel. George loved ice cream. He could eat ice cream several times a day, each day, and never get sick of it.

Which is why when he didn't order anything except a bottle of water, Randy said, "Are you sick or something?"

George hadn't heard him or if he did, didn't acknowledge it.

"George, are you okay?" Randy asked with a nudge.

George didn't answer. He stared off in the distance, eyes glassy, vacant, jaw set.

Randy, Billy and Danny stared at him. Finally, Billy shook his arm and said softly, "George, what's wrong?"

George was certain the voice he heard was his grandfather's. Yet, his grandfather wasn't talking to him, at least not directly. His Grandfather was warning someone, encouraging, and giving directions.

Who?

CHAPTER EIGHTY-SIX

Waukesha, Wisconsin

Stephen went upstairs to take a shower. Gavin and Garrett went back to Wii.

"Anybody hungry?" Mark shouted down the stairs.

A chorus of, "Yeah!" or "Yes, please!" came back at him.

"Mike, come on up and order pizza," Mark answered with a laugh.

That was when Tim saw him.

He wore a plaid shirt and a leather vest, faded blue jeans and dusty cowboy boots. His long gray hair was tied in a single braid. His face was brown and wrinkled and he smiled at Tim.

Tim was certain he was the only one who could see him.

Or hear him.

'Yá'át'ééh.'

It was clear. It was loud enough for anyone in the basement to hear. But Gavin and Garrett didn't hear it, and Mike was on his way upstairs.

Tim nodded.

'The dark boy and the blond boy are in danger.'

'From who?'

'He's almost here. You need to go up and protect them.'

'Will you be with us?'

The old man smiled and nodded.

Tim licked his lips.

"Guys, I'm going up to help Mike."

"Yup," Garrett said without turning around.

Gavin didn't answer, but turned for just a second to give Tim a smile.

Tim loved Gavin's smile. It was sweet and innocent and kind and good. His eyes disappeared behind thick eyelashes. He wondered if he'd ever see that smile again.

CHAPTER EIGHTY-SEVEN

Eureka, Missouri

George stood up slowly and dropped the bottle of water on the table, spilling part of it in Billy's lap, who jumped up out of the way.

"What the hell?" Billy said.

George made no move to mop up the water with napkins like Danny and Billy did. Instead, he stared off in the distance, mouthing words of a language the three boys didn't understand.

"George, what's wrong?"

CHAPTER EIGHTY-EIGHT

Waukesha, Wisconsin

Mark and Mike were hunched over either side of the counter with the phone in Mark's hand. He spoke into it, ordering two large pizzas, one with extra cheese, and one with extra cheese and pepperoni, along with an order of garlic cheese bread and marinara sauce.

"Where's Stephen?" Tim asked.

"Shower. End of the hall, last door on the right," Mike answered.

Tim walked down the hall and knocked on the door. "Stephen?"

"Yeah?"

Tim opened the door and shut it behind him. "You almost done?"

The water stopped and the shower curtain opened and Stephen said, "Yup."

"You trust me, right?"

"Yeah, what's up?" Stephen said slowly.

"I'm not sure, but dry off, get dressed and stay back here somewhere out of sight."

Stephen grabbed a towel, dried off his face, but stared at Tim.

"Okay?"

Stephen nodded, fear evident in his eyes.

'Be careful. He's here.'

Tim left the bathroom, shut the door and walked down the hallway towards the living room. When the doorbell rang, he stopped in mid-stride.

CHAPTER EIGHTY-NINE

Eureka, Missouri

George snapped out of it. He spun in a slow circle, searching the faces of the people near them. He saw who he needed several tables away and quick-walked over to him.

"You're FBI, right?"

Tom Albrecht looked to his left and right and then back at George.

"Answer me," George demanded quietly.

"Waukesha County Sheriff on loan to the FBI. Why?"

George bent low so only Albrecht could hear him.

"Mike Erickson, Stephen Bailey and Tim Pruitt are in danger. Right now."

Seeing the urgency in George's face, Albrecht hesitated only a second. He took out his cell and speed-dialed Graff.

CHAPTER NINETY

Waukesha, Wisconsin

Mark had finished ordering and went into the living room to answer the door. Mike followed.

Tim appeared at Mike's side and held his arm preventing him from advancing beyond a step or two. Mike looked up at him curiously.

Mark opened the door and took a step back and said, "Oh . . . hello, Doctor Frechet."

Mike shrunk at Tim's side. Tim took one step in front of Mike shielding him.

"What can I do for you?" Mark said puzzled at the house call.

"I'm sorry for bothering you this evening, but I wanted to check on Mike to see if he's okay. And I thought that as long as I was here, I'd give Stephen a quick physical. I want to make sure he's okay."

"Mike's fine," Mark said. Puzzled, he said, "Give Stephen a physical?"

"Yes, make sure he's okay," Frechet said with his charming smile.

Stephen appeared in the hallway and Tim gestured slightly for him to stay where he was. Stephen crouched down against the wall.

And in that moment, Frechet and Tim recognized each other.

Tim said slowly and deliberately, "I know you!" Pointing at him, he repeated, "I know you!"

Mark half-turned towards Tim.

It gave Frechet an opportunity to step into the living room, drop his medical bag and pull out his gun.

CHAPTER NINETY-ONE

"Graff, this is Albrecht. Something's going down at . . ." He turned to George and said, "Where?"

George hesitated and then shook his head, not knowing the answer.

Albrecht turned back to the phone and said, "Do you know where Mike and Stephen are?"

"Erickson house. Eiselmann's there. Why?"

"Not sure. George said the Erickson boy, Stephen, and a Tim are in danger."

"On my way."

Albrecht was left with dead air.

He turned back to George and said, "Come on," and led him back to the table where the twins and Danny sat.

"We need to get back to the hotel," Albrecht said as he began walking and speed-dialing his partner.

"Brooke, where are you?"

"Balcony outside our room. Why?"

Albrecht explained the little he knew and then shut his phone.

"Guys, let's hustle," Albrecht said over his shoulder, jaywalking across the street.

The boys followed in a tight group with George bringing up the rear, eyes taking in every pedestrian, every parked or passing car and wishing he had his knife with him.

CHAPTER NINETY-TWO

"I saw you at the soccer game but I couldn't place you," Frechet said nervously.

Mark said, "What's going on?" He never took his eyes off the gun in Frechet's hand, thankful that Jennifer, Sarah and Laura weren't there, but worrying that they'd walk in on this.

"Be quiet and move back."

"What do you want?" Mark asked.

'Keep him talking. Help is coming.'

Tim said, "This is one of the fuckheads from Chicago. He examined us and then fucked us."

Mark whipped his head at Tim, at Mike, and then back to Frechet. The realization hit him like a punch. "What did you do to my son, you sonofabitch!"

The gun in Frechet's hand shook, but it was still lethal. Perhaps more so because Frechet was nervous.

"I said get back."

Mark backed up trying to place himself between the gun and the boys.

'You are Stephen?'

Tim saw the old man talking to Stephen who stared at him with mouth open and eyes wide. He nodded.

'Stay where you are.'

"Fuckhead, Mr. Erickson asked you a question. What did you do to Mike?"

Frechet's face was slick with perspiration. He licked his lips, stared at Mike and said, "We had a little fun today, didn't we, Mike?"

"Fuck you!" Mike yelled.

Gavin and Garrett had come up from the basement and stood in the kitchen listening to the conversation in the living room. Frightened, Gavin motioned for Garrett to get down and both of them crouched low.

"Frechet, put the gun away and leave before someone gets hurt," Mark said through clenched teeth.

"Not without Stephen. He and I are going to spend time together."

"The fuck he will!" Mike shouted.

Frechet cocked the gun.

The old man turned and stared at Tim. His expression was sad. There weren't any words. There was no direction or command. The two stared at one another, frozen in both time and space.

And Tim understood what was going to happen. And what he needed to do.

CHAPTER NINETY-THREE

Eureka, Missouri

"George, what is it?" Jeremy asked.

Randy, Danny and Billy stood off to the side with Jeff slightly in front of them. Albrecht and his partner, Brooke Beranger, stood behind Jeremy.

George had a vacant, unfocused, and glazed look on his face. He shook his head.

"George," Jeremy said again.

"Dad, wait," Randy said. "I think it's his grandfather."

CHAPTER NINETY-FOUR

Waukesha, Wisconsin

"Eiselmann, what's happening?"

Eiselmann stared out the windshield at an empty street. The only traffic was the white Escalade that pulled up in front of the Erickson house. He had called dispatch and had them run the plate and it came back as Blaise Frechet, a doctor. Eiselmann figured the doctor was just checking on Mike.

"Nothing. It's quiet."

"You sure?"

Eiselmann twisted around in his seat, stared out the back, then out both sides and said, "Nothing. Why?"

"A report that something's going down."

"There's nothing, but I'll do a once-around the house. I'll be in touch."

. . .

"I'm not leaving without Stephen," Frechet said in response to Tim's urging that he leave.

"Stephen, wherever you are, stay there! Don't come out here! Don't make any sound. If you're in the kitchen, go out the back door and find the red-haired cop that's watching you."

"Shut up!" Frechet said.

"Go up and down the street and look in each car. Tell him a pervert has a gun and he's in the living room by the front door."

In the kitchen, Gavin looked at Garrett and whispered, "That's us. Tim knows Stephen's taking a shower."

They stayed low and tiptoed out the back door, but the screen door shut a little too loudly.

"Hear that? Stephen's going to find the cop that's protecting him. You better leave while you can," Tim reasoned.

Frechet licked his lips and nervously glanced out the front window.

"You need to leave before someone gets hurt," Mark said.

"I want to know what you did to me!" Mike said defiantly.

Frechet focused on him and said, "You enjoyed it."

Mike started forward, but Tim held out his arm preventing him from doing so.

•   •   •

Gavin and Garrett stood at the end of the driveway looking in both directions, not seeing anyone.

"Garrett, go that way. Look in every car. I'll go this way. If you see someone, a cop or somebody, tell them what's happening."

As the boys turned to leave, a red-haired, freckle-faced man walked up to them.

"Where are you boys going?"

Graff rounded the corner and pulled diagonally to the curb, cut the engine and jogged out of the car in time to hear Gavin say, "There's a man inside with a gun."

"Where inside?" Graff said.

"By the front door," Gavin answered.

"Where did you come from?"

Garrett pointed and said, "Back door. It goes to the kitchen."

"You're the one that had Stephen and me kidnapped!" Mike spat.

Frechet licked his lips. It was taking too much time. He wanted- *needed*- Stephen, and he wanted him *now*.

"Stephen! Come out here!"

"I already told you, he's outside looking for the cop," Tim lied. "You need to leave before he gets here."

"You're a sick fucker!" Mike yelled.

Eiselmann said, "I'll take the back door. Give me fifteen seconds on my mark. Go!" And he took off.

Graff looked over his shoulder, and then said, "You two, get across the street and around the side of that house. I want you face down in the grass and don't raise your head. Got it?"

The two boys took off on a sprint.

•   •   •

"Stephen wants me. I came for him."

"You sick sonofabitch," Mark said quietly.

"There's no fucking way Stephen wants you, Asshole!" Mike shouted.

This angered Frechet.

This was the Erickson boy's fault. If it weren't for him, he'd be with Stephen now.

He extended his arm and took aim.

Tim knew that Mike's father would step in front of Mike to take the bullet. Tim couldn't let that happen. He shoved Mike and took a step forward in front of Mark as the gun went off.

Eiselmann burst through the door to the living room too late to stop Frechet from firing, but he hit Frechet center-mass with four shots at the same time Graff fired three shots at an angle through a side window hitting the doctor in the chest just below the neck.

Frechet flew back into the closed front door, dead before he hit the floor.

Tim fell on top of Mike and the two of them lay in a pile behind Mark.

"You okay?" Tim said thickly.

"Yeah, I'm okay," Mike answered.

Tim didn't move. He lay on top of Mike, eyes shut and said, "I need to catch my breath."

"Tim? Tim?"

Mike lifted his hand, saw blood. "God! Tim! Dad, help!"

CHAPTER NINETY-FIVE

Eureka, Missouri

George grabbed his stomach and fell to his knees. Jeremy went to the floor to help him, and Randy and Billy flew over the bed to help. The two detectives didn't know what to make of it, so they stood well back watching intently.

"George! What's wrong? What happened?"

George recovered slowly, reaching out to Jeremy for support, looking at him with tears in his eyes.

"What, George? Tell me?"

"My dream," George stammered. "It wasn't me. It was Tim and Mike."

"What happened?" Billy asked.

"Mike and his dad are safe. Stephen, too. My grandfather was with them."

"What happened to Tim?" Randy asked.

George looked up at him, shook his head, and wept.

About the Author

After having been in education for forty-four years as a teacher, coach, counselor and administrator, Joseph Lewis has retired. He is the author of seven novels, using his psychology and counseling background in crafting psychological thrillers and mysteries. He has taken creative writing and screen writing courses at UCLA and USC.

Born and raised in Wisconsin, Lewis has been happily married to his wife, Kim. Together they have three wonderful children: Wil (deceased July 2014), Hannah, and Emily. He and his wife now reside in Virginia.

Note from The Author

Like *Taking Lives* and *Stolen Lives*, *Shattered Lives* is a work of fiction, but it is based in fact. One just has to read headlines or watch the news to find our children caught up in the most heinous crime of Human Trafficking. It is my belief that to force a child to engage in sexual activity is unconscionable. This should not, must not, happen.

I began to research the topic of child abduction, child sexual abuse, child safety, prevention, and education because of the case of a missing boy from St. Joseph, Minnesota, Jacob Wetterling, who at age 11, was taken at gunpoint by a masked man in front of his younger brother, Trevor, and his best friend, Aaron. I began speaking to parent groups, student groups, teachers, and faculty about the topic and how we can keep kids safe. It wasn't much, certainly not nearly enough, but I did what I could.

Taking Lives, which is the prequel of my *Lives Trilogy*, was first released in August 2014. The first book of the *Lives Trilogy*, *Stolen Lives*, was first released in November 2014. As I stated above, these are works of fiction, yet based upon years of research, as well as the stories that kids and parents shared with me over the years. But it is a work of fiction, first and foremost. The statistics quoted in the stories are true, taken from the National Center for Missing and Sexually Exploited Children website. And while kids are abducted, some for a long time, kids do make it back home. We've read news reports about kids who do and we rejoice. Sadly, some kids don't make it back home. Some kids are found dead.

Taking Lives and each book of the trilogy, *Stolen Lives*, *Shattered Lives* and *Splintered Lives* are meant to be stories of hope, a story of survival. Each of these books pays homage to law enforcement and other caring individuals who work to bring kids home safely.

I want to thank Jamie Graff, Earl Coffey, Bryan Mabry, and Jim Ammons for their expertise in police, FBI, and SWAT procedure; James Dahlke for sharing his forensic science work with me; Jay Cooke, Dave Mirra and Bill

Osborne for their IT expertise; and Sharon King for patience with all my medical questions. I also want to thank the folks at Sage and Sweetgrass, Robert Johnson, and various personnel at the Navajo Museum for taking the time to answer my questions about Navajo culture, tradition and language.

I want to thank Winona Siegmund for her patience and her editing skills on each of the books. I want to thank Stacey Donaghy of Donaghy Literary Group for guiding my early writing career, Natissha Hayden and the folks at True Visions Publications for giving me my first opportunity to see my books in print, and Reagan Rothe and the team at Black Rose Writing for re-issuing the trilogy and prequel.

Lastly, I can't tell you how supportive and encouraging my family has been. My wife, Kim, and my kids Wil, Hannah, and Emily have been so understanding and encouraging, never letting me give up and pack it in after each rejection. They stood by my side and supported me and whatever great or little success I might have as a writer, I am truly blessed for having been a husband to Kim and dad to my kids. I love you guys.

To you, the reader, thanks for taking a chance on an unknown writer, a guy who loves putting words on paper and seeing what might be made from them. I hope you enjoyed the prequel, *Taking Lives*, and the first book of the Lives Trilogy, *Stolen Lives*, and I thank you for your willingness to continue the journey with me through the trilogy and beyond, and I hope I never disappoint you.

Word-of-mouth is crucial for any author to succeed. If you enjoyed *Shattered Lives*, please leave a rating and a review online—anywhere you are able. Even if it's just a sentence or two. It would make all the difference and would be very much appreciated.

Happy and Thoughtful Reading!
Joe

For fans of Joseph Lewis,
don't miss the final book of *The Lives Trilogy.*

Splintered Lives

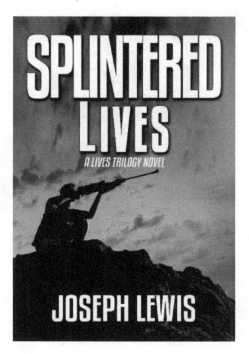

CPSIA information can be obtained
at www.ICGtesting.com
Printed in the USA
BVHW071156180521
607630BV00003B/168